The Raven Witch of Corfu

A fantasy romance

by

Effrosyni Moschoudi

Effrosyni Moschoudi

In loving memory of my Great-Aunt Rini Tsatsanis from
Messonghi

Contents

Prologue

Messonghi, Corfu, Greece

Twenty years earlier

Lizzie ran out of the cave and thundered past the gnarled olive trees, her heart pounding in her chest. Bees and mosquitoes buzzed around her, and ear-piercing cricket sounds echoed from the trees.

Her legs felt wobbly, but raw primal fear kept her running, somehow, away from the mortal danger she'd just escaped from.

The strong sunlight felt hot on her skin when she emerged through the olive grove and stopped for a moment to gasp for breath. Then, she resumed running, downhill now, along the mountain road, desperate to get home, if only a moment sooner.

Her brother's wails still rang in her ears. She couldn't help Tom, she couldn't save him, no matter how hard she'd tried. The witch had said she'd keep him for twenty years... and then, only then, would she be willing to release him if Lizzie, and only Lizzie, came back alone to claim him.

The witch... that vile creature who'd introduced herself as Phoni. Where had she come from? Where had she returned back to, taking Tom away with her? She had laughed at Lizzie when she started to yell, calling for help, telling her there was nothing she could do; that no matter what she did, or whom she called, no one would ever find her brother.

Tears flowed from Lizzie's eyes as she continued to run in the scorching heat, her gasps, mixed with her sobs, burning her throat.

Through bleary eyes, she made out the guest house in the distance. Her mum and dad were inside, none the wiser... Mum, no doubt, about to set the table for lunch, Dad reading his paper on the porch. How could she tell them that Tom was gone? And who would ever believe her?

You have to love the Greeks

Messonghi - Present day

Lizzie stepped out of the taxi and stood at the dusty roadside, feeling dazed. Ever since she'd arrived at Corfu airport an hour earlier, she'd been feeling odd, as if this was a dream. Throughout the taxi ride to Messonghi, she had trouble believing this was true. But it *was* true. The day she'd been waiting for, for twenty whole years, was finally here. She had returned to the place where the nightmare had begun, to claim her brother back.

Closing her eyes, Lizzie breathed in the refreshing cool breeze, the sunshine hot on her face and naked shoulders. The heat felt wonderful, familiar, taking her back. It stirred in a second, it seemed, a host of old holiday memories. This was her second visit to Corfu. The first time, she'd been only twelve, spending a whole month's holiday here with her parents and her twin brother Tom.

Tom... my dear, precious brother... Will I see you again? For the past twenty years, she'd found it impossible to forget him... to forget what happened here, in this tiny village of Corfu. Unlike her parents, she knew... she knew what had happened to Tom. She'd told everyone the truth but no one had believed her. She had paid a dear price for that, but Lizzie didn't dwell on that any more. All that mattered to her now was to find her brother again.

Lizzie took in another deep breath and tried to shake the painful memories away, just as the taxi driver put down her luggage before her. She forced a smile, then took out her wallet and paid the fare.

As soon as the taxi rolled away, she began to walk down the road, trailing her luggage behind her.

Her face brightened when she approached the first shops and tavernas on the way. The familiar, yellow post box in the corner made her smile. Not much had changed in Messonghi all this time. She welcomed this eventuality. It gave her an odd sense of comfort.

Across the street, she recognised the café that she used to visit with her family on the way to the beach. Her parents would have a coffee, and she and Tom would enjoy an orange juice and a bun.

Sometimes, they'd skip breakfast and all have a *bougatsa* instead. Tom used to ask for absolutely loads of cinnamon on his... so much so that it made it taste bitter but he still loved it.

Lizzie's eyes misted over at the memory, her mind revelling in the thought of the luxurious hot custard sprinkled with cinnamon. She gave a soft sigh and turned left at the first corner.

The path led to the beach. This spot was where she used to swim with her family. She had booked online a room close by. When she arrived at the boarded walkway that ran the length of the beach, she left her luggage there and ambled to the edge of the shore in her flat, open sandals. She stopped so close to the water that her toes got splashed with every feeble wave that came to lap on the sand.

She didn't mind. It felt like a welcome, but it caused her heart to constrict with feeling too. She could almost see her brother before her in the shallows, the way he used to paddle there as their parents watched from the sand.

Tom had the knack of hiding coins in the pockets of his swimshorts, then placing them on the sand near her when she wasn't looking. He'd sit there patiently talking or playing with her with a ball until she noticed the spare change glinting on the seabed. Then, he'd tell her it was mermaid gold... that it was going to give her luck all day. It was something he'd come up with on his own and loved to play this charade with her, just to make her smile.

Tom had always enjoyed making up stories to entertain her. He was fanciful like that, believing in the impossible, in magic and fairy tales. It often struck Lizzie, the irony of it, that eventually he was taken from her by something that didn't belong to this world.

Taking a deep breath, Lizzie turned away from the water and looked around her, her eyes scanning both sides of the beach. It was still too early for the holiday makers to arrive here in droves – just gone nine o clock. They were probably in their beds still, sleeping off the extra glasses of alcohol from the night before, or snoozing, half-awake, making plans in their blissful minds for another day in paradise.

Her bittersweet thoughts ended when her eyes drifted to the distant view of the bay. The two familiar mountain tops were too imposing and magnificent to ignore. First, her eyes caressed the tall mountain of Chlomos to the left, her eyes widening on spotting two antennas on its top, something that wasn't there during her last visit.

Her breath caught in her throat when she shifted her gaze to the right. The pyramid-shaped mountain of Martaouna stood there, robust and lush, a beauty to behold, no doubt admired by so many who didn't know the kind of evil it nurtured at its core.

The idea brought a bitter taste to her mouth, and she scrunched up her face looking down at her feet again, to find her sandals were half-sunk in the golden, wet sand.

'Hey, is this yours?' echoed from behind her, and she turned to see a woman in her late twenties. She was standing on the walkway pointing to Lizzie's luggage.

Lizzie approached and gave a tight smile. 'Yes, it is.'

The woman's expression turned cheerful. 'I take it you've just arrived. Welcome!'

'Indeed, I have. Thank you.'

'Are you looking for accommodation? My family owns a guest house right there.' She pointed to a line of business establishments across from a pier.

Lizzie saw a small guest house where the woman was pointing. Her booked accommodation was supposed to be around there too. *This could get awkward!*

'Our guest house is called Pitsilos Apartments. It's very nice. Come! I'll show you!' insisted the woman and began to beckon urgently.

Lizzie gave a frown. 'Pitsilos, you said?' She took a folded piece of paper from her shoulder bag and opened it. 'Why, that's where I've booked!'

The woman's face lit up. 'Wonderful! What's your name?' She took Lizzie's luggage by the handle and began to pull it along speedily, beckoning her to follow.

Lizzie hurried behind her along the wooden walkway to catch up, a bright smile on her lips. It amazed her, her own ability to feel amused, given the circumstances. Where had her light-heartedness come from? Perhaps Messonghi had inspired it... Being here made it impossible to stay in low spirits long enough, and the jovial locals certainly helped with that. *You have to love the Greeks! So spontaneous, so easy-going!*

The woman looked over her shoulder to speak, snapping Lizzie out of her reverie. 'I do all the bookings at Pitsilos. We're expecting two young ladies today. Are you Miss Roberts or Miss Doherty?'

Lizzie smiled. 'I'm Miss Roberts.'

'Pleased to meet you. I am Nia.' She looked up ahead again as she continued to stride along.

'Nia?' asked Lizzie to make sure she'd heard it correctly. She found it hard to keep up with the Greek woman in the heat and was about to ask her to slow down when Nia halted abruptly, much to Lizzie's relief.

'Yes. It's short for Evgenia...' the woman said as she stood, two hands on her hips, before an ancient-looking white-washed building. It had beautiful cypress-green shutters and a flight of stairs that led to the upper floor. Its banister made of polished dark wood glinted in the sunshine like fresh tar.

The front door of the property was wide open and cypress-green in colour as well. Terracotta flower pots, mainly with geraniums, daisies, and basil, lined the front path. A bright pink bougainvillea stood on the far corner, creeping up the front wall, the edges of its branches reaching up to the terrace on the upper floor. The place looked so quaint that Lizzie couldn't help but smile brightly.

'Your room is upstairs, but it's not ready yet. I'm sorry. You've come very early,' said Nia.

'Yes, I know, I'm sorry.' Lizzie apologised, absurdly enough.

Nia waved the apology away. 'Don't be. But you won't have to wait for long. My aunt has already started cleaning the rooms upstairs. I will go now and start preparing yours. The guests left last night.' She pointed to a taverna next door. 'You can go there and have a drink while you wait. Come back in an hour. You may leave your luggage here, if you wish.'

Nia pointed to the taverna, then to the guest house with an air of authority, her voice firm, causing Lizzie to admire her for many things. Not just for her impeccable command of English, but also for her confidence, the general way she carried herself... as if nothing could sway her, as if no matter what life could ever throw at her, she could handle it.

Lizzie felt a pang of jealousy inside. She hadn't had much confidence or self-assurance while growing up. Lost in her thoughts, it took her a while to realise Nia was looking at her intensely, her head tilted to the side. 'Is it okay? Are you happy to wait at the taverna, Miss Roberts?' she asked with a twirl of her hand mid-air.

'Yes, of course. Sorry, Nia. See you in an hour.' Lizzie gave a quick wave and walked to the taverna. It was a small establishment with a covered porch at the front where the seating area was. It looked idyllic. The simple notion that Messonghi hadn't been marred by mass tourism delighted her enough to put a spring in her step.

She sat at one of the tables near the sand and placed her shoulder bag on the chequered tablecloth, a huge sigh escaping from her lips as she sat back in the chair.

I've made it here. I can't believe it. Her eyes drifted to Martaouna again. Only she knew what the mountain meant to her. What it had taken from her. *Tomorrow is the day. Tomorrow I'll get my brother back.*

Thoughts of Tom flooded her mind. They had been staying at a guest house in Spileo back then, a tiny village nestled on the foothills of Martaouna. They used to play outside daily, in the mountain groves mostly. *Oh, it was heavenly there... until that dreadful morning, of course...*

A single tear rolled down her cheek, and she bent her head, brushing it away. She looked up again, just as a burly, elderly man came to stand before her. His piercing blue eyes and shock of salt-and-pepper frizzy hair caught her eye before all the rest did. He wore a tattered shirt and cotton trousers, a pinafore tied loosely around his midsection, and a huge smile on his face.

He was too old to be a hired waiter so Lizzie guessed he was the owner. His smile never fading, he took a pencil from behind his ear and placed the tip on the tiny notepad in his hand. 'Good morning,' he offered in pidgin English, 'Yes, please?'

'*Kalimera, ti kaneis*?' she said, savouring the sound of the first Greek words she'd uttered in twenty years. She'd spoken English to the taxi driver earlier, but now that she was in Messonghi she felt compelled to switch to her basic Greek with the locals.

The man's eyes turned huge. 'Very good Greek! You from England? You here before?'

Lizzie looked away and gave a wry smile. 'Yes. Many years ago. A coffee please?' she said, eager to change the subject.

'Greek coffee? Frappé? Capuccino?'

Lizzie didn't have to think. She knew what she wanted. 'Greek coffee, please. *Kafe. Glyko.*'

'Sweet?' he asked for confirmation.

'*Ne, glyko. Efcharisto.*' She'd tasted the honey-sweet Greek coffee only a couple of times during her last visit, having begged her parents to let her try it. She'd been waiting eagerly for the moment where it would touch her lips again.

'Okay. And I bring you *koulourakia*. My woman make now. I bring you two. For welcome!'

As soon as the man dashed back into the building, she fished her pocket dictionary out of her bag to look up the unknown word. Now that she was here she wished she'd learned some Greek back home all those years but, of course, all this time, the very thought of Greece or anything Greek had been impossible to bear.

She looked up '*koulourakia*' and couldn't help a tiny giggle. *Cookies! How sweet of him... Oh, my! How I've come to miss the Greeks and their generosity with food!*

Have I seen you before?

Lizzie had almost finished her Greek coffee. The small plate of warm, delicious cookies the owner had brought was now empty. She'd dunked them in the hot, velvety liquid, the way she'd seen the locals do so many times all those years ago.

Sitting back in her chair, she watched the world go by as holiday makers began to arrive, spreading out on the sand beach mats, towels, and even deck chairs. The sea view was spectacular, the water sparkling, the soft susurrus echoing from the water's edge reaching her ears like the sweetest angel song.

Just as she reached for her phone to check the time, she noticed a small fishing boat arriving to moor at the pier nearby. The boat had a cheerful azure colour and a white stripe running across its hull at the top. A tall, bearded young man wearing a fisherman's hat skipped onto the pier from it, then took two crates from the boat. Even though they brimmed over with fish, he piled them onto his shoulder effortlessly as if they weighed nothing.

Lizzie leaned forward in her seat and watched as he made his way along the pier towards the shore. She felt magnetized by him and admired his lank figure and beautiful olive skin. He was wearing jeans, but their tight cut suggested he had a muscular body. His bulging arms and shoulders confirmed that. He wore a flimsy, tattered t-shirt, its neckline grown out of shape. As he walked, a long black fringe danced before his eyes in the gentle breeze.

He was holding the crates in place on his shoulder with both hands, the muscles in his biceps and neck tightening and flexing as if little mice lived under his skin and scurried about.

The notion made Lizzie chuckle as she continued to watch him, transfixed. He was walking on the sand now and, to her delight, was coming towards her.

Sitting up in her chair, she looked away just as he stepped onto the seating area. As he hurried past her, she tossed back her mane of long auburn hair, her eyes darting at him again as soon as his back was turned to her. Now, he was making his way into the taverna, the sight of his muscular retreating form making her skin prickle and causing a rush of heat to course through her.

Lizzie fanned her face just as the owner inside greeted the man cordially. She was sitting directly opposite the door and could actually see them. She couldn't understand much from the volley of Greek they tossed at each other and wondered if the fisherman had come to sell his catch.

As if on cue, he rested the crates on a table inside, and the owner handed him a few notes. Next, the two men came to stand at the threshold, where the owner gave the fisherman a friendly pat on the shoulder. The latter smiled cordially and put the notes in the back of his jeans pocket. When he caught Lizzie looking, his smile froze in place.

Startled, Lizzie looked away, but not before registering a glint in the man's eyes in the split second that he'd captured her gaze.

The whole thing had made her heart beat in a crazy rhythm. She willed it to calm down and ventured another look his way to find him chatting to the owner. Lizzie gave an inaudible gasp when the owner said something and pointed vaguely towards her. Before she knew it, the handsome stranger had come to sit at the next table to hers.

Sitting back, he let out a long, luxurious sigh. Lizzie threw a surreptitious glance his way and saw that he'd just taken out a pack of cigarettes, placing it on the table. Bemused, she looked away, twisting her lips. She was allergic to cigarette smoke.

Even though she'd seemed mesmerised by the look of him earlier, the very idea that he smoked was enough to put her off him at once.

She wondered if she should complain to the owner, imagining it must be illegal to smoke in restaurants in Greece just like it was in England. She darted her eyes at the threshold only to find the owner had gone back inside.

How about asking the man not to smoke? She could ask nicely. After all, he wouldn't like it if she started coughing uncontrollably as soon as the toxic smoke reached her nostrils. He had a kind face... surely he would be thoughtful enough to put it out if she asked? Or... she could move instead. But why should she? It was a matter of principal, after all. He was the one breaking the law.

'Excuse me...' she piped up, turning to face him, and leaning towards him somewhat.

The man turned to her, a startled look in his eyes, but she was sure there was a hint of something else in there too. Intrigue? Admiration? She couldn't tell. But it gave her more courage to continue. She'd caught him right on time. Both his hands were hovering mid-air, one holding a cigarette between two long, surprisingly well-manicured fingers for a fisherman, the other hand about to strike a lighter.

'Yes?' he answered, a ghost of a smile playing on his lips.

'I wonder if you'd be so kind as to not smoke here? I am allergic. Or perhaps you could sit a little further away?' She waved her hand vaguely towards the tables at the far end of the seating area.

To her surprise, alarm ignited in his eyes, cigarette and lighter disappearing from view. 'Oh, I'm so sorry!' He ran a hand through his thick black hair. 'How thoughtless of me!' He leaned forward and gave an awkward smile, his neck muscles rippling.

Lizzie thought her throbbing heart would jump right out of her chest. She froze, captivated by the rugged lines of his jaw, his high cheekbones, and sparkling green eyes. *What's wrong with you, girl? Five minutes ago, men were the last thing on your mind!*

'Have I seen you before? You look familiar...' he said in perfectly enunciated English, his eyes twinkling in the streaming sunlight. Sitting right at the edge of the porch, showered by the soft morning light, he seemed nothing short of a bronze Greek god.

As well as admiring him, Lizzie also wondered how a fisherman could speak her language so well. Finally, she cleared her throat and said, 'No... I don't think so.'

He gave a grin so huge in response that his mirth reflected in his eyes. 'One thing's for sure – you haven't been here long.' He leaned back in his chair and tilted his head. He seemed to study her now, playfully, and it made her mad.

Lizzie huffed. 'What makes you think that?'

He looked away, then shot her a meaningful look, his hand pointing at her with a little wave. 'For one, you're pasty white. And there's the other thing...' He seemed hesitant and looked away again.

Lizzie gave a frown. 'What other thing?'

He gave a soft sigh, then turned to her and said, 'Well, to tell you the truth, you seem a little... how do you say... worked up?'

Lizzie's brows shot up. 'Do I?'

'Yes, you do.'

'And? What if I do? How did you surmise from that that I haven't been here long?'

He threw out his arms. 'Well, isn't it obvious? Messonghi is a paradise. And I don't think there are stressed people in paradise, if you know what I mean?' He gave an irresistible smile that made her stare for a few moments, despite her annoyance.

Finally, she tore her eyes away from his face. For a moment, she wondered how he could be causing her to fume with vexation and to gawp with admiration at the same time. 'Excuse me, but this is not very nice,' she mumbled, venturing a look his way again.

He wrinkled his brow. 'But why? I was merely stating a fact.'

'No you weren't, you were being rude! And let us not forget you were about to light up a cigarette a while ago! You didn't even plan to ask me if it's okay to smoke, did you?'

He put up both hands, eyes widening. 'Hey! I've apologised for that.' He winked at her, a lopsided smile spreading on his face, head tilted playfully.

There was something in the way he eyed her then that made her blood boil. 'You apologise but you're still being an arse, excuse my French!'

'French? You don't sound French!'

Despite herself, Lizzie chuckled. 'It's a saying...' She gave a dismissive wave and looked away, making a point of ignoring him by turning in her chair towards the beach. She was mad at him but, at the same time, she scolded herself. *Have I gone too far? It's not like me to be on a short fuse...*

Just at that moment, she heard the owner's cheerful voice. He was saying something to the handsome man behind her. She heard the chink of porcelain, a soft thud, then footsteps. Turning to take a peek, she saw the owner walking back inside. He'd just served the man a Greek coffee and a glass of water.

She threw another furtive glance towards the stranger, catching him as he emptied the long tumbler of iced water in one go. Droplets of condensation ran down the glass, then onto his hand as he held it drinking, and she felt a stir inside at the sight of

ianly hands. He had his eyes closed as he drank, his long
iesmerizing, as thick and dark as his eyebrows.

panicked as he opened his eyes and put the glass down,
having just enough time to look away as she heard him say, 'Well
if I caused any offense, I apologise. I was merely stating what I
saw.'

She turned to meet his gaze, happy to accept the apology. She'd
come here to try to end a torment that had lasted for years on end.
Of course, she wasn't happy or relaxed. Why would she hold it
against him?

She let out a soft sigh and said, 'Okay... Maybe we started on the
wrong foot. I apologise too. I went a little crazy on you back there.
Truth is, I am a little stressed. And yes, you're right. I've only just
arrived here...'

He smiled broadly, his laughing eyes sending butterflies to
dance before her own. But, somehow, she managed to conceal the
spellbinding effect he had on her. Her ability to appear collected
even in the most difficult situations was a gift she owed to her
long years of service at state hospitals as a nurse back in England.
It takes a lot to faze a nurse... thank goodness!

'Miss Roberts!' came a voice from behind her.

Lizzie turned in her chair to find Nia beckoning to her from the
front patio of Pitsilos Apartments.

Lizzie jerked upright and brushed her cheek with an urgent
hand. It felt hot as if she'd been sitting by a raging fire. 'My room's
ready?'

'Yes! It's ready. Come!' said Nia as she waved frantically.

Lizzie nodded, then turned to give the man a little wave. 'Bye,
nice to meet you...' she said breathlessly as she picked up her
shoulder bag from the table.

'Are you sure... that it was nice?' he asked with a lazy smile, an
arm draped over the back of his chair.

'Absolutely!' She gave a wicked grin. 'And, lucky you... Now that
I'm leaving, you can smoke to your heart's content!'

She turned away just as his eyes ignited with amusement. A
visceral sound rose, filling the air behind her, and he erupted in a
loud belly laugh just as she began to walk away.

It's wrong to feel blissful in this place

Lizzie had had a quick lunch—just a toasted sandwich from a café and a cup of tea—then enjoyed a cooling swim. Next, she rented a deckchair and, at some point, fell asleep with the warm rush of the sea breeze caressing her skin. It felt delicious... A feeling she was overjoyed to recapture after so long.

Upon waking, she thanked herself for choosing to rest under a thatched umbrella. Without it, she'd have burned under the merciless sun during her siesta.

In the late afternoon, she returned to her room and had a shower. It helped her to feel refreshed and rejuvenated, but not without a measure of guilt too. It struck her as wrong to feel blissful in this place. She wasn't here for a holiday. She was here on a mission; to end the tragedy that had befallen Tom and herself... once and for all.

Her room had a small balcony with a stunning view of the mountains. The village of Spileo was clearly visible on Martaouna at this hour, its houses resembling tiny white birds nestled on a leafy tree.

But, the beauty of the view was lost on her. That wretched mountain hid at its core a curse that no one, other than she, knew about.

A soft rustle, then a metallic sound, broke her reverie. She turned her head to the right to find a woman about her age—early thirties—standing on the next balcony. She didn't look Greek.

'Hi, there!' came the confirmation from the woman in a heavy Irish accent. She leaned against the railing and gave a huge smile.

'Hello,' replied Lizzie, smiling pleasantly.

'Isn't it fantastic here?'

Lizzie swallowed hard, then said, 'Yeah...' hoping the woman wouldn't notice her lack of enthusiasm and call on it, in the way that handsome Greek had done earlier today.

As it turned out, the woman was too exuberant to notice Lizzie's damp spirits. She kept talking, flailing her arms and rolling her eyes, telling Lizzie how much she loved Messonghi. This was where she'd met her husband twelve years earlier. They'd come back this year, after all this time, with their ten-year-old son in tow.

'Wonderful. Does your son like it here?' asked Lizzie, genuinely pleased to see the woman's excitement. It helped her to forget her own misery.

The woman rolled her eyes for the umpteenth time. 'He adores it! And we only arrived yesterday. We're off to the north of the island the day after tomorrow, visiting Paleokastritsa, then Corfu town. We can't wait! We're staying for three weeks and intend to go around a lot—'

'That's nice...'

A boy came out onto the woman's balcony, cutting her torrent of enthusiastic talk short and taking Lizzie by surprise. Had she not said her son was ten, Lizzie would have thought he was a teenager. He was far too tall and large for his age. That's when his father came out too, to confirm who the boy had taken after. He was a mountain of a man.

The woman gave a cheer and beckoned them over to make introductions. 'This is my boy, Derek, and this is my husband, Brian. I'm Janet, by the way.' She offered her hand.

Lizzie approached to shake hands. 'And I'm Lizzie. What a lovely family you are!'

Brian and Derek shook hands with Lizzie, then Janet asked her if she'd like to join them for a drink in a bar later on.

Lizzie had planned to have a quick dinner, then go to bed early to try to rest properly, not just physically but also mentally. Her mind was all over the place. But perhaps a drink and a fun conversation before bed could work wonders for her.

'Sure!' she piped up in the end, mirroring Janet's bright expression. 'I'm grabbing a bite next door a little later. Should be back here by eight... so anytime after that would be fine by me.'

'Great!' said Janet, and all three waved, then disappeared inside, leaving Lizzie alone once again, hostage to her thoughts, but this time she knew not to gaze at the mountain any longer.

With a deep sigh, she turned about face and headed back to her own room to unpack her bag, then head down for her dinner. The ventilation pipes of the taverna next door were filling the air with tantalising smells of tomato sauce, grilled cheese, and roasted meat. They had long begun to torture her senses. But, far from those, she had her mind set on trying again the delicacies she had most come to miss.

'Oh, how I've missed fried *kalamari*! And *dolmadakia*... Yeah, these and a Greek salad will do me just nicely,' she mumbled to herself as she opened the tiny wardrobe in her room and began to unpack her bag.

Bad, bad bird

The cocktails Lizzie enjoyed in the company of Janet and her family had helped her to relax and to spend her first evening on the island with surprising ease of mind.

She'd managed to sleep soundly and, the next morning, awoke feeling rested, an unexpected feeling of hope blooming inside her heart.

She washed her face, then changed into her swimsuit and beach dress. As she combed her hair she caught herself humming a tune that she'd listened to in the bar the night before.

'What's the matter with you?' she scolded herself, her brow creasing. She shot a fiery look across the mirror at her reflection. 'Poor Tom is gone for twenty years, going through god-knows-what and you're singing? Really?'

Disgusted to look at herself any longer, she grabbed her beach bag and stormed outside. Once on the terrace, though, the gentle early morning sunshine came like a cheerful child to greet and caress her face.

Despite herself, she allowed the corners of her mouth to curve into a thin smile. Teetering between guilt and a growing feeling of elation, she skipped down the cement steps to the patio, then glided to the taverna next door.

The owner, who was serving chilled coffees at a table in the far corner, turned to her as she came in, his face the epitome of excitement. '*Kalimera!* Welcome, lady! Come sit!' he said in his broken English, and she let him guide her to a small table by the boarded walkway that ran across the façade.

'*Kafe parakalo.*'

'Same yesterday?' he asked with a tilt of his head.

'Yes, same as yesterday. *Glyko.*'

He nodded heavily. 'Of course! Remember I, remember!' With that, he disappeared inside.

As soon as she was left alone, Lizzie checked her watch, then turned her gaze towards the pier. The blue fishing boat wasn't there. She'd checked earlier, on her way to the taverna, and had felt a little disappointed. Yesterday, at this hour, that man had already arrived and was having his coffee here. *I wonder why he is late today... Unless he doesn't come here daily?*

Lizzie pressed her lips together, then looked away, tossing a silky strand of hair behind her shoulder. She fiddled with her sunglasses on the table. *So what if he doesn't come? What do you care? It's not like he was kind to you. Rude... That's what he was! What do you want to see him again for?* The little voice inside her head kept going, telling her it didn't matter, but her mind was still full of images of him... Green eyes, full lips, and that dark fringe that kept dancing in the breeze over his tall forehead. The way he squared his shoulders, the bulging hips under his jeans, the pronounced biceps.

Lizzie shook her head as if all the tantalizing images had just conjured up an argument against that inner nagging voice that spoke against him, and she felt compelled to take sides. She should really forget that man; she had enough to worry about as it was.

As if feeling guilty over the loss of her brother all those years ago hadn't been enough, her love life had always been a disaster. No man had lasted long enough around her. Her fixation about her lost brother and her ever-lasting depression meant that no man could ever handle her. They had all fled in the blink of an eye, it seemed. Why bother? Why open up her heart to another man again? It was futile. And that straggly little voice knew it.

Still, it was hard not to think of that man. Especially because he was rather mysterious. His hands, for one, didn't look that rough, which meant that perhaps fishing wasn't his main profession... this might also explain why he hadn't delivered any fish here again today. And there was the other thing: his English was impeccable. Surely, this wasn't the case with the Greeks who caught fish for a living.

The taverna owner's cheerful voice forced her out of her reverie. She raised her head and smiled readily as if she'd been thinking about happy things. But Lizzie had spent twenty years building walls that stopped others from knowing what she was thinking, how she was feeling. By now, it was as easy to her as a-b-c.

'Thank you, you're so kind. *Kalos anthropos*! A good person!' she said, surprised that the Greek words she once knew were coming back to her so easily. The man had placed a *koulouraki* on the saucer beside her coffee cup.

'*Efcharisto*! *Ki esi, kalo koritsi*! And you, a good girl,' he replied with a little laugh, but then his eyes widened with horror as they darted to something behind her.

Taken aback, Lizzie turned back in her chair, following his frosty gaze, to see that a raven had come to perch on the railing. It was very close to her, just behind her chair.

'Oooh!' she squealed with delight, despite herself. 'It's so beautiful! Is it all right to touch it?' she asked, her hand hovering mid-air near the bird. It didn't seem afraid of her. As for her, she felt enchanted by it. Its black wings and neck glistened in the sunlight in a mesmerising way.

The man's eyes ignited with alarm as he began to wave both hands frantically. '*Ochi! Ochi!* No touch! This, bad! Bad bird!' he said and, to her surprise, came around the table to approach the raven, making loud shooing noises and waving his hands fiercely.

The bird flapped its inky wings and flew away, disappearing from view in an instant.

Lizzie turned an inquisitive gaze towards the man, who was now shaking his head. 'Bad, bad bird. No touch. They bird for the dead, you know?'

'The dead?' Lizzie asked, her blood chilling. A hand flew up as if of its own accord to clutch her chest.

'Yes, oh... how you say?' His eyes lit up as he remembered the word he wanted, 'Grave! They go to grave. People no want raven. *Koraki*, we say. Bad bird! Only for the dead.'

'Oh. I see...' said Lizzie, relaxing somewhat and taking a deep breath. She couldn't imagine how the ravens could be connected to the dead in Greece, but she had to respect he believed that. She didn't want to upset him.

'Of course, thank you,' she said, then remembered she didn't know his name. 'By the way, I am Lizzie,' she added, offering her hand.

The man gave a huge grin and wiped his hand on his apron before offering his hand to her. 'Petros! Thank you,' he responded, and Lizzie thought that what he lacked in his command of English he compensated for with his earnest, jovial expression and the fervour of his handshake.

Lizzie smiled at him for a few more moments, then asked, 'And what is the name of your taverna, Mr Petros?'

'*Gorgona!*' he said, lifting an arm to point to the large painting on the wall beside the entrance. It depicted a beautiful, shapely mermaid with small rounded breasts, a wistful smile, and long flowing hair.

'*Gorgona*? It means, mermaid?' she asked for confirmation, smiling widely.

'Yes. *Gorgona*. Alexander sister.'

Lizzie tucked back her chin and frowned. 'Sorry, who's Alexander?'

'Alexander the Great, of course!' he said matter-of-factly with a satisfied smile, causing her to gawp, puzzled for a few moments, but he didn't seem to notice. He took his tray from the table and returned inside before she could express her mystification about his reply.

She sat back in her chair and began to laugh, a snort at first, then a titter, and it soon turned into a mad giggle that she found hard to suppress behind her open hand. Eager to stop herself before any onlookers might think she was nuts, she took a sip of her coffee, then removed her book from her bag and buried her nose in it.

She began to read but found it hard to concentrate, and her eyes began to jump all over the open pages. Waves of gaiety rose to her throat, causing her to giggle again at the thought of what Mr Petros had said. How can a mermaid be connected to Alexander the Great, she didn't know. But it filled her with intrigue that she found rejuvenating, hilarious, and she counted herself lucky to have found this quaint little taverna.

She tried to read but kept bursting into nervous giggles from time to time. At least, with a book in her hand she looked like she was enjoying a funny read.

Of course, she was still mad with worry about her brother, and this was exactly why she found the quirky Greeks a godsend at this dark hour. Thanks to them she could keep her sanity, at least for now, as she waited for the moment when she would see her brother again. If the witch had spoken truly, this would happen very soon.

※ ※ ※ ※

An hour later, Lizzie was in the water, enjoying a long, refreshing swim in Messonghi's shimmering blue waters. Afterwards, she lay on a rented deckchair to read her book under a thatched umbrella. She was in heaven there, happy to stay for hours, the temperature perfect, the sea breeze gentle, delicious on her skin.

Out of the blue, she heard the sound of a child crying. She looked up and saw a little girl, who seemed to be screaming with pain. A woman, perhaps her mother, was sitting beside the girl on a towel.

Another woman, well into her 70s, who Lizzie imagined was the little girl's *yiayia*, had just left them in a hurry, much to Lizzie's bewilderment. From what she had gathered from their short exchange, the little girl had been stung by a bee. She knew the word for bee. *Melissa*. The woman who sat with the child spoke to her in an intriguing mixture of Greek and English.

The little girl continued to cry, the woman looked helpless, and the older woman hadn't returned yet, so Lizzie decided to help. She shot upright and began to rummage in her bag. Seconds later, she found what she was looking for. It was an ammonia stick. She rushed to the others, taking the cap off. 'Hi! Here! Try this!' she said to the woman.

'Oh thank you!' The woman, a beautiful blond in her late twenties with translucent olive skin, took the stick and applied the ammonia to the girl's arm.

In a few moments, the child stopped crying, her breathing slowing down. The woman wiped the little girl's tears and kissed the top of her head as she held her in her arms. Finally, she looked up at Lizzie and returned the stick, her face bright.

'Thank you so much. I don't know what I would have done without that!'

'It's nothing. I always carry one with me. I'm a nurse... and tend to take precautions, you know?'

'Good for you! Silly me, I never plan ahead. But I've learned my lesson now.' She pointed to the stick in Lizzie's hand. 'That thing is more efficient than the ice my mother-in-law just rushed off to get. I tried to stop her, telling her it won't help, but she was too panicky to listen.' She flicked her wrist and rolled her eyes. 'Oh! The Greeks are so dramatic!'

Lizzie smiled at that. 'Are you married to a Greek?'

'Yes.'

'And you live here?'

'Oh goodness, no. I'd have killed myself if I had to live here in the winter. I'm a Londoner. A city girl. This peace and quiet is fine in the summer, but winter here is quite different. I couldn't stomach it, and I only stayed for a week the only time I've ever braved spending Christmas here, I tell you.' She scrunched up her face, then gave a little wave. 'Besides, living in England all winter puts enough space between me and the *petherika*, you know what I mean?' She offered a meaningful smile.

Lizzie frowned at the unknown word. '*Petherika*?'

'Sorry. I meant the in-laws.'

Right on cue, the old woman rushed back with Mr Petros in tow. From the short and rather fervent conversation that ensued among the three adults in Greek, Lizzie gathered that the *yiayia* insisted on trying the ice even though the child was calm now, and didn't need it any more.

In the end, to keep the peace, the mother allowed the old woman to place the ice for a little while on the girl's arm. The moment the *yiayia* looked away, the mother turned to Lizzie and whispered, 'I rest my case!' causing Lizzie to place a hand over her mouth to stifle a giggle.

The little girl seemed to enjoy all the attention and was now giving gappy smiles all around, clearly no longer in pain. She was about six or seven years old.

As soon as Mr Petros returned to Gorgona, the *yiayia* joined a friend nearby for a little chat.

The girl's mother rolled her eyes and offered Lizzie a knowing smile. 'The Greeks are such drama queens, aren't they?'

Lizzie shared a laugh with her about that, even though she had nothing bad to say about the locals. She found them endearing, no matter their quirks, but imagined that for an English woman, having a Greek mother-in-law must be quite a challenge, in many ways.

Lizzie patted the little girl on the head and returned to her place. She sat on her deckchair and, as she swung her legs over to lie down again, she heard someone call her name.

It was Janet. She'd just halted before her with an open smile, her husband and son trailing behind her. They were all clutching bags that brimmed over with beach paraphernalia, clearly just descended from their room and about to hit the water.

After a short exchange, they were off, but Lizzie could still see them from where she sat; they were fussing about as they laid down towels and beach mats, then Janet helped her husband and child put suntan lotion on. As she watched them, not without a sense of envy for Janet's obvious family bliss, she couldn't help but pay the most attention to her son, Derek. How young and happy he looked! His whole life ahead of him... Inevitably, Lizzie's mind wandered to her darling Tom again.

If only she had never suggested that they enter that cursed cave... if they'd run out the moment they saw the witch, Tom might have grown to be a big lad like that too... And today, he'd be thirty-two, perhaps a married man with a son that looked just like Derek...

Lizzie's eyes misted over but, like she often did, she fought back the pain. Shaking her head, she checked her watch one more time. *A few more hours to go.* Her heart leapt at the very thought of seeing her brother again.

A plethora of unsettling thoughts

After a light lunch, Lizzie returned to her room, her anticipation becoming unbearable once indoors, somehow. After a quick shower, she began to feel the walls closing in, so decided to get out again and have a walk up the mountain. Slipping on a patterned short summer dress and her most comfortable sandals she dashed outside. Once she began to walk, or rather stride determinedly, she felt herself breathe more freely again. *I'll do anything but sit indoors till midnight twiddling my thumbs! That would drive me nuts!*

It was the early afternoon and the heat was ferocious but she'd put a hat on and was braving the uphill climb with gusto, telling herself she used to do this all the time as a child. This was going to be a fun walk... just killing time. Yet, she knew, what she was really after was to catch a glimpse of the cave again in daylight.

A plethora of unsettling thoughts had long begun to creep into her mind that maybe she wouldn't be able to remember where it was, or that it might be difficult to locate it in the dark. What if the locals had sealed its entrance? Surely they knew there was a cave by that grove. What if someone had found out about the witch and told everyone, and they'd taken measures to ensure that she had no way to contact the living any more?

Panic rose inside her at the very thought, but she set it aside. She had learned in her life to swat away negative thoughts like pestering flies. There was no other way she could have functioned all this time.

Soon, she was sauntering happily again, marvelling at the shady olive groves on either side of the road, and breathing in the fragrant, fresh air. Every so often, she halted to admire the stunning vista of the bay. It grew less and less obstructed by the trees as she made her way up the mountain.

When the first houses of Spileo came into view, she gasped at the sight, realizing it all seemed just as she remembered it. It pleased her, the thought that time hadn't touched this place, just like it hadn't touched Messonghi either. This gave her hope, making her feel closer to Tom, somehow.

As she continued to amble along, she came upon a particular house she remembered all too well. It was the guest house where she'd stayed that fateful summer with her family. It was adjacent to the private house of the family that owned it. At first glance, she noticed that, unlike most of the other properties, this one had suffered greatly from the passage of time.

All the windows and the main entrance of the guest house were shut, and the lettering on its large sign had nearly faded away completely – so much so that she wondered why the owners bothered to keep it on the front wall.

It was clear to her that the guest house was closed down, but the air of neglect hung over the private dwelling beside it as well. Its façade looked derelict, and if it weren't for the washing line where a pair of jeans and two t-shirts flowed gently in the breeze, she'd have thought that this was uninhabited too.

The off-white front wall was strewn with ugly patches of damp here and there and was generally in dire need of re-painting. Large pieces of the plaster covering were missing in places as well. The same was the case in the front porch where the railing had rusted for the most part and the black paint had peeled away here and there. There was no car or other vehicle parked in the drive, and the tall garden gate before her was closed and chained.

In the garden, the only flowers were roses, but they were in need of pruning and watering. None of the colourful blooms she remembered from the past filled the flower patches these days. Two herb bushes stood in their place—rosemary and sage—and the soft soil was dotted with clumps of purslane. In the far corner, a lemon tree and a pomegranate tree stood side by side, their leaves rustling in the soft breeze.

Lizzie's gaze returned to the front porch of the private house. *Why did they leave this place to come to this? Did something happen to them? They were such a lovely family...* She remembered their names well. Mr Lambros and Mrs Penelope Katsaros, and their little son, Stamatis, who was one year older than her and Tom. He was a good boy but naughty too... teasing her all the time, often making her lose her patience with him. Lizzie smiled wryly at that. *They were all such happy people... even the* pappou *and the* yiayia *who lived here with them. What happened to them all?*

With a heavy sigh, she resumed walking, leaving the sorry sight behind her.

Lizzie reached the end of the village and continued to walk uphill along the winding road, past a couple of guest houses she hadn't seen before. It was then that her breathing grew laboured, but not because of exhaustion or the sweltering heat.

Her eyes were focusing far now, at the dense olive grove that was coming up ahead. She quickened her step, her breath catching in her throat, but she was too intent on getting there if only a moment sooner; just to make sure the cave that stood on the other side of that grove was still accessible.

She took a dirt path off the road and entered the grove, now hurrying through the trees, aware that she was palpitating and getting thirsty. And even though she chastised herself for not having brought with her any water, it never crossed her mind to turn about face.

She neared the far end of the grove, the song of the cicadas deafening. The sound reverberated inside her, urgent, along with the thumping of her heart and the hum of her own blood rushing through her temples.

Lizzie stopped short when she arrived at the familiar clearing. Thick clumps of thorny bushes lined the precipice to her left, but she wasn't in the mood to go there and enjoy the view of the bay. Instead, her eyes were pinned on the cave in the rock face across from her. Its entrance was unobstructed, gaping open like a hungry mouth, expectant, unquenchable.

Letting out a huge sigh of relief, she looked all around her. No one was about, just she, alone in the serenity. All she could hear was the buzzing of bees, the tweeting of birds and the long-drawn cries of a raven that swooped and circled overhead.

A thought of Mr Petros and what he had said about ravens made the tiny hairs on the back of her neck stand on end. But this wasn't the time to ponder upon the man's superstitions. She had something more important to deal with.

Slowly, she walked up to the cave and stood at the entrance, gazing at the dark abyss inside. Because of the strong sunshine, she couldn't make out anything. She inched inside a couple of steps, just enough so she could inspect the space a little better.

After a few moments, she still couldn't see much. She had started to contemplate venturing a few more steps inside, to make sure the spring was still there, when something peculiar happened.

A conspiracy of ravens arrived from seemingly nowhere, circling low over her head and cawing at an ear-piercing volume. Instinctively, Lizzie crouched over and placed her arms over her face, howling with distress. Somehow, they had flown into the cave, straight at her. *How is that even possible? Why are they doing that?*

Seeing that they wouldn't go away, she began to panic and brought an elbow over her eyes, raising the other to wave it in mid-air while making shooing sounds. 'Get away! Go!' she commanded a few times, her voice sounding frail and desperate in her own ears.

In those moments, she could hear an eerie rush of wind as the wings of the ravens flapped over her head. Every now and then, she would feel the softness of feathers brush against her waving hand, her arms and shoulders.

Seeing that the ravens didn't seem to be deterred, she dashed out of the cave and headed for the olive grove, all the while keeping her head low and protecting her face with her arms. As she made her way, her heart thumping in her chest, she felt thankful that the ravens, somehow, weren't hurting her with their beaks and claws.

The very thought of the possibility made the blood chill in her veins, but at the same time, she wondered... *Do ravens attack humans? They don't, do they?*

Stumbling blindly ahead, she made it back to the grove and hurried under the dense canopy. A moment later, she brought her arms down, eyes widening, when she realized the ravens hadn't followed her there. Instead, they had flown high and away in seconds, it seemed. And now, they had disappeared from sight altogether, the last echoes of their shrill cries fading in the distance.

Lizzie stood straight again and threw her gaze at the cave across the clearing. Right then, the ravens returned to stand before the cave, a glistening mass of blackness before the entrance, laid out like a carpet that rustled and breathed. Other ravens stood in small groups on the rock face over the gaping hole, turning their heads this way and that, their eyes on her as if willing her to take a step closer.

Lizzie's thoughts returned to what Mr Petros had said… that the ravens were the birds of the dead. *What did he mean?* But, whatever he'd meant, and whether there was truth in it or not, one thing was certain: the way these birds were acting wasn't normal.

She wasn't going to risk taking another closer look. After all, she'd got what she wanted – she'd ascertained that the cave was still accessible. She would return at midnight when she was supposed to.

Mystified by the ravens, but certainly not deterred, Lizzie turned about face and ambled back to the road.

I assure you I don't have cooties

Lizzie walked downhill along the road towards the village of Spileo, her mind racing from the scare she'd just had.

The heat, hammering down upon her with ferocity, was welcoming now. It helped her to restore in her a rudimentary sense of normality and sanity. *Back to the real world... What was that back there? The edge of the Twilight Zone?*

Suddenly, she heard a honk coming from behind her. Her shoulders jumped, eyes popping out, as she looked over her shoulder to see a motorcycle rushing towards her, a man its only rider.

Her heart began to race and she froze for a moment, realizing in horror that all this time she'd been walking down the middle of the road. She hurried to the side and ran a hand through her hair as the motorcycle approached.

The man stopped the motorcycle and took his helmet off just as she waved with a faint smile, about to apologise for being so careless.

The words never came out. Instead, her heart gave a thump to see his face and bright smile. *It's him!* It was the Greek fisherman from the taverna, and he looked just as handsome as he had the previous day. He had a mischievous glint in his eyes. Clearly, he had recognised her.

'Hi, there! You ought to be more careful, you know. I'd have hated to run you over,' he teased with a toothy grin.

Lizzie twisted her lips before replying, 'I know, sorry...' He must have read something in her expression then, because his face dropped. 'What's the matter? Are you okay?'

'Yes, thanks... It's just too hot... I think I've had too much sun, that's all.' She forced a smile.

'Maybe you got sun stroke...' Alarm coloured his face, and he reached for a plastic bag that hung from the handlebars. He rummaged through it, past what looked like a small power tool, and took a small bottle of water in his hands, offering it to her. 'Here! Drink! I've had a sip, but I assure you I don't have cooties.' He winked. 'And I didn't smoke before drinking either, scout's honour,' he teased with another wink.

Lizzie froze for a moment or two, mesmerised by his bright green eyes. He shook the bottle in his hand, without a word this time, just intensifying that smile that made her weak at the knees, even weaker than a conspiracy of ravens ever could.

Somehow, she jerked into motion and took the bottle. The water inside splashed against its plastic confines, sparkling under the sunlight like liquid diamonds, making her mouth feel even drier than before, and she realized just how badly she wanted it. She opened the top and tilted her head back, drinking thirstily, like a Bedouin who's just reached an oasis.

'Wow! You certainly needed that!' he said when she closed the bottle again. She'd emptied it to its last drop.

Lizzie felt silly, having been caught in this state; not just half-dead from thirst but unsettled too from her earlier encounter with those nasty birds. Her afternoon had had a turn for the worse, and she was thankful he had come. *And he's incredibly handsome!*

The way he was smiling at her now was irresistible, showing perfect pearly whites. Even his beard seemed okay on him, and she didn't like facial hair on men. But he was so drop-dead gorgeous she could only stare. Longer than she was happy to, it seemed.

At last, he spoke to break the awkward silence. 'Are you staying in Messonghi or here in Spileo?'

'In Messonghi.'

He tilted his head. 'Do you need a ride?'

'No, no thanks. I'm happy to walk.' She had said it without thinking and already regretted it. *What's the matter with me? Why did I say no?*

He furrowed his brow. 'Are you sure? It seems to me that you've had too much sun for one day. Not safe for you to walk down the mountain in this state, trust me. Besides, you needn't worry. I'm a good man. Promise.' He put up his hands, then pointed at himself with a sharp thumb. 'Not an axe-murderer.' Then, with a slow, sweet smile he beckoned. 'Come on, I'll take you to your hotel.'

Lizzie gave a beaming smile but hesitated still. 'Are you sure I wouldn't be putting you out?'

He half-closed his eyes and shook his head from side to side. 'Of course not. I'm not working tonight. I was just coming from Agios

Dimitrios visiting a friend, and now I'm off to Messonghi to see another.'

The word 'friend' made Lizzie wonder if he meant a lady or a guy, but she didn't show it. Instead, with a grateful smile, she got on the motorcycle to sit behind him. He offered her his helmet but, as there was only one, she insisted that he should wear it since he was at the controls.

Reluctantly, and seeing that she was adamant, he put it on and started the engine.

As its hum reached her ears, she realized in panic she didn't know what she was supposed to do with her hands. *Should I hold on to him or would he deem it rude?*

To her relief and much excitement, he spoke then as if on cue. 'You'd better hold on to me with both hands. There are several potholes on the way. I'd hate for you to jump off the motorcycle and onto our path like a rabbit out of a magician's hat!'

Lizzie gave a chortle and put her hands on either side of his waist. The motorcycle began to roll down the road slowly, then to gain speed. A cool rush of air hit her face, rejuvenating her, and her hair began to fly around her, flaming red strands twirling about her face like the tentacles of an octopus.

Lizzie took deep breaths, feeling more alive with every passing second. She'd never been on a motorcycle before, but that wasn't the only novelty that made her feel elated. It was also the lush green views that rushed past her, the vast blue sea in the distance, and the salty breeze that she could smell all the more as they made their way down the mountain.

But, most of all, it was the feel of his warm flesh against the palms of her hands, the sight of his bulging thighs, and the musky fragrance of his cologne that tantalized her in ways she found too irresistible to ignore.

❋ ❋ ❋ ❋

As soon as they reached the main road at Messonghi, she tapped his waist and asked him to stop.

He obliged her and put his feet down on the tarmac. 'Here?' He looked over his shoulder.

'Yes, thank you. This is fine.'

He took off his helmet to reveal a puzzled expression. 'Are you sure? I can take you to your hotel, it's no problem.'

Lizzie slid off the motorcycle to stand before him on the roadside. 'No, it's okay, thank you so much. I am not going to my room anyway. I think I'll go to a bar to gaze out to sea for a while and rehydrate myself adequately.'

Despite herself, she winked at him, then let out a high-pitched laugh. If she didn't know better she'd have thought it had come from a girl who had no worries in the world, unlike her. *What's wrong with me? I didn't come here to flirt!* Her awful guilt had returned with a vengeance to gnaw at her insides.

He scratched his head. 'Oh, okay. But make sure to drink plenty of water! Not alcohol. That would dehydrate you further.'

'Yes, doctor,' she teased, then sobering up, 'Look, I'm very grateful. You literally saved me back there. I don't know what I was thinking traipsing like that in the heat.' She twirled a strand of her hair as she spoke, but stopped when she realized he was staring at it as if hypnotized.

Now, he was gazing into her eyes, a lazy smile on his face, causing her heart to race again. His facial features were chiselled to perfection, his green eyes specked with gold. The effect they had on her was mesmerizing.

Her mind returned to just a few moments ago when she was still holding him by the waist. His flesh had felt hard like a rock... and, all the while, the view of his muscular back had caused her to hyperventilate.

Now, she was fanning her face again, feeling stupid. At least, he wasn't staring any more. He was scuffling the dirt with the front of his trainers now, looking up ahead. 'Well, okay then, have a good evening... And maybe I'll see you around.'

She cleared her throat, threw him a fleeting glance, then looked up ahead too. 'Yes. See you around. Take care now... and make sure you don't jump off the seat and onto the road like a rabbit!' she teased.

'Yes! Out of a magician's hat,' he added for her, taking her eyes hostage as he offered another irresistible smile.

'That's right. I forgot that bit,' she said, giggling, despite herself.

'My mother used to say that to me for years, ever since I bought my first motorcycle. I guess it stuck.' He shrugged.

'It's cute. I like it...'

He was gazing into her eyes still, not making a move to go, and she wondered what that was all about. She shook her head, then gave a little wave. 'Well! I'll let you go then, thanks again!'

Her voice had sounded a little urgent, and that seemed to jerk him into motion. He put his helmet back on, and with a wave, he was gone.

She stood on the roadside for a while, just watching him go till he disappeared behind the oncoming traffic. He had left her at the corner where she'd arrived by taxi the previous day. *Look at me! I've only just arrived, haven't even seen my brother yet, and I'm flirting! Shame on you, Lizzie! Where are your priorities?*

Scolding herself still, she crossed the street without further ado and made a beeline for the café she knew from her happy days. She sat at the nearest free table and, as she waited for the waiter, made plans for her evening. *A* bougatsa *and a sweet* Frappé *for now... A couple of glasses of water... Then, this evening, a light dinner... and some alcohol for Dutch courage.*

Just the thought that she needed courage made her cringe inside, wondering if she had enough. She wasn't looking forward to entering the cave or seeing the witch again. But she had to. To get her brother back. Tonight she had to be at her best, the strongest and most fearless she could ever be. Tom needed her. And she would do anything, absolutely anything, to get him back and keep him safe this time around.

A horror mask of ugliness

The next couple of hours were a torture, and she grew all the more restless as the time went by. At Gorgona, she ordered a Greek salad and *dolmades* for dinner but hardly touched them. Even the jovial face of Mr Petros, and the small talk he engaged her in with his basic English, couldn't cheer her up.

Afterwards, she went to the nearest bar where she downed a cocktail and a gin-and-tonic while she waited for the time to pass.

Dressed in a t-shirt, jeans, and flat shoes, she must have looked like a random tourist to the other patrons at the bar, just a woman holidaying alone perhaps, but only she knew she was anything but. She tried not to look around too much, in case she caught anyone's eye and gave the wrong impression that she was looking to be picked up.

So she made a point of checking her watch and glancing at the door every now and then, hoping it would give the impression that she was waiting for someone. Whether this had helped or not she didn't know, but no one did approach her and she was thankful for that.

When not checking her watch or the front door, she browsed through posts on social media on her phone, but nothing seemed to entertain her or take her mind off the task at hand.

In the end, the wait got too much to bear, and she thought she would scream her head off. And even though the witch was expecting her in the cave at midnight, she left the bar too early— just gone eleven—telling herself she'd walk uphill really slowly.

Thanks to the street lights as she made her way to Spileo, a tote bag flung over her shoulder, she could see comfortably up ahead, and the sparse traffic made her feel safe.

Lizzie had put a small torch in her bag, which she'd bought at a supermarket earlier that day. She had noticed in the afternoon that after Spileo there were no street lights along the road. This meant the olive grove would be in total darkness at night. The very idea that she'd be entering the cave with that little plastic torch as the only thing slicing feebly through the gloom, brought a shiver to her spine. Meeting a supernatural being under these circumstances seemed unthinkable. And yet, this was exactly what she was going to do. *For Tom.*

The witch, who had introduced herself as Phoni, had given her specific instructions. Lizzie had to visit her on her own, and thus, she couldn't consider taking a taxi to the grove. What if the witch found out and minded that? She couldn't risk it. Besides, walking helped her think. The fresh night air was chilly, heavy with moisture. As she walked uphill she felt her clothes begin to cling to her flesh.

※ ※ ※ ※

Leaving Spileo behind, Lizzie steeled herself for the darkness up ahead. She passed by the last street light on the way and kept going. Some locals in the village had given her funny looks. Others, who were sitting on their porches, had whispered to each other as she passed by. They'd probably thought she was mad traipsing uphill alone in the semi-darkness.

Darkness... the word echoed ominously inside her head as she stared into the abyss before her, the cries of crows and the hooting of owls the only sounds to reach her ears.

Aided by the light of a waning moon, she found the olive grove; she could just make out the top branches of the trees waving eerily in the gloom against the silky sky. They looked like lost souls begging for redemption. The soft rustle of their swaying movement made the hairs on the nape of her neck stand on end.

Somehow, she'd forgotten she'd been carrying a torch until now. She fished it out of her bag and turned it on, a soft sigh of relief escaping from her lips. It had a much stronger beam than she'd expected. It made the olive trees look silver; a beautiful, yet forlorn sight.

Lizzie stepped off the road and onto the dirt track, then headed for the trees. Now that she was off the road, it felt like a dip into the sea, like a long dive that you had to do while keeping time, lest the air in your lungs would run out.

The very thought kick-started her mind and body in ways she hadn't thought imaginable. A rush of heat rose from her legs as she started to rush forward, then it spread onto her chest, down her gut again, and from there it mushroomed in an explosion of energy.

She felt herself glide as she ran now, impossibly fast, and she was no longer afraid, no longer worried. Now was the time she'd been waiting for. She could be seeing and holding Tom in her arms any moment now.

As she hurried along the path, the witch's words echoed inside her mind, for the millionth time, again:

'Twenty years after today, not a day earlier or later, return at midnight, if you wish, and claim your brother back. But come on your own! This, I demand!'

❋❋❋❋

By the time Lizzie had reached the cave, her heart felt like it was about to explode. Sweat ran down her face, and her legs tingled all the way down to her toes. Her body was pumped with adrenaline – an exhilarating feeling. Fearing that it might subside anytime soon, she dashed into the cave without hesitation, her torch shining strongly to reveal grey, mossy walls.

The water spring was there, as expected, and it looked eerie at this hour. That fateful day, its water was murky, unlike any fresh water spring you would imagine. Green, and strewn with moss, leaves, and twigs, it had looked repulsive the day she and Tom had seen it during their first and only visit to the cave.

Yet, their adventurous spirit and curiosity had been strong. Tom had suggested they take off their sandals and wet their feet in it, but Lizzie had refused seeing that the water was filthy. They began to disagree and Tom was about to take off his shoes to get in on his own when a baby goat dashed into the cave, taking them by surprise.

Lizzie gave a deep frown at the memory of that poor goat. The moment its feet touched the water and it lowered its head to drink, that nasty creature had emerged from the spring, snatching it, then plunging it into the water... never to be seen again.

Lizzie shook her head and, steeling herself, took a step closer to the spring. Cradling the torch with both hands, she began to inch closer and closer, while shining the light on the water surface but detected no movement upon it.

She checked her watch. It was quarter to midnight. As good a time as any. 'Phoni! Where are you? Phoni!' She began to shout, knowing that no one from the village or the road could possibly hear her. She shouted even more loudly now. The sooner the witch came out to give her back her brother, the better.

No movement on the surface. Where is she? Restless, she made about face and began to explore every inch of the cave with the torch. All she found was rocks, startled spiders that scurried away from the light, and a large green lizard. It eyed her back with beady eyes before disappearing through a crack in the rocks.

Lizzie heaved a deep sigh and returned to the spring, her gaze resting on the murky water as her mind raced.

The last time, the witch had emerged through the spring just as the baby goat had come into contact with the water. Darling Tom had gone in with his sandals as soon as she'd snatched it, trying to get to it, to save it from her grasp, even though he'd seemed just as shocked as she was at the sight of Phoni. But he was too late. The witch had plunged the goat underwater before he could get close enough to save it.

Lizzie replayed the scene in her mind again. The poor animal had entered the cave and approached the spring without stopping for a moment as if magnetized by it. Lizzie had long worked out that it must have been some kind of trick... so Phoni could snatch it and lure Tom into the water in the process.

Lizzie had made a few assumptions about Phoni over the years. She was also convinced the spring was her gateway between this world and the underground one she obviously lived in.

Thoughts of the baby goat and the way it was captured returned to her mind. *What if Phoni can sense movement in the water?* Lizzie picked up a small stone and threw it in. She swallowed hard and pricked her ears for a few moments. Nothing.

Ok. Maybe if I touched the water? What if she only responds when something alive comes into contact with it?

She took off one shoe and dipped her toes in. Again, she gave it a few moments, only to ascertain this was futile too. As she put her shoe back on, she considered getting one of the spiders from the rocks and throwing it in but decided that was a bad idea, even for someone as desperate as she was. If her toes couldn't do it, a spider never would. Besides, how could she risk the life of another creature, no matter how small, and call herself an animal lover?

She was getting agitated now and was about to call out the witch's name again when a screeching sound made her cower, then shudder, and she turned around, her eyes huge.

A raven stood at the cave's entrance, its feet scuffling in the dirt, its eyes glowing milky white in the light of the torch. Now it was cawing at an ear-piercing volume, causing Lizzie to back-step onto some rocks behind her.

Was it the raven that screeched just now? Do ravens do that? It sounded almost like a human scream. Impossible!

She didn't have time to ponder about it much longer, because the raven then flapped its wings and took flight, circling around the cave and cawing loudly, the sound reverberating against the cave's walls.

Lizzie dropped the torch on the ground, a cloud of dirt rising into the air as she fell to her knees, holding her ears with both hands. She began to scream for it to stop, to go away, but the raven was relentless, and it continued its flight and wicked song until Lizzie thought she was going to go mad.

Then, a sound like water boiling in a pan echoed from the spring. The sound got louder and louder and, as it did, the raven began to cry more and more softly, flying lower and lower, until it landed by Lizzie, then waddled onto the edge of the spring. It turned its head back to look at her, an intelligent look in its eye as if it were willing her to do something.

And Lizzie did, as she gazed back at the raven, realizing that boiling sound in the spring meant the coming of the bird's mistress. Surely the ravens were connected to the witch. And now it made sense why they'd tried to stop her from visiting the cave sooner than she was expected to come.

Lizzie set her jaw and moved to stand by the bird, just as Phoni began to emerge from the spring. The water shimmered and bubbled, an outwardly yellow hue rising from its depths, making it look like it was on fire.

A vile smell of sulphur, mixed with the stench of decay, reached Lizzie's nostrils, causing her to scrunch up her face with disgust. Then, somehow, a rush of cool air came in from outside, clearing the air. Taken aback, Lizzie looked over her shoulder through the cave entrance to find the branches of the olive trees swaying madly outside. She could just make out the movement under the feeble moonlight. *How? It's not windy tonight!*

Lizzie turned to look before her again, her mystification fading as trepidation mushroomed inside her.

Phoni stood in the middle of the spring, the water up to her waist. She was looking straight at her, eyes narrowed into slits.

The witch's face was a horror mask of ugliness, and Lizzie remembered it well. It was made up of leathery wrinkled skin, large hairy ears, a twisted mouth of rotten teeth and milky eyes that were full of malice.

She was dressed in a sack cloth that revealed only her gnarled hands and skeletal legs. Her feet were bare and almost black, long black talons at the end of her toes to match those at the end of her fingers.

Phoni began to walk out of the water, glaring eyes trained upon Lizzie, a tight-lipped smile on her face that conveyed no trace of gaiety, only spite.

With every passing second, Lizzie grew all the more restless because she had noticed two things: First, that the witch's skin, long white hair, and garment were as dry as hay on a summer's day. And secondly, that she was alone. *Where is Tom?* Alarm ignited in her eyes. *It can't be! She cannot deceive me!*

Instinctively, she took two steps back, raising a hand before her. 'Stop! Don't come any closer!'

Phoni let out a wicked cackle, revealing an open mouth of inflamed gums and rotten teeth. 'What's the matter, Lizzie? I thought you'd be happy to see me again. It has been a long time, after all...' She tilted her head, toying with her.

Lizzie felt her blood boil in her veins. 'Don't ask me any questions, Phoni! I don't care to talk. I just want my brother back. That's all. Like you promised.'

Phoni gave a smug smile and continued to approach, stopping right at the edge of the spring, where the water licked at the dirt. The witch looked down at her own deformed toes, then back up, but didn't move or say anything. She only looked at Lizzie intently as if she was studying her.

Lizzie lost her nerve, her voice rising a few notches, arms flailing about as she said, 'What's this? Where's my brother? You told me to come back and claim him. I'm here! So give him back! Now!'

Slowly, Phoni raised her chin, then shot Lizzie a look that was heavy with indignation. 'You don't tell me what to do! You hear?'

'But you promised, Phoni! I've waited for twenty years—'

Phoni scowled at her. 'And you shall wait another twenty if you don't show me respect, little girl!'

Lizzie stepped forward. 'I'm not a little girl! Not any more! You don't scare me, witch!' She tipped her chin. 'Where's my brother?'

Phoni let out a guttural sound of amusement, then eyed Lizzie sideways. 'I like you, Lizzie... You should know that.'

'Really? You mean, you like me enough to steal my brother from me?'

'No... I like you enough to have let you go back to England. I could have taken you too... but I didn't.'

'Trust me. You've left me with half a life all the same. But don't change the subject. I am here for Tom. Where is he?'

Phoni brought her hands on either side of her head and started to sway, mimicking Lizzie, making fun of her. 'Where is he? Ooh! I cannot wait! My brother... my brother—'

Lizzie saw red. She lunged forward, reaching out with her arms to get to Phoni, to do whatever she could to deliver some punishment for the pain she'd been causing her all this time.

Except, Phoni was faster. In the blink of an eye, she had moved back to the centre of the spring from whence she'd come, impossibly fast, and that was not the only surprising thing about it. Now, she was standing on the surface of the water, somehow.

Lizzie couldn't believe it. She was still gawping when another malicious laugh from Phoni came to offend her ears.

'That wasn't nice, Lizzie. But I'll let this one go. Just this once. Now, listen. Here's what I need you to do. You will go back to Messonghi, and you are going to find a place to stay.'

Lizzie's brows shot up. 'What do you mean? I *do* have a place to stay!'

Phoni sneered. 'Not a hotel, Lizzie! A proper place of your own. You're not getting your brother yet.'

'What?' shrieked Lizzie, not believing her ears. 'No! You can't do that! You promised! You told me—'

Phoni rushed forward, fast and effortlessly, gliding over the water, like a leaf travelling down a stream. 'I told you what, Lizzie?'

Lizzie brought up her arms before her, like a boxer ready to fight, hands balled into fists. 'You told me I could get him tonight!'

Phoni gave a slow smirk and put up a gnarly finger. Its nail had long been lost, to rot, no doubt. 'No... I didn't say you could get him. If you recall, I said you could *claim* him.'

'What?' Lizzie turned on her heels, took a few paces, running her hands over her face, through her hair, and grunting like a caged animal. Then, she turned to the witch again, her face alight with ire.

'Claim him? Claim him, like, *how?*'

Phoni stood up straight, as straight as her huge hump could allow, and twirled a hand in mid-air. 'You really didn't think I was going to give him back to you so quickly, did you?'

'Tell me!' came Lizzie's thunderous response, causing Phoni to sober up, her expression afire with wickedness, as she replied, 'You have to prove your loyalty first—'

'Loyalty?' Lizzie huffed. 'Loyalty to whom? You?' She raised her chin. 'I don't owe you any!'

'Call it what you wish. But you're not taking him back unless you stay here a while longer. I need to...' She hesitated.

Lizzie took another step forward. She was now near the edge of the spring. 'You need to *what* exactly?'

'I need to be certain you won't do anything you're not supposed to do, like, in a hurry. Your brother will need to spend some time on the island to get acclimatized to your modern world again. You can't just take him back to your country overnight! So you'll need to stay here for a while... to just, take time.'

She put up both hands and began to move her fingers in a shooing gesture, her eyes full of scorn. 'Go get a place to stay... long-term. And come back here in a week.'

'A week?' Lizzie shouted, her cheeks flushed.

Phoni nodded once. 'Yes. That's right. At midnight.'

'And then you'll let me take him with me?'

'Yes. Yes, I will... If you promise to keep him on the island for a while first, that is.' She shook a sharp finger at Lizzie. 'And don't you try to trick me! I will know if you try to leave the island! I have ways to spy on you.'

'Yes, I know...' sneered Lizzie, looking around for Phoni's wretched bird, but it was nowhere to be found.

'Good. We understand each other then,' said Phoni, and began to sink into the water slowly, a satisfied smile playing on her lips.

Lizzie widened her eyes and shot up a desperate hand. 'Wait! Don't go yet!'

Phoni stopped short. 'What do you want?'

'I want to see him. Just for a moment. To make sure he's okay. I won't try anything. Please!'

'I don't think that's a good idea. And he's not here. I've... sent him on an errand.'

'Let me come with you then. For a while. Just to see him, then you can bring me back here.'

The witch gave a devilish smile. 'What makes you think I'll bring you back once I've taken you away? Aren't you afraid, little girl?'

'I told you, I'm not a little girl! And I'm not afraid either.' She shrugged one shoulder. 'Besides, if you wanted to snatch me, the way you did with my brother, you would have done it by now. Am I right?'

Phoni gave a crooked smile, her eyes glinting with merriment. 'I like you, Lizzie. Oh, how I like you!'

Encouraged, Lizzie took another step, this time into the water, her shoes getting soaked. 'Take me with you then! Just to see that he's all right.'

Phoni shook her head. 'You'll just have to trust me...'

Before Lizzie could say another word, the bubbling sounds echoed again from the water that shimmered anew. The witch disappeared under the surface, her wicked laughter resounding from the dark walls of the cave long after she was gone.

This guy's full of surprises

Five days later, and with the help of Mr Petros, who seemed to know everyone in Messonghi, Lizzie had moved in to a furnished one-bedroom apartment on the first floor of an old apartment building. It was a stone's throw away from the beach and the river mouth.

From her small bedroom balcony, Lizzie had a quaint view to a whitewashed courtyard below. With its herb bushes, vine trellises and flowers of vibrant colours it was a joy to behold. A second apartment building stood across the courtyard. On its top floor lived an elderly lady on her own. She was Lizzie's landlady and owned both buildings.

Mr Petros had explained to her in his basic English that the landlady detested noise, so Lizzie made sure never to play music or the TV too loud. Other than that, she felt right at home and considered herself lucky to have found the place.

That morning, a plumber was coming to fix a leaking tap in her bathtub. The time that he was expected to visit was drawing near, so Lizzie went to sit at her bedroom balcony and wait for him to arrive.

Mr Petros had recommended him, saying he'd talk to the landlady, then arrange for him to come. Apparently, the man was very reliable and equally handy for plumbing and carpentry repairs.

As she waited, Lizzie drank iced water from a tumbler. Setting it down on a round table she let out a luxurious sigh. From what she could tell, one of her neighbours on the ground floor was cooking a roast. The mouth-watering aromas of cooked meat and garlic wafted up to her balcony, reminding her that it was close to lunchtime.

Earlier that morning, she'd visited the council to register the utility bills under her name and hadn't had the chance to cook anything. *I'll grab a cheese pastry from the bakery, cut up a tomato... sorted.* She checked her watch. The man wasn't late, and if he appeared now, he'd actually be right on time. The very thought made her chuckle. *A handyman? On time? That will be the day!*

At that moment, a man came into view down on the road. He was opening the low gate to enter the courtyard, seemingly in a hurry. Already, he was making his way up the spiral staircase that led to her front door. As he was wearing a baseball cap she couldn't see his face but guessed he was the handyman she was expecting.

Soon, he came into view again and she stood, ready to call him over. When he reached the landing, he finally looked up, allowing her to see his face for the first time under the brim of his baseball cap. *Oh-my-god!* Lizzie's heart did a somersault when his eyes met her own.

'Hi!' he said, his face breaking into an open smile.

Lizzie stared at him aghast for a few moments. *A fisherman, a good Samaritan on his motorcycle, and a handyman too? This guy's full of surprises!* Finally, she jerked into motion, giving a little wave, her voice sounding somewhat shrill in her own ears. 'Hi, there!'

He put a hand on his waist and tilted his head. 'Is it you Petros sent me to see?'

'Yes, that's right!'

He gave a cute smile. 'That was lucky. He couldn't remember your name, so he only gave me the address and told me to go upstairs.' He looked to his right for a moment, then added, 'I see three doors on this floor. Glad I didn't have to ring everyone's doorbell!'

She flicked her wrist. 'Ah, no worries!' She pointed to her door. 'This one's mine... Well, obviously!' She shrugged and gave an awkward smile. 'Just a moment. Coming to open the door for you!' She dashed inside and, a moment later, hit her shin against the corner of the bed as she rushed around it. 'Ouch!' she mumbled with a yelp.

'Are you all right in there?' she heard him say through the open window, but didn't answer. Instead, she made her way to the front door, at a normal speed this time, while cursing under her breath.

She opened the door, feeling rather stupid, and fought the urge to rub her shin that stung and burned.

He hesitated at the threshold and gave a chuckle. 'Are you okay? I heard a clunk!'

She shook her head. 'No... ugh, it was nothing.' She waved her hands in a frantic manner as if trying to ward off a cloud of bees before her eyes. 'Never mind that... Do come in!' she urged him and he obeyed with a firm nod.

He stood in the hallway, a large metal toolbox in his hand. She looked at it, imagining it must be very heavy. Yet, he was holding it as effortlessly as she'd carry a flower or a spoon. *Oh, my! How strong he must be!*

Lizzie had trouble restraining her eyes from scanning him from head to toe and back again. He looked marvellous in his knee-length shorts and sleeveless t-shirt... his body a heart-stopping sight of strong shoulders and long, bulging limbs.

'Well? Where's the bathroom?' he asked, snapping her out of her reverie.

'Sorry, yes! This way!' She beckoned him to follow her to the single open space where her living room and kitchen were. Past the sofa and her tiny dining table, she led him to the bathroom at the opposite right corner.

As soon as he got in there, he took off his hat, opened the toolbox and within seconds he was busy at work.

Even though Lizzie had no interest in leaky taps and knew nothing about plumbing, she stood beside him, listening to his every word with rapt attention. He began to undo the tap from the wall so he could apply some new rubber 'thingies'—she had already forgotten what he'd called the bits he'd produced from the toolbox—and she admired the rippling muscles on his neck and biceps as he loosened this and that.

His dark hair was cut short, but thick strands fell over his forehead and temples. His lashes, long and dark, fluttered like butterfly wings as he tilted his head to peer at the tap, rendering her spellbound. Even her feeling of hunger had subsided.

Then, it occurred to her that she had completely forgotten to offer him something to drink. *In England, it would be a cup of tea... What do I offer a plumber in Greece? A beer? Retsina?* She shook her head. *Better not offer him alcohol. He might think I'm a soak.*

She cleared her throat but didn't speak. Instead, she admired his muscly back as he fussed with all sorts of minor plastic and metal bits. She couldn't have been watching it with more rapt attention if it were the telly on the night of the Eurovision song contest – the moment the British song comes on.

'Um… Can I offer you something to drink?' she finally piped up. 'Though I don't have Greek coffee… but I have some juice. It's some extra vitamin mixture of apple, carrot, and—'

He gave a little wave and shook his head, taking her out of her misery. It was good that he was concentrating on his work and not looking at her. She'd been hyperventilating and imagined she must have looked half-dead as she spoke as if she were choking from lack of oxygen.

'No, thanks…' he finally said placing a wrench on the floor. 'I'll just get on with the work, I'm fine.' He turned to look at her, only momentarily, before turning to the job in hand again.

She stood there, transfixed, her eyes caressing the back of his neck as he worked on his knees now, leaning over the bathtub.

'Oh! How about some water maybe? I have good water,' she said without thinking.

He turned to her, brows knitted, one hand frozen in mid-air. A rubber thingie was nestled between two fingers, ready to be applied. 'Good water?'

She gave a high-pitched little laugh. 'Sorry. I meant *bottled* water. From Epirus, I think. It's supposed to be the good stuff…' She was aware that she was rattling on like an idiot, but couldn't help it. His green eyes were dancing and all she could do was talk, just to distract herself from the beauty of his face. They made her knees weak and turned her brain into mush. She screwed up her face, lower lip twitching. 'Well, according to the nice man in the supermarket around the corner, that is.'

He gave a chortle. 'I know who you mean. And I'll vouch for him. If he says it's the good stuff, it must be so.'

'So?'

'So, what?'

'Shall I get you a glass?'

Another enthralling interlude of laughter. It had the good vibes of a hundred Tibetan singing bowls put together.

'You have a beautiful laugh…' she said dreamily behind his back before she could stop herself. Horrified, she scrunched up her face as she waited for his response. *Oh, God! I hope he won't mock me or think that I'm a flirt!*

He turned to face her, a slow, crooked smile breaking on his face. 'Thanks. It must be you.'

'Me?'

'I don't normally laugh. At all.'

'I find that very hard to believe.'

He resumed his work, without answering to that. After a few moments, he added, 'I'll have that glass of water if you're still offering. Getting warm in here...'

You don't say... She'd been hyperventilating from the moment he'd stepped into her apartment. 'Of course! Just a moment!' she replied, then dashed to the kitchen.

By the time she'd returned with the water, he had already finished the job and packed his tools. After drinking from the glass, he opened the tap, then closed it again a couple of times, to show her that it was no longer leaking.

Pleased, she thanked him and opened her wallet to give him a tip, but he refused to take it, saying that he was going to settle the matter of the payment directly with the landlady.

He picked up the toolbox and she gestured to him to follow her back out. As she led him to the front door, her mind raced. *I have to see him again! Should I ask him out? Or would that be terribly forward?*

Why is he lingering here?

By the time they'd reached the front door, her mind had gone numb. Now, he was standing outside on the landing and, to her relief, instead of leaving, he leaned over the railing and admired the view of the lush courtyard below.

'Nice place, you've found, I must say.' He turned to look at her. 'You know, I thought you were a tourist here. Had no idea you were renting a property. You're staying for a while?'

'Maybe... I don't know,' she said, looking away, her mind wandering. She'd spoken the truth. She'd sublet her house back home and taken a three-month sabbatical from the hospital, then bought a one-way ticket to Corfu, determined to stay for as long as it took until she and Tom could return to England together. With a shake of her head, she met the man's eyes again. He didn't seem to have noticed her dark thoughts.

'Well, it's a beautiful place and in a quiet neighbourhood too. Far from the noisy bars and so near the water. You're lucky to have found it.'

'I have Mr Petros to thank for that. He's been really helpful.'

'Yes, he's a great guy, very helpful indeed.' A short silence ensued for a few moments while he gazed at the courtyard some more.

She took the opportunity to throw surreptitious glances his way, admiring his form. *Oh. I could sit here and admire him for hours...* Her eyes wandered to the little hairs on the nape of his neck. They were lighter in colour than the rest and quite a contrast to his radiant chocolate skin. His chin was strong and chiselled, lips thick and delicious, cheekbones high and prominent... as far as the beard allowed her to see anyway. *I wonder what his face would look like bare, without the beard... If he ever decided to shave that beard off, he'd be exposing the whole shebang of the rare ragged beauty that he is... in a clean-shaven Gerard Butler kind-of-way.*

He finally turned to her again with a cute smile. He took off his hat and wiped his forehead with an urgent hand, then fanned his face with the hat before putting it back on. 'Phoar! Sure is hot today.'

'It sure is,' she replied with a chuckle. *Why is he lingering here?* He was shifting his weight from foot to foot, a lovely smile plastered on his face. The very idea that perhaps he liked her made her heart race, but it gave her a little more confidence too, enough to start a conversation.

'So, you're not just a fisherman...' she said with a timid little smile.

He waved a hand dismissively. 'I wish! In a perfect world, I'd only be a fisherman as I enjoy it so much. But I also do odd jobs here and there to make ends meet.'

'Oh? What kind of jobs, if I may ask? Other than plumbing of course!'

'Oh, you know... a little building work here, a little carpentry there...' He smirked, eyes twinkling. 'I'm a man of many talents.'

Lizzie's gaze dropped surreptitiously to his animated hands. He kept gesticulating as he spoke, in a typically Greek way, but only now she noticed that he wasn't wearing any rings. Her eyes lit up, despite herself.

'I'm so pleased that Mr Petros sent you over. I'll make sure to thank him when I see him. You've done a great job! I'll definitely call you if I need anything else.'

'You do that!' he replied with a grin. He shoved a hand into his shorts pocket and pulled a face of annoyance. 'Typical! Forgot to bring cards with me today.' He winked, causing her knees to buckle. 'I owe you one.'

Stunned by the delicious warmth blooming in her gut, Lizzie smiled sweetly in lieu of a response.

Unaware, he blathered on. 'I can help with fridges and washing machines too. And cars, sometimes... though I have a hunch you don't have a car?'

'No, no, I don't,' she said, her smile freezing mid-sentence. A raven had just landed on the railing behind him.

The sight of the damned birds made her sick to the back teeth these days. She'd noticed them a few times, on the beach mostly, and felt certain by now that they were spying on her and, somehow, reporting back to Phoni. Just thinking about her caused her high spirits to plummet.

Her distress must have been evident because he turned around, following her gaze, to find the raven standing on the ledge below the railing.

'Aaaargh! You devil!' He lunged forward and away from the bird, then pinched his t-shirt and made spitting sounds, something Lizzie recognized from the past. She'd seen many locals during her previous holiday there, the elderly mostly, make these spitting sounds to ward off the evil eye. Sometimes, they'd pinch their shirts too at the same time.

Lizzie was shocked into silence to see his reaction. *So it's true! Everyone must know there's something evil about these birds...*

He began to shoo the bird away from a safe distance and, finally, with a flap of its wings, the raven took to the sky and disappeared behind the distant trees.

'You don't like ravens, I take it?'

He shook his head fiercely. 'No one does! Nasty things!'

'I know. Mr Petros thinks so too. Says they are only for dead people, whatever that means.'

'Too right. I wouldn't go near them. They are cursed.'

'You know... I meant to say, your English is amazing.'

'Thanks.'

'Did you learn it as a child? In a *frontistirio*?'

'Yes. Like all Greek kids do. But...' He tilted his head, eyes narrowing. 'How do you even know the word *frontistirio*?'

'This is not my first time visiting here. I had a friend once who spoke good English at the age of thirteen. He attended private evening classes in a *frontistirio*. That's how I know.'

'Here? You mean in Messonghi?'

'No, sorry. I meant in Spileo.'

'That's where I live! What's your friend's name? I bet I know him. Spileo's only small.'

'Stamatis Katsaros. He'd be thirty-three now.'

He gave a gasp, eyes huge. 'What? That's *me*!'

Her face ignited with incredulity as she pointed at him. '*You're* Stamatis? *You* own the guest house in Spileo? The one that's derelict now?'

He nodded with a chuckle. 'Yes, that's right!' He tilted his head, eyes narrowing. 'And you are...?'

She gave a broad smile. 'I can't believe it! Stamatis, I'm Lizzie! My family and I had a month's holiday at your guest house when I was twelve. We used to play together, remember? You, me and my twin brother, Tom...' Despite her excitement, her voice trailed off after mentioning her brother. Stamatis knew, his whole family knew, that Tom had vanished.

Stamatis's eyes widened, arms flailing. 'You're Lizzie? I *thought* you looked familiar! But, it's been so long...' His eyes shone as he studied her face intently.

Lizzie twirled a strand of her hair and giggled. 'I guess I didn't wear makeup back then...'

Stamatis nodded slowly, his eyes never leaving hers. Then, much to her excitement, he stepped closer and gave her a hug, kissing her on both cheeks, the Greek way.

When they pulled away, they looked at each other for a few moments, just grinning, lost for words.

'I can't believe I didn't recognize you earlier! It must be the beard,' piped up Lizzie.

He scratched the side of his head and looked down, a shadow crossing his face for just a moment. When he looked up again, his smile seemed forced. 'I'm just as bad. Except for your hair that is a different shade to what I remember, you haven't really changed much. You did look familiar, but so many people do, you know?' He shrugged, offering a mischievous smile this time.

She gave a titter. 'Oh come off it! You have no excuse!'

'What about you? You didn't recognize me either!'

She threw out her arms, eyes widening. 'Hello? You have a beard!'

The same shadow darkened his features as he looked away, an urgent hand brushing his hair. Then, he turned to her, his brow wrinkled. 'So tragic about Tom...'

'Yes... it is...' she mumbled dropping her gaze at her sandaled feet.

'I never saw you or your parents again since that summer... Did you not come back for another visit?'

Lizzie shook her head and looked away, ashamed to put her answer into words. She'd begged her parents to return to Corfu, to try to find Tom, but couldn't get them to do it, couldn't get them to believe what she'd said. The police inspectors had suggested he had drowned in the spring, never to be found again – they said it'd be impossible for the divers to swim through the large fissures of the aquifer below to retrieve his body. So they'd given up. Just like that.

'I'm sorry...' he said, regret colouring his voice. 'I shouldn't have mentioned Tom. This must be a painful subject for you. I'm such an idiot. Forgive me...'

Lizzie saw tenderness in his eyes, and it drew her like a magnet to him. She gave a faint smile. 'No, please don't apologise. Thank you for mentioning Tom. I appreciate it, actually.'

'So, this is the first time you've come here since...'

'Yes, yes...' It sufficed her to say. She'd been aching to return every single year, but there'd be no point in coming before twenty years had passed. She'd only have been close but still unable to save him. It would have been too much to bear.

She looked away, resting her gaze on the building across the yard. On one of the balconies, a woman was hanging bed linen on the line, their ends flapping gently in the breeze.

'I don't blame you. And I'm so sorry this happened to Tom, to *all* of you...'

'Thank you, Stamatis...' Her thoughts returned to his house in Spileo, curiosity spurring her on to ask, 'So, your guest house... I take it that it's no longer in operation?'

'That's right... My father can't run it any more, and my mother has passed away.' He hesitated for a moment, then added, 'And my wife... she'd been helping at the house. She's passed away too.'

She rested an open hand on her chest. 'Oh my God... I'm so sorry, Stamatis.'

He shrugged. 'Thanks... Running the house on my own has proved to be impossible. I didn't want to do it with paid help either so decided to close it down and save on the running costs, at least.'

'I'm so sorry... I had no idea that you were married... let alone that your wife has died.'

'Of course, how would you know?' He gave an awkward little smile. 'And that explains the beard, in case you're wondering. It's because of my late wife, Kiki... her passing, I mean. It's a Greek thing.'

'Is Kiki's death very recent?'

'No, not really… It's been a little over five years… But I guess I got used to having a beard… Saves me from having to shave every morning.' He had made a feeble attempt at a joke, she knew, judging by the weak smile he gave, but it never reached his eyes.

He rubbed his beard absent-mindedly, rendering her mesmerised by the sight of his long fingers running over his jaw. Still, she wondered about his wife. How did she die? Was it a sudden, tragic death? Or maybe a drawn-out, terrible disease? Either way, she could only imagine how distraught her passing must have left him. She didn't dare ask any questions.

'And you?' he asked, his eyes focusing behind her, at her hallway through the open door. 'Are you married? With someone?'

'No, no…' She shook her head profusely and thought she saw a sparkle in his eyes. Taking in a deep breath, she added, 'It's been hard… for me too, you know? Ever since Tom…' She waved a hand dismissively, and he mirrored her gesture.

'Of course, of course, I understand…'

'Thanks,' she said, even though she had no idea how he understood. He was tactful, and she loved that. It helped her to relax around him. She gazed into his eyes and saw a sweet smile blossom on his lips. She felt herself smile in the same way.

He put a hand on his hip, a mischievous grin spreading across his face. 'So… Lizzie! I simply cannot believe we've met again! My dear old childhood friend… and all this time I thought you were a stranger!'

He winked, and she knew that he was trying to lighten the mood after they'd both shared their family tragedies, so she followed suit. She widened her eyes and chortled. 'That's not how I remember things.'

He knitted his brows. 'What do you mean?'

'You just called me a dear old childhood friend, yet if my memory serves me correctly, I wasn't so dear to you back then!' She pointed a playful finger at him and chuckled.

He scrunched up his face, and she added, 'If anything, you seemed intent on annoying me all the time. You didn't even call me by my name – you called me *kontessa*! It took me ages to find out that this is the Greek word for countess!'

He gave a belly laugh, his expression exultant as if the previous awkward conversation had never come to pass. 'In my defence, it suited you perfectly. You used to be all about fineries and comforts!'

'I was not!'

'Yes, you were! You'd start wailing every time your clothes got stained, and you never wanted to sit down on the ground to play with Tom and me. Even when we sat together with our families during our picnics at the olive grove, you refused to sit on the blanket! You made my father carry a low stool just for you to sit on!'

Lizzie crossed her arms over her chest playfully, pretending to look upset, but inside, her heart was singing. She had forgotten about those picnics and their playtime in his family's olive grove. It was a little further up the road after Spileo past the grove where Phoni's cave was. And it had the best view of the bay she'd ever seen.

A host of happy childhood memories came flooding in, filling her mind with images of Stamatis as a young boy, his lean limbs and mop of thick black hair as he played in the fields with Tom and her. Tom's flushed cheeks, his toothy, mischievous grin, and that infectious, giggly laugh of his... all that paraded through her mind in seconds. She heaved a long sigh. 'It all seems so far away now...'

'Yes, it does,' he replied, his expression sombre again.

'So, will you be calling me Lizzie or *kontessa*?' she teased with a smirk, her eyes squinting against the strong sunlight.

He gave a grin and tapped her on the shoulder playfully. 'Lizzie's fine. Unless you prefer me to call you Queen Elizabeth?'

'No! You're not calling me that again! Or *kontessa*!'

'Good! Lizzie, it is then!'

'You'd better behave...' She shook a playful finger at him, '...because I just remembered I used to call you something you hated too.'

'You mean, Stamata! How could I forget? That was cruel, Lizzie!'

'What did you expect with the way you teased me?'

'I'll hand you that, though, with one name you managed to deliver two different offenses. Not only did you call me with the Greek word for stop, but you feminized my name too, as Stamata is one of the feminine equivalents of Stamatis.' He put a hand on his waist and huffed playfully. 'Basically, you were calling me a girl!'

Lizzie broke out laughing. 'What? I didn't know that! I only knew I was using the word for stop.'

He planted a hand on his chest, and gave a pretentious sigh before saying, 'Oh Lizzie... You'll never know how much you've traumatized my poor, boyish soul!'

'Seems to me you turned out all right!' she teased, and he reached out with a hand to pat her on the arm gently.

The gesture made her freeze and she stared into his eyes. That's when a Greek *syrtaki* song echoed from seemingly nowhere, taking her by surprise. *Zorba's Dance? Where's it coming from?*

Stamatis's shoulders jumped, and he dropped his gaze, then fished his mobile from his shorts pocket.

'Excuse me,' he told her, then on the phone, '*Ne?*' A short pause. '*Ne!* Yes! I'm coming! Sorry, having a busy morning!'

Stamatis finished the call shortly after, looking stressed all of a sudden. 'That was my next customer... Sorry, Lizzie! Got to go!' He said a quick goodbye, then began to hurry down the steps.

Lizzie stood at the top of the stairs, watching him go, his loud footsteps sounding like music to her ears, the sight of his long dark fringe waving about with every step he took, rendering her mesmerized. Suddenly, just before reaching the bend, he stopped and looked up. 'Drop in next time you're in Spileo, and I'll treat you to some mountain tea or something. Unless you're willing to suffer my awful *Frappés*.'

She gave a beaming smile. 'Sure, I'll do that!'

'I'm out and about a lot every day, but if you see my motorcycle on the drive it means I'm in. The doorbell is disconnected, and the gate is locked, but if you shout out my name I'll come out to let you in.' He gave a playful smirk. 'But, please, don't call me Stamata from the gate. I have a reputation in the village to live up to.'

She giggled and remained on the landing a little longer, listening to his footsteps as he resumed his descent. He re-emerged from behind the cascading bougainvillea below and hurried to the gate across the yard. She watched until he got on his motorcycle and rode off. When he was gone, she turned on her heels with a soft sigh and walked into her apartment, her mind full of possibilities, a huge smile on her face.

Come... Come with me!

Two days later, Lizzie returned to the cave just before midnight. The witch, who was waiting for her behind the opening of the cave looking out, gave a low guttural sound, a wicked smile on her lips, as soon as Lizzie emerged through the trees.

Lizzie entered the cave with her and, being hyper from her strenuous run through the grove in the darkness, forgot to lower the torch in her hand.

'Put that away!' shrieked Phoni, bringing up two skeletal hands over her eyes, black talons glinting.

'Sorry,' mumbled Lizzie, dropping the torch on the soil. The light was strong enough to allow her to look around and she did so, but couldn't see Tom. She placed her hands on her hips, looking daggers at Phoni. 'Where's Tom? You promised!'

Phoni scrunched up her face, her pronounced chin jutting out even further as she chewed, goodness knows what, for a while, before lifting a finger up slowly to say, 'I haven't forgotten, little girl...'

Lizzie opened her mouth to protest, but then her jaw dropped. The witch had just stepped aside, sweeping her arms with a flourish to point at a little boy. He must have been standing behind her all this time.

He looked emaciated and was dressed in what looked like a scrap of sackcloth wrapped carelessly around his body. It was stained and reached down to his knees. He had short brown hair that was heavily tangled, tiny twigs trapped in it here and there like birds perching in a tree. His face was smeared with dirt, lips trembling, eyes full of trepidation, hands clasped together before his chest so tightly his knuckles looked white. All the while, his eyes were pinned on Lizzie.

Somehow, Lizzie found her voice after a while to say, 'Who is this boy? I don't understand! Where's Tom?' She broke the little boy's gaze only for a moment to shoot a fiery glance at the witch.

Phoni clapped her hands and gave a wicked smile. 'Oh, this is precious!'

'What do you mean?'

'Move, boy! Go to the girl. It's an order!' she commanded him, ignoring her question.

With knees that seemed ready to buckle, the boy began to move forward. This is when Lizzie realized he wasn't as afraid as much as he was weak. He certainly looked mal-nourished, too skinny to be okay.

'What have you done to this boy? And why have you brought him here? I don't underst—' Suddenly, as the boy approached, she saw something in his eyes that made her stop short; something… familiar. She got closer to peer at him and gave an audible gasp, an urgent hand flying to her mouth. 'No! It can't be!'

The witch gave a howl of laughter that rang in Lizzie's ears as the worst possible offense. If it weren't for her strong desire to go to the boy a moment sooner, she was going to attack her, right there and then with all she had, come what may.

Lizzie ignored the witch's cackles and rushed to the emaciated child, her arms around him to hold him, hot tears escaping from her eyes to roll down her face. 'Oh Tom! My sweet Tom! What's happened to you?'

Her hands caressed his pale face, his head, his scrawny neck, his bony back, and shoulders. Wherever she touched him he seemed to be only bone, hardly any flesh on him, and all the while he gazed back at her with those huge eyes, the fear in them palpable, stabbing her at the heart like a knife.

She stood straight and took his hand, pulling him against her, her free hand caressing the top of his head, and he stood there, like a toy, without reacting or making a sound.

Lizzie turned her gaze towards Phoni, her rage bubbling inside her. Her stomach was churning, aching, more and more with every passing moment. It took all her restraint to stop herself from hurting her for what she'd done to Tom. She needed the witch to try to help him. 'What have you done to him? Why is he still a child? I don't understand!'

Unaffected by Lizzie's turmoil, Phoni tilted her chin and tutted. 'Why are you complaining? I never said you'd get your twin back as he should be looking twenty years later.'

'What? Are you serious? But he is thirty-two like I am! Not twelve!'

She shrugged. 'My world is not affected by time.'

Lizzie jerked forward, pulling Tom alongside her. Somehow, she managed to stop a step away from the witch and not touch her. She shook her fist mid-air. 'How could you do this to us?'

'Calm down, little girl... All that is not helping you at all. Touch me and you lose your precious brother forever. Make no mistake about *that*!' She pronounced the last word with malice, exposing a putrid mouth of decayed teeth that smelled like rotten food and sulphur.

Lizzie stepped back, a hand over her mouth, her face scrunched up. She looked down at the boy, her precious Tom, whom she'd been dragging back and forth like a rag doll. Her heart opened, then swelled with love for him, the feeling too much to bear.

She collapsed to the ground, finding herself on her knees before him. She gently pulled him down by the hands and he knelt before her. For a few moments, she held him against her chest, tears falling down her face freely as the witch stood, rigid, watching.

Finally, she pulled back, holding him by the shoulders, gazing into his gaunt face and those huge eyes, her heart aching. She had to do the best she could for him; nurture him back to health, back to an iota of normality. Could the witch make him age, make him look as he should be? She was the one that had ruined his life, after all. She had to! What if she begged her? Would she help him then?

Lizzie didn't have the chance to beg, though, not even to look up to face Phoni. Instead, she heard a splash and turned towards the spring to find the witch was immersed in the water up to her chest, surely about to return to her world.

Lizzie jumped to her feet, and Tom tiredly stood up beside her. 'Wait a minute! Is that it? You're not going to help him?'

'No. Why should I?'

'But—'

'No buts, Lizzie! The boy is a Healer. And a good one too. I am sure he will know how to heal himself from whatever it is you think is wrong with him.'

Lizzie's eyes widened as she pointed to the boy. 'You think he's fine?' She shook her head. 'Wait a minute! What did you say he is? A healer? What kind of healer?'

The witch elevated a little out of the water so that she was visible from the waist up. She tilted her chin. 'A Healer of the Underworld. I've taught him myself.'

Lizzie gave a deep frown. 'Of the Underworld?'

'That's correct. This is what I am as well.' She puffed up her chest. 'The best one of all!'

'Wait a minute! Underworld as in... the world of the dead?' Mr Petros's words about the ravens came to mind again.

'Yes. I heal the ethereal bodies of the dead who are in a semi-living, semi-dead status on their way to the Underworld. But I cannot do that on my own. I needed a helping hand so I took your brother to make him my apprentice. He did a good job, as I stated earlier. But now, now is the time for me to ascertain that I have taught him well!'

Lizzie swallowed hard and took a shallow breath before saying, 'But, what does it matter if he's learned or not? He's free to go back home with me now, surely!'

'I beg to differ. First, I must make sure. He must pass the test.'

'What test?' she said in a feeble voice. Already, she knew she wouldn't like the answer.

Phoni crossed her arms over her chest. 'Well! He needs to heal three souls in the next ten days. If not, I'm taking him back.'

Instinctively, Lizzie pulled Tom closer and squeezed him by the shoulders. 'What? You can't!'

'I think you'll find that I can. I can take him back now, so I'd advise you to show me some courtesy!' Her eyes lit up but then, somehow, her expression softened and she gave a lopsided smile. 'But... I'm a caring soul... and I quite like the idea of reuniting you two.'

She gave a smirk and inspected her talons for a few moments, then shot out an arm to point a sharp finger at Lizzie. 'But don't you test me! You do as I say! Know that I have eyes everywhere! I can take him back to my world in the blink of an eye!'

Lizzie bowed her head, dropping her gaze to her brother, who stood before her, facing Phoni silently. As if he felt her eyes on the top of his head, he turned around and looked at her, causing her heart to melt. It made her determined to do anything she could to free him from the witch's clutches forever.

She heaved a long sigh, then faced Phoni again, her shoulders slumped. 'All right. I'll do what you ask. What do I have to do?'

Phoni gave a smug smile. 'As I said, the boy must heal three souls in the next ten days. The who and how, I leave to you two.'

'And then he's free to go?'

'Certainly! But not an hour before. You two come back here at midnight after ten days, and I will tell you if he's done a good job. So do your best!'

'I understand,' she said, hoping Tom would know what to do. *How do you heal souls? What does that even mean?*

'You'd better! Don't attempt to trick me. And don't try to take Tom away from the island either. I will know in an instant.' She shook a sharp finger their way. 'I am warning you! If you try to trick me you will never see him again!'

Lizzie felt her insides churn at the very idea of losing her brother forever. She nodded profusely, bowing her head, so overwhelmed by the torrent of threats that she had no words. When she heard the splash that signalled Phoni had just made her exit, she looked up again.

The spring was serene, but the cave was anything but quiet. The moment Phoni disappeared, Tom began to wail, calling for her to return and take him with her. Oddly enough, he had spoken Greek, not English.

Lizzie panicked, not sure how to calm him down or to communicate with him. She tried English but he didn't seem to understand, and only when she said '*stamata*' enough times she managed to stop him from shouting.

Then, she remembered she had left in her bag a half-eaten pack of biscuits. She took it in her hands and, the moment the child saw it, grabbed it in two smeared little hands that spoke volumes about his hunger.

He ate most of the biscuits greedily, finishing them in seconds, and Lizzie snatched the packet back from him, fearing he'd choke if he ate them all in this manner. Now, he was on all fours, picking up the leftover crumbs off the floor, shoving them into his mouth, dirt and all.

When he was done doing that, he tried to grab the rest of the biscuits from Lizzie's grasp, but she raised the packet too high for him to reach, asking him to stop that, but to no avail.

He began to jump, as feebly as he could, until he gave up. Then, with the packet in one hand and the torch in the other, she beckoned him towards the opening of the cave, an encouraging smile on her lips as she shook the packet, causing the leftover biscuits to rattle inside. Moving slowly towards the exit, she coaxed him, *'Ela... Ela mazi mou!* Come... Come with me!'

With her limited Greek, and by giving him a morsel at a time to eat, Lizzie managed to lead him out of the cave, through the olive grove and out onto the road.

From there, she continued to lure him in the same fashion. When they reached the streetlights, she put the torch away in her bag and took him by the hand, which made things easier. Little by little, by feeding him a morsel of sustenance every now and then, she led him further down the mountain.

When, just after Spileo, he collapsed from exhaustion, she took him into her arms to carry him the rest of the way through the semi-dark, deserted streets.

Finally, on the brink of exhaustion herself, Lizzie arrived at her lane and carried her brother up the steps and into the safety of her apartment.

A huge victory over Phoni

When Lizzie got in her apartment with Tom and closed the door, she felt a huge weight lift off her shoulders. Her troubles weren't over, she knew, but being in the safety of her home with her precious brother, no matter in what state, felt like a huge victory over Phoni.

Still, when she set Tom down gently to stand before her in the hallway, she could tell he had no idea who she was and what had just happened.

Tom teetered on his feet, then moved slowly to sit down on the floor in the opposite corner, his back pressed against the wall. His bare feet were black with dirt and grime, skinny legs bent, knees held tightly against his chest, eyes bulging with apprehension.

He looked like a stray animal someone had just saved from the street – famished and beaten. Something deep in the pit of Lizzie's stomach caught, then twisted and burst, to see him in this state.

It would be useless to go to him and try to console or reassure him. He didn't know who she was. So instead, Lizzie beckoned him to follow her to the kitchen with the promise of more food and, as she expected, he jumped upright and followed her.

Lizzie took a loaf of bread from a bag and cut him two slices on the counter while he made excited sounds. She handed him the bread and, as he began to devour it, took some Cheddar from the fridge. By the time she'd handed him two chunks of it, he'd already eaten the bread. He made appreciative sounds as he ate the cheese, eyes sparkling and, all the while, he kept skipping on the spot as he chewed, unable to contain his delight.

A glass of milk awaited him on the counter as soon as he'd finished the cheese. He downed it in one go, clutching the tumbler with two grimy hands and gulping with relish as if he were drinking from a precious chalice.

Setting the glass down on the counter, he wiped his mouth and nodded his head with reverence. '*Efcharisto, kyria...*' He kept his head bowed as he spoke.

Lizzie lifted his chin with a single finger to gaze into his eyes. *He called me 'madam'. He doesn't know me...*

'*Parakalo...*' she finally replied with a faint smile. 'Do-you-speak-English?' she added even though she knew the answer.

His eyes lit up, only for a moment, making her think that perhaps he had understood, but then he tilted his head and frowned.

Lizzie's heart sank but she managed a weak smile. 'Never mind. Perhaps you'll remember soon.'

Tom knitted his brows. '*Ti? Then katalava, kyria.*'

She waved dismissively and offered him an encouraging smile. 'Doesn't matter. *Then pirazi...*'

Taking him by the hand, and encouraged by his lack of opposition, she led him to the bathroom, then ran a bath for him. Soon, the small space filled with the soothing aromas of rosemary and lavender. She put a hand in the water to test the temperature and turned when she heard a rustle to find him unravelling the sackcloth off his torso without a hint of shame. If anything, his expression was afire with exuberance as he stood naked beside her, the grubby cloth dropped around his feet.

'*Mirizi dentrolivano! Ke levanda! Ti orea!*' he exclaimed as he breathed in the luxurious herbal scents, his face exultant.

Lizzie guessed he was calling the aromas as they reached his nostrils, aided by the fact that *levanda* sounded a lot like lavender. '*Levanda?*' she asked, pointing to the foamy water.

'*Ne, mou aresi poli. Efcharisto, kyria!*'

Lizzie watched him, speechless. She'd been dreading this on the way home, thinking she'd never convince him to have a bath. Yet, here he was, stripping down unprompted, and now getting into the bathtub of his own accord too.

Tom sat in the tub, the water up to his chest, and rolled his eyes dreamily. Then, his jaw fell slack, head tilted back as he gave a long sigh. '*Aaaahhh... Ti orea!*'

Lizzie wasted no time. She took a sponge and began to wash his back as he continued to make appreciative sounds, sitting limp and doing as she asked without protest. He raised his arms for his armpits to be washed, then stood in the bath so she could wash the rest of him.

The hard part was coaxing him to sit down and lift one leg up at a time, standing still, so she could remove the stubborn dirt stains off his feet. He was too excited to stay still for that. He kept splashing about, squealing, and soaking her top and shorts.

Lizzie laughed and pressed on, Greek words she once knew and thought forgotten coming back to the rescue to get him to hold still. 'Katse kala... siga-siga. Ligo akomi, stamata... Bravo, bravo, kalo pedi...'

Afterwards, wrapped up in a large bath towel, his hair untangled and combed, he was sitting before the TV on the sofa, laughing with the antics of the characters in a Greek comedy.

Lizzie rummaged through her wardrobe and found a t-shirt that wasn't too long and a pair of knee-length sporty shorts that clung to her skin.

She tried both garments on Tom and they fitted him fine, albeit rather loosely. Later, as she watched him laugh in front of the TV once more, she wondered how she could get him new clothes. She could hardly put him on a bus wearing these to buy new clothes from Corfu town. There were no suitable stores on this side of the island.

Then, her eyes lit up. *Janet!* The lovely Irish woman from Pitsilos Apartments had said she was staying for three weeks. *She must still be there!* Her ten-year-old was large for his age. *His clothes would be perfect for Tom!*

Delighted by her idea, Lizzie decided to let go of any worry for now, and just enjoy being with her brother. She made two sandwiches, put some crisps in a bowl and sat beside him to watch the comedy, even though it was in Greek and she couldn't understand it. But Tom did, and that was all that mattered.

It was almost two o'clock but she felt too wide awake to go to bed just yet. Tom seemed just as hyper as she was. Every now and then, he'd turn to her as he giggled, pointing to the TV and hitting his knee with his hand.

Lizzie gazed at his jovial face, her eyes misted over, and told herself the biggest step had already been made. The rest was going to be difficult, she could tell. Yet, she was determined to do as Phoni asked, hoping that, somehow, this nightmare could be over soon, and she and Tom would be allowed to live free of her for the rest of their lives.

Crazy with excitement

The next morning, when Lizzie snapped her eyes open, the first thing she did was give a huge smile as she lay on her bed. The very thought that Tom, her Tom, was in her apartment, sleeping on the living room sofa, made her crazy with excitement. For now, she shoved aside, back to the darkest corners of her mind, all thoughts of Phoni.

Janet! I have to borrow some of her son's clothes today! Then maybe head to Corfu town this afternoon to buy Tom some more... Better leave him here... He's in no state to go around in public yet. And who do I tell people he is? I'll have to think of something!

Her mind was racing as she slipped on a t-shirt and a pair of shorts. Once again, it was going to be a hot day. She loved this certainty about Corfu, about Greece in general – a far cry from the weather in England. She opened the blinds and took in a huge, grateful breath of the humid morning air, the sun on her face warm, not a single cloud in the azure sky.

The breeze caressed her face softly, lifting her spirits even more. Lizzie gazed at the lush view of the bay in the distance. The sea sparkled like liquid silver, the sun reaching down with golden tendrils to bless the world for another day.

Turning on her heels, she left the room, on tiptoe now, to check on her brother. The wall clock outside her bedroom door told her it was only eight. *He must be sleeping still...*

Yet, when she turned her eyes to the living room, she found a sight she didn't expect. Far from sleeping, Tom was sitting on the sofa eating greedily with his hands, head bent. He was holding a chunk of bread and something else that was unidentifiable across the distance. He didn't seem to have noticed her.

Lizzie was sure he had taken the whole chunk of bread left in the bag from last night. *Phew! At least he didn't use a knife!* Her eyes shot to the kitchen counter to find a mess. The bread bag was lying open on there, a handful of carrots and cherry tomatoes scattered beside it. The glass container where she stored the cheese in the fridge stood with its lid firmly on top a little further away.

'Hi there... Everything all right?' she asked as she approached him. On purpose, she refrained from calling him with his name. It was obvious he had some sort of amnesia, and she couldn't risk unsettling him.

Tom looked up, one cheek swollen with whatever he was chewing. He looked like a hamster hoarding food for later, and the thought made her chuckle. But, when her eyes darted to his hands, her face dropped.

'No! Don't eat that!' she exclaimed, trying to take the raw rashers of bacon from his hands, but he pulled them away. 'Not good! *Ochi! Ochi kalo!* You can eat cheese instead! Okay?' She beckoned frantically and he followed her to the counter.

The glass container where she stored the cheese had four flaps on the lid that were very tight. She always found it hard to open the container and imagined Tom had tried but failed. As she forced the flaps open one by one, Tom watched her licking his lips and, as if he understood, opened his hand that held the raw bacon leaving the remnants on the counter.

Gulping, and sick at the very idea that he'd been eating that, Lizzie pulled a face of disgust despite herself to receive a chortle from Tom. He was pointing at her now, giggling.

'Yes... I mean... *Ne. Ochi kalo.* Don't eat that again, okay?' She took the raw bacon in her hands and made a show of throwing it in the bin while scrunching up her face with revulsion.

He gave her a sheepish look and nodded firmly, and Lizzie took him to the sink to wash and dry his hands.

'Bravo. *Kalo pedi.* Good boy. Now eat this cheese while I cook some eggs to have with our tea, okay?'

Tom took a piece of cheese from her and nodded again, even though he couldn't have understood the English part of her phrase. Her heart went out to him, because of how innocent he'd looked just then.

He went into that cave twenty years ago like a lamb to the slaughter... And like a lamb he came out twenty years later, incapable of harm, a benevolent being, unlike the nasty creature that took him. Oh! What am I going to do? How fast can I teach him to speak English again? Or will he remember? If his amnesia goes away perhaps? Let's hope so... But even then, how am I going to explain to him what has happened to him and who I am?

Lost in her dark thoughts as she took eggs, milk and mushrooms from the fridge, she hadn't realized that her eyes were full of tears until Tom approached and pointed at her face.

He was holding the TV remote with the other hand and she guessed he wanted her to turn it on. But, it seemed, now that he'd found her crying he no longer cared about the TV.

In his beautiful blue eyes she saw his sympathy, and it made her heart melt. There was no way she was going to be sad around him. She wiped the tears from her cheeks with the back of her hand until there was no trace left.

Forcing a smile, she took him by the hand, then led him to sit on the sofa. She showed him the button to press while pointing at the TV, and he did it, letting out a shriek of delight when it went on.

He turned to her then, studying her closely for a few moments, and she gave an inaudible gasp when she saw a glimmer of recognition in his eyes.

He opened his mouth, hesitating for a moment, head tilted to the side, then said, '*Mama? Mama, esi* ise?'

Lizzie swallowed hard, then shook her head, a thin smile on her lips. 'No… *Ochi. Den ime I mama sou.* I am not your mum.' She registered the confusion, then the sadness in his eyes, and she patted him affectionately on the head. '*Ime fili sou.* Your friend… Lizzie. Just call me Lizzie.'

'Lizzie…' he repeated slowly, dreamily, huge eyes staring into her own, and she found it hard to keep her composure. He seemed perplexed. But that was better than being upset. She looked away, swallowing hard. She'd said her name without thinking, and it had panicked her for a moment that it might rattle him. Thankfully, that hadn't happened.

Instead, he had already returned his attention to the TV, looking transfixed, even though it was showing adverts at the time. Lizzie showed him how to change the channels and to adjust the volume. He had a go and stopped at the first cartoon show that came on.

Shortly, he began to laugh, that same string of pearls she remembered so well from their childhood. She left him there, lost in his merriment, and returned to the counter to make their breakfast.

Is he playing matchmaker?

Lizzie locked the front door and hurried down the steps, guilt squeezing her insides as she did so. At the bottom of the steps, she looked up at her balcony. *Thank goodness I live on the first floor. He should be safe up there... and he can't get out through any of the windows or the balcony.* She felt bad for locking Tom in, but what else could she have done? She'd left him sitting before the TV watching cartoons, with the promise to get him some new clothes. She didn't intend to be long.

She hurried down the lane and arrived at the beach seconds later. From there, Pitsilos Apartments were a stone's throw away. Janet was in and, after some niceties, Lizzie delivered the speech she had rehearsed well. She was doing a favour for a friend, minding her son, and he'd just soiled his clothes by dropping a glass of juice onto them accidentally.

She went on to say the boy had no other clothes with him, and his mother was coming to get him in the evening. If she would be so kind as to lend her a change of clothes of her son's, she would return them in a day or two, freshly washed.

Janet was more than happy to oblige. Five minutes later Lizzie was back at the entrance of Pitsilos Apartments, carrying the clothes in a plastic carrier bag. Derek's t-shirt and shorts had seemed a perfect fit for Tom.

She didn't leave at once but rather lingered at the entrance, admiring the sea view and the quiet beach, seeing that it was still early in the morning.

Mr Petros came out of Gorgona next door and went straight to a family sitting at a table. As he served them coffee and refreshments, Lizzie approached along the boarded walkway. By the time he'd turned away from the patrons, she had come to stand outside the restaurant.

She raised a hand to wave with a bright smile. *'Kalimera!'*

Mr Petros returned the greeting with equal earnest. 'Hello! Bathroom okay? Stamatis, good work?'

Lizzie nodded firmly. 'Yes, thank you. He fixed the tap in no time. Thank you for sending him to me!'

Mr Petros patted his heart. 'Wonderful!' He scratched his head, then pointed at her. 'Your name? I forget...'

'Lizzie. My name is Lizzie...'

'Ah... Lizzie!' He gave a huge grin, his eyes twinkling under his shock of salt-and-pepper hair.

Then, something caught Lizzie's eye in the distance. It was Stamatis's blue boat that had just moored at the pier.

Mr Petros must have seen something in her eyes because he turned around, following her gaze, and exclaimed, 'I no believe it! He come now!' He checked on his watch. 'How you say? Uh... he come for fish today!'

Lizzie smiled and stood with Mr Petros, watching as Stamatis hurried along the pier, fish crates loaded on his shoulder. As he stepped onto the walkway, striding directly towards them, Lizzie checked her watch once. A pang of guilt squeezed her insides for wasting time there while Tom was alone at home. Pressing her lips together, she promised herself silently that she'd just say a quick hi to Stamatis, then go.

Striding along the boarded walkway, Stamatis was almost there now, his manly form in jeans and a blue t-shirt rendering her magnetized.

Mr Petros tapped her gently on the arm, startling her. She turned to him, and he leaned conspiratorially towards her to whisper in his broken English, 'I sure he order coffee today. Other day you here same happen. He... never do before. You know?' He nodded fervently, not seeming to mind her stunned expression.

She'd understood exactly what he said. So Stamatis had only ordered coffee after delivering fish that day because she was there? *Interesting....* She was so stunned that all she could do was stare mutely back at the old man. *Is he playing matchmaker?* His next words confirmed that her assumption was right.

He winked. 'Stamatis like you. I know! He... how you say? Nice man for you. You want coffee? I bring two. For Stamatis and Lizzie. No money! Okay?'

Before she could respond, he had already disappeared back inside. Now she was panicking. Did he really offer to bring her and Stamatis coffees on the house so they could sit together? What's this? Had Stamatis told him he fancied her perhaps? Or was Mr Petros just assuming? It would be quaint, even hilarious, on any other day, but today she didn't have the luxury of time. Tom was alone and waiting for her. *He's as innocent as a toddler… what if he has an accident?*

Hyperventilating now, and being lost in her horrifying thoughts, she hadn't even noticed Stamatis had arrived, two large crates of fish, full to the brim, loaded on his strong shoulder. Emphasis on strong.

Despite her mental state of disarray she couldn't help but notice how utterly drop-dead gorgeous he looked today, what with his hair tousled by the breeze, his skin taut and smelling delicious from the salt spray, eyes sparkling green like emeralds.

He was eyeing her with a tilted head, though, a light frown on his face, and with panic she realized he must have said hello while she'd been too distracted to notice.

'Lizzie? You okay?' he asked before she could say hi.

Lizzie brought a hand to her chest, the one that held the plastic bag. She ran the other one through her hair, licked her lips, and looked at her feet. 'I am… sorry. I'm not feeling hundred per cent today. I may be coming down with something.' She heard herself chuckle. It sounded foreign. Another glance at her watch. 'Oh! Look at the time! I have things to do this morning and I… I'm running behind. Sorry… got to go!'

'Wait! Lizzie? Are you sure you're okay?' Confusion was ablaze in his expression, but she was already walking away, looking over her shoulder, and she chastised herself when she thought, of all things, that he was carrying those crates like they weighed no more than a bag of crisps.

Just as she stepped onto the boarded walkway, about to wave goodbye, Mr Petros came out to stand beside Stamatis, arms flailing frantically. 'Wait! I make coffee! No leave!'

She opened her mouth to protest across the distance, to say she'd never said yes to that, when the two men exchanged a volley of Greek that was too fast to comprehend. When they turned their gaze back to her, she repeated that she was in a hurry, but Stamatis put up a hand.

'Come, Lizzie. Please. Just a coffee. You haven't come by the house yet so we could talk about the old days.' He tutted playfully, his expression so delightful she felt her heart swell. He smiled, then added with a wink, 'Come on... Petros says it's on the house. I could use a break!'

He looked so cute with his hand extended out like that towards her, and she couldn't have wished for a better thing. But thoughts of Tom, her precious brother, alone at home were weighing down on her.

'I wish I could, but I'm very... busy,' she said, twisting her lips. 'I am sorry... I'll come by the house soon. Promise! Thank you both. Have to run!'

She began to walk away, without looking back once, dreading that Stamatis might mistake her refusal as a rejection. She minded that. A lot. But she had no choice. Her brother was way more important than romance. Even if it entailed someone as wonderful and as knee-tremblingly gorgeous as Stamatis. That's why she'd spent every waking hour with Tom for the last three days since she'd got him back, and hadn't left him on his own to go visit Stamatis.

Lizzie turned a corner and hurried down her lane, then went up the steps like she was being chased. Only when she opened the door to see her brother's eager face, did the frantic beating of her heart begin to subside.

As she watched him open the carrier bag and begin to try on the clothes, she told herself nothing could ever be more important than helping her brother adjust to the world where he belonged.

She'd have to try to make that possible for him, a baby step at a time. This had to be her top priority. Everything else would have to wait.

People need healing all the time

Before she knew it, the morning of the fifth day had dawned, leaving just as many left. Time was pressing now, but Lizzie wasn't sorry. She'd made a point of dedicating all her time to her brother, spending quality time with him at home.

She'd only really left him on his own for a considerable time once so she could visit Corfu town. She'd gone there to buy him clothes and a few bedtime story books in English.

Other than that, Lizzie and Tom had spent the last five days lazily at home, watching TV together, chatting the best they could, and reading from the children's books she'd got for him.

At first, she'd chosen two basic books for toddlers, full of brightly coloured pictures; the rest were for older children. He'd loved them all, and she'd been amazed by how quickly he'd started to speak his native English again. It made sense though; it wasn't like he was learning the language anew, but rather that his amnesia was fading fast when it came to his mother tongue. And he still spoke fluent Greek, having learned it from Phoni, no doubt.

As for his earlier-life memories, they were still lost to him. Now, she'd call him by his name and, much to her relief, he seemed to recognize it as his own. Also, he called her by her name but still didn't seem to realize she was his sister.

That morning, Lizzie was thinking about his amazing progress as she made their breakfast. She took a plate of mini croissants out of the microwave and stole a glance at Tom, who sat on the sofa. He was eating his cereal and watching cartoons, laughing out loud.

Her heart bloomed every time she heard his laugh. Once again, it swelled inside her chest, but the hot plate she was holding issued a rude reminder for her to return to reality.

'Ouch!' she exclaimed, letting the plate drop on the kitchen counter with a clank. Two croissants fell on the counter, and she pinched them between two urgent fingers to drop them back on the plate.

'What is it? Are you okay?' asked Tom, in a perfect English accent.

She smiled sweetly at him. 'Nothing to worry about.' She added a teaspoon of sugar and a splash of milk to her coffee mug, then took it to the sofa along with the croissants.

When Tom saw them, his eyes let off sparks of enthusiasm. 'Whoar!' he said, but didn't make a move to take one. Other than his English, his manners had also made a dramatic improvement.

'Help yourself,' she said gesturing to the coffee table where she'd left the plate. She hadn't finished her sentence when his little hand flew out and grabbed two.

'Thanks! Mmm! How lovely!' he said chomping loudly, making her giggle. She watched him, pleased to see how the wholesome meals she'd been cooking had already helped to improve his appearance. Gone were the bones that used to be prominent around his frame. Even his face looked fuller already.

For a while, he watched TV and ate, and she did the same, lost in her thoughts, her coffee growing cold on the table.

'Lizzie?'

She turned to meet his eyes, her mind in a torrent of thoughts and worries.

'Can we go out today? Please?'

She'd been dreading the moment when he'd ask her that again. He'd asked her on his second evening in the house, and she had a difficult time finding a good excuse in her bad Greek to say no. He had wound up getting angry and not talking to her for a while... but then the bedtime stories had helped them bond, fixing that initial coldness between them.

Now, she was able to communicate with him perfectly but still didn't know what to say. *Will he be okay outside? Will I have to lie to everyone I know about who he is? Yes, I guess I'll have to... Can't keep him indoors forever... And Phoni expects us to heal three people! Maybe he has ideas about how we can do that...* She hadn't mentioned Phoni at all and, strangely enough, he hadn't mentioned her either.

Lizzie shook her head slowly. Eyes focusing far, she was looking at the TV but couldn't see or hear it. *Okay... Let's start with simple things... go outside together for a little walk. Just to the beach maybe, when it's relatively quiet. And I'll take him for a swim today... It's about time he enjoyed himself a little... he's been in here for five days. Poor thing!*

'Lizzie? Can we go out?' he repeated, a little more loudly this time.

His face was bright with hope and when she locked her gaze with his, he obviously saw the answer in her expression because he sprang upright and gave a cheer, then carried on skipping like a kangaroo around the table. There was a kangaroo cartoon character on the screen at the time, so that made sense, and Lizzie began to laugh as she watched him.

Once he'd had enough of skipping and giggling, he surprised her by jumping on her lap, lacing his hands around her neck and holding her tight. 'Thank you, Lizzie! You are my best friend!'

Lizzie froze for a moment, startled, then relaxed and gave him a huge grin. She caressed his cheek, then kissed it, and held him against her, squeezing him tight.

✳✳✳✳

Lizzie helped Tom choose one of the two swimming trunks she'd got him, then she retreated to her room to put on her bikini and a summer dress on top. A few minutes later, she led him outside the door.

They stood in the sunny threshold for a while, taking in the view of the courtyard, Tom making sounds of enthusiasm no matter where he looked. He'd seen the courtyard many times from the balcony but being out there, he seemed ecstatic about it for some reason.

Lizzie watched him go down the steps, his face alight with excitement. '*Oreos kipos!*' he let out, rushing to admire the herb bushes by the gate.

Lizzie held up a finger as she followed closely behind. 'Uh oh! English please! Only English with me, remember?'

'Sorry, yes... Beautiful garden, I meant.'

'Yes, it surely is.'

'Yours?'

'No, I'm a tenant here.'

He tilted his head. 'Tenant?'

'Yes. It means I rent it. I pay money every month to the owner. My landlady. An old woman who lives up there!' She pointed to the top floor on the building opposite theirs, and whispered, 'She doesn't like noise… I think she's a little batty.'

'Batty?'

'Yes, like, she has bats in the belfry?' Lizzie made googly eyes, moving her pupils from side to side, and laughed.

Tom found that hilarious, and opened the gate giggling madly.

They ambled down the lane, then turned into the road that led to the beach. As soon as they got there, Tom kicked off his sandals and ran to the shallows up to his knees, splashing the water on the surface with his open palms and giggling, his face ecstatic.

'I love it here!' he shouted, and Lizzie hurried to the edge of the shore, gesturing frantically for him to get out.

'Come out, Tom! Let's have a walk first, okay?'

He obeyed, his smile never fading, and she took his hand to take him along the beach to the river mouth. She told him she wanted to show him the quaint fishing boats that moored there, and he grew excited, quickening his pace.

It was a short distance away. Lizzie hoped that the place might spark an old memory or two for Tom. During their holiday with their parents, the four of them had strolled along the river bank many times together. A couple of mornings they had boarded pleasure boats from there to visit coastal paradises of sparkling azure waters in Syvota and Parga on the Greek mainland.

Arriving at the river, Lizzie and Tom moved towards two excursion boats that were moored closely together. Many others were missing, having already set off for their daily tours. The two siblings moved to a poster that was mounted on a pillar, and Lizzie took turns with Tom to read aloud the excursion program displayed on it in English.

When they were done, they marvelled at the stunning pictures on the poster. All at once, Tom let out a gasp and murmured, 'Syvota…' His hand flew up, index finger landing on the poster under the specific word.

'Yes, Syvota. It's in Epirus, across the water,' said Lizzie, trying to sound as nonchalant as she could.

Tom looked at the photos again, lips pressed together in rapt concentration, then turned to her, his eyes full of intrigue. 'I know this place…'

'Have you been there, Tom?' she asked, knowing well that he had. With her. But that was twenty years ago. Could it be that he had remembered?

He shook his head. 'Maybe I'm wrong. I haven't been to the sea for so long.'

'I meant to ask you, Tom...' Lizzie took his hand and they sat together on a whitewashed ledge nearby. 'Where have you been living all this time?' She cleared her throat. 'Before living with me, I mean? Do you remember?'

Tom scratched his head, then turned to her, his face scrunched up. 'I don't know what it's called. It was in the mountain... I can't remember in detail. But there were many caves... and tunnels. I've been living with the witch—'

'Phoni?' Just the sound of the name on her lips caused Lizzie to pull a face of dismay. Thankfully, he didn't see. He was staring at his lap at the time.

'Yes. Phoni...' He met her eyes. 'But I don't like her... I am happier with you. Can I stay with you, Lizzie?'

Lizzie put a loving arm around his shoulders and squeezed him against her. 'Yes. Yes, of course you can. But we have to do as she asked...'

To her surprise, he stood up, and pointed to himself, puffing up his chest. 'Yes, I know! Heal three souls. I remember. And that's easy. Just take me to them. Do they live close by? I will heal them. I am very good at this!'

Lizzie stood slowly, pressing her lips together as she realized that by 'souls' Phoni had meant 'people'. 'Did... Did you do that a lot where you were? With Phoni?'

'Yes. All the time.'

'I don't know how we can do this here, Tom. I don't know anyone who needs healing...'

Tom stayed silent for a while, just gazing at her, looking confused. Finally, he shrugged, then said, 'People need healing all the time, Lizzie... I will help you find them. But first, we need herbs. I can't do anything without them.'

'Herbs?'

'Yes. From the mountain.'

Her expression brightened. 'Sure. I can take you there anytime you like.' She took his hand and smiled. 'Come! Let's go have a swim. Afterwards, I'll take you to a taverna that a friend of mine owns. You can have an ice cream there, if you like.'

'Yes, please!' Tom smiled to his ears and began to glide alongside her as they headed back towards the pier.

The resemblance is uncanny

To Lizzie's amazement, it turned out that Tom hadn't forgotten how to swim. Without a moment's hesitation, he'd gone in and swum with her in the deep water, floating and diving like a blissful duck in a pond.

After a spot of sunbathing they sauntered to Gorgona, Tom's eyes bright with the promise of ice-cream. As soon as they sat at a table, Mr Petros materialized from inside, his face full of mystification to see Tom by Lizzie's side.

'*Kalimera!*' he said when he stood before them with a theatrical sweep of his hand.

Tom gave a giggle. '*Kalimera, kyrie!*'

'You speak Greek?' asked Mr Petros, his eyes widening. He tousled Tom's hair, then turning to Lizzie, 'Your friend is Greek?'

'No, no...' Lizzie twisted her lips, '... um, I mean, yes, he is. He is half-Greek, half-English. A friend's son. I'm minding him for her.'

Mr Petros leaned forward and tilted his head. 'Minding? What is, minding?'

'Baby-sitting,' she enunciated slowly, the sting of guilt jabbing her inside for lying to this sweet man.

'Ah! Good! You work now? Money is good?'

'No, no. Just a favour. I'm helping my friend. She works, you see.'

'I understand. You... good friend!' He straightened and gave an open smile.

Lizzie marvelled at the glint of satisfaction in his eyes. All this time, he'd been eyeing her with intense curiosity that had stressed her. She thanked herself for her foresight to visit Gorgona with a ready excuse.

She knew the Greeks only a little, but had noticed they could be nosy and tended to ask questions until their intrigue was perfectly dispersed. Lizzie imagined this happening back in England, questions about money especially, and the thought made her chuckle. No one seemed to notice her joyful expression, though, and she soon realized Mr Petros had turned his full attention to Tom.

'Chocolate syrup?' he asked the boy, which suggested he was already in the process of getting his order.

'Yes, please. Thank you,' said Tom.

Mr Petros patted the boy's head. 'Oh. You English. Very kind. Thank you. No problem.' He turned to Lizzie and she ordered her usual Greek coffee. She had missed it in the past few days and was looking forward to one. She kept telling herself she ought to buy some Greek coffee and a *briki* to make it at home, but she'd heard once that getting it frothy enough at the top was a bit of an art, so the notion was daunting.

Besides, getting the coffee at Gorgona raised her chances of seeing Stamatis again. She still felt bad that she'd turned down his offer to sit together last time she was there. She hoped he hadn't been put off by her refusal. At least, Messonghi was a small place; surely she'd run into him again soon enough.

She cast her gaze over the sea, caressing its cobalt blue vastness with her eyes for a few moments. Then, she turned to Tom to find him fussing with a flyer that he'd picked up from outside a travel agency on the way there. A moment later, she gave a gasp. Tom had just folded it to make a paper boat. Both of them knew how to do that. Back in the day. *He remembers?*

'Nice boat,' she said, adding nothing else that would betray her excitement.

'Thanks. I don't know how I did it... My fingers knew, somehow.' He tilted his head. 'Does this make any sense?'

'Yes, Tom. It does.'

'I think there's a lot I don't remember.' He looked around him, his brow creased. 'I think I've been here before... and that I've been to Syvota too.' He pinned his eyes on her. 'Does this sound strange?'

'No, Tom. Not at all.'

'Not that I mind, of course... But why did Phoni ask me to go with you? Do you know the reason?'

Lizzie looked away, a deep sigh escaping her lips. She took a deep breath to take heart, then turned to him again. 'Tom, when it comes to Phoni I don't really know anything... But trust me when I say, I will do whatever I can to help you remember. Your past, I mean. Everything you have forgotten.'

'Lizzie, do all children have parents? Do they all have a family?'

'Why do you ask?'

'I don't think Phoni is my mother... But I don't remember anyone else. Only her... and you—'

Her eyes turned huge. 'Me? You remember me?'

'No, no. I mean... *she* and you are the only people I know...' He straightened in his seat. Will you help me find my family, Lizzie? My real fam—' He stopped abruptly, a spark igniting in his eyes. Tilting his head, he added, 'Why did you say that? Am I supposed to remember you?'

Lizzie's breath caught in her throat. 'I... I don't...' She looked away and squeezed her eyes shut, willing the tears not to come. Another glance at the open sea helped her to regain her composure. She steeled herself before turning to him again, her voice surprisingly calm when she replied, 'Tom, let's take things slowly. For now, all I can tell you is that I will do everything I can to help you find your family.'

But, Lizzie—'

Mr Petros came out and rushed over to them to deliver their orders, much to Lizzie's huge relief, especially as Tom picked up his spoon and began to eat his ice cream with gusto. Lizzie took advantage of the ensuing silence to breathe more freely.

Mr Petros hadn't stayed for a chat, which was fortunate; she wasn't in the mood to talk to anyone. She sat back in her chair and took a sip of the divine blend in her tiny cup, its exquisite aroma filling her nostrils, its thick, velvety texture going down her throat like liquid silk.

Suddenly, her heart began to thump, and she set her cup down on the saucer as if it had scorched her fingers. Stamatis had just emerged from the threshold of Pitsilos Apartments, his plumber's toolbox in hand.

Stamatis said goodbye to Nia, who stood at the door waving, and as soon as he stepped onto the boarded walkway outside, he cast his gaze over Gorgona.

Lizzie gave an inaudible gasp when she realized he had noticed her. Yet, he seemed to freeze for a moment or two, and she wondered why, then he put up a hand to say hi, but rather hesitantly.

She raised her hand, wondering why he was acting so strangely, and gave a big smile, but then remembered Tom was sitting beside her and her face dropped. *What if he recognizes Tom? From back then? Oh, my God!*

It was too late. Stamatis had seen them both. Her panic rose to new heights as she registered mystification in Stamatis's face. He was walking towards them now, his gaze shifting as he approached, from Lizzie to Tom and back again.

Lizzie turned to Tom for a moment only, enough to see that he hadn't noticed Stamatis. Instead, he seemed to be enjoying his ice cream as if he and it were cloistered together in a bubble, detached from the rest of the world.

Unlike him, Stamatis was fully aware of the boy, his intrigue seemingly rising with every passing moment as he came closer and closer to the table.

By the time he'd halted before them, he was gawping, his eyes trained on Tom.

'Hi...' he exclaimed, to receive a mute gaze from Tom, then turned to Lizzie again. '*Popo!* Oh, my goodness! Lizzie, is this young lad a relative of yours? I can't believe he—' He let out a loud chuckle pointing at Tom, clearly too aghast to even put it into words.

'Hi Stamatis. Good to see you.'

'Hi Lizzie...' He said breathlessly, then pointed to Tom again. 'Well, I'll be damned! If I didn't know better, may God be my witness, I would have thought he... you know... that he was Tom's child... or his clone maybe.' Another chuckle. 'Really! The resemblance is uncanny.'

Lizzie cleared her throat. 'Yes, yes, I know...' Now she was panicking some more. He had noticed the likeness with her brother. Of course he had. *Time for more lies.* 'You are right. Yes, he is a distant cousin of mine. That is, his mother is. Hence the likeness. And, would you know it, his name is Tom too.'

'Really? Oh, my goodness! He looks just like him... it's amazing.' His jaw was gaping open as he stared at Tom some more.

Luckily, Tom said nothing. He just gazed back at Stamatis, a hint of surprise in his expression.

'Well, as I said, he is a distant cousin...' She gave little waves with her hand, praying inside that she sounded convincing.

Finally, Stamatis turned to her, a hand on his waist. 'I had no idea you had family here, Lizzie. Do his parents live here then?'

Great. More lies. 'No… just his… single mum. She works. I'm minding him for her.'

He nodded slowly and seemed to believe her. 'That's very kind of you.'

'Yes. Well…' She tossed a strand of her hair behind her shoulder and fidgeted with her coffee cup, drawing his attention to it.

'You're having a coffee.'

'Yes. Would you like to join us?'

'I wish I could. But I have a lot of work today. Two customers expect me in the next two hours, and I'm running late as it is…' He checked his watch and huffed. 'Ooh. Too late, actually.'

She twisted her lips, then said, 'Bad timing. Again.'

He gave a lopsided smile, eyes twinkling. 'Yes. I wish we had better luck than this.'

'I can always come and visit you at your house as you kindly offered…' It had been daring of her, she knew. It wasn't like her to invite herself even though he'd offered in the past. But now that it was out, she was glad it was done.

'Yes! Do. That would be lovely. And you'll be more likely to find me home in the afternoon, by the way. I'm always rushing in the mornings.'

With that, and a dashing smile, he was gone. She and Tom exchanged a happy glance, then the boy turned his attention back to his ice cream. But, alas, a moment later, he looked up, a deep frown on his face. 'Who was that man, Lizzie?'

Lizzie pretended to admire the sea view. 'Oh… just a friend of mine.'

'Who did he say I look like?'

She let out an inaudible sigh, then turned to face him with a forced little smile. 'No one you know. Now eat up! We're going soon.'

Tom did as he was told, without further questions, and Lizzie felt relief wash over her like a jet of warm water. At least Tom hadn't recognized Stamatis. Glad for this reprieve, she brought the tiny cup to her lips and drank the remaining coffee in a single sip, until the tip of her tongue detected the thick granules at the bottom. It signalled the end of her delicious treat.

'I have to learn how to tell the fortune in the coffee cup,' she joked when she put the cup down on the saucer, her mind still overwhelmed from her exchange with Stamatis earlier. She was talking to herself more than anything else.

'You can do that?' asked Tom.

'People do that here, yes. In England we do it with tea leaves, mind you.'

'In England? That's a place, isn't it? Can we go and see it tomorrow please?'

'That's a little too far, Tom. But maybe another day.'

Tom shrugged, then finished his ice cream greedily. He dropped his spoon in the bowl and licked his lips clean from the dregs, then looked up at Lizzie with a wide grin.

It made her heart swell to see him so happy. 'Did you enjoy that, my darling?'

'Yes, thank you, Lizzie. Can we swim again please?'

'Just a quick dip. Then off to the house for lunch.'

Tom leaned forward in his seat, his eyes bulging out of their sockets. 'Lunch? We'll eat again? I love being here with you, Lizzie!'

'Yes, of course we will eat...' She put out a hand and patted his slim shoulder. 'We need to put some more meat on your bones, don't we?' She winked playfully. To watch her, if you didn't know her inner turmoil, you'd think she was the most carefree woman in the world. Just a tourist, sitting with a little boy, seemingly a mother with her son.

Only she knew what kind of energy it took to act and sound so normal, so jovial. But it was all for him. Anything for him. And Lizzie had come to Corfu well prepared. For years, she'd been telling herself she'd do anything, no matter how hard, to get her sweet Tom back. If anything, so far, things had proven a lot easier than she'd imagined.

Tom's excited voice snapped her out of her reverie. 'What are we having for lunch?'

'Well, I made a quick sauce earlier this morning. I'll boil some pasta when we get home, cut up some salad, and Bob's your uncle.'

'Bob? My uncle? Where?' He looked around, to no avail.

'No, no. It's just a saying...' Chuckling, she caressed his cheek, then called Mr Petros for the bill.

I love syrtaki too!

In the late afternoon, Lizzie and Tom sat on their balcony to enjoy refreshments and even more hot mini croissants. They began to talk about plants, the kinds that could help with various ailments, and Lizzie, using a small Greek-English dictionary, tried to work out the English equivalents for all the Greek plant names her brother kept reciting.

Suddenly, they heard excited barking from the courtyard below and dropped their gaze to find a woman holding a dog by the lead. She was standing outside one of the ground-floor apartments of the building across the yard.

She was in her thirties, tall and voluptuous, with long dark curly hair, wispy strands springing on her shoulders as she moved. She wore a knee-length paisley dress and flat shoes. Still holding the lead, she seemed to be having trouble opening her shoulder bag with her other hand that held her keys. The dog, a medium-sized mongrel with floppy ears barked excitedly, tugging at the lead, its tongue sticking out.

Tom jolted upright to lean over the banister, and let out a squeal. 'Look, Lizzie! Oh, how cute! I love dogs so much!'

Lizzie moved to stand beside him. She'd seen the woman before but never had the chance to say hi. Often, she would spot her in her living room walking about; the lady's windows were netted, and she kept her curtains pulled apart all day.

The woman looked up and raised a hand. 'Good evening! Sorry for the noise.' She gave an awkward smile.

Her accent was unmistakable. Lizzie waved and responded light-heartedly, 'Hey, you're American!'

'Greek-American, to be exact. From sunny California!'

'Wow! What's a Californian girl doing in Corfu?' asked Lizzie.

The woman chuckled. 'I'm no stranger to this place. My grandparents and mother were from good old Messonghi!'

'How nice... You've been here before then?'

The woman gave a little wave, about to speak, then turned to the dog that kept tugging at the lead. She commanded it to sit and it obeyed at once.

Tom let out an exclamation that suggested he was impressed.

The woman turned to them again, her face bright. 'Of course. I've spent long summers here as a child.'

'And you live here now? Permanently?' asked Lizzie.

'Yes! Since the spring.'

'You're enjoying it?'

'Oh yes. And I have family here; cousins, aunts and uncles. So, I feel right at home, you know?' She tilted her head. 'And you? You're English, unless I'm mistaken?'

Lizzie smiled. 'Yes. But a Corfiot at heart, mind you.'

The dog gave a loud bark and the woman shushed it, then gave it a gentle pat on the head and whispered something to it, before looking up again. 'Ah! A kindred spirit! I am Aliki. Pleased to meet you.'

'Lizzie!' she said excitedly, pointing to herself. 'And this is my br—' she raked her hair with an urgent hand, '...my friend, Tom.' She swallowed hard, then added, 'I'm friends with his mother, I mean.'

Aliki gazed up at Tom, who seemed taken with the dog still. 'Are you a dog lover, Tom?'

'Yes, I am! Can I come and pet it please?'

'Of course you can. Come on down!'

At the sound of that, Tom left the balcony and reappeared through the front door at lightning speed. Lizzie watched from the balcony as Tom hurried down the steps.

Lizzie let out a giggle as Tom went on his knees before the dog and petted him fervently, the dog relishing the cuddles, its obvious urgency for a walk forgotten, for now.

'Is it a boy or a girl?' Tom was giving the dog's ears extra attention now, and it kept nudging his hand for more whenever he stopped.

'A boy. His name is Charlie,' said Aliki.

'Oh! Charlie! Good boy!' said Tom. The dog stretched out on the ground, belly up. Tom took the hint to rub his tummy fiercely.

Aliki smiled as she watched, then asked, 'Do you have a dog?'

'Sadly, no, *kyria*.'

Aliki gave a little wave. 'Oh no! I'm old... but not old enough for that.' She giggled. 'Aliki will do!'

'Okay... *Aliki*.'

'So, are you English too?'

'Half-Greek and half-English!' piped up Lizzie from the balcony before Tom could respond. She had told him this lie was necessary but didn't want him to do the lying for her. This was a burden she wanted only for herself. At least, for as long as they could help it. 'Tom's mother is a friend of mine, as I said earlier. I mind him for her while she works.'

'Oh, that's nice of you, Lizzie, to help her like that.'

Lizzie shrugged. 'I enjoy it. Tom is a good boy.'

Aliki tussled his hair. 'Well, Tom, would you like to walk Charlie with me?'

Tom shot a look up at Lizzie. 'Can I?'

'Well, if... if you're not going far...'

Aliki shrugged and waved vaguely to the distance. 'Just to the green patch at the end of the lane really. It seems to inspire him to do his business.' She patted her bag and gave a throaty, infectious laugh. 'I've got his bags at the ready. We should be back in five minutes.'

Lizzie felt her shoulders relax. 'Yes, sure... that's fine.' She watched as Aliki handed over the lead to Tom, who stood up straight and walked the dog with slow, sure-footed steps under Aliki's guidance. They went through the gate and soon disappeared from view around the first bend.

Lizzie felt something tighten, then twist in her gut. But at the same time, she knew it was a breakthrough. Tom was back into the real world, outside, out of her sight for the first time. The next five minutes felt like an eternity as she stood by the railing, her eyes glued to the lane as far in the distance as her view allowed.

They returned to the courtyard less than five minutes later, all big smiles and waving hands.

'This was great! Aliki said I can do this again tomorrow with her! You must come with us next time!' Tom announced to Lizzie, still holding Charlie by the lead.

'Yes, that would be great!' added Aliki.

Lizzie nodded and gave a bright smile. 'Sure, I'd love to do that with you.' Seeing Tom so excited was worth solid gold to her. That was his first day out, and he was already acting like a normal boy, raising no suspicion to strangers. It felt like a miracle. 'That's wonderful!' she blurted out, carried away by her blissful thoughts, only to register a bewildered look from Aliki. It suggested Lizzie's intense enthusiasm had sounded odd to her.

Lizzie put a hand before her mouth and pretended to cough. Her voice came out more contained this time. 'Lovely of you to let Tom walk the dog with you, Aliki. Thank you.'

To her relief, Aliki waved dismissively, then invited her and Tom to her apartment for tea and cookies. 'Come! I've got English Breakfast and everything!' she coaxed with a chortle that Lizzie found irresistible.

Moments later, she had joined them downstairs and was entering Aliki's apartment with them.

※※※※

Aliki's home looked like a set from a 1960s-1970s movie, complete with a beaded curtain at the kitchen entrance, ABBA and The Beatles LPs lying on a cabinet by an old stereo, and brightly coloured, antique light fixtures and throws.

As soon as she led them to the kitchen, Aliki said, 'In case you're wondering, you haven't entered a time capsule. This is just my grandmother's old stuff!' She waved her arms vaguely to various corners of her living space, and let out a giggle. 'I was offered it when one of my cousins inherited our grandmother's house. Her stuff reminded me so much from the old days so I took the lot, then moved it here. Furniture, fixtures... everything.'

Lizzie nodded, then pointed vaguely to the living room behind the beaded curtain. 'That's sweet... and the old LPs? I couldn't help noticing them when we came in. Were these also your grandmother's?'

'Oh no! She only owned a radio, bless her soul! I've loads of LPs and brought them from home, others I got from friends and family here. I love 1970s music, *syrtaki* especially.' She beckoned to the kitchen table. 'Please. Make yourselves comfortable.'

'I love *syrtaki* too,' said Lizzie as she and Tom sat down.

Aliki filled the kettle with water from a bottle and turned it on. 'Did you dance *syrtaki* here in the old days?' she asked as she took mugs out of the cupboard.

'Oh yes! We danced all night!' she said, pointing to her brother without thinking. Alarm flashed in her eyes, and she visibly shrunk before continuing. 'Er... I mean, *I* did. When I was a child I came on holiday here.'

'When was that then? In the 90s? That's when I was here as a little girl,' said Aliki as she got the milk out of the fridge.

'Yes, that's right,' said Lizzie cautiously, worried she might say something untoward again.

'Is *syrtaki* a Greek dance?' piped up Tom.

'Yes! Let me show you my favourite record. It has the best *syrtaki* songs in it. Let's see how many you will recognize, Lizzie!'

In a flash, Aliki had dashed to her tiny living room returning just as quickly with a tattered LP in her hands. She was holding it like a holy relic. 'Here! Read the track list! They're all there!'

The song titles were written in both Greek and English. Lizzie did her best to read out the titles. '*Ky...ra... Giorgaina...* I don't know that one... *Tou Antra tou Polla Vari... Lochias...*' Lizzie stopped then, her eyes scanning the rest of the song list quickly. Suddenly, she turned to Tom, her eyes lighting up. '*Tarzan!* Oh! Tom, you—'

She was so excited to regain a long lost memory from her fond mutual past with Tom in Messonghi that she had slipped again. She shook her head, chuckling, eyes back to the LP to add, 'I... used to dance to this song here... back in the 90s.' She stole a glance at Tom. He seemed oblivious to the song or the mention of *syrtaki* music.

Aliki went to the stereo to put the specific song on. When the first notes filled the air, Tom began to sway his head, eyes twinkling. 'I love this song... How do you dance to *syrtaki*, Lizzie? Is it easy to learn?'

'Oh! It's been a long while since I last did it...'

Aliki didn't comment on that as she brought three mugs to the table, but when she took a seat she said, 'Don't worry, guys. Aliki's here! I'll show you both how to dance to it, if you like!'

Tom cheered at that and Lizzie watched as the two of them engaged in conversation about it. Once they'd all had a few sips from their drinks, Aliki got Tom to stand. They stretched out their arms and held one another's shoulder, then she began to show him the *syrtaki* steps in the middle of the kitchen floor.

'Come, Lizzie! They do Greek nights at the restaurants all the time here. And they dance at the festivals too! Let me help you remember how to do it. You don't want to miss out on the fun!'

Lizzie sprang upright and joined the line, her excited squeals mixing with their own as they tried to synchronize their steps while the music continued to play.

As she copied the moves from Aliki, she willed Tom inside her mind to remember that song, somehow... how he used to love it once. But that didn't seem to happen. She happily settled for his laugh, though, and that beaming smile he gave her, satisfied, when the song had finished and he'd already learned the steps.

When the next song started to play, the three of them danced in near-perfect sync, their cheeks flushed as they smiled brightly at each other.

❋❋❋❋

As soon as Lizzie and Tom returned to their apartment, Tom asked, 'Lizzie? Aliki said she's a vegetarian. What's that?'

'It's when you don't eat meat and other animal products.'

'You mean, never?'

'Never.'

Tom tilted his head. 'But why?'

'It's a choice some people make, that's all. Because they're against cruelty to animals.'

'But we don't hurt animals! Should we be vegetarians too?'

'No. Definitely not.'

'But Lizzie...' He took in a deep breath. 'I want to be like Aliki. I want to be a vegetarian too.'

'Uh-uh. No you don't! You need to get your strength back! Forget it!'

'But Lizzie... Aliki—'

'Please, Tom! We had such a nice time earlier... What is this now?'

'I told you. I want to be like her. I think it's nicer to not eat meat.'

'Tom, Aliki said she's into tarot cards and crystal healing too. Will you get into those things as well?'

'No...'

'Well then!'

'Why are you shouting, Lizzie?'

'I'm not shouting!'

He folded his arms before his chest, his expression hardening as he looked away. 'Yes, you are.'

Lizzie flicked her head to the side, then rolled her eyes. 'I am sorry, Tom. Look...' She took him gently by the arm and led him to sit beside her on the sofa. 'I just want the best for you. And, right now, believe me... It is very important that you do as I say. You need protein to get your strength back. And that is why you must eat meat. You and I both know that Phoni didn't care much about your nutrition...'

'But, Lizzie—'

She put up a hand. 'Do you trust me?'

'Of course I do.'

'And you want to find your family, yes?'

'Yes! More than anything.'

'Then you must trust me. And no buts!'

'Okay. But we are seeing Aliki again?'

'Yes, of course. The three of us are walking Charlie tomorrow evening, aren't we?'

'Yes!'

Lizzie made a move to go to the kitchen when Tom spoke again. 'Lizzie? Did you see Charlie's coat? I didn't ask Aliki, but he seems to have some kind of skin problem.'

'On his side, you mean? Yes, I saw that.'

'It's by his ears and on his tummy too...'

Lizzie tilted her head when he didn't elaborate. 'So? What about it?'

Tom gave a playful grin. 'I think I know how to fix it.'

I think I've been here before

Lizzie and Tom took the path up the mountain early the next morning. Both were excited to be out and about together and, as they went uphill, relished breathing in the cool, fresh air.

Soon, their cheeks were tinted rosy pink, hands flying into the air to point at the lush hills on the peninsula and the deep blue of the Ionian sea. The higher they ascended, the better the sea view became.

Lizzie had promised to take him to a specific spot that had a breathtaking view, and Tom was walking briskly, eager to see it. Lizzie walked cheerfully beside him, her worry about his strange amnesia forgotten for now. It all changed, though, when they reached Stamatis's house in the village of Spileo.

Tom stopped short at the locked gate, his brows knitted, mouth agape, eyes focusing far at the forlorn guest house across the garden.

Lizzie saw his expression and froze. 'What is it Tom? What are you looking at?'

Slowly, he turned his head to face her. 'What is this place, Lizzie?'

She placed a hand on his shoulder. 'Why do you ask, my darling?'

'I think I've been here before... but the gate used to be light blue. It's black now.'

'Yes, yes, you're right. It used to be blue.'

'Where are the bicycles? They used to be propped up against that wall...'

Lizzie gasped. 'You remember that?' Stamatis owned two bicycles when they were kids, and the three of them used to take turns to ride them daily around the property.

'Yes...' He scratched his head, then shook it, 'I think I used to stay here, Lizzie. Were you here too, with me? Back then, whenever that was, I mean?'

'Can you remember when it was? Or who else you were with?'

He turned to the decrepit guest house again, then to Stamatis's family house next to it, his eyes glazed over. 'I remember an old man... he used to sit at a small table by the front door of this house... and an old lady. Sometimes she sat with him. Sometimes she... she brought me and...' Tom drew a sharp breath, then brought up a hand to his mouth, eyes lit up.'

'What is it? What else did you remember?'

'I used to play with a boy here! His name was... Oh, wait a minute... I had a sister! Lizzie! What? Lizzie?' He turned to his sister, the light in his eyes slowly fading, dying, as the epiphany tightened his features.

Lizzie had no words. She was reduced to silence by the devastating sight.

When realization set in fully, his face fell, eyes darkening with upset. 'You're my sister?' He gripped her forearm. 'Wait a minute! If that little girl was you... then... how did you grow up so fast? What happened to you?' He grabbed her arms and pulled her close.

Lizzie crouched over, allowing him to hold her for a few moments. Soon, hot tears began to fall down his face, wetting her naked shoulder.

Lizzie's stomach tightened into a knot, and she found it hard to breathe. She pulled back and caressed his face while he peered at her, his gaze intense.

Taking a deep breath, she managed a thin smile.

'Well? What happened to you?'

'Tom, it's not easy to explain...'

'Okay then, tell me what happened to the little boy! He was our friend, wasn't he? Can we ask if he can come out to play with me? It may spark up a memory! Where is the old man and his wife? Why aren't they sitting outside now, do you know?'

'Those were his grandparents, Tom. I don't think they're around any more.'

'Why? Where are they now?'

Lizzie shook her head, unsure about how much she could say without shocking him. Clearly, he didn't realize it had been twenty years since he was last there.

Tom was tugging at her t-shirt, demanding answers. As much as she dreaded it, she turned her gaze to him, spent. 'Tom... just walk with me. Don't rush your memories. I am here. I promise I will help you remember. But for your own good, we need to take it slow, okay?'

'But you *are* my sister, right? You are Lizzie, the little girl I just remembered?'

She caressed him with her eyes. Her vision was blurred from tears she tried desperately to stop from flowing. 'Yes, yes… I am your sister. But please, no more questions. For now, anyway,' she said, and he opened his arms to embrace her again.

She held him tight, the air finding its way with effort into and out of her lungs as if through a maze. It was so hard to breathe, and to think clearly at that point, but she managed a weak smile when they pulled apart, regardless.

'You're such a good boy, Tom. I've missed you so much! I'm so happy to finally be able to tell you that I am your sister.'

Her brave little brother said nothing to that. Instead, he offered one of his sweet smiles and took her hand. He only threw a single look, full of intrigue, over his shoulder at Stamatis's house, then carried on walking uphill alongside her.

❋❋❋❋

Shortly after Spileo, and a little further from Phoni's cave, Lizzie led her brother off the road and took him through a grove to a beautiful clearing. It was covered with grass, wild flowers and bushes and had a spectacular vista of the bay. Tom was ecstatic to see it but didn't seem to recognise the place.

Lizzie and Tom had been there many times in the old days seeing that it was owned by Stamatis's family. Back then, his parents tended a field nearby where they kept farm animals too. But the field had no shade, so they'd often come to the olive grove for a quick lunch and a siesta while the sun hammered down on the land with gusto.

Sometimes, Lizzie and her family would come up to the grove with Stamatis to join them for a picnic. Occasionally, Stamatis's grandparents would come along too. These memories flooded Lizzie's mind as she wandered around the clearing, picking wild flowers, while Tom looked for plants he could use.

At some point, Lizzie returned to the grove, attracted by the cool shade and the frantic song of the cicadas that echoed from the trees. She ambled under the thick canopy, just enjoying the quiet for a while, lost in her thoughts of Stamatis. But then, somehow, a persistent nagging feeling made her curious about Tom.

Her brother had said something about needing to find a rare herb and had wandered off to the adjoining field asking her to give him half an hour or so before meeting him back at the clearing. It seemed a little strange now, but at the time she'd thought nothing of it.

Lizzie pondered on this some more. Why half an hour? What was he up to? *Perhaps he needs total quiet to concentrate on his search for the right plants without my usual babbling in his ear...* It sounded sensible enough, but that twisting feeling in her gut wouldn't let up, so she decided to return to the clearing to check on him before the half hour had expired.

As soon as she got there, she noticed a few scattered herb cuttings on the grass. As she bent over to pick them up, thinking that maybe he'd dropped them accidentally, her eye caught something. She turned to a bush on her right to find him lying on the ground behind it.

'Tom!' she shrieked, rushing over to kneel beside him. He was lying flat on the ground, eyes closed.

Lizzie shook his arm and yelled his name, her blood running cold in her veins, but to no avail. Unlike the rosy flush on his cheeks a while ago, now, he looked pasty white.

The world began to spin around her. *It can't be! What could have possibly happened? We are too far from the cave. Did she come here? Did she hurt him?* She decided that was far too unlikely, but her head tilted back all the same, a hand over her eyes to shade them from the strong sun as she scanned the sky for any ravens. *Nothing.*

Seeing that shaking him hadn't worked, she tried slapping his cheeks gently this time, shouting his name and, all the while, scanned the ground for any signs of snakes. She inspected his arms, his face and legs, and found nothing. *Would he pass out if a snake bit him? Oh, my God! What do I do?*

'Tom! Please wake up! Tom!'

That's when she noticed a speck of something green on his bottom lip. She put her fingertip on it, and it stuck to it so she brought it closer to inspect it. She licked it. It tasted foul.

'Yuk! What's that?' Just as she turned her head to spit with disgust, she heard a throaty gasp.

Lizzie turned her head just as Tom opened his eyes. Immediately, he shot both hands up and brought them to his head. 'Oh... my head, my head...'

'Tom! What is it? What happened? Tell me, please!'

She helped him sit up slowly while he rubbed at his forehead with a busy hand. 'I'm sorry, Lizzie, I had to do it...'

'Do, what? What did you do?' she shouted, her eyes wild as she held him tightly, now sitting beside him on the ground.

'I took a mixture of herbs and mushrooms to aid my memory. They cause hallucinations sometimes... but I'm all right now...'

'Hallucinations? Oh, my God! Are you okay?'

'Don't worry, Lizzie. It's slowly passing now. The world is still spinning a little, but...' He managed a faint smile, a lopsided one, the one he'd always saved for her for his most mischievous acts. 'It'll stop whirling around me soon, promise...'

A short silence ensued as she watched his face and caressed his hand. Soon, colour returned to his cheeks, much to her relief. She tutted at him, and he gave a sheepish smile. 'Sorry.'

Lizzie shook her head. 'You silly boy... You scared me to death! What did you do that for, huh?'

Tom pressed his lips together in lieu of an answer. He began to take deep breaths, colour returning to his face all the more with every passing second.

She gave him a few more moments to recover and finally added, 'Well? Why put yourself in danger, Tom? You looked half-dead when I found you, for goodness sake!'

He twisted his lips. 'I know... I'm sorry, Lizzie, truly I am. But I had to! And I was so happy when I found both the right herb and the right mushroom that work together.'

'What exactly do they do?'

'They unlock lost memories... from the mind.'

'Phoni taught you about this?'

'Yes, of course. She has taught me about hundreds and hundreds of plants. I know everything there is to know about them, and I remember everything, Lizzie, everything about how to heal with plants... unlike the things that matter mostly to me...' His eyes softened, then misted over as he locked them with hers.

'Your past, you mean?'

'Yes. My past. What happened to me... and you know what happened, don't you, Lizzie? You know and you're afraid to tell me. You're afraid of how much it would upset me.'

Lizzie gave a laborious sigh. 'In essence? Yes...'

'Well, it seems to me I just spared you from that fear. I wanted to do this, Lizzie. So you don't have to worry about it any more. Better to do it in one swift move, I thought... Like when you tie a bad tooth to a door with a thread, then bang the door shut, you know?' He gave a giggle and, once again, she marvelled at how brave he was.

'So?'

'I took a small dose. So I didn't remember everything. But I remembered enough.'

'Like, what?'

'The boy who owned this land, the boy I played with in that house... his name was Stamatis, wasn't it?'

'Yes. Yes, it was.'

'I thought so... And I am guessing he is the man I saw in Gorgona when you bought me ice cream yesterday. It looks a lot like him. It's not a coincidence, is it, Lizzie? That you know him and his name is Stamatis?'

'No, no, it's not...' She goggled her eyes. 'Wait a minute! You recognized him? With the beard and all?'

'Yes... All I had to do was look into his eyes. They've been haunting me since yesterday... Now I know why.'

She sighed. 'Amazing...'

'Lizzie... He's grown up. Just like you...'

She looked away, at the vastness of the blue sea. 'Yes, that's right.'

'So nothing happened to you or him. Whatever happened, it happened to *me*.'

'Yes, Tom.' She turned to look at him this time, but only for a heartbeat. The clear blue pools in his eyes were too much to bear.

'So... Phoni took me away. I know that. But, for how long?'

Lizzie bit her lip for a moment, then gave a deep sigh. 'It's been twenty years, Tom...'

His face fell. 'Twenty years?' he mumbled in a little more than a whisper.

She only nodded this time, meeting his eyes and holding his gaze till her soul wept, but she managed not to cry. He was so brave! It would shame her to appear weaker than him.

'But why did she do that? And why would she return me to you now? After so long?'

'I don't know, Tom... I don't know. I am just thankful she was willing to give you back, period.'

'And what about the three souls I need to heal? What happens if I don't manage this before the ten-day period ends?'

'I don't dare think about that possibility, Tom. And neither should you!'

Tom looked away and kept silent for a while, then shot upright. 'Come! Let's pick up all these scattered cuttings. And there are a few more I must get before we can go home.'

'What will you do with them all?' she asked, standing up too.

'I'll dry some of them; others I will mix and turn into paste. Depends on the affliction or disease. I must have a wide variety of herbal remedies at the ready.'

Lizzie pressed her lips together, saying nothing to that. Instead, she helped him pick up all the cuttings from the ground and put them in a plastic bag she'd brought along. 'Have you got the plants we need for Charlie's skin problem?'

'Of course. They were the first I made sure to pick.'

'Have you healed any dogs before? When you were with Phoni, I mean?'

'No. But I imagine dogs would count, since they have souls too. And I'm sure I can heal them as well as I can heal people, if that's what you're really asking.'

'And what if dogs don't count?' she asked as they left the clearing behind and began to saunter through the adjacent field.

Tom shook his head and moved to a rock formation. Herbs and plants of various kinds had sprouted through the cracks in the rocks. He got to work picking as soon as he got there.

'Tom? What if they don't count?' she repeated after a while when she received no answer.

Tom turned to her as she approached, his face animated with enthusiasm. 'Well, I guess I would have healed the dog. That's something in itself, isn't it?'

'And what about Phoni?'

'We'll have to heal three people, if the dog won't count.'

'And where do you suppose we can find people who need healing?'

'Are you serious? You told me you're a nurse! People need healing all the time! Who doesn't have pains, aches, or ailments?'

'I know, but—'

'Don't be so negative, Lizzie! It will be easy to find people to help. You'll see.'

Lizzie stared back at him mutely and marvelled again at his happy-go-lucky attitude, which she remembered well from the past. Perhaps he had retained it because he'd been frozen in time, unlike her who, as an adult, had lost the inherent positivity that's the natural trait of every child.

She gave a faint smile, then turned her gaze towards the deep blue sea that shimmered and sparkled below. The breeze had picked up and was now caressing her face, warm and gentle.

Soon, the corners of her mouth curled up as if of their own accord. 'That herb you used earlier? It tasted foul... but it surely worked wonders. On me too,' she teased, turning her face away from him so he couldn't see her playful grin.

Tom raised his brows. 'You tasted it? When? How?'

Lizzie giggled, and waved dismissively. 'You don't want to know. But I think it worked some sweet magic on my brain too.' It was a joke, of course, and when she saw his mystified expression she began to laugh with abandon.

And it felt wonderful, at last, to live with hope again. To start to piece her life back together, and her brother's too. If only a tiny bit at a time.

I have a good feeling about this

As soon as they returned home they got to work. They washed each kind of herb, plant, or tree bark separately, then spread everything out on a sheet on the balcony to dry under the strong sunlight.

Early in the afternoon, when everything was perfectly dry, Tom wasted no time. He used Lizzie's small pestle and mortar to make pastes, and her electric blender to grind herbs really fine.

The previous day they had bought from the pharmacy some organic ingredients, oils mostly, for the creams and ointments that Tom wanted to make. At the nearby supermarket, they had bought tiny pickle jars, and tin containers of cheap hand cream. Having been emptied, washed and dried, the glass jars and tin containers were now standing on the counter ready to store away all the healing products Tom intended to make.

As she watched Tom work, Lizzie felt proud of him. He had accomplished so much already, in less than a week. Later, as she helped him put creams and herbs in tin containers and jars, she secretly hoped the four days they had left would be more than enough to heal three souls, and even more, if they could.

❋❋❋❋

In the evening, and with his work done, Tom grew restless to go knock on Aliki's door across the courtyard. He wanted to try the cream he'd made for her dog, but Lizzie was unsure. Wouldn't it be rude to go unprompted and offer this?

They were sitting at the balcony, playing trumps at their plastic table, and throwing ideas to each other about how they should do this. What happened next felt like a sign from Divine Providence.

All of a sudden, Aliki's front door opened wide and there she was, one arm flying upwards to greet them across the distance. 'Hiya, guys! How's it going?' she shouted out in her vibrant Californian accent.

They returned the greeting, asking her how she was and, to their surprise, she pulled a face of mock despair. 'I'm going nuts, to tell you the truth! Charlie's skin is a mess. It's behind his ear, and—'

'Yes, I know,' interrupted Lizzie, standing up to approach the rail. 'I noticed it yesterday but I didn't want to say.' She frowned, trying to look suitably sympathetic but was finding it hard to hide her excitement.

'Yes, me too! He has it on his stomach and his side too, doesn't he?' added Tom brightly, who had shot upright to stand beside Lizzie.

'Yeah, that's right. My poor baby...' Aliki lamented, shaking her head. 'I've tried everything I can! But the pharmacies here don't seem to have anything helpful. Just nasty chemicals, you know? Not even homeopathic remedies. I know I said I love Greece and all, but I really wish I were in California right now! We have all sorts of natural remedies there, and I'd be able to fix my poor Charlie in no time.'

'Sorry to hear that...' said Lizzie as she prepared her little speech one last time.

'Well, I'll be damned if I'm going to give up so easily. I'm off to Corfu town and see what I can get there.'

'Corfu town?' The others said in unison.

'Sure. I can't sit and watch him suffer any longer. He spent all morning scratching his skin away... Gotta go, guys. Catch you later...'

Lizzie exchanged one glance with Tom, who nodded to her, his lips tightly pressed together.

'Wait, Aliki!' Lizzie put up a hand. Aliki was nearing the gate when she stopped short and looked up again. 'Yeah?'

'Speaking of natural remedies... We... Well, I'm a nurse, as you know...'

'Yes, you said.' The odd look Aliki gave her conveyed a mixture of mystification and hope.

'Well, I've taken some courses on natural remedies and...' Lizzie faltered and took a deep breath. She found it hard to lie. But she had to. She couldn't say Tom was involved in this. 'You know, I make herbal remedies for all sorts of ailments. I believe I have just the right thing for Charlie.'

Aliki's eyes lit up like a neon sign. 'You do? Oh, my God! That's amazing!'

✳✳✳✳

Less than a minute later, they were both downstairs, following a very excited Aliki into her house.

Behind the door, Charlie greeted them all with playful yelps and barks. As the two siblings petted him, he licked their hands and made them laugh.

'Bless him! He doesn't seem to know he's not well...' said Aliki with a thin smile, then beckoned to them to follow as she moved to the living room. They all sat closely together on the sofa, Charlie standing before them all, his tongue hanging out as he panted.

Tom had brought the right cream with him. He opened the lid of a small tin container and had trouble keeping it away from Charlie. The dog seemed to think it was some kind of treat and was trying hard to lick it.

All three of them laughed as Aliki held him firmly in place, while Tom applied cream on all the affected areas. All the while, Aliki asked all sorts of questions; what the cream contained and how it was prepared, what other applications it had.

Luckily, Lizzie had stayed with Tom throughout the preparation process and was able to provide all the right answers. With a wide smile, Lizzie ended her last sentence just as Tom closed the lid and put the tin container on the coffee table.

Aliki patted Charlie, her face bright. She left a kiss on his snout, and he licked her chin. 'This thing smells divine! Almost makes me wish I had the same skin problem so I could put it on too,' she joked with a chortle.

'You could use it, you know,' replied Tom. 'It's a wonderful body lotion. Very nourishing and softening.'

'It is?'

'Yes... I mean, that's what Lizzie told me.' He turned desperately to Lizzie, his eyes alight with panic, and she quickly confirmed. 'Yes, perfect for the skin. All skin types. Just use a little less if you have oily skin.'

'Yes, that's right,' said Tom, again unable to hold himself from imparting advice. He still couldn't remember much from his life with Phoni but guessed he must have healed thousands of souls in the past twenty years. It had become second nature to him to do that.

Aliki broke the short silence that had ensued. 'Can I buy it off you? I'd love to try it too.'

'You're welcome to it. And it's a gift. You must apply it three times a day to Charlie. And Tom... ugh...' Lizzie cleared her throat, '*I* can make you some more, if this is not enough for you to use as well.'

'Oh, thank you, Lizzie! That's so generous of you!'

'It's a pleasure, Aliki.' She turned to look at Tom, who was beaming, not seeming to mind at all that she was getting all the credit. She knew, like he did, that the only thing that mattered was for Charlie to get well.

Aliki jumped upright, the tired springs of her ancient sofa making a creaking sound that pulled Lizzie out of her reverie. 'Gosh, it's getting hot! Would you guys like a glass of juice?'

Lizzie and Tom said yes to that. As they waited for Aliki to return from the kitchen, they petted Charlie while minding that he didn't jump on the sofa. As old as it was, it'd be awful if the dog stained the upholstery with cream. The rug on the floor seemed old too, but when the dog lay on it with a loud exhalation, both Tom and Lizzie panicked. 'Aliki! Is it okay if the dog stains the rug? He just lay on it!'

Aliki giggled from the kitchen sink and flicked her wrist at them. She was just visible through the beaded curtain. 'Relax! This house is totally dog-proof and not by accident. There's nothing Charlie can soil irreversibly. I keep my Persian rugs in my other house!' she said with a wink and a playful grin, causing the others to giggle.

Moments later, she returned to the living room with three glasses of orange juice. 'Are you guys walking Charlie with me later?'

Tom brightened up immediately. 'Yes, we'd love to!'

As she raised her glass to her lips, Lizzie said, 'Had you not suggested it, he'd surely have begged you to come along. He just loves dogs.'

'Oh, what's not to love?' Aliki leaned forward to caress Charlie's ears. He lay by her feet and gave a soft sigh as soon as her fingertips touched him. 'Oh! The cream is absorbing well... it's barely visible now.' She put her glass on the table and turned him over gently, confirming that there was hardly any cream left showing on any of the affected areas.

She looked at the others and crossed her fingers, her face exultant. 'I have a good feeling about this! Thank you so much, guys!'

And now, girlfriend... let's talk men!

After they'd had their refreshments, Tom asked if he could go outside and play with Charlie in the courtyard. As soon as the two of them were out, Aliki sat on the sofa by Lizzie and leaned closer, a conspiratorial look in her eyes. 'And now, girlfriend... let's talk men!'

Lizzie scrunched up her face and giggled. 'Men? Please! I just got here.'

'Oh come on!' Aliki winked. 'Surely *one* among all those gorgeous Greek men roaming about has caught your attention! Go on... I haven't sat with a girl to talk guys in ages...' She pulled an over-the-top, imploring face that caused Lizzie to laugh.

Aliki took it as a sign that she had convinced her. 'Thanks! But first...' She stood. 'I'll get myself another glass of juice. You want one?'

'Yes, please,' said Lizzie and finished the dregs in her glass. 'Here!' she said standing to offer it to her, but Aliki put up a hand as she moved towards the kitchen. 'No worries. I'll get you a fresh one.'

A little later, she was back, two full glasses in her hands. She offered one to Lizzie and sat beside her. 'I'll even go first! She squinted her eyes, and leaned a little closer. 'Do you know the dark Adonis who runs the little supermarket in the corner?'

'Yes, of course. Babis?'

Aliki's eyes lit up, then melted like snow cones under the sunlight. 'That's the one!'

'Is he your boyfriend?'

'I wish. He's very shy. A local boy... and a Scorpio! Very hard to fathom, as you know, Scorpios—'

'Well, I wouldn't know...'

Aliki rolled her eyes. 'Oh you wouldn't believe! And he's so incredibly shy. I can hardly get a word out of him. But I know he likes me, I can tell...'

'So, nothing's happened between you so far?'

'Nothing...' Aliki let out a rushed exhalation. 'You know... I buy a few things each time... He punches it all in the register, I pay, he helps me pack the bags, and I go. Rinse. Repeat. Every day.'

'That's all?'

'Yes. And I have to really organize my shopping, to make sure I have something to buy from him every day. You know... a few things at a time... one lettuce, two tomatoes, one tub of yoghurt, that sort of thing.'

'What? Surely he must have realized if you're forever visiting!'

'Sometimes twice and three times a day... I get these strong urges for ice cream very often.' She made air quotes when she said 'urges' and bulged her eyes, which made Lizzie laugh. 'Sorry,' she said, hoping her new friend wouldn't take offence.

Aliki raised her shoulders. 'Oh, I'm pathetic, I know. But he's like a drug to me. I dream of him night and day.' She widened her eyes. 'Help! What should I do? Any ideas?'

Lizzie ground her teeth and looked at her lap. 'Ah, let's see...' She wasn't used to having girlie conversations about men. That would have required strong friendships in her life and she'd never had one. She pressed her lips together, then said, 'Well, are you sure he's single? No wife or girlfriend?'

'Of course I am! I've asked around surreptitiously.'

'Good! And he seems to like you, yes?'

'Yes, I believe so... but he's just shy, you know? Hardly meets my eyes when I talk to him.'

Lizzie scratched her head. 'Really? He doesn't avoid eye contact with me.'

'I know, right? He doesn't with any of the other shoppers either, I've noticed that! He even jokes with some of them! It's only with me that he's unable to string two words together!'

'Oooh! That's a good sign!'

'I know!'

They began to giggle again, sounding more like schoolgirls, rather than two grown-up women.

Aliki sobered up first. 'Your turn now, and don't be shy. Spit it out, girl!'

'Well, there's this local I really like... but he's not a stranger. I actually knew him when we were children.'

'Really? That's wonderful! How long ago was that then?'

'Twenty years ago. I stayed with my parents and my brother in his guest house back then.'

'Guest house? Which one?'

'It's not here, it's up in Spileo. It's closed down now, though... no longer in operation.'

'Where does he live?'

'In Spileo. His house is right next to the guest house.'

'I bet I know him! What's his name and what does he do?'

'It's Stamatis. Stamatis Katsaros. He's a fisherman but also does odd jobs here and there...' It felt wonderful to say his name aloud. It had felt like a piece of silk caressing her tongue, making her wonder how much she had fallen for him. She also wondered if that was the reason she'd been procrastinating so much to visit his house. Was it just because she wanted to dedicate her time to Tom and the task at hand? Or was she a little afraid too? A little too afraid to give love a chance in her life?

Aliki's whooping sounds pulled her abruptly out of her private thoughts. 'Stamatis Katsaros? Wow! I know him! He's a looker!'

In lieu of an answer, Lizzie nodded with a knowing smile.

'I have to hand it to you, girl, you have good taste.'

Lizzie tittered, but her lips froze when Aliki spoke again to add, 'Sadly... so does Nia.'

'Nia?'

'You know Nia from Pitsilos Apartments, right? Tall, skinny, perfect skin and legs?'

'Yes, I know her. I stayed there for a while. Stamatis does odd jobs there sometimes. What about her?'

'Well, they had a thing in the past. When he was single, that is; before he got married to Kiki.'

'A thing? Like a relationship?'

'Yes, but for a short time only. He ended it with her when she foolishly cheated on him with a tourist. She's been regretting it ever since from what she told me in the past...'

Aliki leaned forward. 'Beware of her, Lizzie. She has her eye on him and still has hopes. Plus, she's younger than us. And she can put back a pint of beer faster than you can say Jack Robinson. She's uncontrollable with drink in her... The kind of woman men like for a good time, you know? Don't let her innocent looks fool you, either. She's a minx, that one. An adversary to watch out for!'

'Wow. I had no idea...'

'Well, if you think you stand a chance with Stamatis, you'd better chase him and chase him relentlessly. I know Nia is! She's forever calling him for this and that.'

'She is?'

'Yep.'

'Well, she's got lots of rooms in Pitsilos. I'm sure maintenance work is needed every now and again…'

'Huh! Try every few days! Remember what I told you earlier about me shopping daily from Babis?'

'What? No! You mean she finds excuses to call Stamatis over to Pitsilos?'

'You got it! She told me herself one night in a bar after we'd downed a few cocktails. I'd hate to break someone's confidentiality and all, but in her case I have no qualms to do it. So I am telling you… She bangs the taps, the pipes, wardrobes, shutters… you name it… She uses hammers and anything else she can find to break stuff up so she can pick up the phone to ask him to come over. And she blames it on the guests… careless children, drunken young boys, heated domestics, you get the picture.'

'I can't believe it! She smashes things up in her own business?'

'It's not her own… Nia's not even Corfiot. She's from a small village near Preveza. Left it years ago and came here begging her aunt and uncle to let her stay with them. They own Pitsilos and adopted her, in a way. And don't ask me what happened back in her village. I've no idea; she never told a living soul.'

Lizzie shook her head, incredulous. 'And that's how she repays them for their kindness? Charming.'

'You don't say.'

'And what about Stamatis? Can't he tell that she smashes things up to get him to come in?

'Tell?' Aliki raised her shoulders and chortled. 'Tell, what? Men are naïve, dear. Especially when it comes to making money or chasing skirts. And I don't know if he fancies her still, but this is certainly about his bread and butter. Even if he can tell what she's doing, the work still pays the bills…'

'Oh my!'

'Don't panic. Aliki's here.'

'What do I do?'

'Does he like you?'

'I think so... I mean, he's asked me to visit his house for tea.'

'What? He's practically fallen for you then! He *never* does that! With anybody!'

'Oh come on! How could you possibly know that?'

'Because everyone here knows he's a loner. And he's been like that since Kiki passed away. I mean it's been five years, and he hasn't even shaved his beard yet! You know it's the Greek custom for widowed men to grow a beard, yes?'

'Yes, he told me about that.'

'Well... he should have shaved it after the first year...' said Aliki gesticulating heavily now, 'I guess he's hurting inside but it's not right. He's still young. But perhaps, if he's invited you to his house, it means he's ready to move on. And you've got a good chance there, that's for sure.'

'Maybe he's only extended the invitation because of our past. We used to play together as children, remember?'

'Yes, I know. But I don't think that's it. I think you could be special to him.' Aliki nudged Lizzie on the arm, her eyes lighting up. 'You should go visit him! Tomorrow! I insist!'

Lizzie's heart gave a thump at the very thought of doing this. 'Oh... but how could I? Unless... Aliki, would you be able to mind Tom while I visit Stamatis?'

'Of course. You don't need to ask!'

'Thank you!'

Aliki squeezed Lizzie's arm. 'So you'll go? You'll do it?'

'Yes! Yes, I believe I will...'

'Good girl!' She drank from her glass, then gave a wicked smile and added, 'Nothing will give me greater pleasure than to see that weasel, Nia, lose her chance for good.'

'Why do you dislike her so much?'

'Oh... I have a good reason, believe me. But that's somebody else's secret... so I can't tell you.'

Lizzie nodded and drank from her glass.

'Can I ask you something, Lizzie? I don't mean to pry or anything, but I don't get it. How come you mind Tom all day and all night? Has his mother abandoned him or something? I have to admit, I can't help it, but I can see you guys through the window. He's with you all the time.'

Lizzie twisted her lips. A pang of guilt stung her insides. She hated lying to her new friend, who was so sweet, but she had no choice once again. 'Oh! She's gone to England for a while...' She lowered her head, pinning her eyes on the glass she nestled on her lap. 'For work. And I'm only happy to help her. It's hard for single mothers, you know.'

'You're an angel, Lizzie. Good for you. And I'm here if you guys need anything.'

'Thank you, I appreciate that, Aliki.'

They both turned when they heard the key turn in the lock. The front door creaked open and Tom got in with Charlie, the boy's face animated. 'I think it's time for Charlie's walk, Aliki. He just did a number one in the garden!'

Aliki jolted upright. 'Oh no! Better walk him now before he does a number two. The landlady would have a fit if she saw! Now where are the poop bags?' She rushed to an old cabinet by the door to rummage through the top shelf while the others hovered at the threshold with the dog, giggling.

Fear of deep water

Tom was watching music videos while having his breakfast in the living room. Lizzie stood before the kitchen sink, her mind churning with disturbing thoughts of Phoni as she looked outside the window, empty-eyed, her coffee getting cold on the counter.

Seven days! It's been a week already... How are we going to heal three souls in the next three days? Oh, God! Please don't let Phoni take my brother away!

Excited squeals from the living room made her shoulders jump, and she spun around, her breath catching in her throat.

Tom was jumping up and down to a frenzied dance beat that blasted from the TV speakers.

'Turn it down please, Tom, I have a headache!' Lizzie complained, shooting a hand up to the side of her head. A tiny migraine brewed on her left temple. She always wound up with one of those whenever she was stressed.

She looked at Tom again, who had turned down the volume and stood frozen in the living room, his brows knitted. 'What is it, Lizzie? You're not worried, are you? It'll be all right. You'll see!'

Lizzie marvelled at his optimism, but a knot had lodged in her throat, and the words never came out. She turned to the kitchen window and took a deep breath. 'Of course, of course...' she mumbled, and heard his footsteps as he approached.

She steeled herself in case he pressed with more questions. He had always been able to take one look at her and know what she was thinking. And she desperately didn't want him to know she was afraid. She didn't want to share with him this hell... the hell of dreadful possibilities that plagued her inner thoughts. Optimism was better, she knew. But it was hard. So hard to find it inside her wounded heart and mind.

Luckily, the doorbell rang then, before Tom could come any closer. He hurried to open the door, and she took another steadying breath, telling herself that she had to appear as if this was just another day and not what it actually was: three days to the possible end of all that mattered.

Behind the open door, they found Aliki holding Charlie by the lead. Before either of them could greet her, Aliki began to squeal and bounce, causing the two siblings to gawp.

'Whatever is it, Aliki?' asked Lizzie first.

'It's Charlie! Look, guys!' She pointed to the dog's head.

'Hey! Look at his ears! His coat!' said Tom, cheering.

'I don't believe it!' said Lizzie when she came closer to ascertain that the dog's coat was flawless all over, showing no signs of his terrible ailment. It was a magical thing to behold. Like he had never suffered from it at all.

Lizzie's eyes glazed over, her mind floating somewhere amidst the heavens, unlike the dark pits of hell it'd been roaming in up until a minute ago. Dreamily, she shook her head, then turned to Tom. 'And this happened overnight? This is amazing!' But then, somehow, she remembered that she was supposed to be the one who knew all about the treatment. She cleared her throat and turned to Aliki. 'But, of course, it happens sometimes...'

Aliki didn't seem to notice Lizzie's *faux pas*. 'Thank you both so much! You saved my darling Charlie, and I owe you both *big time!*'

'It was nothing, really,' said Lizzie.

'Happy to help,' added Tom.

Aliki waved dismissively. 'Yeah, yeah. All that's fine, but I must thank you properly. Are you guys going swimming this morning?'

'Yes, we are,' said Lizzie, Tom nodding alongside her.

'Then let's have lunch at Gorgona together today. My treat. For Charlie. One o' clock okay with you guys?'

✵✵✵✵

Lizzie and Tom got to their usual spot on the beach near Gorgona. Aliki said she would be joining them an hour or so later for a quick dip, then they'd go together for lunch.

She hardly ever visited the beach as she worked from home, so they were excited about the novelty of swimming with her today.

After a cooling swim, the two siblings lay on their mats for a while, then sat together, just looking around and shooting the breeze. It was past midday and the beach was packed.

Behind a large family that had practically camped beside them, Lizzie could just make out the familiar face of a woman under a large sunhat. She was applying sunscreen on a little girl's back. She soon recognised her as the child that had got stung by a bee on her first day.

Lizzie stood and beckoned to Tom. 'Come! I'll introduce you to a nice lady. You could play with her daughter if you want, a lovely little girl. Just keep to our story that I mind you for a friend who's in England, okay?'

Tom nodded his assent and hurried behind her.

'Hi, remember me?' said Lizzie when she approached them.

'Oh hi! Of course! How are you?' asked the woman, a wide smile on her face.

'This is Tom. A friend's son – I'm minding him for a few days,' said Lizzie pointing to him. By now, the lie came out more easily; she even managed an easy smile to go with it.

Tom smiled at the woman, who said her name was Brenda. Lizzie offered her name too, then Brenda pointed to the little girl.

'This is my daughter, Mandy.' The two children nodded at each other and smiled.

'Mandy... that's a lovely name,' said Lizzie to the little girl, who gave a cute grin.

Brenda rolled her eyes. 'It's Mandalena, actually. My mother-in-law's name...'

Lizzie gave a titter. She remembered how Brenda felt about having Greek in-laws.

'I had no choice in the matter,' Brenda flicked her wrist, 'But everyone calls her Mandy back home. Only here I must remember to call her Mandalena to keep the Greek dragon happy.' Brenda made air quotes when she uttered the last three words, her eyes wide with mock-dread. 'Oh well! Keeps my man happy, you know?'

'Mum? Have you finished putting the cream on? Can I get in the pool now?' asked Mandy.

Everyone looked where the girl was pointing, and Lizzie noticed for the first time a plastic pool. It was small, and just the right size for the child to sit or even lie on her back in it. It stood on the sand a few paces away filled halfway with water.

Lizzie found it peculiar but was too tactful to ask. It was the kind of thing children used in gardens and balconies to cool off on a hot summer's day – quite an unusual thing to bring to the beach.

'Oh, you have a pool!' said Tom.

'You want to try it?' asked Mandy.

'Of course,' he replied, bright-eyed.

A moment later, it seemed, Tom and Mandy were sitting together inside, splashing about and squealing with delight. Brenda had just offered the information that her daughter was seven years old.

Lizzie's curiosity rose inside her. *All children like to play and splash around as near the sea as possible. This one prefers to sit in a pool that's not even placed anywhere near the edge of the shore. What's going on?*

Lizzie walked up to the pool, willing herself to look as nonchalant as possible. 'Mandy, would you like Tom to help you build a sand castle on the shore? Tom is very good at making sand castles, he can show you!' She pointed to the girl's bucket and spade lying by Brenda's feet, then to the water.

Mandy's face turned ashen. 'No!' Her features grew pinched, and she seemed ready to break into hysterics. Or tears. Or both.

Lizzie took a step back and nodded in silence, wondering what that was all about.

Behind her, Brenda waved a frantic hand. 'It's okay, Mandy, it's okay. You stay there, darling! Play with Tom now, there's a good girl!'

Lizzie rushed to Brenda, her voice reduced to a whisper. 'I'm so sorry... All I wanted was to—'

Brenda put up a hand, all traces of humour gone from her expression. 'It's okay, it's okay. You didn't know.'

'What's wrong? If you don't mind me asking...'

Brenda twisted her lips and looked away.

Sensing this was something distressing, Lizzie reached out and rubbed Brenda's back. 'It's okay. You don't have to answer that.'

'No, no. It's fine. Sit...' Brenda patted her towel and Lizzie sat beside her without a word.

Brenda gave a long sigh. 'A terrible accident started this... This phobia of hers for the sea. It happened when Mandy was three.' She threw a glance at the children. They were laughing in the pool and tossing a tiny rubber ball back and forth.

Brenda gave a thin smile. 'So... where was I? Yes... It happened right here in Messonghi. One of my husband's great uncles took my husband and Mandy for fishing one day. It was springtime. We had come here for the Easter celebrations. The weather was humid but sunny on most days, but that particular morning it stirred up a horrid storm out of nowhere. Gales, lightning and everything. Then a water tornado formed... *"Roufoulas"*, my husband called it. It came right at them in the boat, then swept by at a good distance away from them, thank goodness. Yet, the impact it had in the water sent huge waves their way... Oh! The story they relayed! You wouldn't believe...'

'I'm so sorry... it must have been very traumatic for your little girl.'

Brenda gave a wry smile. 'You haven't heard half of it yet. The boat nearly went over and, what's more, the waves sent Mandy overboard.'

'What? No!'

'Yes... Luckily, she stayed underwater for only a few seconds. My husband dived in straight after her and got her back on the boat. They managed to get to shore safely but... because of this... Mandy has a fear of deep water now.'

'Deep water?'

'Yes. She won't have a bath unless there's hardly any water in the bathtub, for example. Swimming pools are out of the question... as for the sea, she won't go anywhere near it. Only rarely, by coaxing her a lot, I manage to convince her to stand at the edge sometimes, just to pour some water over her with the bucket to cool her down. Then, last week, my husband bought this pool and finally we got her to splash around a little in it today. It's only shallow and it's not even seawater... but it's a start.'

Lizzie arched her brows. 'Not seawater? How did you fill it?'

Brenda turned and pointed to a private property behind them. Their front door was right on the beach, just a few paces away. 'See that? That's where Mandy's *nonos* lives... her godfather. As of today, he's on pool duty. He came out with a garden hose and filled it for us earlier. He'll be emptying, then refilling the pool every couple of days to keep the water fresh. We hope that slowly the pool will help her overcome her fear... enough to get her into the sea again. Before our holiday ends.' She shrugged, lips twisting. 'Well, we do hope.'

Lizzie thought for a moment. *This could count as a second healing for us, couldn't it?* 'Did I tell you I'm a nurse, Brenda?'

'Yes, you did.'

'Well, I read a spot of psychology at some point... Would it be okay if I tried something? To help Mandy?'

Brenda's face lit up. 'Of course! I have full faith in your nurse training... My grandmother was a nurse. So be my guest!' She pointed vaguely towards the children in the pool.

'Not now. I need to speak to Tom first.' She gave an amused smile and squeezed Brenda's arm. 'This plan calls for a little helper... Are you coming here again tomorrow?'

'Yes, of course we are. We've been away for a few days, visiting my sister-in-law, who lives in Ioannina. We came back yesterday, and we'll be visiting the beach every morning in the following week, then we're going back home.'

'Oh, wonderful! This is more than enough, I should think,' replied Lizzie, bright-eyed. *It'd better be. All we have left is three days!*

How could I have been so blind?

When Aliki joined them a little later, more introductions ensued, then Lizzie and Aliki went for a swim together. Brenda stayed behind to mind the children, who seemed oblivious to the world while playing in the pool.

By the time the two women had got out of the water to sit on their towels, the fierce heat had made Brenda desperate for the cool refuge of her mother-in-law's house. She sprang upright and began to pick up her things. 'Come on, darling! Time to get back home,' she shouted out to her daughter.

Mandy did as she was told, but looked rather sad to have to say goodbye to Tom. She stood out of the pool with him, a coy expression in her eyes, her lips twisting, and he eyed her back with fondness, a bright smile across his face.

'It's all right. You'll see Tom again tomorrow!'

'Really, Mummy?'

'Yes! You can play some more tomorrow. Let's go now, say bye-bye!'

Brenda had picked up their things in record time. 'If I don't put my mitts around a glass of water in the next minute I think I might faint.' She fanned her face and took Mandy's hand. 'Bye-bye everybody!' she said in a childlike voice, and the little girl said goodbye too.

'Bye, girls!' said Aliki.

'See you tomorrow, Brenda. See you, Mandy!' said Lizzie with a knowing smile and nodded at Brenda.

Tom was waving goodbye at the time but, all of a sudden, his face ignited with alarm. 'Wait! What about the pool?'

Brenda waved it off. 'The pool stays there... We'll come back this afternoon again. Our house is literally around the corner.'

'But, what if someone steals it?' insisted Tom.

'Steal it? Here in Messonghi?' Brenda laughed. 'No chance. It's safe here. No thieves, no robbers. Trust me. We sleep with the shutters wide open back at the house.'

'You do?'

'Yes. Safest place in the world.'

And with that, they were off.

If only you knew... thought Lizzie, caressing her brother's face with her eyes.

Aliki, who sat beside her still, seemed just as blissfully oblivious to the sheer terror this place hid in the bowels of its mountain slopes.

❈❈❈❈

Once the scorching heat got too much to bear, the three of them made a beeline for Gorgona and sat at a table near the sand. Under the shade, and with a big electric fan blowing at full speed their way, they felt themselves come alive again and began to chatter excitedly.

Moments later, Mr Petros came out in his usual chirpy manner. He chuckled loudly to find that Aliki and Lizzie knew each other, and began to recite the special dishes of the day. Lizzie went for *bifteki* filled with tomato and feta cheese, while Tom chose *souvlaki kotopoulo*. As for Aliki, she opted for *gemista* saying it was her favourite of all Greek vegetarian dishes. They decided to share a *choriatiki salata* among them, and then Aliki ordered *tzatziki, kolokithokeftedes* and *saganaki* too, much to the others' delight.

As soon as Mr Petros went inside, Tom began to talk about dogs. Soon, the three were engrossed in discussing different breeds, deliberating about the one that would be most suitable for Tom.

At first, Lizzie listened to them, offering the odd suggestion, but soon, she turned to gaze over at the pier where Stamatis's boat was moored. Inevitably, her mind drifted to him again. *Aliki is right... I should take him up on his offer and visit him today... But... does he still want me to? What if he thinks that I shunned him? That I'm not interested? But what could I have done? I had to rush back home to Tom that morning when he asked me to have coffee here... Tom is my first priority, but... Oh, what an idiot I am!*

A sudden jab in her ribs made her return abruptly to reality. She heard footsteps then; they echoed loudly from the boarded walkway that ran past Gorgona. As soon as she saw who had just hurried by, the sight causing her heart to skip a beat, Aliki jabbed her again, this time on the arm, before calling out, 'Hey! Stamatis! Over here!'

Stamatis, who was obviously heading for Pitsilos, his metallic toolbox in hand, turned around and cheered. 'Hey, how are you, ladies?' He hopped onto the seating area, rendering Lizzie breathless once she caught a glimpse of his broad shoulders and twinkling eyes. Dressed in a sleeveless t-shirt and faded jeans, he looked good enough to eat. By the time he'd reached their table, Lizzie had begun to hyperventilate.

'I didn't know you girls knew each other!' he said with a grin, then turning to Tom, 'Hi, Tom. How are you? Did you go swimming today?'

While Tom and Stamatis exchanged a few words, Lizzie dropped her gaze to Stamatis's toolbox. It looked like it weighed a ton judging from the flexing muscles and popping veins on his forearm, and yet he preferred to hold it rather than put it down. *How strong these arms must be! Oh... to be held in those arms... to be kissed by those lips...* Her heart gave a thump, beads of sweat prickling on her brow. With a huff, she shot up a hand to brush her fringe away from her face.

'We are neighbours... Of course we know each other,' she said faintly, and only after she'd said it she realized, panicking, that her answer to his comment had come far too late.

Stamatis turned to meet her eyes, for just a few moments, but for her, it felt like an eternity. 'Oh yes, of course. Duh!' He face-palmed himself. 'Sorry, it's too hot today.'

'Well, I keep telling you that you ought to hit the beach and swim like the rest of us,' said Aliki. 'It's not good for you, all this work and no play. You don't want to be a dull boy, now, do you?' She winked at him, and he laughed out loud.

Lizzie watched, shocked into silence. She didn't think Aliki would be like that with men, with Stamatis especially. But somehow, she knew she wasn't flirting with him. Stamatis laughed once more, the sound bringing her deliciously back to reality.

'Dull or not, I've got to eat, dear Aliki.'

'Don't tell me. Off to Nia's?'

'That's right.'

'What is it this time? Don't tell me. Running tap?'

'A shutter.'

'Again?'

'Hm-hm.'

He seemed distracted now, looking away, and Lizzie turned to find that Nia had just emerged from the entrance at Pitsilos next door.

As soon as Nia clocked him she raised a hand, her face ablaze with anticipation.

Oh my God! How could I have been so blind all this time? Lizzie squinted her eyes as Nia shouted out a greeting to her and Aliki. Issuing a thin smile, she watched as Nia and Stamatis exchanged their greetings across the distance. All the while, she felt shocked to have failed to notice Nia's infatuation with Stamatis until now. Nia's whole body language screamed with it, eyes twinkling and lashes batting as if they were powered by a motor.

'Be there in a minute!' he shouted out, then turned his back to Nia to bend slightly over Tom, his hand on the boy's shoulder. 'I still can't believe how much you look like the friend I once had... I did tell you about him, didn't I? Oh, my! You look just like Tom...'

Tom turned to Lizzie, looking lost for words, and she cleared her throat. 'Well, yeah. But he's in the family, so... it makes sense there's a resemblance.'

'Family?' asked Aliki.

'Yes, didn't I say? Tom's mum, my friend, is actually a distant cousin,' lied Lizzie.

Aliki leaned closer to Lizzie. 'Oh, that's nice... It now makes even more sense that you're doing so much to help her.' She turned to Stamatis with a frown. 'But what am I missing? Who is this friend who looks like Tom?'

Lizzie pressed her lips together, then cut in, 'It's... erm... my brother, Tom. He... he... erm...'

'Lizzie's brother disappeared, Aliki... twenty years ago. And...' Stamatis let out a sigh. 'Well, I don't think we should discuss it any more.' He turned to Lizzie. 'My bad... I shouldn't have brought it up, I am sorry, Lizzie.'

His eyes were full of tenderness. It took her by surprise and, even though she had no words, her heart bloomed with feeling.

Aliki broke the ensuing awkward silence. 'I see. I am sorry too, Lizzie. It must have been hard. And I agree, let's not discuss this any more.' She squeezed Lizzie's hand fondly.

Even though all three looked sheepish, Lizzie, on the other hand, was over the moon. She ventured another look towards Nia to find her, to her delight, craning her neck to peer at them through the patrons, and Mr Petros, who strode up and down the seating area.

At the time, Nia was sitting outside in a chair leafing through a magazine. It felt to Lizzie like a little victory that Stamatis kept her waiting to talk to them. She loved the feeling. It made her crave more. It made her want to fight Nia for him with all her might. Also, the tender look he'd given her earlier had stirred her beyond words.

'Stamatis, can I ask you something?'

He turned to her, and only then did Lizzie realize that he'd been talking to Aliki and had stopped midsentence.

'Sorry. Carry on. This can wait,' she said, appalled, waving frantically.

'No, no, it's okay,' he said.

Aliki made sounds to agree, her eyes bulging out of their sockets behind Stamatis's back as she beckoned her to say what she had to say.

Lizzie registered that and it made her smile brightly. She spared a thought for Nia and wondered if she'd seen Aliki do that, but decided that even if she had it was of no importance.

'Right... I just wanted to ask... how about that tea you promised me? Will you be around this afternoon?'

Stamatis gawped for a few moments, then his face lit up. 'Oh! Yes, yes of course!' He bent his knees and left the toolbox on the floor with a dull clanking sound. With both his hands free, he began to gesture wildly. 'You know where it is, right? Get to the road to Spileo, then, after the church, you get to the mini store, then—'

Lizzie giggled. 'Yes, yes, I know where it is. I remember. Plus, I passed by it a couple of times, but I didn't see your motorcycle so I presumed you weren't in.'

'Yes, I'm sure that was the case. Sorry I missed you when you came...' His voice trailed off.

She flicked her wrist and gave an encouraging smile. 'Oh, no problem at all. So, how about this afternoon? Will you be home?'

'Yes! Please, do come. That would be wonderful.' He screwed up his face. 'Though, I may have to get to the shop... What kind of tea do you like? Not sure I have any of the good stuff, you know?'

'Well, I'd like to try your local mountain tea, if you have some,' she said, remembering that's all his grandparents used to have but she'd never had any.

'Oh, I have plenty of that!' He seemed relieved, and it made Lizzie smile all the way to her ears.

'Problem solved then! Six o' clock okay?'

'Perfect! Look forward to it, Lizzie!'

With that, he raised a hand and walked away. When he reached the boarded walkway he spun around to wave goodbye again, causing her heart that was already racing to thump hard. Right then, Aliki reached under the table and squeezed her knee gently, and Lizzie gave a giggle.

As soon as he reached the entrance of Pitsilos, Nia stood like a coiled spring and hurried him inside. Before disappearing behind him through the front door, she cast her gaze at Lizzie's table, looking daggers at them all.

Smooching sounds

When Lizzie and Tom returned home, the latter said he fancied reading for a while, then having a siesta. Seeing that Lizzie was a bag of nerves already in anticipation of her visit to Stamatis's house later that day, she suggested that he lie on her bed while she watched TV on the sofa.

Tom was happy to oblige. After a while, Lizzie saw the light go off behind the semi-closed bedroom door and switched off the TV so that she didn't disturb him.

She opened a book, trying to pass the time, but the words only danced before her eyes. Soon, her mind began to churn with a plethora of worries again; not just about Stamatis, but also about the task Phoni expected them to carry out.

They had already healed one soul. Charlie wasn't human, but surely dogs had souls too, so healing him had to count... Hopefully, they could help Brenda's little girl next, so that would make two. They needed to find a third person who needed assistance as soon as possible... and a fourth one too. Just in case they failed on one occasion.

Lizzie made a mental note to talk to Tom in the evening, to make sure they had a solid plan to help Mandy overcome her fear of the sea. Lizzie had a good idea about what they could do. Tom, being highly fanciful, was bound to turn her idea into a detailed plan in no time.

As she stared absent-mindedly at the open book, she realized Phoni had given them no details... How were they to prove they had cured three souls? Would they have to bring the three along? She shook her head profusely. *No, no way.* Phoni wouldn't want anyone to know of her existence. Then she thought of the ravens and nodded to herself. *Those damned birds! Surely they've been spying on us! They'll tell her...*

Lizzie glanced at the clock on the wall for the umpteenth time and made a mental note to check for any ravens next time she was out. She hadn't seen any for days, then again, their trained eye probably could spot her from a good distance away. Not seeing the birds certainly didn't mean they hadn't been checking on her and Tom all along. *So what? We have nothing to hide...*

✻✻✻✻

At five minutes to five, Lizzie went to the kitchen to make a cup of tea. Miraculously, she'd managed to read a little in the end, and even dozed off for an hour. Tom was still in her room, sleeping. She made her beverage, then took her time to enjoy it with a couple of biscuits. At some point, she went to her room and woke her brother up, seeing that on her way out she'd have to take him to Aliki's so that she could mind him during her absence.

By five thirty she was ready to go and so was Tom.

Dressed in a flowery summer dress that reached down to her knees and left her back half-exposed, Lizzie felt comfortable enough to brave the ascent to Spileo in the sweltering heat.

She put her best flat sandals on and a wide-brimmed sun hat on her head, then stood before the mirror chewing her lips. Her hair fell loosely on her sun-kissed shoulders and curled at the edges like baby snakes basking in the sunshine. The thought made her smile.

That's when Tom approached to stand behind her. He caught her eye through the mirror and chuckled.

Panic struck at her that something was wrong with her appearance. 'What is it? How do I look?' she asked in a frail voice, turning around to face him.

'It's only *Stamata*...' he said with a wicked smile. 'It's not like you haven't spent time together before. Unless... Oh! You're not going to kiss him, are you? Yuukkk!' He pulled a face of disgust.

Lizzie gave a lopsided grin. 'Tom, you talk too much, you know that?'

He stuck his tongue out at her and, giggling, she turned her attention to her reflection. She had already applied light touches of eye shadow, and mascara on her lashes. Now, with a single layer of pearly coral lipstick, she was ready to go.

'It won't stay on that long, so why bother?' he teased, and she pretended to take a swipe at him. He skipped away from her reach, then pretended to hug himself and made smooching sounds. 'Oh kiss me, kiss me... darling, *Stamulu*!'

Lizzie turned away and, with the sound of Tom's laughter in her ears, shooed him out the door, then rushed out behind him.

A messy scatter of flower pots

Lizzie made it to Stamatis's house just before six to find him in his garden pruning a bush. He had taken his shirt off and left it on his motorcycle that stood nearby. He was applying himself to the task with gusto, the muscles of his upper torso rippling with every cut from the shears in his hand.

Lizzie stood at the gate for a few moments, transfixed. It took a while to realize she was just standing there admiring him, at which point she panicked with the idea that he might turn at any moment and catch her gawping like a stalker. She raised a hand. 'Stamatis! Hey! I'm here!'

'Oh, hi!' He came to open the gate and, when she went through it, surprised her by kissing her cheeks. By the time he'd pulled back, her cheeks were on fire, and so were her insides. *The uphill walk has been bad enough in the heat but to have him kissing me while shirtless? Mercy!*

Unaware of her inner thoughts, he was all sweeping arms and open smiles, leading her to the front door of his house. On their way there they zigzagged past a messy scatter of flower pots and garden tools on the concrete path. When they stepped up to the porch, Lizzie removed her hat and began to fan her face.

Stamatis beckoned to the front door but then his eyes lit up with alarm. 'Oh! I left my keys on the motorcycle, excuse me! One moment!' He beckoned her to wait and went back to retrieve his keys through the maze of garden paraphernalia. 'Sorry about that, Lizzie. I'd lose my head if it wasn't screwed on, honestly.'

'Did I catch you at a bad time?' she asked when he came back having picked up his keys and his shirt.

'Oh no!' He waved a frantic hand. 'You came at the perfect time.' He checked his watch. 'I'll say! Six o' clock sharp... a proper English woman!' He pointed to the mess in the garden and scrunched up his face. 'Don't pay any attention to that. I underestimated the time it would take me to finish the job, that's all. I'll finish it later. Nearly done anyway.'

'You sure?'

'Yes, of course. Do come in, Lizzie.' He opened the door and gestured to her to enter.

As soon as the door opened, the smell of the hallway rendered Lizzie speechless. It might as well have been a device to take her back in time. The musty, familiar smell was non-traceable but had remained the same over the years.

They stood behind the closed door, her eyes glazed over when she turned to him. 'I don't believe it! It smells the same like it did when we were children.'

'It smells? Not unpleasantly, I hope!'

'Oh no, of course not.'

She followed him down the hallway, and he led her to the living room that had a view to the front garden. Again, it was just as she remembered it. The fireplace in the corner had the same marble hearth, and the antique painting that stood beside it on the wall depicted the same marvellous sailboat that she'd admired so many times as a child inside its gilded frame.

Stamatis beckoned her to sit on the sofa. He put his shirt on, buttoned it, and only then sat beside her, the right distance away. Respectfully far, but not too far. It was just perfect, and it made her feel comfortable.

Lizzie watched as he fumbled with his buttons, checking that he had done them all up. His head was bent, short black hair trembling in the breeze that came through the open tall window. In the same way, she felt her heart tremble inside her chest.

Despite herself, she reached out and straightened his shirt collar. He looked up then, his gaze deep, penetrating. The impact this had on her was tremendous. It made her thankful she was sitting at the time. This was the kind of look that would cause her knees to buckle if she were standing.

'Here, let me help you,' she said with a faint smile, despite her dizzy spell. She reached out with both hands, and he leaned slightly forward, allowing her to straighten the collar, then fold it neatly outwards. The skin on his neck felt warm under her fingertips; she could swear she could feel his heart pumping, the beat reverberating through her hands, to match the crazy rhythm of her own.

She cleared her throat, then tossed a curly strand behind her shoulder when she sat up straight again.

Stamatis jumped upright and clapped his hands together once. 'Oh, I am unforgivable! You must be thirsty... What can I get you to cool down? Water? Orange juice?'

'Water please, thank you.'

He excused himself and disappeared out the door, and she spent the next minute listening to the sound of cupboards and the fridge opening and closing. All the while, she relived in her mind the feel of his warm skin at the end of her fingertips.

So much for the lipstick...

Lizzie looked around the room while she waited for Stamatis to return. It seemed the world had stopped in this house for the past twenty years. Everything looked exactly the same as she'd left it. Even the vase on the old coffee table. She'd seen his grandmother many times arrange flowers from the garden in it.

Stamatis returned whistling a happy tune, the sound bringing her back to reality delightfully. He was holding two glasses full of chilled water, judging from the condensation on the outside surfaces.

He offered her a glass and she downed it in one go.

'Wow! You were thirsty!'

'Yes, sorry.'

'Why are you apologizing? You poor thing! Have another.'

He offered her the other glass, and she drank half of it greedily, then set it down on the coffee table.

'Well, that wasn't ladylike, was it?' she said, wiping the sides of her mouth with her fingertips. She had drunk so quickly that a few drops had escaped and wet her chin as well. She checked her lap with an urgent swipe of her hand. Her dress was dry, but she saw smudges of her lipstick on her fingers. *So much for the lipstick... Oh, how Tom would tease me if he saw this!*

Oblivious to her thoughts, Stamatis watched her for a little while, then waved dismissively. 'Hey, you don't have to apologize for drinking water, no matter how thirstily. For beer or wine, yes. But not for water. Trust me, I've seen a few ladies in my time lose their ladyship status that way.'

'Yeah? Like who?'

He tapped his nose. 'A gentleman never tells.'

She thought about pushing him a little, to see if he would mention Nia, hoping to discover what he thought of her, but thought better of it. So instead, she tilted her head and smiled. 'Sorry I drank your water too. You'll have to get another one now...'

He cocked his eye at her and grinned. 'You forgot?'

'What?'

'They were both for you. You always had two glasses!'

'When?'

'Whenever we came back home from playing in the heat.'

Lizzie thought for a few moments, then her eyes lit up. 'Oh! Like when we went to your olive grove on the mountain to play?'

'Yes. And every time we returned from the beach. Didn't I always bring you two glasses when you said you were thirsty?'

Lizzie brought a hand to her forehead. 'Goodness me, yes, that's right. I had forgotten all about that.'

'It's strange, isn't it? The things you remember from your childhood...'

'Yes, and the things you forget too. I've always wondered what it is that makes a person retain certain memories from their early life and forget so many others. How is it decided?'

'I don't know that, Lizzie... But I expect the mind protects us from hurtful memories or traumatic experiences. Or maybe it filters out all the things it believes are not important.'

'Believe me... I have my traumatic experiences in my head fully indexed and in technicolour...' She gave a bitter smile.

'I'm sorry... I didn't mean—'

'Don't apologize, Stamatis. Not your fault we lost Tom back then.'

'No, of course not...'

An awkward silence followed and Lizzie tried hard to think of something to say. What she really wanted to do was throw out her arms and announce the big news – that her brother was back! She wanted so much to tell him... Only, she had lied to him, introducing Tom as a distant relative who was his spitting image. She was surprised he had believed the lie... It didn't help to alleviate her guilt, though.

She lay her eyes on him again, and he turned to meet her gaze. Once more, that deep look that said so much kept her captive. Finally, she tilted her head and gave a thin smile. 'So... What else do you remember that I don't?'

He turned away and raised his head, eyes focusing far. 'Ah... let's see... Do you remember our picnics in my family's land on the mountain?'

'Of course, I remember! You know, I went back to your grove the other day. I took Tom along to see the view.'

'Tom, yes... I cannot believe how much he looks like your brother. But...'

'Yes?'

'Don't you mind? Spending time with him, I mean? Doesn't being with him, you know... make you sad?'

'Well, Tom is gone...' She swallowed hard and looked away, '... I have no choice in the matter. And my cousin is a single mother. She needs someone to mind her boy so I offered to do it while I'm here.'

'Since you mentioned it... I hope you'll be staying for a while.'

'Yes, yes, I am...'

'How long?'

'I don't know. I haven't decided yet. But I can give you my address in the UK... We could keep in touch this time if you like, after I'm gone.'

'Yes, I'd love that.'

Lizzie drank the dregs in her glass and had another look around as she put it down on the coffee table. 'It's strange... how this place hasn't changed at all. I'd have thought with a new bride in the house—'

'A new bride? Oh, no. This has always been my parents' home. When I was married, I lived next door with Kiki, not here.'

'At the guest house?'

'Yes, that's right.'

'And you don't live there any more?'

'No... Shortly after Kiki passed away, my mother died too. So I made the decision to close down the guest house, and I've been living here with my father ever since.'

'I see. And your father? Isn't he in today?'

'No... He has developed Alzheimer's, I'm afraid, and I had to put him in a retirement home recently. It's been getting harder and harder over time to leave him here on his own while I'm out and about. But I visit him once a week in Corfu town.' He gave a wistful smile. 'It's always good to see him, especially on the days when he greets me with a smile.'

'I'm sorry to hear that... But he's doing okay, your dad?'

Yes, generally speaking.... He has his good and bad days, you know?'

She gave a faint smile. 'I hope you get to catch him on good days mostly.'

'Well, yes, those days are easier. He lets me give him the odd hug then, and to call him Dad, you know? We even get to play chess together on those days and, knowing who I am then, he doesn't cheat.' He winked and offered a wicked smirk. It made him look adorable.

Lizzie slapped his forearm and giggled. 'Oh come on! Your father never cheated in chess.'

'No, of course he didn't. But you looked so sad just then, I thought a bad joke was in order.'

Lizzie gave a little sigh. 'I miss your dad... I remember him always surrounded by books. His nose was forever buried in some ancient volume, be it history, philosophy or something heavy like that... He loved to share stories with me, I recall.'

'Greek myths...'

'You remember, yes.'

'He surely was a fine scholar. The Ionian University misses him still, just as my family does – aunts, uncles, cousins and the like, I mean. No one else left in this house to miss him but me these days.'

'And your grandparents? I gather they've passed away?'

'Oh... yes...' He scratched his temple, turning his eyes towards the ceiling. 'Granddad left us first, about ten years ago, Granny followed him two or three years after that.'

'It must have been hard. Losing them all in such a short time. Your wife too...'

'Yes...' He lowered his head, pinning his eyes on the floor tiles. 'It has been hard.' He turned to catch her gaze, only momentarily, then looked towards the open window, his eyes filling with sunlight. 'But life goes on... and the living belong to the living, not to the dead.'

'I love that...'

'It's my dad's, actually. He'd reminded me that many times over the years. Nowadays, mind you, only on his lucid days.'

'You never had any children with Kiki?' she asked, throwing a glance at the garden outside. She'd noticed the lack of toys out there but was desperate to make sure.

'God, no!' His reaction startled her. She watched speechless as he shook his head before chortling. 'I cannot imagine having any children right now. I am glad this is not the case.'

He seemed to register her stunned expression and cleared his throat before adding, 'Don't get me wrong. I don't have anything against children. And maybe, sometime in my future, there will be kids. But I'm just glad there are none from my past. For one, I'd have driven them crazy the way I've been since Kiki's passing.'

Lizzie nodded, even though deep down she wasn't sure she understood him fully. She'd have expected that any given widowed husband would be wishing he had children with a loving wife he'd lost too soon.

Then again, she was never one to judge. Giving it no more thought, she changed the subject, asking him about his garden and what he'd been doing there. This caused his face to light up.

Soon, they were chatting excitedly as he told her about the plants he had bought to grow in the pots, and the vegetables he also intended to plant in the ground. He said he hadn't done much gardening in years and was out of practice. She teased him then, causing him to howl with laughter by saying that, from the look of his front path, that was rather obvious.

Act normal, for goodness sake!

Half an hour later, Stamatis led Lizzie upstairs through an internal staircase, then out onto the terrace. She'd never been there before, and he was itching to show her the view.

The terrace overlooked the lush mountains and the bay. Lizzie admired the spectacular view, and he stood with her for a while, then excused himself so he could prepare the mountain tea he'd promised her.

As soon as he was out of sight, Lizzie took a seat in a wicker armchair, relaxing in it, seemingly, in a second. As she filled her lungs with fresh air and her ears with the fervent song of the cicadas, the breeze caressed her face. Silky red strands of her hair began to dance around her face, tickling her cheeks and forehead.

As she tucked the loose strands behind her ears she thought of Stamatis's parting words a while earlier. He'd mentioned he was going to have a quick smoke in the kitchen while he brewed the tea. Lizzie had assured him that it would be fine if he smoked on the terrace while they sat together. There was a light breeze and he could sit further away so her allergy wouldn't be a problem. Finally, she had convinced him but it hadn't been easy.

Lizzie felt her heart melt at the thought of him, how soft-spoken and thoughtful he was. She turned her gaze towards the bay, her eyes taking in the deep blue, her heart lifting. She was looking forward to that mountain tea and felt surprised by her growing sense of joy. *How little it takes to feel happy... even in the darkest times of my life...*

Thoughts of Phoni crept into her mind, but she pushed them aside, willing herself to think of Stamatis instead. As always, she welcomed filling her mind with images of him. At some point, during her reverie, she heard his footsteps on the internal staircase. Moments later, he appeared through the door holding a small tray with two mugs and a porcelain bowl filled with biscuits.

'Sorry. I don't have any proper cookies from a bakery. Hope these biscuits from the supermarket are okay.' He put the tray on the little table before her and pointed to them.

'Oh, that's fine, thank you.' She nodded and smiled sweetly as he placed one of the mugs before her.

He sat across from her and, without further ado, lit up a cigarette from his pack. He took a long drag, then pointed to the mugs with a flourish. 'I hope you like the tea. I pick it myself. From my land!' He pointed towards the lush mountain with his head, his chin hardening as he took another drag, eyes squinting with relish. He turned his face to the side and let out the smoke, an urgent hand fanning it away from her at the same time.

She laughed. 'You don't have to do that. We're outside, it's okay.'

'No, I have to be really careful... Don't want you looking at me sternly the way you did at Gorgona that day. Oh! If looks could kill...' His eyes glinted with gaiety as he pinched the front of his shirt, tugging it repeatedly.

She knew that Greek gesture. The tugging meant he was wishing it away, and it was a joke in this case. His grandmother was forever doing it, whenever she saw bad things on the TV news, like robberies or bad road accidents.

He saw she had got the joke and tilted his head back, laughing uproariously.

She giggled. 'You devil, you...'

He gave a lopsided grin. 'So, you like the view, Lizzie?'

'Oh yes... It must be wonderful to be able to sit out here and see this view every day... You didn't have a terrace in the old days, did you? I don't remember it.'

'No, we didn't. My parents had built only part of this floor at the time, if you recall, and it was uninhabitable. They finished it a lot later. And yes, it is wonderful to have this view. I love Martaouna... The land of my family up there means a lot to me.'

Lizzie registered the look in his eyes as they caressed the mountain. They were glinting with pride, and with nostalgia too. For the old days, she imagined, when his family was whole. When her own family was whole too.

'Oh, I'm sure...' she whispered, turning to look at the dark green mountain too. Except, for her, it seemed threatening, like a terrible foe planning an attack, breathing down on her... its breath, this fresh, cool breeze, the epitome of its deceit that put you at ease when it should be warning you to run for your life.

Martaouna, from what her brother had said, was a treasure of healing plants just waiting to be found by those who could identify them. But, deep in its depths, it also contained the lurking evil of Phoni... something that no one but she and Tom, it seemed, knew about. Stamatis picked his favourite tea up there... and she and Tom had recently collected in the same place many other herbs that meant the world to them ...

'Hey! What is it?'

Lizzie's shoulders jumped. Only now she realized she'd been staring absentmindedly at the mountain. 'I'm sorry... I was miles away.' She offered a thin smile, then dropped her gaze to the mug of clear green liquid that steamed on her lap. She hadn't even realized she'd taken it from the table.

'Hey! It's still rather hot. I'd let it sit awhile if I were you.'

'Yes, of course...' She put the mug back on the table.

She saw it in his eyes then; he could tell she was distracted. The last thing she needed was for him to think she was acting strange. She liked him too much and hoped to see him again... *Act normal, for goodness sake!*

Her mind churned as she tried to find something to say and end the awkward silence. When she found it, her eyes lit up, her features arranging themselves into an expression of nonchalance.

'So... how did you get to be a fisherman? I don't remember your family owning a boat. Did you buy it, or...?'

'Yes, I bought it.'

'Really? So you decided to start fishing? Just like that?'

'Yes, well...' He smiled and scratched the back of his neck, eyes focusing far towards the sea. The Ionian waters stretched out to the distant shores of Epirus and Albania, a velvet sheet of blue and silver. 'I guess you could say that.'

Lizzie smiled and, as she sat back in her comfortable seat, felt herself relax again. It felt like heaven, sitting here with him, surrounded by so much beauty, including his. 'So, which is your main profession? The odd DIY jobs or the fishing, if you don't mind me asking?'

'The DIY, definitely. After all, this has been my main job for years. I only bought the boat as a hobby. I've always wanted to learn fishing and a couple of my friends taught me. Then I acquired a licence that allows me to sell a little to the local tavernas every now and then. It means I can combine my hobby with earning a little on the side.'

'Wonderful...'

'Yes, it is. And being out at sea on the boat is a delight in itself. So relaxing...' A spark ignited in his eyes as he bent forward to extinguish his cigarette in a small ashtray. He tilted his head and gave a little smile. 'Hey. If you like, I could take you out with me sometime.'

She smiled back. 'Yeah, thanks! I'd love that.'

'Great.'

'And the DIY work, where did that come from? Did you go to a technical college to learn all that?'

'Oh no. I learned a lot from running the guest house all those years. Remember, my father ran it before me, so he taught me the basics. Also, here on the island, all the boys go out for work during the winter. Some more than others, but most of them wind up doing some kind of building or technical work. I've done it all. And when I closed down the guest house, I even moved to Ioannina for a couple of years.'

'Really? You did building work there?'

'Yes. I helped build hotels mostly.'

'Did you enjoy doing that?' she asked taking her mug into her hands. The tea smelled wonderful; she guessed it would be safe to try it now.

Stamatis waited, watching her reaction, without answering her question.

'Oh! You were right. This tastes really nice...'

He gave a satisfied smile. 'I'm glad you like it. And, yes, I did enjoy working in Ioannina. A big city like that did me just fine. But, alas, then Dad got sick and I had to come back here to take care of him.'

'I'm sorry... Sounds like you'd have been happier there if you'd had a choice.'

'Well, I did like it there, I won't lie. But I had come to miss my island too, you know? Besides...' He leaned closer and captured her eyes for a few moments, his gaze electrifying. Lizzie felt the effect course right through her, making her fingers and toes tingle.

'Had I not come back, I would have missed you...' He gave a slow, sweet smile. It made her stomach fill with butterflies. 'I am so glad I didn't miss you, Lizzie.'

Lizzie smiled back, still lost in his gaze. 'So am I, Stamatis. So pleased we could meet again.'

He leaned back in his chair, a lazy smile on his lips. He appeared to know nothing about the stir he'd just caused inside her. Or, if he did, he seemed to enjoy doing it. 'So? What about you? What do you do for a living?'

She opened her mouth to answer but he raised an urgent hand before she could make a sound. 'No. Let me guess! Something that has to do with caring. Or teaching. Or both!'

The startled look in her eyes told him he was very close.

'A-ha! So what is it? Teacher? Professor? School principal? Or maybe, a doctor? Or a nurse? Did I get it?'

She drank from her mug and gave him a cryptic smile as she placed it on the table.

He eyed her playfully for a few moments, then said, 'Well? Which one is it?'

She raised her hands. 'Busted! I'm a nurse.'

'A nurse?' He slapped his knee. 'I knew it!'

She leaned forward and planted a hand over her chest. 'How the hell did you guess? I'm speechless!'

He gave a big sigh. 'Oh, you... Lizzie... you have always been a nurse... a natural healer. It was in you from back then, when we were just kids.'

'A healer?' The choice of word was uncanny, setting her eyes ablaze with intrigue. *What is he talking about?*

He must have seen the bewilderment in her eyes because he said, 'Oh come on, Lizzie... Don't you remember? You were always attentive of my ailing grandmother, fetching her a chair whenever she'd come out to sit and watch us play in the garden, or after we'd all gone out for a walk. When my family and yours had picnics on the mountain and the adults had had too much to drink, you'd mind them all by yelling *'Aftokinito!'* whenever a car would come from behind as we walked back home along the road. We used to laugh about that. Don't you remember?'

She squinted her eyes, pushing her mind for confirmation, but had no recollection of this. 'I don't remember any of that, but I'll take your word for it.'

'Trust me... You, Lizzie, you have always been a protector. Oh! And, of course, there's that fateful day...'

Before she could ask what he meant, he leaned forward, eyes softening, to say, 'Surely you remember that afternoon on the mountain when it was just the three of us kids? I got bitten by a snake on my hand while we played hide and seek...'

'Oh, yes. I remember that! That was scary! You were sitting behind a rock, and the snake bit you. It was in the grass, out of sight.'

'Yes, that's right. You used my Swiss army knife and cut my t-shirt... and made a ribbon to tie around my arm, really tight, so tight it hurt. I complained but you told me to shut up, remember?'

Lizzie nodded, a smile growing on her lips slowly, until it reached up to her ears. All the while, the old memories from that harrowing incident flooded her mind.

He mirrored her expression. 'Then, we bolted down the road back home as fast as we could. Dad said you saved my life that day. Had it not been for you, knowing to do that, I might have died, he said.'

'I am sure your dad exaggerated.'

'No. I don't think so. I owe my life to you, Lizzie. And I'm glad you chose to become a nurse. It's the perfect profession for you. I'm sure it comes to you as second nature.'

✳✳✳✳

An hour had passed before she knew it. With every passing minute the setting sun filled the sky with more and more shades of gold, pink and violet, turning the sea into a wonder of pastel highlights. The white cotton clouds over Albania were specked with orange and pink. It was a marvel to watch them as they slowly moved to the north, aided by the gentle breeze, shifting further and further away over the distant mountain tops of Konispoli.

Sitting on the terrace chatting with Stamatis and reminiscing about their childhood had been wonderful. But Aliki was still minding Tom back in Messonghi... so Lizzie stood, albeit reluctantly, and announced it was time to go.

Stamatis stood and said he was sorry she had to leave so soon, the mirth in his eyes of moments ago disappearing. He followed her inside and they stood together on the landing.

'Shall I give you a lift on my motorcycle? I'd be more than happy to.'

'Thank you, Stamatis, but no. Besides, you need to get back to your work in the garden, don't you?'

'He waved a dismissive hand. 'Oh, that! Who cares? I can do it tomorrow morning.'

'Are you sure?'

'Yes. And I'm going to town now anyway,' he said looking towards the window.

'Are you?'

'Yes.' He checked his watch. 'I'm meeting a friend soon. The timing's perfect actually.'

She tilted her head and eyed him playfully. '*Stamata!* That's not true, and you know it.'

'No, really!'

She shook a sharp finger at him. 'I know you, *Stamata!* You're only saying that so I say yes. You're just trying to be gallant, and it's nice, but I don't mind walking.'

'I beg to differ. It's getting dark. There are prowlers around. What is a young lady like you going to do on her own? They'll chew you up for dinner and spit your bones out one by one!'

The last sentence was an old private joke. Just five minutes earlier they had recalled how he used to scare her with ghost stories at night, more often than not using that very sentence. As a young teenage boy, he used to speak surprisingly good English already. He'd take full advantage of it back then to tease her relentlessly.

She let out a giggle, then shook her finger at him. '*Stamata, Stamatis...* that won't work any more!'

'Hey, that's one *Stamata* too many. Don't call me that... *kontessa!*' he retaliated.

'I won't if you don't call me that again!' They laughed, and he teased her some more. She put out a hand to slap his arm playfully as he teased her still, but he turned abruptly and her hand landed on his chest, or rather, on the mounds of his pecs. It slipped through the crack between them, the skin taut and warm, like a valley of bliss, causing a warm sensation to bloom inside her.

She removed her hand from his chest as if electricity had hit her, and used it to brush her hair, as nonchalantly as she could muster. 'Anyway... be good!' she said feebly, looking away.

'So how about that ride?' he asked when she began to walk towards the stairs.

'Oh Stamatis, it's okay. Just admit I caught you lying in order to be helpful, and head back to your gardening. I'll be fine.'

'I'm not lying. Do you want me to prove it to you?'

'Yeah? Like, how?'

'I can tell you who I'm meeting. It's my friend, Babis. He owns a small supermarket near your house. You said you shop there so you must know him.'

'Yes, of course I know him.' How could she not? Aliki wouldn't shut up about him if she paid her. She tilted her head and twisted her lips, before asking, 'Is that where you're going then?'

'Yes. I can leave you outside the supermarket, then you can go home from there.'

'Okaaayy... If you're going that way, I'll go with you, thanks.'

He gave a beaming smile and, in a gentlemanly manner, went down the stairs first, then beckoned her to follow. As she went down the first step, she had an idea. 'Actually, I'll come to the supermarket with you... I just realized I don't have any milk for Tom's breakfast tomorrow.'

'Oh. Right...' he mumbled, then took his phone out of his shorts pocket in a heartbeat. As she continued to go down the steps, she noticed he had changed his own pace, now going down the stairs a lot more slowly than before, and was tapping the keys frantically in what looked like an sms screen. She guessed it was to Babis, or rather, she hoped it was. It would mean he was trying to cover his lie. Hiding her huge smile with a hand in case he suddenly turned to talk to her, she continued to descend.

At the bottom of the steps, he put away the phone, a triumphant look in his eyes. 'Come on, *Your Highness*! Your stallion awaits!' He showed her through the front door with a flourish.

'What did I say? Unless you like the name *Stamata*?' she said with a giggle.

He pretended to slap himself in the face. 'Sorry. Sorry, won't happen again... *Queen Elizabeth*!' he added with a cackle.

She followed him towards the front gate where his motorcycle stood, her amusement rising to new heights. *Men are so transparent...* She rolled her eyes, and had to admit, he certainly looked just as good from behind.

Her eyes lowered to where his cute butt progressed to carry his long muscly legs down the concrete path. *Yikes! A looker and a jester? Exactly what a girl needs!*

A wonderful custom

The motorcycle pulled to a stop right outside the supermarket. Stamatis waited till Lizzie got off, then he parked it and did the same.

'Hi!' said Babis with a raise of his hand as soon as they entered.

Lizzie and Stamatis exchanged a few pleasantries with him. As always, Babis was smiling openly and, once again, Lizzie wondered what Aliki was on about. She couldn't imagine Babis being anything else but chatty with anyone.

Even though she had two full cartons of milk at home, she had no choice now but to go get one. On her way back to the till she found Aliki and Tom turning away from the ice cream freezer. Aliki was holding a basket with a few things, obviously there to get another of her daily fixes.

'Hey, what are you two doing here?' asked Lizzie.

'Oh, there you are! We just finished walking Charlie and thought we'd get some ice cream. My treat!'

'Look! We got you one too!' said Tom, pointing to three large cones in the basket.

'Thanks!' Lizzie gave a frown, then added, 'Wait, where's Charlie?'

Aliki tilted her head. 'He's tied up outside. Didn't you see him on your way in?'

'Why are you surprised, Aliki?' replied Tom in a whisper. 'She's just come back from seeing Stamatis. She has her head in the clouds still!' He rolled his eyes causing Aliki to giggle.

'Hey!' protested Lizzie delivering a playful slap to each of their arms, then shushed them and whispered, 'He's here!' She pointed behind them.

The two turned around and Aliki tilted her head sideways to look behind the crisps display stand. Spotting the two men talking at the till, she put a hand over her mouth. 'Oh, sorry!' she mumbled to the sound of Tom's giggles.

'Now, let's go, and don't you two embarrass me!' Lizzie made to go but Tom grabbed her arm and pointed to the carton in her hand. 'Hey! We have loads of milk back home.'

'Long story,' it sufficed her to say, and the other two sniggered. She hushed them again as they all began to move towards the till.

'Now, behave!' she warned, stopping a moment later, shaking a sharp finger before their animated faces.

'Lizzie... let's see how Babis will talk to me now you're here,' whispered Aliki.

'Why? How does he talk to you?' asked Tom.

'Well, Aliki likes Babis but he's shy,' offered Lizzie.

'Really?'

'Hey!' replied Aliki throwing a mock-dagger look to Lizzie.

'It's not so funny when I share your love story with Tom, is it?'

Aliki grimaced, then nodded. 'Fair enough...'

They resumed walking to the sound of Tom chanting in a whisper, 'I know your secrets, I know your secrets, I know your secrets...'

Both the girls tapped him playfully, one on the shoulder, the other on the side of his head, to make him stop, just in time before arriving at the till.

✳✳✳✳

Stamatis greeted Aliki and Tom breezily, then Aliki turned to Babis and began to place her items on the counter. As Stamatis engaged Tom in idle chat, Lizzie watched the other two, her mystification growing.

Babis was punching Aliki's purchases without looking at her, even though she was talking to him about Charlie and how he loved his walks.

Aliki was clearly doing her utmost to get him to interact with her but her effort seemed futile. *Babis never misses an opportunity to talk to his customers... She's right. He's shy with her! It can't be that he dislikes her... Everyone loves Aliki. So, he must like her. Too much!*

Realizing, Lizzie felt the urge to do something about it. Stamatis and Tom stood near the door. They were looking outside. Stamatis had spotted Charlie tied to the railing. A little girl had stopped to pet him, her mother holding her by the hand, petting him too. It was a sweet scene. But she needed to talk to Stamatis now. This couldn't wait.

'Stamatis?' she asked, causing him to turn immediately as if she'd yelled 'fire'. He moved to stand before her in an instant, his face animated with eagerness. 'Yes?'

'Well...' She side-stepped towards Aliki, stopping right beside her before the till. As if tethered to her by an invisible thread, Stamatis followed to stand there beside her too.

Tom, having watched the scene with a glint in his eye, squeezed past Stamatis to stand between him and his sister, looking expectant.

Lizzie turned to Stamatis. 'You were saying earlier, Stamatis, about your boat... You asked if I'd like to go on a boat ride sometime with you?'

'Yes, that's right.' His eyes sparked with intrigue causing her heart to swell with adoration for him; she could already tell he had decided to say yes, no matter what she had in mind to ask him.

'Well, my friend Aliki here, she loves boats!' She turned to her friend, 'Don't you sweetheart?' She reached behind her friend with one hand, to tap her on the back gently.

Like a mechanized doll, Aliki stood straight, eyes widening. Then, she jerked into full motion, flailing her arms and rolling her eyes before landing an open hand on her chest. 'Oh! Don't get me started on boats! I just *loooove* them!' She turned to Lizzie, an impish smile on her fleshy lips. 'What do you have in mind, girlfriend?'

As soon as Aliki finished her sentence, she turned to Babis but he dropped his gaze in an instant. He was still in the middle of processing her purchases and seemed fascinated by the pack of sugar in his hands. Either that, or he was incredibly shy. But not just with anyone. *Only with Aliki. Fancy that!*

Lizzie saw the plea in Aliki's eyes during those moments. She pressed her lips together and turned to Stamatis with a sigh. 'Well? Would you mind if I brought Aliki over when we have that ride? And, say, you could bring a friend too maybe?'

What followed was a huge surprise. Stamatis's eyes darted to Babis, and the latter's face brightened beyond measure. He looked at Stamatis mutely for a few moments, his eyes shining. It was the human equivalent of a dog begging for a biscuit. *Wait. What just happened?*

Stamatis seemed to realize how keen Babis was. So what he said next, didn't surprise anybody. Not even Tom, who watched this odd four-adult show with growing curiosity, his eyes darting from one animated face to another, a big smile plastered on his own.

'Yes! What a wonderful idea! Babis? Would you like to come along?' asked Stamatis finally.

'Yes, yes I'd love to!' he said, and everyone cheered. Somehow, he managed to give Aliki a fleeting glance then, causing her to smile back sweetly at him. It was evident they were crazy about each other. It warmed up Lizzie's heart no end, and she congratulated herself for her idea.

'Say,' piped up Tom, raising a finger. 'Am I invited too?' Everyone responded to that with pats on his back and his head. Even Babis had livened up by then, now his normal self, and raised a hand to him for a high-five.

Smiling to his ears, Tom said, 'I have an idea! Have you guys seen the posters about the festival in Petriti? They're plastered on the walls all over Messonghi.'

Everyone seemed to have noticed them as they began to nod eagerly. 'Well,' continued Tom, 'Why don't we all go there together in your boat, Stamatis? Wouldn't that be great? It's this Saturday night, isn't it?'

A short silence ensued as everyone turned to Stamatis. In an instant, he thrust out his arms, face alight with excitement. 'What a marvellous idea, Tom! I'll be more than happy to take you all to Petriti!' This caused excited squeals all around.

'Oh! A boat ride at night! How romantic!' said Aliki.

'I can't wait... What a wonderful idea, Tom!' said Babis, and Tom responded with a huge grin.

'It's the annual Varkarola festival, after all,' continued Babis, looking at Aliki for a few moments, then at Lizzie. 'Not just any festival. This one's unmissable.'

'Well, I've never been to a Varkarola, but my Corfiot grandmother did tell me about them many times,' said Aliki, leaning closer to Babis over the till, despite herself.

To Lizzie's surprise, Babis leaned a little closer too as if drawn by her eyes. *Wow, a breakthrough!* For a few more moments, they remained frozen that way, gazing into each other's eyes, until Aliki giggled, straightened and looked away, pretending to check on Charlie outside.

'A Varkarola? What is it?' asked Lizzie, turning to Stamatis.

'It's a wonderful custom. People decorate their boats with garlands and fairy lights, and parade before the spectators on the shore. Locals dressed in traditional Corfiot costumes sing serenades from inside the boats. There are fireworks too. You'll love it!'

Lizzie gave a gasp or two while he talked, then mirrored his bright expression. Finally, she turned to Tom to the sound of everyone's cheers. 'Oh, thank you, Tom, for this wonderful suggestion! You're a treasure!'

Beside her, Aliki looked just as ecstatic and squeezed Tom's shoulder with feeling. While Stamatis and Babis talked to each other, she bent over Tom to whisper, 'You, little devil, you're my new best friend. From now on, ice cream is on me every day!'

Plumage glistening like tar

When the girls and Tom said goodbye to the men and left the store, Stamatis glided behind them a few moments later.

He went up to Lizzie just as she neared his motorcycle and handed her a scrap of paper.

'It's my mobile number. I thought...' He shrugged, then added, 'Next time you visit me, you could ring me and I could pick you up on my motorcycle so you don't have to walk.'

His goofy smile spoke volumes about his embarrassment. *Fancy that...* Lizzie looked at the hastily written number on the paper for a few moments, then back at him. 'Thank you. That's very thoughtful...'

They gazed into each other's faces for a while, without speaking, then Aliki and Tom, who'd just got Charlie, passed them by. Without stopping, they began to saunter towards home.

As soon as they disappeared around the corner, Stamatis turned to Lizzie. 'Tom is such a good boy! It's odd, you know... you take such good care of him... you two look like family. As strange as that sounds...'

'Well...' She twisted her lips and glanced at the supermarket entrance behind him, 'I guess we are, in a way. What with his mother being a distant cousin and all...'

'Oh yes. Right. Stupid me.'

Without thinking, she reached out to put a hand on his forearm. But, instead of touching him, her fingertips rather hovered over his skin, brushing over the tiny hairs there. They felt like silk, the effect bringing a shiver down her spine. She looked up and was immediately captured in his deep gaze. She felt trapped, but deliciously cosy at the same time. He'd just taken her to a place where she'd be happy to stay for an eternity.

'Lizzie, I...' he whispered breaking the spell.

She turned away from him a little and tucked a long strand behind her ear. 'Yes?' She ventured a glance his way again.

'I had a great time this afternoon, Lizzie. We should do this again.'

'Yes. Definitely. And I'm looking forward to the boat ride. I've never been to Petriti.'

'Oh, yes. This should be fun…' He leaned a little closer, his voice lower and deeper. 'I'm looking forward to it too.'

She pretended she hadn't seen it, the desire in his eyes. It was so evident it had cut across her knees, causing them to buckle. With him standing so close, the heady, sensual aroma of his fragrance was causing her to hyperventilate. She brushed her hair back from her forehead and said, 'Well, I'd better go… Oh!' She froze and dropped her gaze to her hands. 'The milk! I don't have it! Did I forget it in the store?'

Stamatis chuckled, then pointed down the road. 'Aliki took it with her shopping, didn't you notice?'

She facepalmed herself. 'Oh yes. Duh. Stupid me.'

'Hey! I just said that about *me*!' He pointed to himself with his thumb and broke out laughing.

She joined him for a while, and it felt good. Their laughter helped to disperse that steam of attraction that seemed to emanate from her, from him, that irresistible desire both of them projected but neither of them dared express first. *This is ridiculous! What am I, five?*

Lizzie took a deep breath, then stood on her toes and put her arms around him.

He froze, she felt it; it was so palpable. For an insane moment, she wondered if he was repulsed by her. But that was an absurd notion. *We are friends, aren't we? I'm only trying to kiss his cheeks… Not exposing myself, am I?*

She kissed his cheeks—both of them, the Greek way—and by the time she'd moved back again she felt him relax. His eyes were laughing now, a sweet smile on his face that was so gorgeous it made her wonder if she dared kiss him again, this time the way she really wanted to.

'Thanks for visiting me, Lizzie,' he said, and she knew the moment was over. 'Well, goodbye then…'

'Goodbye, Stamatis. See you around soon!'

Reluctantly, she crossed the road and turned around to find him still standing by his motorcycle, looking at her.

He gave a little wave, and she waved back. Then, she made about face and began to walk, or rather glide, all the way home.

✳✳✳✳

Lizzie found Aliki and Tom sitting on the bottom step at the courtyard, Tom holding Charlie's leash, the dog curled up on the concrete by his feet.

As soon as they saw her, Aliki and Tom stood upright. 'Well? How did it go? Did you guys kiss?' asked Aliki, eliciting more smooching noises from Tom.

'Oh, it went swimmingly, thank you!' she said to Aliki, a dreamy smile on her face, then turning to Tom, 'Tom, you're allowed to do that, but only today. Just for that great festival suggestion you made!' She beamed at him, then shook a playful finger before his face. 'But no more smooching noises as of tomorrow. You've been warned!'

She turned to Aliki again to the sound of Tom's laughter. 'You and Babis, huh? What a breakthrough!'

'I know, right? Miracles do happen!' Aliki put her arms around their shoulders and squeezed them against her. 'You guys! I love you! You're my lucky charms! We're off to Petriti! Roll on Saturday, yeah!'

They all cheered, then looked up in perfect sync to check the second floor of Aliki's building. They hoped they hadn't been too loud, loud enough for the landlady to hear. To their dismay, they found her standing at the railing of her balcony, peering down at them over her thick prescription glasses.

Aliki raised a numb hand to her first, and the other two followed, their smiles frozen. 'Sorry, Mrs Vlachos. It's only us. *Yassas.*'

The elderly woman muttered a greeting back, then disappeared from view.

'Blimey! That woman can hear a pin drop in Paleokastritsa!' whispered Tom.

Aliki gave a long sigh. 'We got off easily this time, guys... Boy, she's such a pain.'

'Well, it's her house... her rules, I guess,' commented Lizzie.

Aliki shook her head. 'Yes. But her rules aren't always sane... When she came to collect the rent last week she gave me a ten-minute lecture on the importance of turning my light switches on with the tiniest possible pressure. Said if they make a clicking sound when you touch them, it means you're pressing your finger on them too much. Would you believe?'

Lizzie and Tom sniggered, then all three of them began to laugh as quietly as possible.

The two siblings said goodbye to Aliki and went up the steps. The sun had set and the courtesy light halfway up the steps went on as they passed it.

A chilly breeze was blowing from the mountains and, by the time they'd reached the first floor, Lizzie was rubbing her arms to warm up, one at a time, eager to get in the house a moment sooner.

Yet, when she reached her front door she saw something that chilled her blood even further. She saw it first, and froze, and only then did Tom notice it too. On the ledge, across from their front door, a raven stood, its pitch black plumage glistening like tar, one beady eye fixed upon them both.

Tom approached it, much to Lizzie's anguish, but she was too shocked, too paralyzed, to ask him to stop. Tom stood before the bird, then turned to Lizzie and pointed at it.

Strangely, he had a huge grin on his face. 'Look! Lizzie! It has a pebble in its mouth!'

Somehow, his voice jerked her into motion, and she took a single stride forward, grabbing his hand to tear him away from the raven. 'Tom… keep away from that thing!'

Tom was chuckling, though. She didn't understand why. Again, he pointed to the bird. 'It's okay, silly. It's a message from Phoni.'

As soon as he said these words, the bird, that had remained immobile all this time, suddenly let the pebble drop to the tiled floor.

In the eerie semi-darkness, the rattling sound made Lizzie's shoulders jump. Shocked, she watched as Tom bent over and picked it up. Again, she wanted to warn him, to ask him to throw it away. What if it was some kind of spell? But she was glued to her spot, rendered speechless.

Approaching her, Tom showed her the pebble in his open palm. It was perfectly smooth, and all black in colour. 'It's ours. Our trophy! It signifies we got one healing under our belt. For Charlie.'

'Really?' Lizzie heard the sound come out, but it had echoed like someone else's voice, like she wasn't in her body any more but floating into space somewhere, as far from Phoni as possible.

Somehow, Tom's laughing eyes brought her back to the here and now. Where she should be. For him. And she had to be strong. To *stay* strong. And right now, he was being stronger and more level-headed than her. The thought made her bow her head in shame.

'What is it, Lizzie? Aren't you happy? It means what we did has worked!'

She looked up again. 'Yes, yes, of course! But how do you know the pebble means this?'

'With every day that passes, Lizzie, I recall more and more fragments of memories from my life in the mountain, as you know... and I can tell you this: Phoni used the ravens to supervise me and all the other children that were there. The ravens watched us work and used pebbles to keep score so they could report to her on our successes each day.'

Lizzie gave a deep frown. 'I don't understand. What did it matter in a desolate place like that to keep score on your progress? You were all her prisoners, away from home, from your loved ones...'

'That may be so, but trust me, prison is better when you have better clothes and more food to eat. Only the ones who excelled had those. We constantly struggled, therefore, to do well, to please her...'

Lizzie felt her heart constrict, then twinge with upset. 'Those poor children... wonder what kind of hardship they're enduring right now...'

'I know, Lizzie... I think about them all the time. But, we can't help them, no one can. My heart is breaking for them, but that's the way it is... I was lucky Phoni allowed me to return to you, even after twenty years. I can't understand why she made that exception for me, but I'm surely glad she did...'

In lieu of an answer, Lizzie pressed her lips together, then turned her gaze to the raven. It remained on the ledge, watching them intently. The laser-focus of its glassy eyes, as it turned its head this way and that, felt like a burn on her skin.

When it got too much to bear, Lizzie leapt forward to push the bird off the ledge, her palm coming into contact with velvet-soft feathers for an instant before it flapped its wings and flew away into the dark sky.

She turned to Tom, only to register a look of sheer disbelief in his eyes. She tilted her head. 'What is it?'

'Why did you push the raven, Lizzie?'

'Why did I push Phoni's minion, you mean?' She raised a single brow. 'Need you ask?'

He chuckled. 'A fair point.'

'Come!' she said as she rummaged in her shoulder bag to find the keys. 'It's chilly out here. Plus, you and I have plans to make. We need to get two more pebbles before our time is up! That's only three days from now.'

'Yes. Let's start with Mandy tomorrow! I conjured up a little plan in my head this afternoon and I'm dying to tell you. I'm sure that you and I can perfect it together... Mandy may fear the sea now, but wait till we work our mermaid magic on her!'

'Mermaid magic?' Lizzie's eyes lit up. 'I'm intrigued! Does it involve the infamous mermaid gold, by any chance?' Lizzie opened the door wide.

'Of course, it does,' said Tom with a mischievous smile. 'After you, *kontessa*!' He winked, and beckoned her in with a theatrical flourish, causing her to chortle.

A gift from the mermaids

Lizzie and Tom set out for the beach earlier than normal the next morning. They were both eager to put their fully formed plan into action so Mandy could overcome her fear of water.

They made a stop at Babis's supermarket on the way but didn't find what they were after. They tried a couple of souvenir shops that sold beach stuff and finally acquired the perfect thing: a plastic ball that depicted cartoon mermaids on it.

Tom held it in his hands like a trophy as they ambled along the boarded walkway, the zipped up pocket of his swim shorts jingling with spare change.

They greeted Mr Petros when they passed by Gorgona, then lay their mats at the usual spot. Brenda and Mandy hadn't arrived yet. Anticipation pulsed through them like a living thing, and they went in the water to enjoy a cooling dip while they waited.

A few minutes later, they were floating about in the sparkling water like two blissful sea otters when they spotted Brenda and Mandy arrive.

Unable to contain their excitement any longer, they got out at once to join them. Brenda greeted them in her usual breezy manner and placed her and Mandy's things by their towels.

Tom then showed the ball to Mandy and suggested they play with it. Much to his delight, she accepted saying she loved mermaids. As she took the ball in her hands, Lizzie exchanged a glance with Tom that was full of hope.

The two women sat together on the towels and Lizzie began to relay her plan to Brenda while they both kept their eyes on the kids, but only surreptitiously.

In the meantime, Tom beckoned Mandy to follow him to the pool. It stood in the same spot as the previous day, half-full. As soon as they got to it, he turned to her, a glint in his eye. 'Mandy, I have a big secret to tell you. But you must promise not to tell anyone.'

The girl's eyes widened. 'Of course!'

'Cross your heart and hope to die?'

Mandy nodded frantically and crossed herself to swear.

Tom leaned in closer, pointing at the ball she held in her hands. 'This ball is very special. There's no other in the whole world like it.' He brought his voice down to a whisper to add, 'Shhh… don't tell. It has magic in it.'

As he straightened again, Mandy's eyes narrowed into slits. 'I don't believe you. It's just a ball.'

'No, it's not! I'm telling you… it's got magic and it's very powerful.'

'Liar liar, pants on fire!'

Tom turned away to stifle a snigger, then looked at her again, crossing his arms over his chest. 'Huh! If that's the case, then I won't tell you. And you'll never know.'

'Know, what?'

'What the ball does, silly.'

She leaned closer. 'Okay. So what does it do?'

Tom raised his chin and looked away. 'Sorry. Too late. You had your chance and you blew it.'

Just as he'd expected, now Mandy was dying to know all about the 'magic' ball and was begging him to tell her.

'Please!' she shrieked, eyes pleading.

'Oh, all right!' he pretended to relent, then put up a rigid finger. 'But no more calling me a liar, or I won't tell you all about it!'

In the distance, Brenda was growing excited as she watched with Lizzie, and the latter worried that the little girl was going to realize this was all pretend if she caught her mother watching and grinning like that. Beckoning frantically, she stood and urged Brenda to follow her into the water for a swim. They could watch the children from afar.

By the time they'd left, Tom and Mandy were sitting in the pool. Now, Tom was holding the ball, and Mandy was looking at him intently, waiting to hear more. She hadn't even brought her dolls into the pool with her, like she'd done the previous day. All she seemed to care about was the ball, her eyes fixated on it.

When Tom began to speak, she seemed to hang from his lips for a few moments, then asked, 'What do you mean it makes you brave? How does it do it? Please tell me, Tom! I want to know!'

'Okay. But you can't tell anyone. You must promise me that. The magic of this ball is too strong for the whole world to know.'

'Yes! I promise!' she said, eyes bright, arms flailing about.

Satisfied that he'd worked up her excitement to a frenzy, Tom leaned closer as he sat up in the pool, and she did too, until their foreheads were almost touching. Finally, he began to speak in a little more than a whisper. 'This ball is a gift from the mermaids...'

'The mermaids? Really?'

'Yes. They gave this ball to a friend of mine a long time ago. Back then, she was a very scared little girl. She was afraid to swim, you see.'

'Afraid to swim?'

'Yes. And all her friends teased her. So it made her very unhappy. But no matter what she tried she just couldn't float. One day, she was sitting on this beach, right there...' He pointed to the edge of the shore, '...and a mermaid came out to talk to her!'

'What?' shrieked Mandy as she gawped at the shallow water.

'Quiet! What did I say?' Tom looked around him, in a mock-conspiratorial fashion, and Mandy eyed him sheepishly, a hand over her mouth. She looked like she'd just been caught with her finger in the marmalade jar. Tom found it hard to keep himself from laughing.

Finally, she piped up, 'Sorry... So, what happened then? What did the mermaid say?'

'Well, she listened to the girl's troubles, and gave her this ball, telling her it had the power to make her brave, brave enough to do anything she wanted, including to learn how to swim.'

'And did she? Did the little girl learn how to swim?'

'Yes. The ball helped her in no time.'

'But how?'

'Well... the ball helps you float.'

'It does?'

'Yes. But that's not all; every time you float with it, the mermaids send a little mermaid gold out of the ball and into the water.'

'What? Mermaid gold? What's that?'

'Don't you know? Mermaid gold is the most precious gold in the whole wide world. It's the kind of gold pirates loved to steal the most in the old days.'

'Pirates? Really? I didn't know that.'

'Well, yes,' he said matter-of-factly.

'But... how does the gold come out of the ball?' Mandy put out her hands, and he allowed her to take the ball so she could inspect it. She turned it this way and that, then looked up, twisting her lips. 'I can't see a hole. How can the gold come out if the ball doesn't have a hole in it?'

'Magic balls don't need to have a hole, silly. The mermaids make it happen.'

Mandy gazed at it for a few moments, then looked up, her expression pleading. 'Please? Can you show me?'

'Oh, all right then. Do you know how to swim?'

She squirmed. 'No... I don't.'

'Oh, I see. So that's why you want to know so badly... Tell me, do your friends tease you about it?'

She lowered her eyes. 'No, they don't. But, sometimes, when they say they've been to the pool or to the sea, I feel jealous... that they can play in the water... and swim.'

'Why? What's stopping you from swimming too?' He raised a shoulder, then pointed to the shore. 'It's only there... Just get in. Do you want me to go in with you and help you learn?'

Mandy's eyes lit up with horror. 'No! I don't!' She tilted her head, her expression softening. 'But maybe you can show me in the pool... With the ball?'

'I see...' He cocked his eye at her. 'So you want me to help you? Are you sure?'

'Yes, please. You said the ball can make me brave... brave enough to swim. That's what I want.'

'Sure, Mandy. I'll help you.'

Mandy erupted in cheers, clapping her hands together. 'Thank you, Tom! Oh, thank you!'

'Okay. Now, let me show you how it's done...' He got out of the pool to kneel on the sand. 'Now sit in the middle of the pool... right here... that's it...'

✳✳✳✳

As she listened to Tom's directions, Mandy grew so thrilled she was reduced to silence. When she sat up in the centre of the pool like he asked, he handed her the ball telling her to hold it with both hands, then planted a firm hand on her back.

'Now, you're holding the ball which means nothing bad can happen to you. But I'm holding your back at the same time, which makes you even safer. Okay, Mandy?'

'Okay, Tom.'

He tilted his head. 'Do you trust me, Mandy?'

'Yes, Tom. Please show me the mermaid gold...'

'Yes, yes I will, but first—'

Mandy scrunched up her face. 'What now?'

'Before we start, I must choose a mermaid name for you. I can't call you Mandy while we do this. The mermaids are listening as we speak. You need a proper mermaid name, otherwise they may not give you their gold.'

'A name? What name?'

Tom placed a finger on his chin, then his eyes went alight for an instant. 'Aha! I got it. Your Christian name is Mandalena, isn't it?'

'Yes.'

'I know for a fact that that's a proper mermaid name. I read it in a book once. So I'll call you Mandalena from now on, if you'll agree.'

'Yes, yes, of course.'

'Well, okay then, Mandalena, let's start. But please understand. Your new name has a lot of power too. It'll all add up to help you learn to swim, as you asked. The magic mermaid ball will make it all happen.'

She gave a deep frown. 'Tom, can I see the gold now?'

'Okay, okay, sorry. Here we go. Start leaning back till you float on your back, okay? As I said, I'm holding your back and you're holding the ball so you're perfectly safe. Got it?'

'Yes. Yes... Tell me when the gold comes out, I want to see it, Tom!' Slowly, Mandy raised one foot from the bottom of the pool and began to float higher. At the same time, she leaned back slowly, more and more, as Tom praised and urged her.

Surprise ignited in Mandy's eyes as her hands continued to hold the ball and she realized, now that neither of her feet were touching the bottom, that the ball was indeed very special. With her confidence heightened, she leaned back fully until her body was perfectly straightened out on the surface.

'Relax now... *Bravo, Mandalena*... Breathe slowly...' soothed Tom, still holding her back firmly. 'As soon as I let go of my hand from your back, you will be on your own, floating with the ball. Just you and the ball. And when that happens, Mandalena, the mermaids will send you their gold right away. Are you ready for that?'

'Yes. Do it now, Tom. Take your hand away... I want to see the gold!' whispered Mandy, her eyes closed to protect them from the strong sun.

The pool was slightly shorter in length than she was and her bare feet were resting on the plastic edge of the pool. She felt the plastic, heated from the strong sunlight, burn the underside of her toes, but she was so excited she hardly registered the uncomfortable feeling.

And, just like that, Tom removed his hand. Mandalena heard a jingle, and it sounded like music from the heavens. She heard it for only an instant, her body tensing, but she didn't take her hands from the ball. It was still doing its magic to keep her afloat.

Then, she heard Tom speak. 'Look, Mandalena! There's the gold! The ball worked like I said!'

She jerked forward to a sitting position, letting go of the ball, while frantically looking around her in the pool. A handful of coins were scattered by her side. She picked them up, one by one, and studied them closely, then turned to Tom, her brow creased. 'What's this? Where's the gold?'

'This is it, Mandalena!'

'What do you mean?' She screwed up her face with disdain. 'That's not gold. These are euros. I am not stupid.'

'Mandalena, you're wrong. It *is* mermaid gold. You just can't see it. The mermaids make it look like euros.'

'But why? Why would they do that?'

'So you can use it to buy things, silly!'

'Whaaaat?' She grimaced, and looked at the coins in her open palm for a few moments, frozen in place like a statue.

Tom scratched his head and laughed. 'From the looks, you got enough there to buy an ice cream. I say that's a good gift from the mermaids for one day. If you ask me, they must have been pretty impressed by you. They don't normally give more than two coins at a time, three tops.'

'Really?' A wicked smile crept up Mandy's lips. Next, she jumped out of the pool and ran to her mother, who had come out of the water with Lizzie in the meantime.

✳✳✳✳

Both Lizzie and Brenda had been watching all this time from the water, the latter keeping her fingers crossed so tight they'd begun to hurt. They'd come out immediately once they'd witnessed Mandy float on her back. Brenda was in tears but wiped them away quickly, settling on the towels with Lizzie and chortling as they watched Mandy pick up the coins from the pool.

'Look what I found in the pool, Mummy!' said Mandy when she arrived to sit by her mother. 'Can I buy an ice cream with it on our way home, please? And can you call me Mandalena from now on? I think I like it better!'

For the remainder of their stay on the beach that morning, Mandy kept getting into the pool to float on her back, intrigued to know all the ball's secrets. Then, she'd go back to her mother to show her even more coins, then back again.

In the end, when Tom realized he was running out of change, he told her that was enough for one day and she, eager to do as he asked, accepted it without protest.

Finally, Brenda stood to pick up their things so they could go, and Tom took Mandy aside to tell her she'd done surprisingly well for a first day, causing her to beam. Then, he promised to bring the ball back the next day and the next one after that, until the ball had done its magic to the full to make her brave. Then, and only then, he promised, he would also give it to her to keep forever.

As they watched mother and daughter go, Lizzie and Tom sat on their towels and wished that the two days they had left would be more than enough.

Too late to take the words back

On their way home, Lizzie and Tom passed by Gorgona without stopping seeing that Mr Petros wasn't in sight to say hello to. Walking past it, much to Lizzie's dismay, they found Nia sitting outside Pitsilos Apartments.

Nia seemed idle, just watching the world go by, and noticed them immediately, her features pinching when she spotted Lizzie. She jerked upright from her chair and moved, seemingly with a single stride, to the edge of the porch, by the walkway. 'Hi! Great to see you,' she said breezily, but the intense look in her eyes said otherwise.

'Hi, Nia,' said Lizzie, feeling herself tighten to the core. *Why is she looking at me like that?* Beside her, she could feel Tom tensing. He hadn't greeted Nia, nor had she seemed to notice him.

Nia leaned against the railing at the entrance and squinted her eyes. 'Did you have a nice swim?' She offered a toothy grin, but there was no warmth in it. Her eyes darted from Lizzie to Tom for just a moment, then back to Lizzie.

'Yes, it was lovely, thank you. How are you?' said Lizzie, even though she wasn't at all interested to know. She forced a thin smile.

Nia straightened with a pout, then asked, 'Have you seen Stamatis around?'

'No, sorry.'

The hard quality in her eyes deepened. 'I see... And do you know where he is?'

Lizzie exchanged a curious glance with Tom, before replying, 'Well, his boat is moored at the pier, as you can see, so he's not out fishing today. That's all I know. Why do you ask?'

'He's late. He's never late.'

'Oh, for work, you mean? Maybe something held him back. Another customer, I'm guessing...'

Nia huffed, her eyes narrowing into slits. 'You are... guessing? You mean you don't know?'

Lizzie scrunched up her face. 'Yes, of course I'm only guessing. How would I know for sure where he is and what he's doing, Nia?'

She gave a fake smile that made Lizzie nauseous. 'Oh... You seem to know a lot about Stamatis lately.'

Lizzie put her hands on her hips and huffed. 'What?'

Nia looked away and twirled one of her locks between two urgent fingers for a few moments, then turned to Lizzie with an icy gaze. 'You know.... I thought I'd ask you because you and Stamatis seem to be stuck together lately, like two little stickers.'

Lizzie knitted her brows. 'Stickers? What do you mean by that?'

Nia chortled. 'Oh, nothing! It's just a Greek saying...'

'Yes, but what does it mean? I demand to know. To be frank, I don't like your tone of voice at all...'

Lizzie felt her ire bubble inside her as she waited for an answer. Her eyes burned with intensity as if they were shooting thunderbolts at Nia. Lizzie balled her hands into fists by her sides. *Go on! Answer me! What's your problem, you mad cow?*

Nia's face contorted with malice, her voice loud when she finally erupted, 'I see what you're doing, Lizzie!' Her expression was sour, face ablaze with scorn, a finger pointing sharply at Lizzie as she added, 'You! English girls! Coming here, stealing our men! It's not right. Why are you lingering here anyway? I checked on my booking register! It's been a fortnight since you came here! Why don't you leave? Why don't you go back home and leave us alone?'

'What? Excuse me?'

Tom pulled Lizzie by the arm. 'Come on, Lizzie. Let's go home. I'm starving!' he lied, clearly to get her to move away from that toxic woman.

But Lizzie wasn't going to back down. She opened her mouth, about to give Nia a good piece of her mind, but she beat her to it.

'*Skase esi ore*! You shut up!' shouted Nia, crouching over Tom, a furious hand raised over him, causing Lizzie to step aside and shield Tom with her body. 'What the hell are you doing?' she screamed, pushing Nia away.

Nia's face turned scarlet red, or maybe it was the strong sunshine that made the effect so amplified. Beads of sweat began to trickle down her forehead, and she put up both hands, backing away into the porch. 'No! You horrible English woman! I will not sink down to your level, I won't!'

'Horrible? You, of all people, are calling *me* a horrible woman? That's rich!'

'You shut up! Shut up and listen! You cannot just come here and take our men from us Greek women!'

'And by "men", I suppose you mean Stamatis?'

'Don't you pretend you don't know what I'm talking about! I know you've been riding with him on his motorcycle. And yesterday evening you were standing outside Babis's supermarket chatting in the street together like two little lovebirds!'

Lizzie put her hands on her waist. 'Oh yeah? And what if we were? What's it to you?'

'Stamatis is my friend. I have known him forever and a day. You can't just barge into his life like that, then go back to England. He's a widower. I don't want him getting hurt.'

'And by that, you mean, you want him for yourself. But I'm in the way...'

Nia sneered, a glint in her eyes. 'You're a clever one, aren't you?' Then, glowering, she added, 'You stay away from him! You hear?'

'Or what? What will you do, Nia?' She pointed at the apartments building with a deriding smile. 'Are you going to break up some more doors and windows in there so you can get him to come over here even more frequently? Just how pathetic can you be?'

Nia's jaw dropped, eyes widening. '*What* did you say?'

'You heard!' Lizzie had blurted out the retort without thinking. Now, her heart was sinking. She'd just exposed Aliki, who'd told her this in confidence. Shame began to mushroom inside her, and so did the dread that came with it. *Too late to take the words back.*

'Aliki! I should have known! You two have teamed up against me! She's telling you lies, you hear? Stamatis and I go way back. You don't understand. And if you had any decency you would leave Stamatis to me.'

'No, Nia. I won't...' said Lizzie tiredly with a small wave of her hand. 'Deal with it. As far as I'm concerned, Stamatis is fair game. I owe nothing to you. And he's free to choose as he pleases. Got it?'

Before Nia could utter a word, Lizzie grabbed Tom's hand and marched down the walkway, the seconds feeling like hours until they reached the corner to leave the beach behind. All the while,

Lizzie could almost feel Nia's malicious stare burn her retreating back.

❋❋❋❋

When Lizzie and Tom arrived at their garden gate, she reached out to open it, beckoning him silently to go through first. Her anger from the episode with Nia had subsided somewhat, but the sting of guilt still pricked her insides. She had to confess to Aliki what she'd done. Deep in thought, she moved towards the steps, her head hung low when Aliki's voice rang in her ears cheerful and urgent. 'Hey, guys! Come on over!'

Lizzie turned to find Aliki standing on her doorstep with a young woman she didn't recognize.

Tom had already walked up to them so she followed suit, trying to keep her disquiet aside for now.

Aliki's face was bright. 'Hi guys! Meet Popi. Popi, these are my friends that I was talking to you about. Lizzie and Tom.'

Popi offered her hand to them both, and quick pleasantries followed in Popi's limited English. Aliki then explained that Popi lived nearby. She'd been amazed by Charlie's swift recovery. His coat looked fantastic. She wanted to know more about the ointment they'd used on him.

Then Aliki said, 'Look, guys. Popi needs some help too...' She put a hand on the woman's arm and turned her slowly around, lifting the back of her t-shirt to reveal a plethora of angry spots on her skin.

Aliki went on, 'She got them after a camping holiday she had last week. They won't go away. They're all over her back as you can see, and a few more on other parts of her torso. But mostly on her back.' She turned to Lizzie and asked, 'So, can you help? Is there some kind of ointment you could give her?'

Lizzie and Tom examined the girl's back some more, then she exchanged a few glances with her brother. From his bright expression and firm nods, she realized he could help the young woman. But, of course, they had to maintain the pretence that she, rather than Tom, was the one who had the knowledge to do it.

'Yes, yes, we... I can help.'

Popi spun around and clapped her hands. 'Thank you! Me, very happy,' she said in pidgin English.

'I can make the cream today...' said Lizzie.

'I'm sure you will have it ready by this afternoon if you don't go to bed for a siesta,' said Tom with a wink.

'Yes, yes, I'm sure I can do that.'

'Super. I can get it, then bring it to you, Popi,' replied Aliki.

Over the moon, Popi said goodbye and walked away. As soon as she was out of earshot, Aliki's eyes brightened and she turned to Lizzie, her hand clutching her friend's arm with feeling. 'Oh! Babis and I chatted a lot in his store today! He's like a different person! What do you think happened?'

'I don't know... maybe he and Stamatis talked? Or because he's enthused that you'll be going out to the festival together? But who cares? I'm so happy for you!'

'Oh yes, the festival! I'm so excited!' Aliki's eyes twinkled as she gesticulated wildly. Lizzie knew it wasn't the right time to tell her what had just happened with Nia.

She put an arm around Tom's shoulders and raised a hand to say goodbye. Aliki said she'd visit in the late afternoon to pick up the cream for Popi. Lizzie smiled thinly at that. She would get her chance to confess her guilty secret then.

She wasn't looking forward to doing it, but it had to be done. If Aliki was a true friend, and she had a feeling that she was, she would forgive her for her indiscretion, and help her keep Nia at bay too.

That girl was unhinged. And she had no dignity either. A most dangerous adversary. To think she had fooled her into thinking she was a nice girl when she'd first met her... *It goes to show you never really know someone at first glance. Takes years to really know anybody. And even then, people can always surprise you. The Greeks have a great saying for that... "A man's soul is an abyss"...*

Lizzie thought about her own secret then... Knowing about Phoni when no one else did and keeping this dark secret from all those she knew. With her own point taken, she began to go up the stairs with Tom, her mind churning with a torrent of thoughts, her love for Stamatis and Tom, Tom and Stamatis, the unmoving axis in the middle.

This day is getting worse and worse

Lizzie headed for the kitchen to prepare a quick pasta meal as soon as they got home. The sauce entailed just four ingredients: courgettes, cheese, olive oil, and garlic.

While Lizzie got things ready to cook, Tom opened a large plastic box on the counter to inspect its contents – his inventory of dried herbs that he'd collected from the mountain. Moments after he'd opened the box, he gave a shrill cry.

Lizzie nearly dropped the olive oil bottle that she held. Her hand froze mid-air over the frying pan.

'What is it, Tom?' she asked breathlessly.

'I'm missing an herb to make Popi's cream! I must have used it all for Charlie's ointment... I need to get some more.'

'Is it the same cream you need to make?'

'No... her ailment needs a different concoction.' The dried herbs inside the box were neatly put away. It took him another quick scan to make sure and add, 'I have all the other ingredients I need. It's only that one I'm missing.' He turned to Lizzie, his chin hardening. 'There's nothing for it. I'll just have to go now and get some. This can't wait.'

'You're going to the mountain? Now?' Lizzie's eyes darted to the wall clock. *This day is getting worse and worse by the minute!* She shook her head, then turned to him, her voice frail. 'It's too hot now to get there, Tom...'

Smiling, he waved away her words. 'No. Not going to the mountain, silly. It's a very common herb I'm after. I've seen plenty of it around the fields here and on the river bank. I'll be back in a jiffy. By the time you get the meal on the plates, I'll be here with bells on.'

'You're going on your own?' She whirled around, following him with her eyes as he strode to the front door and took the keys from the lock. Just seeing him by the open door, about to go without her, caused her stomach to churn.

Across the distance, he tilted his head, eyes full of tenderness. 'You have to let me go out into the world on my own sometime, Lizzie...' He gave an encouraging smile. 'It's safe here anyway. What could possibly happen to me?'

Lizzie nodded, a smile creeping up on her lips. 'You're right. I'm sorry... But be back soon!'

'Sure!' he said brightly and closed the door behind him.

❋❋❋❋

True to his word, he returned just ten minutes later, with time to spare till the food was on the table.

After lunch, Lizzie did the dishes while Tom washed the herb cuttings and patted them dry with a towel. Then, with Lizzie's assistance, he began to prepare the ointment.

While they milled about in the kitchen, they discussed their progress with Mandy. The plan was going well. The little girl had hung from Tom's lips and believed every word he'd said. Tom was hopeful that the next day he might be able to impress her enough to lure her into the sea proper.

Lizzie, on the other hand, doubted that would happen so soon. But they still had a second day till the time was up. If all went well, and Popi's skin problem disappeared too, then they'd be laughing in two days from now, their three required healings done.

Tom was standing at the counter now, mixing herbs in a bowl with shea butter, beeswax and a couple of other ingredients while Lizzie watched, amazed by his skills. He seemed so proficient and confident... Once again, she swelled with pride and love for him.

And then, it dawned on her that Stamatis had grown to be just as important to her. This felt like a betrayal to Tom at first, but she still knew... Soon, no matter what happened with Stamatis, she'd have to go back to England with Tom. Even if it meant breaking her own heart and Stamatis's too. Because Tom had to return to his country and get reunited with his long-lost family. The whole family... which included her too. It couldn't be any other way.

❋❋❋❋

The doorbell rang just after six p.m. Tom was lounging on the sofa watching an old Greek movie. As Lizzie rushed to answer the door, Tom giggled at something the protagonist had said.

Aliki appeared at the door bright and breezy. 'Hello!'

Lizzie greeted her back, albeit numbly, and beckoned her in. Tom raised a hand from the sofa, then returned his attention to the movie.

'I'm here to pick up the cream for Popi, if it's ready.'

'Yes, I've got it right here.' Lizzie's lower lip twitched as she pointed to the kitchen and beckoned her to follow. 'Aliki, I need to talk to you about something...'

Aliki moved closer, a shadow crossing her face. 'What is it, darling? You look upset.'

Lizzie realized she hadn't smiled at her just then, preoccupied as she'd been all day about having to tell her what had happened with Nia. She felt terrible about the way she'd exposed her friend. Never before had she done anything of the sort. She managed a feeble smile, only for Aliki to frown once again.

'That bad, huh? What is it, sweetie? Stamatis said something to you?' Aliki stopped before the counter with Lizzie and put a gentle hand on her arm.

'No, no... Haven't even seen him today.' Lizzie waved a hand in the air. 'Anyway. Here's the cream...' She picked up from the counter a reused cosmetic cream container. 'Popi will find relief tonight with this. Her spots must be particularly itchy in the evening...'

'Yes, she did say that! How did you know?' said Aliki as she took the cream. She paused for a moment, dropping her gaze to the counter behind Lizzie, then added, 'She keeps applying a panthenol-rich lotion but it doesn't do much, she said...' Her voice trailed off, and that's when Lizzie turned around to see what Aliki was gazing at with obvious intrigue.

Lizzie's blood turned cold. Aliki was peering at Tom's notebook where he recorded the plants he picked, noting dates and places. He'd said it was an old habit since Phoni had had all the children record everything. He'd put in the same book the preparation instructions for both creams he'd made so far; for Charlie first, then for Popi. He'd even added drawings of all the plants he used with their names, both in Greek and Latin. *Oh, God! We forgot to put it away!*

'What is that?' asked Aliki, her eyes wide, when she turned to Lizzie.

'Oh, it's nothing... Just some notes,' she said in a hoarse voice.

'But that's Tom's handwriting, isn't it?' she asked pointing at the open pages. 'I know, because we played word games the other day back home, and I'd recognize that right slant and his elongated l's anywhere... And the drawings... they're exquisite! *He* drew these?' Aliki looked at Lizzie, only to receive a muted gaze, then darted her eyes at the back of Tom's head. He still watched TV, unaware of her mystification.

Once again, she pinned her eyes on Lizzie, her brow furrowed. 'I don't get it.' Her look deepened, a faint smile on her lips. 'Is it Tom that made the cream for Charlie? For Popi too? How come?'

'No, of course not! What a ridiculous notion!'

But there was no fooling Aliki. Everyone had their strengths and one of hers was reading body language. Lizzie had moved away to gaze out of the kitchen window with empty eyes.

Aliki went to Lizzie and put a tender hand on her back. 'Hey...' she whispered.

Lizzie turned around, eyeing her sheepishly.

'Look, Lizzie... It's okay if it's Tom and not you who made the ointments. I won't tell...' She shook her head profusely. 'But why would you lie about it?'

'I... look... yes. It's Tom who made them. I'm sorry, okay?' Lizzie buried her face in her hands. She'd been feeling bad all day about the way she'd exposed Aliki to Nia... But it wasn't just that.

For two weeks now, she'd been doing nothing but bury her feelings and the truth from everybody. She'd been smiling and laughing despite feeling terrified, carrying on with life as normal when all she wanted to do was scream her agony away. She'd been lying to everyone she respected and liked, and it all felt ridiculous all of a sudden... A ridiculous situation in a ridiculous world that might take her brother away from her again in just two days, this time forever. Just the possibility of it caused her knees to buckle.

Lizzie removed her hands from her eyes and turned to Aliki, spent. 'I'm so sorry... I'm a mess right now. You should never have seen me this way. I apologise.'

'It's okay, Lizzie,' soothed her friend. 'We all have bad days. And I'm sorry for all the questions. It's just that...' She stole a glance at Tom who, none the wiser, watched TV still. 'Well, it's amazing that a twelve-year-old boy has this knowledge. Where did he learn?

How can—?' Aliki's face froze mid-sentence, eyes glinting with alarm, her hand covering her mouth.

Her next words were muffled: 'Oops. Forgive me, Lizzie. There I go, stupid me, asking even more questions. Just ignore me. Or maybe tell me another day when you're feeling a little better.' She winked.

Lizzie gazed at her, relieved by her tactfulness, and wondering if she could postpone her confession to her for another day when the world didn't seem to be conspiring against her. She opened her mouth to speak, to tell her she was a great friend, when the impossible happened. A thrashing sound came from the open window, and she turned to find a raven on the sill.

'Aargh!' came her shrill response, but her feet were glued to the ground.

Aliki grabbed a kitchen towel that hung on the wall and, from a distance, began to wave it at the bird. 'Shoo! Shoo!' In response, the bird started to caw at an ear-piercing volume but refused to budge, causing Aliki to get annoyed and shoo it even more loudly.

Lizzie stared, shocked, her senses numb. All she could register was that the damned bird didn't have a pebble in its mouth. *Is it here just to spy on us?*

Tom heard the commotion and rushed to them. 'Lizzie? What's that doing here? Did it bring another pebble?' he said when he approached her, forgetting that Aliki would find that peculiar. It was no surprise that Aliki's brows shot up in response. At least, she'd stopped asking questions.

'No...' Lizzie answered, 'And it won't go away. What does it mean?'

'I don't know... maybe it's just checking on us!'

Aliki watched this exchange in silence, looking stunned. When Lizzie and Tom stopped talking, all three turned to peer at the raven for a few moments, the bird gazing back at them all, its glassy eyes glinting in the strong sunlight with a mesmerizing effect.

After a few moments, the sight grew unbearable for Lizzie and, just as she thought she was about to scream, she grabbed the towel from Aliki's hand. Unlike her, instead of waving the towel to shoo the bird away, she actually hit it with it, albeit gently. 'Go away, you evil creature! Go and never come back!'

As soon as the towel landed on its side, the bird opened its wings and flew away, its shrill cries reverberating against the kitchen walls long after it was gone.

Like steam bursting out from under the lid of a pressure cooker that had been opened carelessly, Lizzie's upset exploded. With a single heart-rending sob, she broke down crying.

'Lizzie... hush... don't cry,' soothed Aliki, her arms around her friend.

'It's okay, Sis...' burst out Tom, without thinking.

Aliki turned to him, then to Lizzie, her mystification palpable.

Alarmed, Tom turned to Lizzie, and she pressed her lips together, shaking her head. Then, she brought her hands to her face, trying to wipe away the hot flood of her tears. 'It's all right, Tom. It's just as well. Come, you two. Let's go sit on the sofa... and I'll answer all your questions, Aliki... Tom and I will. Together. Yes, he is my brother...' said Lizzie, avoiding her friend's eyes. She picked up two napkins from the table to wipe her face, then beckoned them both to the sofa where she sat first.

Reduced to silence, Aliki and Tom followed, sitting on either side of Lizzie and waiting for her to start speaking as she wiped the last tears from her eyes.

❋❋❋❋

Lizzie spoke non-stop, Aliki listening astounded as Tom nodded along. Every now and then, Aliki turned to him, her eyes wide, seeking confirmation in his eyes for all the unbelievable truths that Lizzie lay bare before her.

At the end, Lizzie apologized for lying to her all this time. Aliki understood, even though she had trouble believing what she'd heard. Then, Lizzie relayed what had happened with Nia and offered her apology for that too.

Talking about Nia after the harrowing revelations about Tom and Phoni seemed unimportant and laughable by contrast. As a result, Aliki dismissed the incident saying she didn't mind Lizzie's indiscretion at all.

When the two girlfriends said goodbye a little later at the open door, they shared a warm embrace. Before leaving, Aliki offered to help, in whatever way she could, so Lizzie and her brother would be freed from the clutches of the evil mountain creature if only a day sooner.

Aliki hurried down the steps, the container in her hand, eager to visit Popi to offer relief and, in effect, to help her two precious friends as well. The deadline was in two days and, in her heart, she felt already committed to helping them acquire a second pebble.

Where did you get it? I need to get some

The next morning, the two siblings rose from their beds like coiled springs, their hearts soaring with a renewed sense of optimism. The sun seemed brighter today as it streamed through the kitchen window, the sky a stunning cobalt hue, and the birds sang more sweetly than ever before in the tree branches below.

After breakfast, they grew restless and dawdled in the apartment for as long as they could bear it, then headed for the beach.

Brenda and Mandy weren't there when they arrived, which made sense as it was so early, so they had a swim, then sat on the sand to talk excitedly. They only had this day and the next one left... Who else might need help?

They couldn't think of anyone, even though they mentioned to each other all the people they knew, including the shop owners they greeted around Messonghi. One thing was for sure: whoever it was that needed help next, they had to assist them promptly.

This is why Tom had brought with him a little freezer bag; it contained different creams and lotions that he'd made. It was like a portable first-aid box, so he could treat anyone on the spot who might need assistance.

When Brenda and Mandy finally arrived, Lizzie took Brenda into the water again so they could watch the kids in the pool from a distance. But, there was one problem today. Mandy wasn't happy.

As Lizzie had asked Brenda the previous day, the girl's *nonos* had come out of his house early in the morning to empty the pool, move it a good distance towards the edge of the shore, then fill it halfway again with the garden hose.

Predictably enough, the moment Mandy saw where the pool was placed that day she'd begun to complain, refusing to go anywhere near it until someone moved it further away from the water.

While the two women watched surreptitiously from the sea, Tom, who held the ball, took Mandy by the hand and led her to stand beside the pool, then said, 'I don't understand why you're acting like this! I thought you said you wanted to be brave!'

'Yes, I do… But not if the pool is going to be so near the water,' she said scrunching up her face.

'But, Mandalena, it has to stay here! It was the mermaids who moved it near the water overnight.'

'The mermaids?'

'Yes, of course! Didn't I tell you they're watching? They're helping you along. By going in again today, even though it's near the water, you'll be proving to them you're making progress.' He raised his chin and gave a cute grin. 'And just think of all the mermaid gold you'll be getting today!' He licked his lips. 'Yum! More ice cream for you!'

Despite herself, Mandy gave a beaming smile, then bent her head, twitchy fingers scratching her nose as she mulled it over.

'Hurry and decide, Mandalena. Don't let the mermaids see you hesitate so much.'

Mandy looked up finally, chewing her lips for a moment, then said, 'Do the mermaids only move the pool overnight? Or will they do it again this morning? I don't want them to take it all the way to the water today. I'm not ready yet!' Her voice had turned into a shriek at the last sentence, eyes lighting up with feeling.

Tom patted her shoulder. 'Relax, Mandalena. It won't happen today if you don't want it to. But eventually you will get in the sea, won't you, Mandalena? Because I can tell… You want to find the courage and swim like the mermaids, right?'

'Yes, I do… but maybe next week?'

Tom twisted his lips. 'Didn't I tell you? The mermaids only help little girls who have a lot of courage. They only give three days, no more. So if you don't feel ready to get into the sea today, there's tomorrow too, and that's it. What do you say? Can you do it?'

She cocked her eye at him. 'Will they give me gold every time I float again today?'

'Yes, yes of course! And, when you finally get in the sea tomorrow, they…' He scratched his head. He guessed that Mandy needed a little something extra to entice her. 'Well, if you do it tomorrow, they will give you a special gift too.'

Mandy's eyes sparkled. 'What gift?'

'A… piece of jewellery. Mermaid jewellery.'

'What kind of jewellery?'

'How do I know? But I'm sure it will be very nice.' He smiled, trying to seem as confident as possible while wondering if he could get a little something in one of the souvenir shops that might appeal to a little girl. 'Maybe a necklace... with nice colourful beads?'

She twisted her lips. 'I like bracelets better... I had one that I really liked but I lost it... Oh! I'd love to have a bracelet!'

'Well, if you're a good girl and you do as I tell you, you'll be ready by tomorrow to get in the water. And I'm sure the mermaids will grant you your wish then. Now, are you ready? Let's float!' He handed her the ball, then pointed to the pool with an enthusiastic smile, offering his hand.

Mandy gave her hand to Tom as she held the ball against her chest with the other. Like a princess aided by her prince to enter her horse-drawn carriage, she stepped into the pool with her head held high. At the same time, she threw fleeting glances up and down the beach and towards the water, probably wondering if the mermaids were watching.

Tom knelt down, his spare change jingling in his swimshorts pocket as Mandy sat up in the pool, ready to float again with his assistance.

✳✳✳✳

For the next hour, Mandy kept floating on her back as she held the ball. During her last five attempts, she'd done it without Tom's hand supporting her. It was a huge breakthrough for her that had given her tremendous confidence, adding to her enthusiasm.

Every time she floated, the bottom of the pool filled with scattered change. She shrieked with excitement on every occasion as she scooped up the coins, then ran to her mother to show her.

Both Brenda and Lizzie had long come out of the water. All the while, they'd been sitting on their towels, their eyes pinned on the children.

When Brenda announced it was time to go and began to pick up their things, Mandy took Tom to the side and whispered, 'Tom, tell me something... Where will the pool be tomorrow when we come back here?'

Tom scratched his head. 'From what I know, tomorrow it will be right at the edge of the shore.' He peered at her worried expression for a few moments, then added, 'But you'll be okay with that, won't you, Mandalena? See how far you've come already!' He pointed at the pool and smiled widely.

Mandy pouted for a moment, then asked, 'Do I have to get into the sea to get the bracelet?'

'Of course!'

'Isn't it enough to do it in the pool when it's at the edge of the shore?'

Tom shook his head. 'No way. You cannot cheat with the mermaids. They are too clever. They will tell.'

'Oh, all right... Tomorrow then...' Her voice trailed off.

Detecting her uncertainty, Tom gave a dazzling smile and squeezed her shoulder gently. 'I'm so proud of you, Mandalena! The magic ball has worked wonders on you. It gave you all the confidence you needed. Just think! Tomorrow you'll have both the magic ball and a bracelet! Two mermaid gifts for floating in the sea. Seems such a little thing to do for getting these precious gifts, don't you think?'

'Yes, I think so too! See you tomorrow!' said Mandy and ran to her mother, who was standing a few steps away, waiting, holding her oversized beach bag.

As soon as Mandy came to stand before her, Brenda reached down and caressed her head, her face beaming. 'My princess! What a good girl you are! What a good girl!'

When the two were gone, Tom lay on his towel beside Lizzie, and they sunbathed for a while. Then, Lizzie announced she needed to cool off and went for a quick dip in the shallows.

Left on his own, Tom cast his gaze over Gorgona. It'd been a couple of hours since breakfast and he was getting hungry. Tantalizing aromas of tomato sauce and grilled meat wafted in the sea breeze, torturing him for a while. A little later, Mr Petros came out to stand by a vacant table at the edge of the seating area, a hand on his lower back. He seemed to rub it fiercely, his features pinched with discomfort.

Tom jolted upright, just as Lizzie returned, to tell her that Mr Petros might be needing help. By the time she'd followed his gaze to spot the old man, Tom had already left her side, the freezer bag slung over his shoulder as he strode over to Gorgona.

※※※※

'Hello, Mr Petros! How are you? All okay?' asked Tom in his perfect Greek as soon as he hopped onto the seating area.

'Hello, Tom. Not good, I'm afraid,' he complained, shaking his head and rubbing hard at his lower back with one hand.

'What is it? Are you in pain?'

'It's my sciatica... It hurts from time to time. I picked up some crates around the back earlier. They proved to be too heavy for an old man like me.'

'Come, Mr Petros, sit here for a little while. I have a cream that will help.'

'A cream? On you? How come?'

'Oh... I... My mother has this problem.'

'And you carry it on you?'

'Oh, Mr Petros. You're so full of questions! It's a good cream. The best in the world. You want to put some on your back or not?'

'Yes, yes, thank you... Argh! *Oh, Panagia mou!*' he exclaimed, sitting down in a chair with a wince, and placing the name of the Virgin Mary on his lips, the way all Greeks do in times of need, upset, worry, and any possible kind of discomfort.

Tom took out the right container, opened it and put it on the table. 'Here, Mr Petros. Help yourself. It will really help, I promise!'

Mr Petros did as he was told, applying a small amount of cream on the affected area. Soon, in a little more than a whisper he said, 'Oh, that's so nice... so warm and soothing. Where did you get it? I need to get some.'

'It's not from here... it's... it's from England,' said Tom, but Mr Petros seemed too caught up in his sense of relief as he massaged his back to notice the boy's awkward expression.

'Put some more on, Mr Petros. Rub it in circular movements, that's it...' instructed Tom, and the old man did as he was told. Moments later, he announced, incredulous, that the pain had simply disappeared.

Tom wasn't surprised, though. The precious mountain herbs had done their magic again, numbing the pain. He gave a bright smile. 'Glad I could help you, Mr Petros. Now, please bring me a little coffee cup, and I'll put in it some more cream for you to rub in tonight before you go to bed. Tomorrow, same time, I'll come over so we can do this again. You'll be fine by tomorrow, you'll see!'

When Mr Petros stood, he informed him that he felt as if he'd just risen from bed, all revitalized and rested.

As Tom waited for Mr Petros to return with the coffee cup, he raised a hand and gave a thumbs up to his sister across the distance. She smiled in response, raising her own thumb aloft, her face alight with hope.

Better nip this in the bud

Tom returned to Lizzie holding what looked like kitchen paper in his hand. Mr Petros had placed four *dolmadakia* and four *keftedes* on it, as a snack for Lizzie and Tom, to say thank you for treating him.

They sat on their towels quietly for a while, just munching away. As soon as they finished, they heard Aliki's excited voice. Taken aback, they turned to find her rushing along the shore towards them.

'Hey, guys! Guess what?' she said as soon as she arrived, then sat on her haunches to match their eye level, her eyes sparkling. She was wearing an enormous sunhat and a long summer dress, the crystal beads in her bracelets rattling against each other as she gesticulated.

'What is it?' asked Lizzie, breathless.

'Is this about Popi, by any chance? Please say it is!' said Tom, shaking his fists with impatience.

'Yes, it is!' said Aliki, putting both hands down on the sand to right herself. She was so enthused she nearly fell forward when she replied.

'Is she better?' asked Lizzie.

'Better? Only better? I can't see any spots on her back! They're gone! Like, completely! She's just left my house and she's over the moon about it. Says she owes you both big time!'

The two siblings sprang upright and huddled with Aliki, jumping up and down like partying teenagers, while ignoring the onlookers who gave them funny looks.

They picked up their things and strolled down the beach to return home, and Tom told Aliki all that had happened earlier with Mandy, then Mr Petros. If either of them could be healed just as quickly as Popi and Charlie had been, then by tomorrow they would have all three of the healings they needed to pass the test, if not four.

They were still whooping when they left the beach. Turning into the street where Babis's supermarket was, they saw the man himself outside chatting with none other than Stamatis, who had a lit cigarette in his mouth. Both men stood by Stamatis's motorcycle, their backs turned to the others.

As they approached, Lizzie and Aliki steeled themselves at the sight of the special men in their lives while Tom, predictably, began to make smooching noises to tease them both. The girls sniggered, then delivered playful slaps on Tom's arms in perfect sync.

'Hey!' said Babis, who turned around first to see them, no doubt upon hearing their soft laughter.

The three returned enthused greetings and so did Stamatis. As soon as he saw them, he dropped his cigarette and extinguished it under the sole of his shoe.

'I hope you didn't do that on my account...' said Lizzie when she came to stand before him.

Aliki went straight to Babis, and Tom hovered somewhere between the two couples, pretending to read the announcements of various local festivals that were pinned on the store's entrance.

'It's okay... don't worry about it,' said Stamatis with a killer smile. His eyes were dancing, and he took another step towards her, now too close for comfort.

Oh my... he's gorgeous! Oh, stop it... get a grip, Lizzie. Don't let him see what he's doing to you! Lizzie tossed a long strand behind her shoulder, then gave a confident smile, happy that she could appear cool when, inside her chest, her heart was about to explode. 'That cigarette looked almost intact. You didn't have to do that, Stamatis. I'd have been fine out here.'

'Oh, no... remember what happened at Gorgona that day? We were outside there too, if I recall.' He gave a cute, lopsided grin.

Lizzie cringed and wished he'd stop reminding her of that unfortunate incident, even though she knew he was being light-hearted. But she felt bad about it. She'd been unfair to him, and so upset that first day, her mind full of disturbing memories and trepidation about what was to come.

'I shouldn't have done that, I'm sorry.' She bent her head, pinning her eyes on her sandaled feet for a few moments.

He put two tender hands on her arms, causing her to look up, startled.

'Hey, it's okay...' he said in a whisper, a sweet smile across his face. 'I was joking... What is it, Lizzie? Everything okay? You never had a problem to tell me off before.' He winked. 'Remember when we were kids? You had the best retorts!'

She tried to smile, her mind whirling. He looked so handsome, so irresistible. Right then, it dawned on her that all the hours she'd spent dreaming of him were futile. *What are you doing, you stupid girl? Even if he begs you to have him as your lover, what will you do then? You're not the kind of girl to sleep with a man for a night or two, then leave him. Let alone this one, a widower, a man you've known as a child... If all goes as planned, tomorrow you and Tom will be free of Phoni. Free to board the next flight back home together at last! Where will that leave you with Stamatis? Huh? You'll only hurt him. And yourself. So stay away. For both your sakes...*

'Lizzie? What's wrong?' echoed Stamatis's voice. Gentle still, but a little urgent now.

Lizzie came to from her reverie with a start, but she found herself looking away from Stamatis, her gaze on Tom, who had his back to her and was still facing the festival signs on the wall. He had read them all to her the other day. So what was he doing reading them again?

Then, she realized. Tom was being tactful as usual. It just went to prove he wasn't really twelve years old... He was a thirty-two-year-old trapped in the body of a child. That was her brother. What she had on her hands was a human tragedy. And what was she doing about it? Flirting.... With a man whom she'd have to leave behind soon.

'Lizzie?'

It was Stamatis again. She finally turned to meet his eyes and found them full of mystification.

'Are you okay?' he said softly.

'Sorry, Stamatis...' She brought up a hand and rubbed her temple. 'I... I've had too much sun today, and I'm a little headachy, if you must know.'

'I'm sorry to hear that,' came his reply, his voice even more gentle now. 'Just take a painkiller and have a siesta. That should fix it. Works for me...'

Lizzie imagined he was smiling now, but she didn't know for sure. She had dropped her gaze to her sandals again, this time scuffling the dirt aimlessly, the pretence of a smile on her lips.

All these lies she'd been telling him... so many lies. She couldn't help them, even though she detested them. Really... all she'd been doing was setting them both up for a lot of heartache in the near future. *Best to stay friends...* But even if she made herself the promise to try, she knew it'd take a mountain of self-control to be around him and not feel faint at the sight of his perfect, manly form. And those eyes, those eyes that told her so much...

Lizzie wondered if it'd be best to make an excuse and not go to Petriti at all. *Saturday's only two days away... And Tom is looking forward to it a lot. So is Aliki. How can I back down now?*

'Lizzie?'

She straightened and turned around. It was Aliki calling her this time.

'Babis is going to close shop for an hour and go grab a pizza. I'm going with him. You guys want to come?'

Tom and Stamatis said they'd love to, but Lizzie shook her head. *Better nip this in the bud! Petriti festival and that's it. Nothing else.*

'Sorry, I'm not feeling so good. Maybe some other time. But thanks.'

'Why, Lizzie? What's wrong?' Tom's face was alight with mystification as he began to approach.

'She has a headache, Tom,' replied Stamatis, his voice heavy with regret. He turned to Lizzie and squeezed her arm gently. 'Would you like me to get you anything from the pharmacy, Lizzie?' He pointed down the street.

Lizzie managed a feeble smile. 'No, thank you, Stamatis. I have paracetamol at home...' She turned to her brother, who eyed her curiously. 'Come on, Tom. Let's go...' She beckoned but, strangely, instead of following her, he opened the zipper of his freezer bag and rummaged through it for a few moments. Mystified, the others watched, and more so Lizzie, who wondered why he was looking through his medicine.

Tom took out a small package wrapped in newspaper. He opened it carefully to reveal a few small compact balls made of dried herbs. Lizzie remembered them from when he was making them back home. He'd said they were helpful for many things, a sore throat being one of them. Intrigued, she watched as he picked up one of the herbal balls between two fingers and showed it to Stamatis.

'Speaking of pharmacies,' he said, 'Would you like to try these?'

Stamatis took the herbal ball in his hand and sniffed it. 'You're not trying to sell me dope, are you, Tom?'

Matter-of-factly, Tom responded, 'I would never do that...'

'Relax, Tom. I'm only joking. That smells minty, if anything.'

'Yes, strong mountain mint is one of the ingredients.'

Stamatis rolled the ball carefully between his fingertips and tilted his head. 'What's it for?'

'Oh, it's great for a lot of things... But especially for you, it will be very helpful with your awful smoking habit.'

'What? You mean I should smoke it?'

Tom tittered, then said, 'No, Stamatis. It will help you *overcome* the habit. Just chew these balls, one a day, first thing in the morning, preferably after a cup of green tea or mountain tea, and it will put you off smoking for the whole day.'

Stamatis sniffed the ball again, his eyes a little brighter. 'Really?'

'Yes. If you want to quit smoking, that is.' Tom smirked and, despite himself, darted his eyes to Lizzie. Lizzie's look was intense, and Tom frowned, then turned to Stamatis again, only to find that he was looking at Lizzie too.

Tom gave a playful smile. 'Well? Do you want to quit? Because I can tell you now, these herbal balls won't work unless you want them to.'

'Yes, I'll give it a try, thanks. I've been meaning to quit anyway.' He threw Lizzie a fleeting glance, then turned to Tom again, who handed him the pack of herbal balls.

'Thanks, Tom. So many! Where did you get them?'

'Oh. They're from England!' he said breezily, and Lizzie felt a stab in her heart. *The damned lies... they're never-ending!*

Aliki and Babis brought up the subject of Petriti festival then, and Stamatis cheered as he expressed his anticipation for their upcoming evening together.

When he met her eyes again, Lizzie gave a tight smile, then looked away and brushed her brow with an urgent hand.

Tom looked just as enthused, and she told herself it was going to be fun. But it was going to be the last time she'd ever go out with Stamatis. That, she knew for sure. It couldn't be any other way. *Honestly, what kind of future could we ever have? What was I thinking?*

✳✳✳✳

Lizzie and Tom left the others outside the supermarket and turned into their lane to walk home. Once they were out of earshot, Tom hurled a torrent of questions at his sister, but she felt too overwhelmed to get into a discussion. He couldn't understand why she didn't want to go for pizza with the others, or why she didn't sound so excited any more about the Varkarola in two days' time.

Lizzie used the headache excuse to get him to stop, but Tom wouldn't buy it and insisted. He was still demanding answers when they reached their front door. But, when they got there, what they saw made them both freeze, their dispute instantly forgotten.

Another raven awaited them on the landing. Lizzie's heart did a backflip just as Tom let out a squeal of excitement. Both of them stood, transfixed, watching the bird as it hopped, then waddled for a short distance towards them. Much to their excitement, it had another pebble in its beak. With a short, quiet caw as if in friendly greeting, it let it drop, the rattling sound of the impact on the tiled floor reverberating against their apartment's front wall.

Without waiting for a reaction from them, the raven flapped its wings and flew high up, then disappeared over the roof, no doubt heading straight back to the mountain of Martaouna and to Phoni.

Tom bent over and picked up the pebble.

'Our second one!' he said triumphantly, hopping up and down.

Lizzie bent over to peer at it as he held it in the palm of his hand. It was black and perfectly round and smooth, like the previous one, identical. 'Which one is that for, do you think?'

'For Popi, no doubt. Can't be for Mandy, can it? It's too soon.'

'It might be for Mr Petros. You did say he no longer felt the pain.'

'Yes. For now. But muscle and nerves are much more difficult to heal than skin. One application isn't enough. But if he applies some more cream tonight, and with using some more tomorrow morning, we may get a pebble for Mr Petros too. So even if we don't succeed with Mandy, we could still be home and dry.'

'Better not take any chances. We should do our best with both of them.'

'Of course, Lizzie. Which reminds me... This afternoon, you and I need to find a suitable bracelet for Mandy. You know, her mermaid gift?'

'Of course.'

Lizzie got the keys out of her beach bag and made a move to put the key in the lock when Tom leaned towards her and put his hand on her arm. 'Lizzie? What is it? I know there's something troubling you.'

'Oh Tom, don't worry your little head about it.' She opened the door and walked in.

'You forget that I'm not little, Lizzie. I am as old as you are. Never forget that,' said Tom as he followed her inside.

Fairy tales are not lies, they are life lessons

The big day had come. Tom was holding the beach ball in his hands like a trophy as he and Lizzie walked, side by side, down their lane to get to the beach.

Tom was whistling a tune, bright-faced, but Lizzie was deep in thought, mind churning with memories of the previous morning.

Tom was right. He was thirty-two. Not a little boy. She needed to remember that. But the whole thing was a mess. How could she ever fix it? Even if she got to return with Tom to England how was she going to introduce him to the family? Wouldn't her parents have the shock of their lives to see him looking the same as if a single day hadn't passed since the day he'd gone missing? Would they believe it was him? Judging from their actions of the past, she guessed they wouldn't…

Maybe Phoni could make him look right for his age. She was the one who had caused this mess, after all. The least she could do was to fix it before she set them free… If all went well tonight, and Phoni granted their freedom, she would ask her then if she could give him the appearance that matched his years.

But, whatever happened today, Tom had to stay her first priority. The visit to Petriti tomorrow night had to be her last time socializing with Stamatis. Romance with him could never have a future.

'Lizzie… if you don't want to tell me what's bothering you, that's fine. But please try to perk up, at least. This is our big day! Come on!'

His urgent request snapped her out of her dark thoughts, and she nodded firmly, chastising herself inside for her perpetual worrying. 'Yes, I'm sorry, Tom…'

Tom stopped short and turned to her, a shadow clouding his features. He spoke in a whisper, so no one could hear, but his eyes were intense. 'We have to get Mandy in the water today, Lizzie. Let's do our best, yes? You and me! Tonight, Phoni awaits us at midnight. We can't afford to not have the third healing under our belt. I won't go back there, Lizzie!' He brought a hand up, just under his chin, and balled it into a fist, eyes afire in the morning sun. 'I won't!'

Lizzie opened her arms and squeezed him against her. 'You won't, Tom. Of course, you won't. She'll have to go over my dead body to take you away from me a second time.' Tom was nestling against her, holding the ball with one hand, the other arm around her.

He pulled back and bounced the ball in his hands, then offered her a cheeky grin. 'Let's not talk of dead bodies, okay? If there's someone that needs to kick the bucket, that's Phoni. She won't break us apart again. We'll have our three healings by tonight, no matter what.' He hardened his chin and added, 'And then, once Phoni says we're done, we'll be back to England like a shot. I've missed Mum and Dad, Lizzie... the whole family. Corfu is great, but we can't stay here forever. This has to work!' He patted his freezer bag that he carried on his shoulder. 'I'm not leaving the beach today till Mr Petros says his pain is gone for good. I'll spoon-feed him the cream if I have to.'

He winked, then gave a chortle, causing Lizzie to break into hysterics, the sound of their elation reverberating around the decrepit walls of the old village houses on either side of their path. They resumed walking, hand-in-hand now, past sweet-smelling yards that brimmed over with herbs, flowers, and cascading trellises. All the while, Lizzie tried to keep the smile on her face, and to contain inside her looming sadness over the prospect of leaving the island and Stamatis behind.

They arrived at the beach in high spirits, only for their faces to drop to find Brenda and Mandy there looking glum.

'Hi... What's the matter?' asked Lizzie as she approached them with Tom, her brow heavily furrowed.

In lieu of a response, Brenda pressed her lips together and gave a rueful shake of the head, while Mandy didn't acknowledge them at all. She was sitting beside her mother on their towel playing with a doll.

The pool stood right at the edge of the shore half-full, where the girl's *nonos* was instructed to place it that day according to the plan. Lizzie thanked her lucky stars the man's garden hose was long enough for the task but, once again, her heart sank when she turned her gaze back to Mandy. She looked positively vexed. This had to be bad.

Tom stepped closer to Mandy, bouncing the ball in his hands. 'What's the matter, Mandalena?'

The little girl raised her head and eyed him sideways. 'Nothing,' she said with a pout, then looked down at her doll again.

Lizzie and Tom exchanged a curious glance, then they both turned to Brenda, who looked sheepish and still said nothing.

Lizzie sensed the girl was on the defensive for some reason, and that her mother had decided to do nothing about it. Trying to test the waters she asked, 'Are you coming for a dip with me, Brenda, while the kids play in the—' She pointed to the pool, but Brenda waved an arm desperately, stopping her short, her eyes igniting with alarm.

Before Lizzie could speak again, Mandy began to wail. 'Nooo! I don't want to go in the stupid pool or use the stupid ball *ever again!*'

Tom let the ball drop on the sand and knelt before Mandy, then placed a hand on her shoulder. 'But, *Mandalena mou*, what are you saying? Today is the day—'

Mandy shook his hand away. 'Stop calling me Mandalena! I don't like it!' Her features were hard, her cute pointy chin so tight it had shrivelled to nothing.

'Okay, if that's what you want...' said Tom, his eyes seeking understanding when he darted them to Brenda.

Brenda swallowed hard. Lizzie had come to sit beside her and was rubbing her arm as she sensed she needed comfort.

At last, Brenda spoke in a little more than a whisper. 'I'm sorry. She doesn't want to play with Tom today. She didn't even want to come to the beach. I convinced her to come, just for a while, but she made it clear she won't go in the pool today.'

'I won't!' quipped Mandy from beside her.

'Mandalena...' soothed Tom.

'Mandy!' she insisted with a scowl.

'Okay, sorry... Mandy. Why don't you want to play today? Today is the big day! Don't you want to be a brave girl and get the big present from the mermaids?'

'Mermaids don't exist!'

'What? Who told you that?'

'My friend, Jenny! She visited last night and when I showed her my mermaid gold she laughed at me! She said you told me a pack of lies. I don't like you!' She dropped her doll and crossed her arms over her chest, then looked away, her face all screwed up.

Tom shook his head fiercely. 'Lies? Of course, they're not lies. You saw, with your own eyes, the mermaid gold appear in the pool every time you floated!'

'Jenny said you tricked me! To laugh at me!' she shouted at him, her eyes brimming over with tears.

'No, Mandy. That's not true...'

A heart-breaking, awkward silence ensued for a few moments, while Mandy broke into sobs, then wiped tears from her eyes. Tom tried to soothe her by putting a hand on her arm, but she shook it away. 'I'm sorry, Mandy, if you feel that way. But the mermaids do exist. And they're waiting for you. Right there...' he pointed to the edge of the shore, '...where the pool is. They put it there for you... And they have that big gift to give you today, remember? You've been doing this for two days. They're waiting for you to make the final step today. Why disappoint them now?'

Brenda let out a laboured sigh. 'She won't do it, Tom. She's a stubborn little thing.' She rolled her eyes. 'I hate to say she's taken it from her father's side. He's the same. And his mother... Ooh! Don't get me started on her!'

'But, Brenda, we can't give up now...' whispered Lizzie in her ear.

'What else can I do?' Brenda whispered back, shrugging her shoulders. 'I tried all I could. Nothing works. I might as well accept it... My Mandy will never be right again. It's okay, you know? It's not so bad. She doesn't have to get into the water. Or to swim. Why should she? She can live a perfect life without the sea. You know, I think if—'

Lizzie did something out of character then, and simply shushed the woman. Brenda stopped her pathetic rant and pursed her lips, allowing Lizzie to think in peace and quiet for a while.

This was preposterous. The child's mother was sulking worse than the child itself! Lizzie had zero tolerance for defeatist people and defeatist attitudes. She knew well that you get nothing out of life by giving up. She wasn't there today, reunited with her brother, because she'd given up once. No. She was there with him because she'd been holding on to a twenty-year-old decision, fighting tooth and nail to make it happen.

And then, a brilliant idea flashed in her mind, and it made her jolt upright so fast that it caused Brenda's shoulders to jump, a hand rising to land on her chest with a thud. 'Oh my goodness! What's got into you, girl?'

'No! What's got into *you*?' Lizzie pointed sharply at Brenda. 'Your child is being told lies by an obnoxious little girl called Jenny, and you're just standing there, not setting things straight? Why did you allow her to tell Mandy these things? When you know for a fact they're not true? When you know for a fact that mermaids do exist? Like any other grown-up knows!'

Lizzie stopped short when she realized that the others were staring at her speechless, jaws dropped. Only then did she realize she'd been babbling without thinking, gesticulating madly with her hands.

Her eyes darted to Gorgona and to the beautiful mermaid that decorated its façade. Mr Petros believed in mermaids... like all the other Greeks. Tom had told her of a Greek legend the other day; he'd said that the sister of Alexander the Great was a mermaid... According to the legend, the mermaid approaches passing ships hoping to hear news of her brother. All the Greek seamen know to lie to her if asked, that he's still alive and ruling the world. Anyone foolish enough to tell her that her brother has passed away would soon find himself sinking into the depths of the sea along with the ship.

No! No way! thought Lizzie. *Who is this snooty little girl who dares challenge us, who dares destroy Mandy's happiness? Fairy tales have magic for a reason! Children take them to heart for a reason! Fairy tales are not lies, they are life lessons!* Anger boiled inside her, and she finally turned to face the others. All three gazed back at her mutely still.

'You!' she said, pointing at Brenda. 'You and I are going for a dip! Now!' As Brenda stood numbly, Lizzie crouched over Mandy, dropping her voice a few notches, her voice velvety when she said, 'And you, my little princess, whether your name is Mandy or Mandalena, you get to decide today. But before you decide, I'm going to show you that mermaids do exist! Will you get into the pool if I promise that you'll see one today?'

Mandy gave a gasp, then nodded once slowly, her eyes twinkling with delight.

On either side of her, Tom and Brenda exchanged a curious glance before turning back to Lizzie, their expressions ablaze with intrigue.

What is it you need? I'm all ears!

Lizzie slipped her sarong over her swimsuit and left the others behind for a while. Before her quick swim with Brenda, she'd had a brilliant idea and now it was time to put her plan into action.

She found a shady spot outside a building and leaned against the wall to make two phone calls. She dialled the first number to talk to a local girl, who worked at a small hotel nearby. Even though they hardly knew each other, a minute later Lizzie ended the call, thrilled. The girl had accepted to grant her odd request.

Now, with that arranged, she dialled Stamatis's mobile number. She'd put it in her contacts shortly after he'd given it to her that evening outside Babis's store. He answered after three rings, his voice sounding rushed on the other line, but cheerful.

'Hi, Lizzie!' he said as soon as he picked up.

Lizzie was surprised at first that he knew who it was, but then remembered that she'd texted him later that same evening so he could have her number too. It had been a moment of weakness and she'd scolded herself for it. He had responded immediately to thank her again for visiting his house, and that was the last time they'd communicated via phone.

He had obviously stored her number in his contacts too. The thought made her heart skip a beat, but she willed herself not to get excited about it.

'Hey...' she finally replied after the first few moments of astonishment had come and gone.

'What a pleasant surprise! Where are you?'

'I'm on the beach...'

'Really? So am I! Well, in Pitsilos, so at work, to be exact.'

Lizzie's head whipped around to Pitsilos Apartments. *She's invited him to her lair, has she? No doubt, she's been banging the taps and the wardrobes again!*

'Lizzie? You there?'

'Oh... yeah, sorry. I need a favour, Stamatis.'

'Sure! Anything for you, Lizzie. Hold on, this is ridiculous! I'm coming out. Meet me outside Pitsilos? I'll be out in a second!'

Before she could speak, to tell him she'd rather not stand out there, anywhere near Nia, he'd already hung up. So now she had no choice but to go there. Luckily, there was a huge mulberry tree at the entrance and she could hide behind it, hidden from view. As soon as she arrived outside Pitsilos she saw him stride through the entrance. 'Hi! In person, this time! What can I do for you?'

He looked radiant, much to Lizzie's chagrin. In fact, more gorgeous than ever. He was wearing a light green t-shirt and tight-fitting faded jeans that accentuated his slender hips and long legs. The sight made her lightheaded. The muscles in his biceps rippled as he threw out his arms in greeting.

He stopped before her, a hand touching her arm for a moment, ever so lightly, and then he took it away as if he'd regretted it, to place it on his waist. But his eyes, all the while, were dancing, his lips stretched in a wide grin.

Lizzie smiled pleasantly, then glanced behind him at the entrance to find Nia had just come out, a malicious look in her eyes. Her lips were pressed together so tightly that her mouth looked like a single line etched across her face.

She sat in one of the chairs that were forever left outside and picked up a magazine from a small table. She pretended to browse through it but kept throwing dagger looks at Lizzie. Stamatis had his back to her and probably hadn't realised she was even there.

Lizzie cleared her throat, then took Stamatis by the arm and tugged gently, steering him towards the tree. 'Can we, erm, stand here please, in the shade? I've... had too much sun today.'

'Sure. No problem! So, what is it you need? I'm all ears!'

He looked so eager to help that her heart felt like singing. They were hidden from view now, thanks to the rich foliage of the tree. Nia couldn't see them there. Not that Lizzie cared about her, but that woman was so toxic it was uncomfortable to be around her. And it was best not to feed her malice further by having her watch her talk to Stamatis.

Lizzie pushed all other thoughts aside. She had no time to lose. She gazed into Stamatis's eyes and spoke in a little more than a whisper. 'You know Elena, don't you? The girl who works as an entertainer at the family hotel around the corner? The one with the pool?'

'Yes, of course I do. I was in school with her brother. Why?'

'I just phoned her. I need her to do something for a little girl I know. And to do that, I need your boat too. Or, rather, you on the boat with Elena. It shouldn't take much of your time. Ten, fifteen minutes tops. Can you help? I'm willing to pay for your trouble, of course!'

Stamatis waved his hand dismissively and scrunched up his face. 'Pay me? Don't be daft!' He leaned closer and whispered, 'It's for a little girl, you say? Do I know her?'

'I don't think so... Her name is Mandy. She has a fear of deep water, and Tom and I have been trying to help her overcome it... to get into the sea for her first swim. She's right there, see? She's with Tom on the beach.'

They turned around, and Lizzie showed him Mandy, who was still in the pool, Tom clapping his hands as he encouraged her, getting her ready for her big feat.

Stamatis was more than happy to oblige. Lizzie asked him to take his boat from the pier and to meet Elena, who would be waiting for him to pick her up from the river mouth. She knew what they were supposed to do and would tell him all about it.

Stamatis dashed into Pitsilos Apartments to pick up his keys and sunglasses, then came out in a rush just moments later. Without breaking his stride, he announced to Nia curtly that he was coming back soon. Hurrying past Lizzie with a bright smile, he strode along the boarded walkway to get to his boat.

Nia's eyes gave off lightning bolts as she watched him go, then she sprang up and rushed behind Lizzie, who was about to walk away too.

'Wait!' she shouted.

Lizzie spun around, but not before arranging her features into an expression of mild interest. 'Yes?' She was thankful, at least, that Nia had stopped at a good distance away from her.

'What is this game you're playing at now? Because I'll have you know, if it's war that you want, you will have it!'

Without moving an inch from her spot, Lizzie gave a long sigh. 'Oh, Nia... You think you're so important, but you're not. I assure you, I didn't come here to steal Stamatis from you. But he and I are old friends. And I just needed him to do something for me. That's all. He'll be back soon, to fix whatever you need fixing...' Lizzie pointed vaguely to Pitsilos and rolled her eyes.

'What's that supposed to mean?'

Lizzie chuckled. It felt wonderful to know she could wind her up like that.

When she received no answer, Nia moved closer, stopping at a distance of about two feet from Lizzie, then shook a sharp finger at her. 'That's a lie, and you know it. I know you're trying to steal him from me.'

'Believe what you must, Nia. Either way, I don't give a damn. But do take my advice – it's not worth it, having a fit every time you see me go near him...' Lizzie saw the malice in Nia's eyes, and it pleased her some more. This woman had no shame and was relentless in her pursuit of Stamatis, but no matter how she tried she would never win.

Clearly, Stamatis didn't have a romantic interest in her. Stamatis wanted *her*, not Nia. But it didn't matter. Neither Nia nor she would ever have him. Which made Nia's futile efforts to win him over all the more entertaining.

Lizzie smiled. 'Relax, Nia. And chin up, will you? In a day or two, I'll be gone anyway. You're welcome to do with Stamatis whatever you want then!'

She turned about face, but only after seeing Nia's face ignite with surprise first, then hope.

Smiling to herself, and full of anticipation, Lizzie returned to the others. The mermaid she promised little Mandy was about to appear and save the day, and she didn't want to miss it.

Everyone knows everyone in Messonghi

Lizzie approached the others to find Tom pleading with Mandy, his hands clasped together before his chest. 'Come on, Mandy! Come into the shallows and try to float in there. The mermaids are watching!'

Mandy was sitting in the pool at the edge of the shore, a deep frown on her face. Brenda was watching from a good distance away where she sat, chewing her lips.

'I don't know, Tom...' mumbled Mandy, then turning to Lizzie, 'You promised the mermaid would come if I floated in the pool today. I've done it lots! Where is she?'

'Yes, I did say she would show up. But you need to try a little harder first, my darling.' Lizzie moved to Tom, pointed to his pocket and winked. Mandy had turned her attention to her doll, playing with her in the water. 'Now... Do it... Throw a few coins in the shallows...' Lizzie urged Tom under her breath.

Tom made sure Mandy wasn't looking, then did as his sister asked. The coins landed slowly beside the pool, one by one, on the soft golden sand. They were all fully visible under the clear, shallow water.

Lizzie gave a thumbs up to Tom, then turned to the little girl. 'Come on, Mandy. Do as Tom asked. The mermaids expect you to be brave today. Show some courage while they watch.'

'But they're not here, are they?'

'But they are... They're watching from the deep water. We just can't see them, Mandalena!' cut in Tom.

Mandy ignored him and kept her eyes on Lizzie, her cheeks glowing red. 'I want to see the mermaid! You told me you'd show me one! Prove to me that you aren't lying!'

Lizzie let out a long sigh, then gazed to the left, where the river mouth was. Stamatis had taken his boat to go meet Elena a good five minutes ago. *What's taking them so long? It's only there!*

'Lizzie? Did you hear me?'

'Yes, darling. I did. Give me a sec... I'm sure we will see her any minute now... But, wait, what's this?' she said, pretending she'd only just seen the coins in the water.

Startled, Mandy stood in the pool and shot out, following Lizzie's gaze.

By the time she'd come to stand beside her, Lizzie had already picked up a couple of the coins to show her.

Mandy was standing in the water now, her ankles fully submerged, and didn't seem to notice, let alone panic about it. Chuckling, she bent over to inspect the coins before her feet. 'How did they get here? The last time I floated in the pool was ages ago.'

'The mermaids must have left the gold for you here...' said Lizzie.

'Yes! To give you encouragement to get in the shallows. And you did! Well done, Mandy!' Tom patted her on the back, but Mandy didn't seem to notice him. She was scanning the deep water in the distance, obviously hoping to spot a mermaid or two, a hand over her eyes to shield them from the glaring sunshine.

'Where are the mermaids? I can't see them!' Mandy said after a while. She turned to Lizzie, her eyes wide, but Lizzie was lost for words and could only exchange mute glances with Tom.

Brenda approached at that point, enthused to see her child in the water, but Lizzie put up a hand, pleading with her eyes for her to stay away a little longer. The woman had a full-blown negativity chatterbox running in her brain. It was too risky to let her come near at this crucial point.

The sound of Stamatis's fishing boat echoed then, and it sounded like angelic music in Lizzie's ears. She turned around to find it approaching fast, Stamatis and Elena sitting inside, the latter dressed in the mermaid costume she used to entertain the children at the pool where she worked.

The costume didn't have a tail, but a shiny long skirt that was heavily covered with sequins. They gave the impression of scales and had a dazzling effect in the strong sunshine. Little shells and scraps of net-like fabric decorated the costume on one side of the skirt where a deep cut was.

Elena's long, curly dark hair reached down to her sleeveless top. The top was covered with even more sequins and had two large shells made of fabric, one over each breast, fake pearls stitched all around them.

As soon as Mandy spotted Elena she froze in place, her jaw dropping. When Elena began to wave to them all, Mandy erupted in movement, throwing her hands in the air, hopping around and squealing with delight. Brenda rushed to her side and began to wave frantically too.

Stamatis steered the boat a little closer so Elena's voice could be heard but not too close to spoil the illusion. Now, they were floating past, like a boat on parade, catching the attention of all the other holiday makers too, children waving and cheering all over the seafront.

Elena waved back to everyone, laughing, and so did Stamatis. When they passed by the spot where Mandy and the others were, Elena spoke out: 'Hey, Mandalena! Are you ready?'

This was all Lizzie had asked her to say and it had worked!

Still standing in the water, Mandy looked ecstatic. She bent over and picked up the rest of the coins Tom had thrown in the water. She took them in both hands and shook her fists in the air. 'Thank you, Miss Mermaid, thank you! Yes, I am ready! I'll do it now!'

They all stood and watched while Stamatis steered the boat a little further out, then turned it around and began to move back towards the river mouth.

Tom, not wanting to let time pass and Mandy's enthusiasm to wane, turned to her, stooping low, his hands on her shoulders. 'If you're ready, Mandalena, then let's go! This is it!'

'Of course, I'm ready!' Mandy looked down at her feet in the water for the first time. With a crooked grin, she added, 'Thank you, Tom. Now I'm in here I realize there's nothing to it, after all.'

Her mother patted her head, reduced to silence. Her eyes were streaming with tears.

Mandy turned to face her and tilted her head. 'Why are you crying, Mummy?'

'Oh, nothing, darling. I am just so happy you got to see a mermaid today,' she said in a wavering voice, then turned to Lizzie and Tom, the look in her eyes speaking volumes about her gratitude.

A silence ensued, while the three stood around Mandy, their hearts swelling with feeling.

'What's the matter?' she asked, perplexed. 'Why are you all looking at me like that?'

'We're proud of you, darling, that's all,' said her mother.

'That's right,' cut in Tom.

'And Mandy... We can't wait for you to get your mermaid present,' added Lizzie.

Mandy gave a cute smile and tilted her chin. 'It's Mandalena, actually.'

All three chortled, then Mandy went to the pool, picked up the ball and hurried past them to stop a little further out, the water up to her calves. In a heartbeat, she was sitting in the shallows, then floating on her back, the ball in her hands.

Her mother gasped and brought her hands over her mouth, while Lizzie cheered. Tom, on the other hand, didn't have the luxury to stand and watch. He barely had time to dig out the bracelet from his pocket and throw it by Mandy in the water before she could shift to a sitting position again.

When she found the bracelet, she gave an excited squeal. She took it into her hands and held it up, the beads catching the light. 'Thank you, mermaids! It's beautiful!' She stood and moved to her mother. 'Look, Mummy! Look what the mermaids gave me for being brave!'

Lizzie found the opportunity to approach Tom with a titter. 'Cats and pink ribbons? I thought you were going to buy a bracelet with dolphins and blue eye beads.'

'Couldn't find one like that in the shops, after all. Brilliant move with Elena, though. I'm surprised she obliged us. We only met her a couple of times at the poolside café.'

Lizzie nodded, a wicked smile on her lips. 'When I mentioned Stamatis she was more than happy to help... I offered to pay her for her time but she wouldn't have it.'

'I'm starting to think everyone knows everyone in Messonghi!' said Tom, just as the other two joined them.

They got out of the water cheering around Mandy and when they returned to their laid out towels, Tom handed her the ball.

'It's yours, Mandalena. You won it fair and square.'

'Thank you, Tom. But I don't need it any more. You can give it to another girl that may need help.'

'But, won't you go in the sea again after today?'

'Of course, I will! Every day!'

'So? Why don't you want the ball? It will help you float.'

Nah... My *yiayia* has many swimming rings and armbands at home for me. She's been asking me to take them to the beach... I was afraid before, but not any more. I'll show them to you tomorrow!'

'Good girl!' Tom was about to tell her again how proud he was of her when Mr Petros's deep voice boomed from Gorgona.

'Hey, Tom! A word with you!'

Tom grabbed his freezer bag. 'Shoot! I forgot all about him!' he told Lizzie under his breath. He exchanged a hopeful glance with her, then went off like a shot to finish the last task of the day.

❋❋❋❋

'Mr Petros! I'm sorry I didn't come sooner. I got caught up helping Mandy learn how to swim,' he said in immaculate Greek when he joined him on the restaurant's façade.

'It's okay, my boy. Can you spare any more of that cream?'

'Of course!' They were standing at the edge of the seating area, a cluster of vacant tables beside them. Tom led Mr Petros to one, took out the container and handed it to him.

As soon as he started to apply a small dab of cream to himself Mr Petros said, 'Ah, Tom, what a treasure you are! Do you know, the pain is nearly gone today. Last night, I rubbed in some more, like you said, and I slept like a baby! Fancy a boy your age knowing stuff about medicine, let alone carry some around. How come you do that, Tom?'

'Oh... uh... my father is a herbalist. I've been watching him work. Herbal medicine fascinates me... And I don't like to see people suffer from aches and pains.' Tom's guilt abated somewhat when he realized that part of his answer held a lot of truth.

'But that's amazing! You're so talented for a boy your age... I owe you so much for this, Tom!'

'I'm just glad I could help you, Mr Petros. And you owe me nothing...'

'Sure I do! When you finish your swim, you and Lizzie must come back here. Lunch is on me today! My lamb roast just came out of the oven and it's to die for!'

Damned bird! What's it playing at?

After their hearty meal at Gorgona, Mr Petros treated them to halva for afters and didn't stop patting Tom on the back, expressing his gratitude for his help. He was completely pain-free and dashing up and down the seating area like an adolescent. Lizzie couldn't remember ever seeing him so sprightly.

Despite their high spirits, when they arrived home the two siblings got a little deflated not to find a raven outside their door. They'd been hoping one might deliver another pebble for their third feat. Still, they were seeing Phoni at midnight, so perhaps she was going to announce the results of their efforts herself. They knew they had succeeded with Mandy, so they took their success for granted. If anything, they hoped Mr Petros's prompt recovery might earn them extra credit.

To pass the time after their midday siesta, they had a long walk to the village of Moraitika along the road. After a stop for a refreshment at a café near the river bridge, they headed home. They had a light supper, then sat in the living room, planning to spend the next few hours watching TV or reading till it was time to set off to the mountain.

Just as a TV movie started to play and they relaxed on the sofa together to enjoy it, they heard a tap on the closed kitchen window. Taken aback, they both turned to find a raven on the sill behind the glass. It was too far to tell if it had a pebble in its beak or not, so they hurried there to check, their faces animated.

The first thing Lizzie noticed was that this raven didn't look like any other she'd seen before. A white streak ran across its middle, starting from between its eyes, to continue over its head, down the nape of its neck, alongside its back, and ending at the tip of its tail.

'Wow! What's this?' said Tom first, chuckling loudly.

Lizzie's stomach constricted with an eerie feeling. The bird had two pebbles in its beak. Her initial reaction had been to feel just as excited as her brother, but the white streak made the bird look sinister, somehow. *Why doesn't it look like the rest? Why send us this odd-looking one today? What's she playing at?*

'Lizzie? What's wrong?'

She turned to throw a glance at Tom, to see him gazing at her curiously.

'What's the matter, Lizzie? Do you want to open the window or shall I?'

'I don't know, Tom...'

'But, Lizzie, it's brought two pebbles! See? We have healed four souls! Even more than we had to! Why aren't you happy?'

Before she could reply, the bird tapped the window again using the pebbles in its beak. The sound echoed sharply in Lizzie's ears, causing her to flinch. 'Okay. Stand back. I'll do it.'

'Stand back? What's the matter?'

'Stand back, Tom! Please! Just humour me. I have a bad feeling about this, okay?'

'Okay. Just don't shoo it away. We have to see Phoni tonight, remember? Be nice to it or she may not like it.'

'Okay, I'll be nice to her evil minions...' she said under her breath.

'Lizzie!' he reprimanded.

'Okay, okay. I promise.' Lizzie let out a long exhalation and opened the window.

The bird hopped onto the window frame and eyed them both curiously for a few moments.

There was a ledge on the inside as well and Lizzie expected the raven to let the pebbles drop on there and leave. Except, this bird didn't do that. Instead, it surprised them both by flapping its wings and flying over their heads, to land in the middle of the kitchen floor.

The two turned about face, taken aback. 'Hey!' said Lizzie, darting her eyes at the pinafore she'd left draped over the nearby chair. *If need be, I'll grab that and throw it over it, then bundle it out of the window. Damned bird! What's it playing at?*

Tom exchanged a glance with her that spoke volumes about his own unease. He opened his mouth to speak but then both he and Lizzie got the shock of their lives.

Black smoke emanated from the bird, swirling up, higher and higher, until it reached up to Lizzie's height. Then, it disappeared in a heartbeat, Phoni manifesting before their very eyes.

'You! What—?' said Lizzie, taking a step back and reaching out to clutch her brother's arm. Poor Tom had frozen and, when she yanked him close to her, he stuck right against her in an instant.

Phoni raised her chin, opened her putrid mouth and let out a cackle, her eyes twinkling with glee. 'Look at you! Looking so surprised...'

I knew that bird was trouble...' murmured Lizzie.

'I like you, Lizzie. You speak your mind. Even when it's not in your best interest,' replied Phoni, taking a step towards her.

Lizzie gritted her teeth and clutched her brother to her side with both hands now, but didn't step back again. Where would she go anyway? They both stood a step away from the sink. 'Why are you here, Phoni? You didn't have to. We were going to come to the cave tonight like you asked...'

'Yes, I know...' She pulled back her lips exposing yellow, rotten teeth. 'But I couldn't wait. I am too excited to wait.'

'Why?' asked Tom, moving away from his sister a little and standing straight. 'I don't understand.'

'Because it seems I taught you well, little one!' Phoni moved forward and opened her hand. Two black pebbles, smooth and shiny, lay in her open palm. 'Take them. You won them. Four healings! You two exceeded my expectations, I must say!'

Lizzie watched as Tom took the pebbles from Phoni's hand, then turned to the witch, her voice cold, to say, 'We didn't want to take any chances.'

'Oh Lizzie, you have a way with words... I'd like—' Phoni stopped short and put out a hand to touch Lizzie's shoulder.

Before she could do it, Lizzie recoiled. 'Don't you touch me! Stay away from us!' she shouted, pulling her brother again to squeeze him against her.

Phoni let out a howl of laughter, then, just as quickly as it had come, her amusement left her face. Her brows knitted, eyes igniting with determination when she said, 'I don't have time for this. I'm here to give you my decision.'

'Yes. By all means, tell us whatever you will, and then get the hell out... or fly out...' said Lizzie, sarcasm dripping from her lips. 'Do whatever you want, but do not touch us ever again!'

Phoni twisted her lips, then tipped her chin to say, 'As I said earlier, you have succeeded in healing four souls... and quite resourcefully, if I may add, seeing that one of them wasn't even human. You two have healed skin problems, a bad back, and even a phobia. I have to give it to you, you surely diversified with your efforts... So, yes! As I promised, your brother is free, Lizzie! Free to go back to England!'

Lizzie and Tom froze for a few moments, too stunned to hear such good news coming from the vile being before them. It sounded too good to be true, but they'd done the work and she had said it, after all. Soon, they burst into peals of laughter and held each other tight, their hearts swelling with relief.

Phoni then cleared her throat and they turned their attention swiftly back to her.

Lizzie pinned her eyes intently on the witch, hoping inside that her exit would be as swift as her entrance had been. *As soon as she goes, we'll be out painting the town red!*

But, when she registered the wicked glint in Phoni's eyes, and her lips that were arranged into a smug pout, she knew that her understanding couldn't be further from the truth. The witch was anything but done with them.

Tom must have realized too because he turned to Lizzie, his expression ablaze with panic. They exchanged a single look and clung to each other again, their eyes mirroring each other's dread.

Phoni gave a cunning smirk. 'What's the matter, you two?'

'You tell us, Phoni!' Lizzie took a steadying breath and let go of her brother. Stepping forward to stand protectively before him, her hands slightly raised at her sides, she cocked her eye at the witch. 'What are you playing at? Why are you still here? You said that my brother is free to go! So we're done! Aren't we?'

Phoni gave a sardonic smile. 'Oh, Lizzie... I thought you were a clever girl! Your brother's freedom has a price, of course...'

'A price? What price?'

'Can't you guess, Lizzie? Oh, come on, isn't it obvious? Surely you can guess!'

'Guess, *what?*'

'That, all this time, it was *you* that I wanted to have...'

'Me? What do you mean... have *me?*'

Phoni threw out her arms, eyes widening. 'As my replacement, of course! I can't be doing this forever. I need to retire and rest my bones...'

Lizzie huffed and did her best to contain the raw panic that grew inside her. She'd never let the witch see that she was afraid. She sneered and squinted her eyes. 'What? And you expect me to follow you into the mountain to take your place in whatever it is you're doing? Just like that?'

'No... Not just like that. But you will do it so your brother can return to England. Isn't that what you wanted?'

Tom leapt forward, grabbed Lizzie's hand and stood beside her. 'No! That will never happen!'

Lizzie held his shoulder firmly, a pleading look in her eyes. 'Please, Tom! Let's see what she has to say...' She turned to Phoni. 'Why me? What makes you think that I'm the right candidate anyway?'

The witch chortled. 'I didn't just decide, Lizzie! I can assure you... I wouldn't choose my replacement lightly. But I watched you that summer when you first came here... You were a protector... taking care of everyone you came across on the mountain. One day you even saved a boy's life after he was bitten by a venomous snake. I saw you... I knew then that you'd be some kind of healer in your life. I thought you'd become a doctor, but you're a nurse, aren't you? That will do me just as nicely...'

'How do you know all that? How—' Lizzie stopped short when she realized. *Those damned birds!* They'd been listening in to all her conversations, watching her every move since she came.

Phoni tittered and said, 'Yes. My faithful companions are my eyes and ears on the island.'

'So why did you take Tom instead of me when we were kids? If it was me that you really wanted?'

'Oh come on, Lizzie. You're a clever girl, you can work it out...'

'She wanted you to get your education first!' cut in Tom, then turning to Phoni, 'Am I right?'

'Bravo, boy! You guessed it.'

'And you took my brother so you can blackmail me twenty years later? Is that it?'

'Well done, Lizzie.'

Lizzie balled her hands into fists and lunged forward. She stopped an inch from Phoni's face, shaking her fists in the air. Tom moved closer and grabbed her by the waist to pull her back, but there was no stopping Lizzie from yelling, 'How could you? How could you play with our lives like that?'

Phoni scowled and raised her arms high over her head, her black talons long, like hammer nails. 'Easy now, little girl! I'm telling you for your own good! Don't try to antagonize me!'

Somehow, Lizzie thought of Tom, that he needed to be kept safe. He was no longer holding her, but was urging her to calm down, his voice desperate. She stepped back to stand beside him again, rubbing her mouth with an urgent hand as she tried to think.

The witch tilted her head, her gaze intense, a gnarled finger pointed at Lizzie. 'Well? What is your decision?'

I'll never let this happen!

Lizzie struggled to contain her angst as she gazed into the witch's face for a few more moments. Her mind whirled with possibilities, but she found no way out.

The witch issued a guttural sound heavy with vexation, then said, 'Well? Your answer, girl! Time is of the essence!'

Lizzie heaved a long sigh. 'What answer? I have no answer! And I can't believe you expect me to just follow you into the mountain. You must be out of your mind!'

Phoni sniggered. 'I beg to differ, girl. I know you'd do anything for your brother. I promise to let him go, to forget I ever laid eyes on him if you agree to take his place.'

'I'll never let that happen, you hear?' shouted Tom, squeezing Lizzie's arm so tightly that it hurt.

'Please, Tom! Let me think!'

'But, Lizzie—'

'Stop. Please, my darling...'

Tom saw his sister's pleading eyes and decided to stay silent for a while. But he had his eyes trained on Phoni and had surreptitiously hidden behind his back a small knife that he'd found on the counter. If need be, he'd use it if the witch tried to take his sister away, if she had magic tricks up her sleeve to do that. He'd get there on time, he knew. He wouldn't hesitate.

Lizzie took a deep breath, let out a sigh, then took another, trying to put her mind in order. Finally, she cocked her eye at the witch to say, 'Wait a minute... If it was me you wanted all along then why this circus? Why did you waste time asking Tom and me to heal three souls? Why didn't you just take me the night I came to claim him from you, huh?'

'Consider this your preparatory exam to getting the position in my practice, my dear.'

'But I didn't do the work, *Tom* did!'

'Yes, of course he did. He's been trained by the best, after all.' Phoni raised her chin with the air of a duchess.

'I still don't understand.'

'I took my time to assess you during your stay here. I now know for a fact that you love him enough... enough to do anything for him. And you've been so loving, so protective of him. Like you are with everyone else. And I must say... this is a true sign of weakness on your part, Lizzie...' She gave a malevolent smile, baring her rotten teeth, then gave a little laugh that turned into a snarl. 'But, of course, no one's perfect...'

Lizzie felt nauseous, her voice a little more than a whisper. 'A weakness? Caring is a weakness? You nasty—'

'Careful of your words, Lizzie!' shrieked Phoni, scowling. 'And yes. It *is* a weakness! If you loved no one, as is the case with me, no one would be able to use you. See? But you're like putty in my hands now, aren't you?'

Phoni gave a titter while Lizzie and Tom watched, speechless. How could anyone be so cold, so void of sentiment and regard for others? It boggled one's mind.

Phoni gave a cackle and put her hands on her hips, eyes glinting with malice. 'So, where was I? Oh, yes! Thanks to my birds I know you don't have any family here, Lizzie. No one will bother to look for you if you go missing. Except a friend or two, you have no one else. But, in my experience, when there is no immediate family, no one really cares to find a missing person.'

'We have family in England!' piped up Tom.

Phoni sneered, her eyes glinting with glee. 'You mean the parents who left you to your fate and went back to England all those years ago, never to return?'

'Wait a minute! My parents were devastated! They—' protested Lizzie.

Phoni raised a hand. 'Enough! I want your answer, Lizzie. And if you say no, then I'm afraid I'll have to take your brother back. It's as simple as that!'

'Suppose I do as you say...'

'Lizzie, no! I won't let—'

'Please Tom!' Lizzie squeezed his hand in hers with feeling, and he lowered his gaze, a tear escaping his eyes, but, secretly with the other hand, he squeezed the hilt of the knife behind his back.

The sight of him broke Lizzie's heart, but she had to explore all eventualities.

'Go on, Lizzie. You were saying?'

'Yes... If... I come with you... will you give Tom back his lost years?'

'Whatever do you mean, child?'

'I mean, he still looks twelve! How can he go back to his family and present himself like their long lost son? He should look thirty-two! Can you do it?'

Phoni brought a talon to her lips, her eyes shrinking into slits, as she pondered on this for a while. She bent her head, and stayed like that for a few more moments, rubbing her chin with slow movements.

The others waited, Lizzie hoping with all her heart she would say yes. If only she could give Tom back his freedom and the looks he should have today, then he could lead a normal life. No one back home would ever need to know the disturbing truth.

Finally, Phoni looked up. 'I'm sure I can... I have to check. I'll get back to you in a week—'

Lizzie raised her brows. 'Check? Check, what?'

'I don't know every single spell! But there are others in my world who can help. I'll seek their assistance. I'm sure it can be done...' Her voice trailed off, then her eyes lit up and she added, 'I'll tell you what! I can surely remove all his memories... so he can be spared from knowing what happened to him in the past twenty years. Seeing that he has remembered how to speak your language again, he'll be able to lead a perfectly normal life back in your country.'

Lizzie pondered on her promises for a while, then said, 'Yes, that sounds perfect for Tom...' She gave a pleading look to her brother, who was about to protest again. He respected her wish to be quiet and pursed his lips.

Lizzie turned to Phoni anew. 'So... we'll talk again in a week when you know for sure what you can do for him.'

'Agreed. And you two can use the week to decide which one of you is going to be my apprentice. Now, ideally, it will be you, Lizzie. But I'll take Tom if I have to. He's done a great job here. It's just that I'd need to train him for a few more years before he could be ready. You, Lizzie, on the other hand, with your nurse training, in less than a year you'd be ready to take over and I could retire at last...'

'You're both crazy!' thundered Tom, unable to contain his distress any longer. 'I'll never let this happen!' He turned to his sister dropping his voice down a few notches. 'I know you, Lizzie. I know what your decision will be, and you can forget it! I will never let you sacrifice yourself for me!'

He turned to Phoni, his eyes emitting fire. 'You know something? I say we don't need to decide! You can go to hell, witch! Because neither you nor your stupid birds can stop us if we decide to leave the island! What are you going to do? Have them circle over the taxi all the way to the airport?'

Phoni took two steps forward, a lingering sneer on her lips.

Despite his angst, Tom felt thankful the others hadn't noticed the knife he still held behind his back. Its blade was concealed under his t-shirt, his hand gripping the hilt even more tightly now. It took all his self-restraint not to reveal it and threaten the witch with it.

Finally, Phoni shook a gnarly finger at him and gave a deriding smile. 'This is where you're wrong, boy! My birds can stop an airplane... All I need to do is command them to!'

Lizzie's blood froze to hear this but, somehow, she jerked into motion, stepping forward and waving her hands madly. 'You wouldn't!' she retorted, hoping to sound defiant, but she could hear the frailty in her own voice.

'Oh yes, I would... I'd send them flying over to your plane, like, *that!*' Phoni snapped her fingers and gave a maniacal laugh.

In an instant, a multitude of long-drawn caws echoed from outside. Then, an unkindness of ravens stormed in through the open window and began to fly in circles low over their heads.

'Aaargh!' Lizzie and Tom began to shriek in panic, shielding their faces with their hands. That seemed to entertain Phoni, who erupted in even louder evil laughter.

'Stop! Tell them to go away!' shouted Lizzie.

'Enough! Go! You heard your *mistress-to-be!*' shrieked Phoni pointing to the window, and the birds obeyed immediately, bolting outside to disappear as swiftly as they'd come.

An eerie silence ensued for a few moments while Phoni eyed the other two with devilish glee.

Lizzie spoke first. 'You proved your point... But you'd put a plane full of people in danger just to stop us?'

'In danger? Oh, I'd do more than put them in danger! I'd send *hundreds* of ravens to your plane. I'd kill *everyone* on board if I had to! And then, you'd have *everyone's* blood on your hands!' She shook a sharp finger at them. 'So don't you dare trick me! Only *one of you* gets to fly back to England! If both of you board a plane, mark my words, it will be the last thing you'll ever do!'

'Stop! Enough!' shouted Lizzie, placing her hands over her ears, her stomach clenching. The deadly mixture of anger and panic inside her had been too much to bear, and she'd begun to shake like a leaf.

Phoni didn't seem to notice that, or if she did she didn't care. 'As long as you realize that I mean it... Believe me when I say, I'll kill everyone on board, and I won't bat an eyelid about it!'

Tom shook his fist at Phoni. 'But then you'd kill us too! Both of us! How would you win then, you psycho?'

Phoni hooked her mouth to one side, huffed and said, 'But you wouldn't have won either then... And, for me, that would be all that mattered...'

Aghast as they both were, they remained numb for a few moments, just watching her move slowly away from them. She turned around, to stand in the middle of the room where she'd appeared at first. She brought a hand to the side of her head, rubbing her temple, and twisted her lips. 'Well, this has been long, and I'm an old woman. I don't have the energy I used to. Which is why I need to find a replacement soon... Remember! I'll be back in a week and then you'd better be ready to name which one of you is going away with me!'

Before they could reply, she was gone, turning into black smoke again. They followed it with their eyes as it began to swirl mid-air, drifting through the window, then they heard the flap of wings and saw the raven fly away, its shrill cry wafting in the cool evening air.

As soon as Phoni was gone, Tom closed the window as his sister watched, dazed.

He raised his other hand and put the knife back on the counter, causing Lizzie's eyes to ignite with alarm when she saw it. 'Were you holding it all this time? What were you going to do with it, Tom? Are you crazy?'

'Never mind that, Lizzie! And please tell me you're not considering what she just asked of you!'

'To take your place in the mountain? Of course, I am! Tom, you've spent twenty years in there! It's your turn to live! I've had my life.'

'What are you talking about? What life? You're only thirty-two!'

'But you're twelve!'

'No, I'm not! I'm as old as you are! You know that! Plus, I've been living there already... it'll be easier for me than it will be for you to adjust!'

'No way, Tom! I won't discuss it with you any further. I'm doing it. For you. And that's final!'

'No, it's not! I won't let you do this!' Like a shot, he rushed to the front door.

Stunned, Lizzie watched for a few seconds, then, somehow, her feet unglued themselves from the spot as if of their own volition. She bolted behind him but was too late.

In a heartbeat, it seemed, Tom had grabbed the keys from the door, opened it, and dashed outside, shutting it behind him with a deafening bang.

Lizzie grabbed the handle and tried to open the door, but sensed the resistance of Tom's pulling effort from the outside. The door opened just a smidgen, then clicked shut again.

Lizzie froze when she heard the sound of the key turning in the lock. She fell to her knees before the door, limp, yet her mind exploded with alarm. 'No! Tom! What are you doing?' she screamed.

A short silence ensued, then Tom's voice echoed from the outside, frail, gentle. 'I'm sorry, Lizzie... I have to do it...'

'Please, Tom... What are you going to do?' she said breaking into sobs.

'I'm going to the mountain... To tell Phoni I'm volunteering. I'm sorry, Lizzie. I won't let you ruin your life for me.'

Know your enemy, isn't this what they say?

Lizzie tried the handle, only to confirm that Tom had locked her in. With her heart racing, she heard his hurried footsteps as he began to walk away.

She jerked upright and rushed to her bedroom, then out onto the balcony. He was running down the stairs and then, in an instant, disappeared from view around the bend. 'Please! Wait, Tom! Don't do it! Let's talk about it! Please, come back!'

The sound of his hurried descent stopped in response to her pleas. He was out of sight now, so all she could do was prick up her ears, praying inside he would reconsider and climb the stairs back up.

Her reprieve lasted for only a few seconds. The horrifying sound of his footsteps as he resumed going down the stairs caused Lizzie's panic to return. Then, she saw Aliki's door open. 'Oh thank God! Aliki! Aliki, please! Stop him! Stop Tom! He's leaving!' she cried, a frantic hand shaking as it pointed to the bottom of the stairs.

Aliki froze in place, her expression dumbfounded, but then, when Tom came into view dashing from the bottom of the steps to the garden gate, she jerked forward and rushed to intercept him. She reached him just as he put his hand on the gate and got hold of his arm. 'Hey! What's going on, Tom?'

Lizzie's breath caught, and she thanked her lucky stars Aliki could be so quick. 'Please, Aliki! Don't let him go! Tom, please! Come back! Let's all talk about it!'

Tom wasn't answering Aliki, who was speaking to him gently, asking where he was headed and what was going on. Instead, he had his eyes pinned on Lizzie, despair alight in his eyes. She knew then that he wasn't going to go. He looked spent, just as much as she did.

Her huge relief chased away the panic inside her, then settled gently in her heart like a springtime butterfly on a rose.

'Thank you, Tom... thank you... please come up! Open the door...' Lizzie called out from the balcony, her voice breaking.

Across the distance, as Aliki patted him on the shoulder, Tom's tears began to fall, just as Lizzie's eyes brimmed over too.

The landlady's shrill voice echoed from the second floor in Aliki's building. '*Ti ginete? Ti fasaria ine afti?* What's going on? What's this racket?' she demanded, one hand gripping the railing as she shook the other in the air frantically.

Embarrassed, Lizzie looked away from her and down at the others. Aliki turned to the old woman, her voice breezy. 'Oh nothing, Mrs Vlachos. The boy had a little quarrel with Lizzie, that's all...' She tousled Tom's hair. 'You know how young boys can be sometimes.'

'Don't I know it? They're nothing but trouble, the lot of them! You be a good boy, you hear? Or you can go live with your mother! I don't like trouble and noise in my house!' the old woman told Tom, shaking an accusing finger.

Tom sounded very apologetic when he assured the landlady that this wouldn't happen again. Lizzie couldn't see his face but imagined his upset must have made him look sheepish enough to seem convincing.

Satisfied, the old woman turned around with a grunt and disappeared through her balcony doors without another word.

As soon as she was gone, Aliki took Tom by the hand and led him quietly up the steps.

Lizzie rushed to her front door to wait for them to come. The very idea that she could have lost Tom so unexpectedly made her knees buckle. She plonked herself down on a low stool, raking her hair with an urgent hand, her eyes pinned on the door as she heard the sound of footsteps growing louder and louder. With that, her all-too-familiar, heart-wrenching sense of loss subsided again, for now.

Five minutes later, they were all sitting on the sofa, the two siblings relaying to Aliki what had happened starting from when the raven had appeared outside the window. As the story progressed, their friend grew all the more horrified.

When they were done, Aliki shook her head and thrust her arms out to gesticulate heavily. 'I cannot believe she tricked you this way! And now she has the gall to put you in front of this impossible dilemma?'

Lizzie and Tom nodded but said nothing, spent. They were holding each other tight, Tom's head tucked in the crook of Lizzie's neck, her chin resting gently on his head.

'So, she's a shapeshifter... I didn't expect that.'

'Well, I guess she surprised us all,' said Lizzie with a wry smile.

Aliki tilted her head. 'You reckon she's a *Nagual* then?'

'A what?' asked Lizzie with a deep frown.

Beside her, Tom knitted his brows and looked at Lizzie, then Aliki.

Aliki did cartwheels with her hand. 'You know... a *brujo*, some kind of wizard or shaman.'

'I guess so...' Lizzie gave a faint smile. 'Though I didn't get all the words you said.'

'Sorry, it's the Californian in me. We love this kind of stuff over there. Or, at least, I do. I've always been keen on spiritualism and read the books of Carlos Castaneda when I was young. He was an infamous mystic writer from Mexico and—' She must have registered their blank expressions then because she waved dismissively and added, 'Oh, never mind!'

Tom moved gently out of Lizzie's embrace to sit up on the sofa. 'Regardless of what she is, I say we fight back! Surely there must be a way we can defeat her!' He shook his fist before his chest.

Aliki gave a little cheer then said, 'I agree with you, Tom! And surely there must be a way. But in order to find it, first, we must get to know her better... Know your enemy, isn't this what they say?'

The other two nodded and made appreciative sounds.

Aliki squinted her eyes, a hand rubbing her temple. 'I wonder... if there are any folklorists on the island... or mystics even, like Castaneda was back in Mexico...' she rolled her eyes, 'Well, anyone really who's likely to know what Phoni is and how we can protect ourselves from her magic.'

Lizzie felt hope ignite, then surge through her, soothing her to the core. 'You think so? That there may be people on the island that know these things?'

'Yes, why not? I dare think Tom is not the only child the witch has ever abducted! She's old, you said... Surely she didn't start now! And Tom did say that there were many other kids in the mountain healing people alongside him. What if they were all stolen like he was? Surely, word must have gone around every time, and I'm guessing she's appeared before other people too.

Hopefully, some of them may know more than we do about her. I say we try to find these people.'

The three of them grew silent for a while. Lizzie's mind whirled with possibilities. Who could they ask? Were there any folklore magazines they could contact? What if they borrowed from the library all the books of local folk tales and legends they could find? Could they get their hands on the police records of any children that may have gone missing in the past?

She was willing to ask everyone, going from door to door all over Messonghi and Spileo if she had to. Now, she had a vivid image on her mind that depicted Tom, Aliki and her leading a horde of locals that wielded torches and pitchforks as they marched to Phoni's cave to deliver her comeuppance.

Aliki's excited squeal snapped her out of her reverie.

'Yes! Of course!'

'What is it, Aliki?'

'Well, I've been sitting here wondering what to do to get answers in the physical world, and I'd forgotten all about the Internet! Duh!' She facepalmed herself.

The revelation flashed in Lizzie's mind, causing her to put both hands on her head. *Of course!* Aliki worked from home as a graphic designer but was also an avid blogger. Her blog, where she rambled about her life in Corfu, had visitors from all over the world including thousands from Greece. Perhaps she could get in contact with the right people to find out more about Phoni. Lizzie leaned closer to Aliki and put an urgent hand on her arm. 'Tell us your idea, Aliki!'

Aliki's eyes danced as she giggled. 'Well, there are a few social media groups about Corfu... I'll get on them tonight. And I'll ask some of the people I've met through my blog. I have a few in mind who share my enthusiasm about spirituality, the metaphysical, you name it. Leave it with me. I'll get on it straight away!'

With these words, Aliki sprang upright and put her hands on Tom and Lizzie's shoulders. 'Hang in there, guys... I should have answers from these people very soon. Try to stay positive. We'll fix that nasty witch, you mark my words! Aliki's taken over now, so may God help her!' She pointed to herself with a sharp thumb, a wide smile on her face.

Lizzie gazed at her friend, this tall, big girl before her. She was all curly hair and twinkling eyes and looked nothing short of a fairy godmother. Lizzie turned to Tom, and they exchanged encouraging smiles.

'That's the spirit!' said Aliki, patting them heavily on the shoulders. 'You guys have a good night's sleep tonight and we'll talk again tomorrow. And, Lizzie…' She winked at her and gave a wicked smirk. 'Petriti tomorrow night. Forget everything else for now. No more upset. Let's live a little, huh?'

A hunk and a gentleman? Be still my heart!

Lizzie, Tom, and Aliki walked down the pier. Tom was dressed casually in a t-shirt, shorts and sandals, but the women had dolled themselves up.

Lizzie had an azure strappy evening dress on that reached down to her calves. It had a modest cleavage and accentuated her slender figure. A ribbon of the same colour, stitched with gold thread, was tied in a bow around her narrow waist.

A necklace, matching earrings and a bracelet, all adorned with aquamarine stone, completed her look. Golden sandals with medium-height heels made it a little difficult to walk. She was accustomed to wearing flat shoes so had to make a conscious effort to walk in a straight line. As she did so, she smiled breezily, hoping Stamatis wouldn't notice the trouble she was having.

He was waiting at the end of the pier near his moored boat that was adorned with blue and white ribbons all around its hull, just for the day. When Lizzie stopped before him with a heartfelt greeting, to her surprise, he bowed slightly and took her hand to kiss it.

Lizzie's free hand flew to her chest. *Oh, my! A hunk and a gentleman? Be still my heart!* Just like in a movie that had just started to play in slow motion, his gallant gesture seemed to last forever. She saw his freshly washed hair dance in the cool evening breeze as the feel of his lips, tender like rose petals, warmed her skin and sent arrows of warmth to her inner core. Tiny hairs shivered on the back of his neck in sync with her heart inside.

Finally, he straightened, a relaxed smile playing on his lips. 'It's as if we'd arranged it beforehand!' He tugged on the front of his shirt. 'Look! I'm wearing the same colour as you are.'

Lizzie laughed, feeling herself hover a few inches off the boards under her feet as Stamatis turned to the others. He complimented Aliki for her patterned evening dress. It suited her voluptuous figure to a tee. A fake flower in her long curly hair and a pearl necklace with single pearl earrings completed her look.

Stamatis kissed Aliki's hand, and even though Lizzie wasn't jealous, she began to wonder. *Does he do that with all the lady friends he goes out with in the evening? Or maybe... he only kissed*

Aliki's hand to muddy the waters? Maybe he wanted to kiss my hand but didn't want to show that he did... So kissing Aliki's hand too made kissing my hand something trivial... Is that what he intended?

'Lizzie?' she heard suddenly and gave a start, realizing she'd been staring absently at the distant shoreline. She turned to find them all looking at her. Stamatis, who'd just spoken, gave a titter. 'You okay?'

'Yes, yes...' She pointed to Petriti across the bay. 'Just looking forward to seeing the Varkarola!' She broke into a giggle.

'So, are you ready to go?' he asked them all pointing to the boat.

'What, *now?*' said Aliki, a shadow crossing her face. 'Babis is coming too, isn't he?'

Lizzie exchanged a fleeting glance with her that was full of concern, then darted her eyes to Stamatis hoping he had good news to tell. *Poor Aliki... what if he's not coming?*

Stamatis chortled. 'Oh! You know Babis. Mind like a sieve!'

'He's not coming?' asked Aliki, her lower lip twitching, yet she managed a thin smile.

'No, of course he's coming!' replied Stamatis, putting an end to the poor girl's misery. 'But he only told me that he changed his plans less than an hour ago. He's on his way to Petriti on his motorcycle. Said he had to help the people there with the preparations.' He drew three circles with his index finger next to his ear. 'Babis is the epitome of the *trello-Kerkireos*! A typical batty Corfiot! His mind's all over the place. I'm surprised he remembered to call me as it is, to tell me not to wait for him.'

Aliki chortled at that, then emitted a soft sigh and looked away, smiling brightly at the lush peninsula across the bay where they'd soon he headed.

At the same time, Lizzie and Tom turned away from Stamatis to stifle their sniggers and exchanged a knowing smile.

Stamatis didn't seem to notice any of that and, with a bright smile, clapped his hands together once. 'Right! Ladies first! Come on!'

When Lizzie approached, he offered his hand. 'Hop on!'

Lizzie took his hand and stepped in, then crouched a little as she inched forward to get to the closest available seat. She'd always been unsure on her feet inside small boats. This one wasn't as small as the ones she'd been in before, but it still rocked as she moved.

During that first holiday with her family, they'd often take a tiny rowing boat across the river mouth to walk to the neighbouring village of Moraitika along the shore. And even though the ride across involved a little more than a single move of the oars back and forth, it had always made Lizzie nervous. Tom used to laugh, and now, as he took a seat across from her, he offered her an impish grin. 'You're all right, Lizzie?' He winked, sticking his tongue out.

'You little devil,' she retorted before turning to look at Stamatis again.

With Aliki in the boat too, sitting beside Tom, Stamatis was the last one remaining on the pier. He was now untying the tether so they could depart. He had rolled up his shirt sleeves, revealing the veins on his strong forearms that popped as he pulled the rope. His dark fringe flowed in the breeze, long lashes opening and closing like a butterfly on a flower.

Lizzie pressed her lips together, spellbound by the sight of him. *He is so beautiful! I hope he finds someone new... he'll make her so happy someday. Whoever she is...* Lizzie was still trying to convince herself to let him go. Whether or not they could escape from Phoni, Tom belonged with his family back in England. And duty called her there too. *What was I thinking? But he is so handsome, so unbearably wonderful... Oh! This is so hard!*

Stamatis hopped in with a dashing smile and started the engine and, to the sound of excited chatter, they soon began to sail across the bay to Petriti. The white and blue ribbons around the hull billowed, swirling and flowing in an enchanting dance with the salty spray. On the distant horizon, the sun had started to set, the sparse clouds tinted pink and violet.

The sea was serene like a dark-blue velvet sheet. As the boat cruised along, streaks of silver and gold on the water surface writhed alongside them like playful snakes that raced them to the festival.

❊❊❊❊

Stamatis had taken a seat next to Lizzie. Across from them sat the other two. For a while they'd all fallen silent, captivated by the beauty of their surroundings. He spoke first, turning to her with a look of concern. 'Hey, Lizzie, do you reckon Mandy... the little girl we helped... will be at the festival tonight?'

Lizzie gave a frown, then replied, 'I have no idea. Why do you ask?'

'Elena will be dancing with two other entertainers there tonight to keep the children amused.' He cocked his eye at her. 'She'll be in her mermaid costume...'

Alarm flashed in Lizzie's eyes. Beside her, Tom seemed just as concerned. 'Oh! I hope Mandy won't be there!'

'Well, don't worry, Lizzie. If she's there and she clocks Elena, we'll think of something.'

Lizzie gazed into his eyes for a little while, then said, 'You think of everything... Thank you, Stamatis, for being so thoughtful.'

He gave a little wave. 'Oh, it's all right. It's nothing...'

'No, it's not. You're still looking out for Mandy... Even after that wonderful thing you did for her. Thanks to you that little girl is now healed from her phobia. That is a big thing.'

Tom nodded fiercely, his face bright.

'Yes,' piped up Aliki. 'You've been amazing, Stamatis.'

'Hey, cut it out you three. I'm blushing here!' he said in a mock-protest fashion. They all laughed, then he turned to Lizzie, his expression solemn. 'It was my pleasure to help.'

A comfortable silence ensued for the rest of the short journey. Everyone seemed to enjoy the ride, taking in the stunning beauty of the seascape as the last remnants of sunlight faded around them.

Finally, Petriti came into view, the lush peninsula silhouetted against a darkening sky and illuminated by lights on the buildings, on the coastal road and from the passing cars. The seafront at Petriti seemed whimsical at this hour, causing the girls and Tom to break out in exclamations of delight as the boat approached the shore.

A small crowd was already standing on the beach, even though it was still early for the festival to begin. A scatter of people stood on a large pier where about a dozen boats were moored.

Lizzie let out a gasp of excitement, guessing they had to be the ones taking part in the Varkarola. They were all adorned with fairy lights that twinkled to a magical effect.

Stamatis pointed at the boats as if on cue, saying that they were going to parade along the beach and that the show would end with fireworks.

Tom cheered in response, his face exultant, and Lizzie and Aliki smiled to their ears. They were nearing the pier now and had fallen silent before the alluring spectacle.

The moored boats varied in shape and size but were all suitably lit up. At the very end of the pier head, Stamatis found a free spot to moor his boat. Moments later, they were all hopping onto the pier, Stamatis offering his hand to help the girls. Tom declined the offer and got out unaided, puffing out his chest and smiling brightly when he did so.

While Stamatis tethered the boat, the other three fanned out at the pier head. Chatting excitedly, they admired the boats and the generous vista of the bay while pointing at the strings of twinkling lights at Messonghi, Moraitika, Benitses, and even Corfu town at the far end.

Lizzie had never been to Petriti before. She'd only heard about it. During that first holiday with her family, she'd visited the area of Boukari nearby. They had enjoyed the food and the ambiance in its wonderful fish tavernas more than once. Petriti seemed just as lovely, from what the gathering crowd allowed her to see.

The festive boats looked even more dazzling at close quarters. Stamatis had now joined the others, and they lingered there some more, taking it all in. The hum of the captains and their crew filled the cool evening air.

With every passing minute, darkness continued to engulf everything around them, but the fairy lights allowed them to see comfortably still. Along the coastal road in the distance, street lights, tavernas and shops provided ample light as well. Now that the time was drawing near, people began to arrive in large numbers, parking their cars closely together on both sides of the road.

Lizzie threw her gaze behind the standing crowd on the shore, noticing a scatter of tables and chairs and what looked like a large serving table at one end. A few people milled about there, some holding trays of food. 'What's that over there?' she asked Stamatis, pointing.

'Oh! That's where we're eating after.'

'We're eating on the beach? I thought we were going to have a meal at one of the tavernas here.' She wasn't disappointed, just taken aback.

He chuckled. 'Oh, sorry. When I said earlier on that we were eating on the seafront after, this was actually what I meant. But we can go to a taverna instead, if you prefer. It's just that the council offers free sardines tonight. Salad and wine too. And it's good wine, from my experience.' He winked. 'Shame to miss it.'

'Oh, how wonderful!' said Lizzie, clasping her hands together. 'Let's do that! How generous of the council!'

Her excitement attracted the attention of Aliki and Tom. They'd been standing nearby chatting between themselves all this time.

'What did we miss?' asked Tom, his eyes wandering from one to the other, then back again.

Lizzie relayed what Stamatis had just told her, causing Aliki and Tom to agree that the free offering from the locals sounded too wonderful to miss.

'I love fried sardines!' said Tom licking his lips. We used to have them at Boukari! Remember, Lizzie?'

Lizzie's eyes glinted with alarm, and Tom chewed his lips when he realized what he'd done. He'd been recalling more and more of his early-life memories with every passing day. Sadly, he had the tendency to mention them in the most unfortunate moments.

'I mean... my mother and I... before she went away to England for work... I've told you about that, Lizzie, haven't I?'

He looked so unsettled that Lizzie felt sorry for him but was a little annoyed with him too for being so careless. *Oh, Tom!* Her eyes darted to Stamatis but, luckily, he showed no signs of mystification. 'Yes, I remember you telling me...' she said finally, her panic subsiding.

As for Aliki, she looked amused, if anything, by Tom's mistake, then his awkward attempt to fix it. Lizzie served her brother a meaningful look behind Stamatis's back. He responded with a firm nod and a sheepish look, and she reached out to caress his cheek, his mistake already forgiven.

Aliki's eyes twinkled with mirth to watch the silent interaction between the two siblings. When she turned away, she leaned closer to Stamatis, gave a long exhalation and said, 'You know, I'm fascinated by the number of festivals held around Corfu throughout the year. And free food is offered in so many of them... How generous of the Corfiots!'

'Well, speaking about the Varkarola festival, in particular, it's the least we can do. It commemorates one of our *Agios's* miracles, after all. One of his greatest ones, in fact!'

'*Agios*? Saint? You mean, Saint Spyridon?' asked Aliki.

'Of course. Who else?' Stamatis gave a little wave and smiled.

What miracle do you commemorate today? I'd love to know,' cut in Lizzie.

'Well, this one dates back to the eighteenth century when the Turkish fleet tried to conquer Corfu. During the siege of the town, it is said that Saint Spyridon appeared before a bunch of Turkish military men in a vision. Our Saint was holding a torch, and they were so terrified, spreading the news among the men so fast, that the Turks left the island a few days later.'

'Really?' Lizzie asked as the other two listened, looking equally impressed.

'And that was only one of many visions, I'll have you know.' He took a deep breath and resumed talking, mentioning other legendary sightings of St Spyridon. He looked so charming and spoke with such eloquence that Lizzie could only hang from his lips.

Stamatis carried on, 'On another occasion, our Saint saved the island from a plague that had taken countless lives. Legend has it, that St Spyridon chased the plague away from Corfu and made it swear never to come back. The sign of the cross that the plague made on the Old Fortress wall to swear is still visible today—'

Stamatis's voice was suddenly drowned out by Aliki's high-pitched squeal. They all turned to follow her gaze to find Babis rushing towards them.

'Hi there!' he said when he stood before them, bright and breezy. He was dressed similarly to Stamatis – in a white shirt and dark jeans. He put his arms around Aliki first, kissing her on both cheeks, the Greek way, then did the same with Lizzie. He smelled of musk and lemon, very pleasant.

Lizzie exchanged a surreptitious glance with Aliki to find her rolling her eyes dreamily, her cheeks flushed pink. Babis and Stamatis were chatting with Tom at the time.

A little later, Aliki struck up a conversation with them all, but Lizzie soon turned away to saunter further down the pier on her own. It was quieter there, her mind returning to the Saint Spyridon stories Stamatis had just shared.

A heartbeat later, it seemed, she felt a warm hand on her forearm and turned to find Stamatis looking at her with a crooked grin. 'Hey, what's up? I didn't bore you out of your head earlier with my old tales, did I? I do apologise!' He pointed at her in a mock-accusing fashion. 'But I blame you, missy. You should never ask a Corfiot to talk about St Spyridon unless you're prepared for a long speech!'

Lizzie gave a giggle and waved away the absurd notion that he had bored her. She was fascinated, if anything. Whether these stories were true or not, it seemed that Corfu wasn't new to lore about apparitions and supernatural events. *This blessed island of breathtaking beauty surely entails much more than meets the eye...*

'Hey, I mean it! Chin up, or I'll have to apologise for my badly timed local legends!' This time he nudged her, his eyes crinkled at the edges, the way she remembered from when they were kids.

Caught in the moment, she smiled and patted his upper arm. It felt so muscly, like a concrete wall, and she removed her hand as if electricity had hit her. *Oh, Stamatis... it was never meant to be...*

She looked away, composed herself with a steadying breath, and turned back to him to say, 'Aw, don't be silly. I loved your local legends, thank you...' She turned away again, the sight of his laughing eyes too tantalizing to bear, and noticed a few youngsters dressed in traditional Corfiot costumes. They looked resplendent.

She gave a gasp, then heard Stamatis say, 'Great! Our folklore dancers are here! The Varkarola is about to start!'

'Dancers? How wonderful!' chimed in Aliki, who arrived with the others to join them. She stood closely with Babis, her fluttering eyelashes forever turning to meet his own eager gaze.

They all fell silent for a while, admiring the folklore dancers in their colourful costumes. They were huddled together talking to one of the captains. The men looked charming enough in their black-and-white vests, black baggy breeches and straw hats, but the girls were a true beauty to behold.

The colours of the girls' traditional attire varied largely among them, but they were all a marvel of red and black velvet, golden-threaded vests, ornate jewellery, and lace. Their headdresses stole the show, though, as they bore an orgy of colourful flowers that framed their young jovial faces perfectly.

All of a sudden, a captain shouted out something that caused a big commotion on the pier. A din rose in the air as the folklore dancers got separated into small groups and began to get on the boats. Then, a few guitar and mandolin players arrived from the beach in a rush to hop on the boats as well.

Stamatis checked his watch. 'We're in the way here, everybody! Let's join the crowd on the shore. The Varkarola's about to start!'

Stick with the Greeks. You'll be all right!

Standing at the edge of the shore amidst the crowd and waiting for the Varkarola to begin made Lizzie so thrilled she felt tingly all over. Shrouded by the semi-darkness, only with the street and shop lights far behind her for illumination, Lizzie admired the wondrous sight before her. The shallows were dotted with floating candles. Their feeble lights flickered in the breeze, the sea almost perfectly still.

High up in the sky the waxing moon was nearly full, tinted dark orange. Its gentle light caressed the sea, setting it alight in the far distance with a mesmerizing liquid fire.

The sea murmured gently in Lizzie's ears, and it was easy to hear it since it was so quiet; so many people stood hushed to silence around her, equally enchanted. As for those who had something to say, they chose to whisper it, so as not to break the spell.

A man shouted something in Greek from the pier and then, the first boat began to move away from it to float gently towards the crowd. The nostalgic chords of a mandolin echoed from the boat, and the crowd fell perfectly quiet to listen.

One of the two mandolin players standing on the prow broke into song. His melodic voice, strong vibrato, and the sweetness of the music caused a thunderous applause to rise from the shore as the boat began to float past.

On the stern, sat a single firework that emitted a sparkling red light and smoke, causing frantic clicking from people's cameras. Just as the firework began to fade away, the boat drifted past the edge of the crowd where it seemed to come to a stop.

Now, only its twinkling fairy lights overhead illuminated it, and it looked so quaint against the dark sky that many among the spectators raised their cameras and phones to capture the scene.

When the last chords of the mandolin song faded away, the people erupted into cheers and applause, and some of the locals, who obviously knew the singer, shouted out words of praise and whistled to him. In return, the man smiled to his ears, patting his chest and offering thanks as the boat began to turn around, then floated past again on its way back to the pier.

As soon as all that had ended, a second boat approached. This one was much larger than the first one and, other than its captain, it also carried three men and one woman, who wore traditional outfits. The men were playing their guitars, and the woman accompanied them with an exquisite singing voice. It echoed in the air in a perfect, smooth legato, her face dreamy, eyes closed, as she gave it her all.

It was the kind of singing you'd happily pay to enjoy in a concert hall and was so sensational it brought shivers down Lizzie's spine. Overwhelmed, she threw a fleeting look on either side of her to find her friends and Tom looking at the boat, equally transfixed, their faces serene, eyes glazed over.

The spectacle and even more fine singing continued with the rest of the boats coming up in line slowly. All of them looked whimsical in the semidarkness, their lights illuminating the surface of the water with streaks of yellow, red and orange.

People clapped, whooped and squealed with elation every time a song ended. Some of the locals, from what Stamatis explained, teased their friends on the boats, resulting in short bursts of banter shooting back and forth between the boats and the shore. Uproarious laughter occasionally erupted on both sides, rising into the air to drift in the salty breeze.

When all the boats had floated past, and as the last two made their way slowly back to the pier, an impressive display of fireworks filled the sky and people erupted into cheers and audible gasps.

Lizzie marvelled at the beautiful starbursts that exploded in the sky with silver, gold and red tendrils. As for the rockets, they rendered her speechless; some of them whistled on their way up, and others burst into stunning displays with rainbow effects in many different colours. All she could do was hold her brother closely to her, an arm around his shoulders, and try to swallow the huge lump that had lodged in her throat as she looked at his exultant little face.

They laughed together and took turns in pointing to the sky, making excited sounds, and gasping with wonder. It felt wonderful to share these fun moments with her brother for a change, after all this upset. The recent memory of him locking her in the apartment to go offer himself to Phoni and save her crept up in her mind, but she pushed it aside.

Lizzie squeezed Tom's shoulder with feeling and resumed making happy sounds, losing herself in a time and a place where there was just she and Tom, making a truly happy memory together, as siblings were meant to do.

So lost was she in those moments that when she heard Stamatis's voice her shoulders jumped.

'Lizzie, are we eating here on the beach? You're still all right with that?'

She turned to find Aliki and Babis were standing beside him, waiting for her answer too. Before she could speak, Tom wiggled out of her embrace and squealed with delight. 'Sardines! Yummy!'

Lizzie gave him a sweet smile, then Stamatis pointed behind her. 'It's over there, Lizzie!'

She spun around to find that only a few people were left standing on the beach. Craning her neck to look in the distance, she grimaced against the glare of the floodlights put up at the seating area on the sand and raised a hand to protect her eyes. 'Oh! I see it, yes...' she mumbled even though she could hardly make out the tables against the strong light. Yet, from the din of the crowd it was evident that they were filling up fast.

She faced the others and beckoned. 'It looks great! Let's go!' All together, they sauntered towards the tables and sat at a vacant one by the coastal road. Being plastic and white, the tables and chairs were the typical garden furniture everyone seemed to use on the island in balconies and yards, and even in some hotels.

After a few moments, Babis slapped himself on the forehead and jolted upright. 'Oh! Stupid! Back soon!' he said, without offering an explanation, then hurried towards the edge of the seating area where the large serving table was. A couple of local women stood there frying sardines and serving them in large platters. About two dozen people had formed a queue there waiting to get served.

Lizzie turned to Stamatis, who'd taken a seat beside her, much to her delight. 'Should we go and join the queue?'

He made a patting gesture in mid-air with his hand. '*Siga-siga...* No need to hurry. Let everyone go and have their plate of food first. They got tons of it. We'll go when it's less crowded over there.' His eyes lit up and he gave a playful grin before adding, 'Why stand when we can sit, huh?'

Everyone made sounds that suggested his logic made sense, and Lizzie cast her gaze towards the serving area again to find that, within seconds, the people waiting to be served had almost doubled in number. Plus, some locals were trying to jump the queue and a quarrel had broken out. 'I see what you mean,' said Lizzie with a little laugh.

Stamatis tapped his temple three times with an index finger and gave an irresistible smile. 'Stick with the Greeks. You'll be all right.' He winked, then gave a charming smile, and she lost herself as she gazed into his face. Once again, he'd reminded her of the little boy he once was. Behind the beard, she imagined he'd be looking just the same. *Who knows? I might get to see him clean-shaven before I leave the island. I hope to have this little treat at least...* she thought with a twinge from her heart.

A young girl approached with a breezy greeting, snapping Lizzie out of her reverie. She carried a dozen or so small wine glasses on a tray. She placed one before every adult at the table, and Aliki raised a hand to ask for an extra one for Babis. He was still out of sight behind the crowd.

A teenage boy approached the table just as the young girl turned away. Holding a large carton of wine with its own spout he filled all the glasses.

Lizzie took some change out of her purse and gave it to Tom to get a juice from one of the shops lining the road, then turned to the other two and raised her glass to meet theirs.

Tom made to go to buy the refreshment but then plonked himself back down on his chair. He nudged Lizzie on the arm and smiled wickedly. 'Food's coming now. I'll go later!'

Right on cue, Babis materialized through the mass of people who came and went around them. He was holding a plastic plate, which he set down on the table with a ceremonial gesture. 'I see you got me a glass, thanks!' He toasted to everyone's health and took a few gulps, then gave a little sigh. 'Oh, that was nice. Now, look what I got you all! Courtesy of my Aunt Voula. Help yourselves!'

The plate was full and consisted of two different kinds of Greek delicacies. One of them Lizzie could easily identify. 'Oh!

Dolmadakia!' she said and took one of them, taking a bite. The rice filling was soft and minty, the vine leaves it was wrapped in tasted divine, the tang of lemon so delicious she could almost feel her pallet emit a silent "thank you". *Oh, what a treat!* Until now she hadn't realized how famished she was.

'Yum! Delicious!' she said, then noticed everyone else was eating, each one lost in their own sense of bliss that was equal to hers, it seemed. All of them were rolling their eyes and making appreciative sounds as they munched. Tom was eating a pastry, his eyes closed. A long-winded "mmm" sound emitted from his person as he chewed.

'Are these spinach pies?' she asked him when she thought she saw a spot of green in the filling.

Tom snapped his eyes open and nodded. '*Spanakopitakia*, yes.'

'Go on, try them! Aunt Voula's *spanakopitakia* are the best!' said Babis and she obliged him, now making the same kind of noises as Tom.

'That's why Babis came to Petriti on his own,' said Stamatis with a bright smile as he leaned closer to Lizzie. 'He'd promised his auntie to come early and help her carry her roasting tins of *spanakopitakia* from her house to here.'

Aliki turned to Babis, her eyes twinkling. 'Oh, how kind of you to help your auntie!' She reached out and squeezed his arm gently.

Babis, who sat beside her, leaned towards her in response, a sweet smile on his lips.

Lizzie brought a hand over her mouth and chuckled. *These two are crazy for each other!*

'And the *dolmadakia*? Who made these?' asked Tom.

'Oh! That's another local lady. But she's a friend of my aunt's so I helped her carry her tray over here too. That's why they let me take a full plate and bring it to you.' Babis tittered, then his face ignited with mock-dread as he pointed in the direction of the serving area. 'A word of warning! Never mess with these ladies. They are watching the platters with hawk eyes. Try to jump the queue and get to the food earlier and your wrist will be slapped faster than you can say *Pastitsada!*'

The others burst out laughing but he wasn't finished. He raised a finger, pointed it to himself and sat up straighter in his chair. 'But you got me, guys, so never fear! These elderly ladies love me…

You'll all eat well tonight!' He winked at Aliki first, then Lizzie, and began to chortle, causing everyone to join him.

Just then, the sweet sound of a *bouzouki* rose in the air, catching everyone's attention. They all turned to the opposite side to find that three musicians had taken seats there. Two *bouzoukis* and a *baglamas* began to echo melodically as a woman opened her mouth to sing, shaking a tambourine in hand.

It was as if the moment had signalled the beginning of the feast. Many of the people who had been standing all this time chatting to friends and family moved to settle in their seats to enjoy their meals and the music.

Lizzie took another *dolmadaki* and sat back in her seat to enjoy it as sweet melodies of music and laughter reached her ears.

Oh, sorry! Wasn't I supposed to eat that?

The food had almost disappeared from the plate. Only a *dolmadaki* and a *spanakopitaki* remained.

Stamatis pointed at the food. 'Go on, girls. We guys have to be gentlemen, no matter how hungry. It's only fair that you have the last two.'

Lizzie and Aliki looked at each other, smiling. 'I don't mind, Lizzie, you choose!'

Lizzie didn't have to think. She was about to go for the *dolmadaki* when a hand materialized from over her head and grabbed it before she could. Startled, she turned back in her seat to find Nia looming over her, two oily fingers hovering before her lips as she chomped.

Lizzie squinted her eyes and willed herself to act civil. That wasn't nice, barging over here, stealing that. It was only a bit of food, of course, but just how rude was she?

'Oh, sorry! Wasn't I supposed to eat that?' said Nia, a rigid hand hovering over her mouth in obvious mock-embarrassment. Her heavily made up eyes wandered to all the faces around the table in quick succession.

Babis was the only one to respond, albeit rather numbly. 'It's okay, Nia. I can get more for everybody. No harm done.' He smiled then, a frozen smile that Lizzie had never seen on his face before. It filled her with satisfaction to see she obviously wasn't the only one who disapproved of what Nia had done.

Nia gave a little laugh. 'Oh good. From the look on your faces, it seemed to me for a moment that I had spoiled your evening.'

'No, of course you haven't, Nia,' mumbled Babis but kept his eyes on the table this time.

Right then, Elena came over to the table. She was dressed in her mermaid costume, just like Stamatis had said.

'Hi! I didn't know you'd all be here!' She slapped Stamatis's arm playfully. 'You didn't tell me!'

Stamatis gave an easy smile, and Lizzie guessed from their body language that they were good friends.

Elena turned to everyone and smiled. 'So, how are you, guys?' she said brightly, a vision of blue eyes, pearly whites, satin, and sequins.

'I love your costume,' Aliki told her after everyone had exchanged a few words with her. Everyone but Nia. From the sour look on her face, it was evident that she didn't really like Elena.

Lizzie couldn't believe her eyes. *Is there a woman Nia actually likes? God!*

'Thank you!' said Elena to Aliki with an amicable smile. 'I am here for the kids tonight...' She pointed at the far end of the seating area where a large oblong table stood. A dozen or so children were sitting there eating, a man dressed like Poseidon, plastic trident in hand, sitting with them. He was pulling faces, heavily gesticulating, making them giggle.

'Good old Poseidon and I are doing a sketch for the kids tonight, then we'll all be dancing together.' Elena turned to Tom. 'Come on over a little later! I'll make sure to find you a dancing partner.' She winked at him, and before he could respond everyone began to tease him.

Tom smiled but avoided Elena's eyes. 'Thanks, we shall see. I may come if it looks like fun...'

Lizzie could tell he was embarrassed, in a typically boyish way, which she found cute, so she cut in to change the subject, for his sake. 'It's wonderful, what you do, Elena, working with the kids—'

She was interrupted suddenly by Nia, who tipped back her chin and cackled.

Everyone turned to her, startled, and she eyed them with disdain.

'You've all turned out to be one fine little group of friends, haven't you? And it all seems to have started with *you*, Lizzie!' She ended her sentence with a screech, then a huff.

Lizzie gave a deep frown. 'Excuse me?'

'You heard! You've come here to stay and...' she twirled a hand in the air, her face scrunched up, 'You think I can't see? Just what are you doing here Lizzie?' She leaned forward, looming over her, her features pinched. 'What were you doing the other day getting Stamatis to leave my apartments so he can participate in one of your silly stunts, huh?'

'What silly stunt?' interjected Stamatis, putting out an arm to land it along the back of Lizzie's chair, like a border between the two women.

Lizzie realized he was protecting her, taking her side. It caused her heart to melt, but for now, she had more pressing matters to face. Staying in her seat, she willed herself to remain calm. 'What on earth are you talking about, Nia?'

But Nia ignored her. Instead, she pinned her eyes on Stamatis. 'You know what I mean, Stamatis! You and Elena on the boat parading in her mermaid costume. Huh!' She put one hand on her hip and pointed sharply to Lizzie with the other. 'To please her royal highness over here and that little girl she befriended.'

In the ensuing silence, everyone looked appalled and lost for words. Lizzie struggled for something to say, but her mind drew blank in the face of such rudeness, such impropriety. *Where to start? No social graces whatsoever. What a psycho!*

Aliki spoke first, her eyes alight with indignation. 'What's wrong with you, Nia? Why can't you be nice for a change?'

'Me? Are you serious? If there's someone that should play nice, then that's your dear friend over here!' she retorted, pointing at Lizzie again with a rigid index finger, her manicured scarlet nail glinting under the strong lights. Next, she pointed at Aliki in the same manner and added, 'And don't you think I don't know that you two have been talking nastily behind my back!'

Before Aliki could respond, Lizzie jerked upright, the faint rustle of the chair legs that dragged through the sand sounding too small a protest for the magnitude of her fury. She put a hand on her waist and took her turn to point a finger. 'Now look here! I haven't done anything wrong. How dare you come here and spoil our fun?'

Nia took a step back and began to sneer.

Stamatis stood too, putting up his hands before his chest. He offered a pleading look to Lizzie, mouthing to her that it was okay. Then, he turned to Nia, his features hardening. 'I say you go now, Nia. And if there are any grievances you have with me personally, for leaving my work at Pitsilos for a little while to do a pressing favour for a friend, then you can let me know next time I visit you, okay?'

'I have no grievances with you,' she said coldly, avoiding his eyes, and only glancing at him for a moment, her jaw set.

'Well, whoever you have a problem with, you'll need to discuss it with them at another, more appropriate time. As Lizzie said... you're spoiling a fun evening. I suggest you leave.' He reached out and held Lizzie's shoulder.

Lizzie's mind whirled. Even though the tender touch of his flesh on her skin felt amazing, rendering her disoriented, she managed to register a momentary scowl on Nia's face. It was directed straight at her.

Nia smiled coldly, then turned around and beckoned to someone from a far table. It was a tall man in his thirties that Lizzie hadn't seen before. He rose readily from his seat, giving the impression that he'd been watching all this time, waiting for Nia to call him over.

Standing tall and walking loosely, smoothly, the way only a perfectly fit, athletic body like his could muster, he approached to stand by Nia, his honey brown eyes sparkling, a broad smile across his face.

He was dark-skinned and dashing, dressed in a white shirt and pants, the fabric of the shirt flimsy, almost see-through. Lizzie could swear she could see his pecs rippling across his chest as he approached just then.

His hair, raven-black and well-gelled, glistened under the electric lights, a long fringe reaching down to his long thick lashes.

Lizzie fell silent, captivated by the guy's striking beauty. He looked like a model from those aesthetically perfect, Italian perfume adverts filmed in the Mediterranean. But even though her stunned response was to be expected, Lizzie couldn't understand why Stamatis and Babis looked so lost for words in the long, awkward silence that hung in the air.

All at once, Nia struck a pose of elegance and spoke excitedly to make introductions as if her awkward exchange with the others had never happened earlier.

'This is Tassos, everyone. An old friend of mine. Some of you may know him, of course.' Her eyes darted to Stamatis for a split second, then back to the others. 'He's been living here for a few years, after all.' Towards the end, her voice took on a strange, almost daunting tone.

She clung to Tassos as if she owned him, and he smiled pleasantly, an irresistible grin that brought a shower of stars to dance before Lizzie's eyes. Still, he seemed the type who knew exactly how much charm he possessed and how to use it.

Lizzie turned to her friends to find that all of them, except Elena and Tom, seemed numb. Actually, the other three didn't appear to know where to look, their eyes darting all over the place. Anywhere seemed to be a good place to look except at Nia and Tassos.

To her further mystification, Stamatis, who still stood beside her, had turned into a pillar of stone. His features had hardened, brow deeply furrowed, head hung low. *What's that all about? Unless... Unless, he fancies Nia, after all, and he's jealous? No, it can't be that!*

Tassos, who had been smiling, undeterred, despite the reaction from the others, sought refuge in Lizzie's open smile when she politely offered her hand. *No reason to be rude to him just because he's friends with Nia.* It was clear her friends knew him, just didn't seem to welcome his company, for some reason. No doubt, Aliki would tell her all about it later.

Tassos began to chat to Lizzie and Tom ignoring the others. He mentioned he was from Athens and had lived in Messonghi for over a decade, declaring it his home.

Nia cut in then to point out that he was a single man, a popular bachelor, and that it would be one lucky girl to tie the knot with him someday. As she said these words, she rolled her eyes and laced her hands around his muscly arm.

Lizzie had a quick scan around; the looks on the others' faces told her they felt just as nauseous as she did. They had even turned away by then, facing each other, every so often mumbling something in hushed tones.

Finally, seeing that no one invited them to sit down with them, Nia announced they were going to queue for their meal. She looped her arm ceremoniously around Tassos's, and they turned on their heels to walk away.

As soon as they were gone, a collective sigh emanated from Elena, Babis, and Aliki. The last two exchanged a mute glance, their spirits dampened. As for Stamatis, he sat down numbly and began to play with his fork on the table.

When Elena left to return to the kids, an awkward silence set in among the five until Babis suggested that he and Aliki go to get plates for everybody. Aliki accepted gladly, urging Tom to come along.

When Stamatis and Lizzie remained alone at the table, she didn't know what to do with herself. He still seemed uncomfortable somehow, his head hung low, shoulders slumped, a deep frown on his face as he played with his fork.

'Hey... are you okay?' she asked in a whisper.

He raised his head and, when he looked at her, his eyes seemed vacant and clouded over. 'Yes, sorry...' He brought a hand to his forehead and rubbed hard, then swept his hair backwards with an urgent hand. 'People on this island can be toxic. I keep forgetting that...'

Lizzie chuckled, despite herself. She leaned towards him. 'Toxic? Whatever do you mean? Do you mean... Nia? Don't let her get to you. I don't.'

He turned to her, his eyes intense, penetrating hers deeply. 'Lizzie, it's not that simple for me. There are things... things that...' He shook his head and looked away. 'Oh, nothing. Just ignore me.'

The others returned quickly enough with the food, and everyone began to eat, chomping appreciatively on the selection of bite-sized treats on their plates. Other than the familiar *dolmadakia* and *spanakopitakia*, every plate had a generous serving of fried sardines with salad as well.

'Eat up!' said Babis. 'Aunt Voula has already started frying the *loukoumades*. We don't want to go there last!'

'What's that?' asked Tom.

'Dough balls covered in honey syrup,' offered Aliki, causing Tom to start chewing even faster, eyes dancing.

Lizzie listened to this exchange trying to seem as happy as possible and, all the while, watching Stamatis. He was eating, but didn't seem to enjoy it and when Babis gave him an encouraging look, he didn't seem to acknowledge him. It was evident to all by now that his spirits had plummeted since Nia and Tassos came over. And it seemed to Lizzie that the others knew what the reason for that was.

She and Tom were the only ones who didn't know, and her mind whirled as she tried to guess but nothing made sense. She still believed it couldn't be because he fancied Nia and perceived Tassos as an antagonist. The way he had talked to her earlier strongly suggested he didn't care for her much. So maybe, it was Tassos's presence that had upset him... Could it be that they had differences of some sort? But Tassos hadn't seemed annoyed with Stamatis at all. He had offered smiles to them all, including him.

The enigma still tortured her, and when Stamatis reached out and touched her hand, she realized her food was gone. His plate, on the other hand, was almost full still. He'd hardly touched it.

'Lizzie...' she heard faintly and turned to look at him. His expression was sombre, eyes misted over with deep sadness.

Startled, she waited for him to speak and leaned over a little to get closer. The live music was deafening. People were dancing to *syrtaki* music and singing along, and it was hard to talk and be heard.

Stamatis opened his mouth a little, hesitated, then leaned over too and whispered in her ear, 'Would you like to go for a walk with me?'

She nodded eagerly, and he announced that they were going to have a little stroll down the seafront, to be back soon. Babis suggested they go after they'd had some *loukoumades*, but Stamatis gave a dim smile and said they wouldn't be long.

They turned away from the table, and Stamatis led her around the cluster of tables to their right, and not on a straight line to the beach, past the one where Nia sat with Tassos and a few others.

Lizzie realized why they went around but didn't comment on it. She also noticed that Nia kept staring at them across the distance, her features pinched with something that bordered on malice. *Has she been watching us all this time since she left?*

Tossing her hair back and tipping her chin, Lizzie looked away from Nia and turned her focus on Stamatis again, the gorgeous man who made her heart sing. *Why should Nia matter? She doesn't...*

She followed him through the tables as he made his way to the beach. She was thrilled that he'd asked her to be alone together with him and hoped he would help her understand why he'd become so upset.

As soon as they left the din of the feast behind them, their senses were soothed by the quiet, and the beauty of the night.

Walking along the shore, they could hear the susurrus of the sea and, as they distanced themselves from the strong lights, the sky began to reveal a breathtaking tapestry of twinkling stars.

A lunatic, in a rabbit-stewing kind of way

They walked side-by-side without touching, quietly, just taking it all in, enjoying the serenity. He seemed deep in thought so she waited.

When they reached the pier they hopped onto it to saunter to the end. The sea breeze picked up, caressing their faces. The boats of the Varkarola, vacant now, floated in the semidarkness. Gentle plopping sounds echoed from the boats, and the pillars underneath, as feeble waves came into shore.

Halfway to the end of the pier Stamatis stopped and turned to her, gazing into her eyes.

Lizzie returned his gaze, her mind still full of questions. Only the waxing moon illuminated his face that looked pale. In his eyes, she saw sadness but tenderness too.

As if he guessed her bewilderment, he raised a hand and rubbed his temple, lips twitching. 'I'm sorry for being so enigmatic, Lizzie. I'm not usually like that. Oh, God...' He swiped his face downwards with a cupped hand, then looked up at the moon.

Lizzie took a step forward. 'Whatever it is that's troubling you, you can talk to me. I won't tell anyone, Stamatis. I will listen, if it helps.'

'Thank you, Lizzie. It means the world to me that you're offering to listen to my troubles...'

'Hey... that's what friends are for,' she said, following him down the pier.

He turned and eyed her with sorrow. 'Friends?'

'Yes... yes, of course,' she said, pretending she hadn't perceived his frustration. She knew he wanted her. But she had already made her difficult decision. It wasn't right to give him hope.

He let out a laborious sigh when they reached the spot where his boat was moored. 'Do you want to sit in the boat and talk, or are you happy to walk a little more?'

'I think I've eaten a lot.' She patted her stomach. 'I could use a walk down the beach, if that's okay.'

He smiled faintly and gestured to her to follow him back to the sand. As they began to walk along the edge of the shore he made a joke that she was so skinny she'd still stay the same if she were to eat the whole stock of *loukoumades* at the elderly ladies' serving table.

His face brightened with gaiety, and her heart leapt. She slapped his chest with a playful hand, about to tease him, but his reaction was quick and silenced her before she could speak.

Stamatis captured her hand in his, then did the same with her eyes. 'Oh, Lizzie... If only I could tell you all my secrets...'

She tilted her head, her voice soft. 'Why don't you?'

'You've come here for a holiday, not to hear my sad stories.'

His look strayed from her and, as they continued walking, he loosened his grip on her hand, about to let it go, but she clutched his this time, the urgency in the gesture causing him to stop walking and face her.

'Hey!' she said as they locked eyes together, 'You think I'm here for a good time? Believe me, what I'm experiencing in Messonghi is anything but! Things are not always what they seem, Stamatis.'

'Still... You're here today and gone tomorrow. Sadly, I am stuck here, forever, it seems. Here, in a place where I am not allowed to ever forget my past. My pain, my losses...'

'You've lost your wife, and I'm sure it hurts... but in time, you will heal... Hang in there.'

'I am not talking about my wife. Well, not *just* about my wife, Lizzie. There are people here who will never let me forget...'

'Forget, what?'

'Oh, it doesn't matter... It's too painful to discuss. Too bloody ugly.'

'Then, I don't understand. Why did you bring me here? You said you wanted to talk to me. What do you want to talk about?'

He looked at her, the sadness lifting, as he emitted a huge sigh. In the short silence that hung between them, the murmur of the sea lapping on the shore by their feet amplified. The only other sound was the distant echo of *bouzouki* music from the festival.

'Well?' she finally asked, still lost in his eyes.

'I just wanted to explain about Nia. She and I... well, we had a thing a few years back. Before I was married. But she acted all weird on me. I dumped her, not because I'd found someone else, but because she cheated on me. Besides, she was just too clingy, you know? Bordering on besotted, to be exact.' He rolled his eyes.

'And I don't think she ever got over me, to tell you the truth. I thought I'd explain it to you. You must be wondering why she seems to be so weird. It's because in the recesses of her twisted, cra-cra mind, she seems to think we're still an item.'

'You're not then?' asked Lizzie. It was a joke and she smiled wickedly to make it clear.

In the semidarkness, he probably hadn't seen her expression clearly, because he put up a furious hand, the other still holding hers, and began to wave it before her eyes.

'Oh no! God forbid. That woman is a lunatic, in a rabbit-stewing kind of way.' He winked and they laughed out loud together.

'Poor Nia!' said Lizzie, and they resumed walking, now hand-in-hand.

'Yes. And she can hope all she wants, you know? I just put up with her.'

'But you work for her. Are you sure you're not leading her on?' she teased.

'Yeah! I bet in her batty mind my turning up for work whenever she calls equals saying yes to a date.'

She cocked her eye at him and tittered. 'You think?'

'Oh please don't laugh, it's not funny! She's really started to annoy me.'

'So why do you do it?'

'Why do I, what?'

'Turn up for work when she asks.'

'It's not easy to turn her down, Lizzie. I wish I earned more money so I didn't have to.'

'Yes, I guess that makes sense...'

His eyes lit up when he added, 'But I do hope to be able to open the family guest house again someday... You know, if I ever manage to have a family again, so to speak...' He made air quotes with his free hand when he said "family" and chuckled.

Lizzie saw something warm and tender, like liquid chocolate, melt in his eyes. And even though it called to her, loud and clear, she decided to pretend it had evaded her. She was holding his hand still, but that meant nothing. That was just her being there for a troubled friend; that was all... Or, at least, that's how she justified it to herself. In the end, she looked away and said, 'Sounds good...'

'Yes. Back to the family business. Be my own boss. That's the plan.'

'I wish it for you, Stamatis. You deserve happiness.'

'Thank you...'

Lizzie stopped suddenly and threw her head back. 'Oh, what a beautiful night! Just look at the stars...'

'Yes, yes... very beautiful...' she heard. When she looked down again though, she found him looking into her face, not at the sky.

'What are you doing, Stamatis? The sky's that way,' she teased, a finger pointing above.

He leaned closer, the look in his eyes deepening. 'Oh that may very well be so, but when it comes to beauty, I'm fine with what I'm looking at, thank you.'

Without thinking, she stepped back and slapped his wrist. 'Hey. Stop teasing. We're friends, remember?' She pointed over her shoulder. 'You don't want Miss Fatal Attraction to hear you say things like that!'

To her surprise, he placed his free hand on her shoulder and leaned in, too close for comfort. By the time she'd realized he wasn't going to stop she had frozen. All she could do was bat her eyelashes, unbelieving, until his lips, warm and tender like silk, touched her own in a passionate kiss. Lost in the rapture of their embrace she lost all sense of time and space as his kiss set her body on fire. *Oh, God... no, no, no... This can't be happening!* Still, she couldn't resist it, and her hands, both free now, gripped the shirt fabric on his back as she clung against him.

They pulled back at the same time. He seemed just as breathless as she was, his chest heaving, eyes dancing, mouth half-open as he gasped for air.

'Oh Lizzie...' he murmured, placing a hand behind her head, drawing her closer for another kiss.

Lizzie felt limp as his strong arms squeezed her against him again, her body set ablaze with passion. His lips, hot and wanting, pressed against hers and, at the end of their kiss, he caught her bottom lip and tugged teasingly. He delivered an ever-so-soft bite before releasing it, shooting warm arrows of desire down to the pit of her stomach.

By the time he'd pulled back, Lizzie felt so lightheaded she was thankful his arms were still holding her tight in case she lost her balance and fell.

'Wow...' she managed with difficulty, then stared into his eyes.

He issued a wicked grin. 'My thoughts exactly.' He caressed her cheek, then smoothed her hair. 'Do you know for how long I've been meaning to do that?'

'How long?'

He gave a lopsided smile. 'Since the day I fixed your bathtub.'

'Really?'

'Yes... and you? If you wanted to kiss me, that is...'

'Me? Yes... I...' Lizzie moved away and resumed ambling down the beach. She couldn't think clearly. This had been wonderful but it was a mistake. He had complicated things. She'd been prepared to abandon all her hopes for a romance. Because, what was the point anyway? But he'd kissed her and... *Oh, God, what do I do now?*

He hurried to her side to saunter alongside her, gesticulating frantically. 'Lizzie? What is it? I thought what just happened was—'

'Amazing.'

'Yes. That's what it was. So, what's wrong? I don't understand.'

She stopped walking and gave a soft sigh. 'Oh, Stamatis... Can't we just be friends? I can't have any more complications in my life right now.'

He put a hand on her arm and sought her eyes. 'But I don't expect you to do anything, Lizzie. I don't expect you to stay here forever. I know you'll want to go home at some point. I understand. But... while you're here, can we just experience this?'

He took her hands in his and brought them to his lips for a tender kiss. Holding them still, he gazed into her face, his eyes melting with adoration. 'You are... the best thing that's happened to me in a long time, Lizzie! Ever since you came back, ever since I saw you... You changed everything for me! Everything! I'd been hoping for so long to get closer to you. And I know you want me too... Please don't deny it. If you do, I'll know you're lying. I felt it in your kiss. You want me as much as I want you.'

Lizzie raised her brows. 'Want? Is that what this is?'

'Can I tell you the truth?'

'Yes. I expect nothing less of you.'

'Then I'm going to be totally honest with you, Lizzie. I love you. There it is, I've said it. I love you. In fact, I'm crazy about you! Since I saw you again it's been impossible to get you out of my mind... And tonight, what just happened between us, it's made me the happiest man in the world. But if you don't love me, just say it. If it's just lust for you, I'll still take it. I want you, Lizzie. No strings attached.'

She'd been staring, unbelieving, while he spoke. Now that he'd stopped, she felt lost for words. Somehow, she found her voice to ask, 'You love me? But why me? I don't understand.'

He let go of her hands and raked his hair furiously for a few moments. Then, he pulled her gently to him to say, 'Because you've made me feel alive again, Lizzie. Since Kiki died I never thought it would be possible again. But you made it happen. With your sweetness, your beauty, your intelligence, your kind heart. I love everything about you! For years on end, I've been feeling so alone... And I've only been feeling worse by bumping all the time into the same nasty people who reminded me...' He shook his head, his voice trailing off.

She placed a gentle hand on his chest. It felt warm under the fabric of his shirt, his heart beating fast. 'What nasty people? And what did they remind you of? Sorry, I'm not with you.' She sought his eyes.

'Oh never mind! It doesn't matter... Nothing of that matters any more.' He took her hand and squeezed it in his, his eyes brimming over with feeling when he met her gaze. 'So what's it going to be? Will you have me as your man, Lizzie? For however short or long that might be?'

Lizzie felt the warmth of his hand, and his pleading expression was impossible to resist. She wanted, *needed* to believe that, somehow, she could get rid of Phoni. Then maybe, just maybe, she might be able to live even a short romance with Stamatis. He had said she made him feel alive. He certainly had done the same for her too.

She owed herself that much – to feel alive again, even for a little while, especially if fate planned to be cruel to her in the near future again. Love, no matter how short-lived, is hard to ignore when it comes knocking.

With that last thought in mind, Lizzie tipped her chin and gave Stamatis a sweet smile that was so full of happiness he got the message.

With a squeal of delight, he took her in his arms and lifted her high off the ground. Then, bringing her back down slowly, he kissed her tenderly, the sea sighing at their feet as their hearts swelled with feeling.

I got a mouth on me. But I got a fist too

Lizzie and Stamatis returned to the table hand-in-hand, faces beaming, to find only Tom sitting there. When he saw them holding hands he gave an impish smirk.

As soon as they sat, Stamatis moved his chair closer to Lizzie's. He put an arm around her and sighed with relish before saying, 'Where are Babis and Aliki? Are they dancing?' He turned his gaze to the dancing crowd and squinted. 'I can't see them.'

Tom rolled his eyes and leaned closer so they could hear him over the loud music. 'They went to the beach for a walk to find you two.' He raised a single brow. 'That's what they said anyway.'

'Oh!' said Lizzie. She and Stamatis exchanged a knowing smile and burst into titters.

Tom twisted his lips. 'Great. I am surrounded by amorous adults... Maybe I should join Elena's table, after all. The kids over there wouldn't make me feel queasy like you guys do.' He pretended to leave sloppy kisses on the back of his hand and they all laughed. Then, Lizzie put an arm around his shoulders, squeezing him against her.

Stamatis leaned in and said to Tom, 'If you didn't look so much like Lizzie's brother and weren't her distant cousin too, I'd be jealous, and you'd be in deep trouble!' He pointed to his own eyes with two sharp fingers of one hand. 'But I'll be watching you, just to be safe!' He winked.

Tom smiled brightly, enjoying the banter, then his eyes caught something in the distance, his face beaming. The others turned to look and saw Babis and Aliki approaching. They were holding hands, looking elated.

'Great! More lovey-doviness. Lucky me!' joked Tom.

All three were still giggling when Babis and Aliki came to sit side-by-side across the table from them.

'Where did you two go? We never saw you on the beach!' said Babis as he put his arms around Aliki, who grinned from ear to ear. She exchanged a penetrating look with Lizzie, and they beamed at each other.

Everyone began to chat, mainly about the festival and how it was a great success. Soon, Lizzie got lost in her thoughts and her sense of newfound happiness.

'So! Are we going to get any *loukoumades* or what?' piped up Tom all at once, his face animated.

'What? Didn't you have any while we were away?' Stamatis asked the other three.

'No. After you guys left, these two followed closely behind,' said Tom with a cunning smirk. 'I wonder why. They didn't even get me any *loukoumades* first. I call this child abuse, I do.' He gave a mock-grumble and crossed his arms over his chest as he sat back stiffly in his chair. 'I ought to sue really. Wait till my mum hears this, Lizzie. Leaving me to go hungry while you go away on an impromptu date. Really!'

'Oh shut up, you little rascal!' said Stamatis and stood. He squeezed Tom's shoulder playfully and shook him, causing him to burst into a guffaw.

Stamatis turned to Babis. 'Come on then. Let's get *loukoumades* for us all! Put on your best smile and get your auntie to give us generous servings. Especially Tom. We don't want him fainting or anything.' He rolled his eyes causing fresh rounds of laughter to erupt around the table.

Tom went with the men to the serving area and returned on his own a few minutes later. He brought three plates of *loukoumades* for the girls and himself but advised them not to start on their desserts just yet; the guys were coming soon bringing even more food.

Mystified, the girls waited, as Tom wouldn't give any details. Soon, the two men came back with their own plates of *loukoumades* plus a big paper package.

'Yum!' said Aliki when Babis tore the bag open so everyone could dig in. '*Kalamaki* and bread! Where did you get them?'

'There's a shop down the road,' said Stamatis.

'Why did you call it *kalamaki*, Aliki? Isn't this *souvlaki*?' asked Lizzie picking up a wooden skewer with chunks of pork meat on it, a piece of grilled bread in her other hand.

'Yes, you can call it that too,' replied Aliki as she chomped. '*Kalamaki* is just the name we give the skewered meat.'

'What's *gyros* then?' asked Tom after swallowing a big bite.

'That's the shavings off the rotating chunk of pork you see roasting in the shops,' said Stamatis, the meat on the skewer he held almost gone. 'That is served with pitta bread, obviously, not on a skewer. We call this *gyro pitta.*'

Before anyone could comment on that, Babis set a meatless skewer down on his napkin, smacked his lips with relish and said, 'Who cares what it's called when it tastes so good? Eat, everybody! Eat before it gets cold!'

Everyone laughed, then obliged him, silence ensuing at the table until the bag was empty. Without a moment's rest, it seemed, they began devouring the *loukoumades.*

'Oh my goodness! How crunchy is this? Did your auntie make them?' Lizzie asked Babis a little later, her eyes huge.

'Yes! She always volunteers and, as she's so good at it, not one in the council ever turns her down.' Babis pointed to his plate. Only two dough balls were left on there already. 'That's her own honey produce on them, you know! And she is generous with the cinnamon powder too, can you tell?'

In lieu of an answer, the others issued a collective "mmm" sound as they munched. Moments later, Lizzie sat back and let out a sigh, her plate half empty. 'Oh my goodness! I don't remember ever enjoying a meal so much! And eating so much too. Somehow, it only happens in Greece!'

Everyone laughed at that, including Tom, who continued to enjoy his dessert and even stole one *loukouma* from Lizzie's plate after emptying his.

Lizzie watched as he took the dough ball, then ate it, honey syrup trickling down his chin. With a napkin in her hand, she wiped it clean, an open smile on her face. She hadn't seen him so happy, so content, ever since they were children, right here, in Corfu. *This island... has always had a way to lead us to happiness. Let's hope, after all the upset in between, that it will grant us perfect happiness a second time, somehow.*

Stamatis must have been watching her as these bitter thoughts entered her mind. He stroked her cheek with the back of his hand, and she turned to him as he said, 'What is it, my love? Are you tired? Sleepy? You want to head back?'

Lizzie saw the surprise in his eyes, then his face animate with mirth, when she gave a beaming smile and said, 'Are you kidding? We haven't even danced yet!'

❈❈❈❈

And dance they all did, on and off, in the following couple of hours. Tom was delighted to be able to dance to *syrtaki* music after the lessons Aliki had given him. All the while, wine flowed freely as the waiters kept going around the tables to refill the glasses.

Inevitably, people's merriment reached new heights, their inhibitions numbed, which meant that everyone danced, even Stamatis, who said he hadn't done it since his wedding day.

At some point, Lizzie stood to visit the Ladies' in a taverna across the road. On her way there she saw Nia and Tassos sitting alone at a remote table that had a few empty bottles of beer on it.

They looked glum as they smoked, eyes focusing far, without speaking to each other. Lizzie wondered what was wrong with them looking like that on such a magical night. As she hurried past them to cross the road, she didn't look their way to avoid any further confrontation with Nia.

When she came out of the taverna a little later, she was surprised to find Tassos on his own leaning against the front wall, a sleazy look in his eyes. She ignored him, and moved to rush past him when he detached himself from the wall, and shouted, 'Hey! Wait! Why are you in such a hurry?'

'Excuse me?' she asked, raising her brows, then threw a glance across the road where she'd earlier seen him with Nia to find the table was vacant.

When he didn't give an answer, her expression hardened. His leering look made him look disgusting. She guessed he must be drunk, and one of those men who are better left alone after a few drinks. Seeing as he didn't seem willing to explain himself, she moved to go but then he leapt forward and grabbed her by the arm.

Lizzie swivelled around and pulled her hand away from his grasp. 'Hey! What are you doing?'

He put up both hands and gave a stupid grin. 'Sorry... I just wanted to ask you something.' He was slurring, not a good sign.

Lizzie looked across the road towards the crowd, instinctively trying to locate Stamatis and the others, but she couldn't see their table from this angle. 'What is it? What do you want?' she asked with a huff.

He gave a satisfied smile, then leaned against the railing, tilting his head. 'I just wanted to know what a pretty girl like you is doing on her own.' He straightened. 'If you were my girl I wouldn't let you out of my sight for fear that someone else might snatch you from me.' He leapt forward again and gripped her wrist. 'Like *that*!' He threw his head back, without letting go, and gave a howl of laughter.

Lizzie made a fist with her free hand and struck his own that held her wrist captive. She did it repeatedly and shouted. 'Let me go! Let me go, you moron!'

'Aoow!' he exclaimed, then moved away, hobbling as if she'd stabbed him in the leg with a knife.

She curled her top lip with disdain, her hands on her hips. 'You're pitiful, you know that?'

'Pitiful as I may be...' he slurred, but kept away from her this time, 'I'm a lot better than that loser you're dating.'

She took a step forward, an accusing finger pointing his way. 'Who I'm dating is none of your business, you hear? And Stamatis is anything but a loser! Stamatis is a wonderful, caring man. The kind of man you'll never be. So excuse me if I think that you're only putting him down because you know you'll never be the kind of man that he is.'

'Wow! You got a mouth on you, missy! You got spunk, I love it!' He began to clap, mockery alight on his drunken face, but it didn't deter Lizzie one bit. This girl hadn't flinched at the sight of an evil witch that had taken her brother away from her for twenty years; she certainly wasn't going to back down before a drunken shadow of a man who thought he could belittle her Stamatis.

She lunged towards him, her head raised, and he lowered his to meet her eyes. His breath was vile and made her nauseous but she didn't flinch. And she didn't care if he was a head taller than her. To her, he looked shorter than a midget. If he tried to grab her again, she knew what to do.

'That's right! I got a mouth on me. But I got a fist too.' She shook it before his glassy eyes. 'And I'm not afraid of you! Next time you try to touch me, this will wipe that stupid grin right off your face! You and Nia stay away from me, you hear? I don't know what game you two are playing at, but I've had enough!'

With that, she turned on her heels and walked across the road. When she arrived on the other side, she turned only once to see if he was still there.

Lizzie gave a silent gasp. Nia had just joined him on the roadside. She probably had been watching the scene all along hidden in some dark corner, behind the trees by the entrance, no doubt. But no matter where she'd been hiding, one thing was for sure: she'd put him up to it – to try to annoy her. *What kind of sick person would do that?*

You don't give me enough credit, do you?

When she returned to the table, she found only Tom and Stamatis sitting there.

'Where are Aliki and Babis?' she asked, forcing a thin smile, and trying to calm down after her encounter with Tassos.

'There!' said Stamatis and she followed his gaze to a long line of locals and tourists. They were dancing a *Kalamatiano,* and she easily spotted the two among them.

As soon as she sat down, Tom leaned closer, his face exultant. 'Stamatis is going out fishing tomorrow afternoon and is asking if we'd like to go with him!'

Lizzie turned to Stamatis to find him nodding firmly.

'Oh, I'd love to do that!' she replied, turning both ways to mirror their enthusiastic expressions.

'Come here, missy...' Stamatis put an arm around her, magnetizing her with his eyes. As he leaned in slowly for a kiss, the last remnants of her vexation over what had just transpired on the road with Tassos evaporated into nothing.

'Eeewww!' exclaimed Tom, before their lips could touch. 'Don't do it! Not in front of me!' He shrieked playfully, his hands over his eyes, causing them to explode into uproarious laughter.

❋❋❋❋

It was well past three a.m. and everyone was getting sleepy around the table, taking turns to stifle their yawns. Aliki had put her head on Babis's shoulder, their hands entwined, and she had shut her eyes, causing the others to throw the odd glance at her and titter.

At some point, a song Lizzie knew from the past blasted from the speakers. It was a fun song she used to dance to with Tom on the island. The moment its notes filled the air, Tom jumped upright. 'They're playing *Dirlanda!*' Come, Lizzie!' It was no surprise he'd just remembered it. These days, he kept recalling old memories really fast.

Lizzie doubted she remembered the steps. 'It's been a long time, Tom. Are you sure we can do it?'

Stamatis tilted his head. 'A long time? Tom, you're only twelve! How do you know this song? It's ancient!'

'Oh, we... My mother taught me...'

Stamatis turned to Lizzie with a frown. 'And you danced to this song with them? When? Did you come here in the recent years?'

'No, no... We danced to it in a Greek restaurant. In England... My cousin came with Tom one year...' Lizzie looked away and twisted her lips, pretending she was watching the dancing crowd. Inside, her guilt landed in her gut like a ball of fire, burning her insides.

She ventured a glance at Stamatis after a few moments, relieved he seemed satisfied with the explanation.

Tom insisted again that they should go and dance so, despite feeling tired at this late hour, she yielded to his pleas and followed him to the other side of the seating area where a dozen or so people danced to the cheerful song.

'Come on, Lizzie! Let's go!' Tom shouted over the blaring music as soon as they got there, and they began to clap their hands along with the others.

Lizzie stood in line and, as her brother did, watched the sequence of the movements as the locals danced, and followed suit. Soon, they had remembered all the moves and were doing them perfectly in sync with the others.

It felt wonderful to recapture the joy of dancing to this song as Lizzie clapped her hands and tapped her knees and heels in sequence. Tom's jovial face made the moments as precious as gold. She turned to her right, as the dance demanded, and was about to slap her right heel when she felt someone cup her breast. *What the—!*

Lizzie whirled around to find Tassos standing there, his hand in mid-air, a toothy, slanted grin on his highly intoxicated face.

'You!' she shouted pushing him away.

'Come on! Let's dance together!' he insisted, grabbing her by the waist.

Lizzie saw red. She pushed him away with all her might, and this time also slapped him hard across the face. The music stopped and Nia materialized from behind him to stand between Tassos and Lizzie, hands on her hips, as the crowd that surrounded them watched, aghast.

'What's going on here?' demanded Nia. Her slur was just as bad as his.

'He had it coming,' said Lizzie. She felt Tom's grip on her arm and turned to look at him. Now that the music had stopped his good spirits had vanished with it. It made her livid that those two idiots had caused that to happen.

She turned to Nia and Tassos, about to launch into a proper speech this time, to give them a good piece of her mind, but she was stopped short.

Stamatis rushed to the scene, ignoring Nia. He went straight to Tassos, grabbed him by the shirt and landed a punch on his face.

'Aooowww!' screamed Tassos as he fell backwards, his pert backside landing on the sand with a soft thud.

Everyone fell silent, including Stamatis, who stood rigid, his hands by his sides balled into fists.

Tassos rubbed his jaw that had taken the blow. 'You bastard!' he screamed. Two men came forward and got hold of his arms to lift him up, but he shook himself away from their grasp.

Tassos took his time to stand back up on his own while Stamatis waited. Nia, who had remained frozen all this time unglued herself from her spot and rushed to Tassos's side.

She shook a finger at Stamatis first, then at Lizzie. 'You! How dare you hit him? What kind of savages are you both? You've ruined the party! I've got everyone here as witnesses!'

Nia had spoken in Greek. While Tom translated for Lizzie what she'd just said, Stamatis took a step forward. This move caused Nia to step back and hide behind Tassos, who now stood numbly.

Stamatis put up a hand. 'Don't worry. I am not going to hurt you, Nia. But your friend deserved what he got. As for Lizzie, I'm sure she had a sound reason for hitting him.' He turned to Lizzie, his voice down a notch or two. 'What did he do to you? Did he offend you in some way?'

Lizzie felt numb and embarrassed beyond words. All she could manage to do was nod once, in silence. Just as she did, Aliki materialized from behind the crowd and rushed to put an arm around her shoulders.

Nia watched the two girls and Tom, who stood together, and scrunched up her face, then looked away in disdain. 'She's lying!' she said, to no one in particular.

'No, Nia!' insisted Stamatis. 'Enough.' He moved to Lizzie and offered his hand to her, causing Tom and Aliki to step away.

Lizzie gave a little sigh and took his hand. His tender gaze told her she meant the world to him. His love helped her to relax, to feel a little better, despite the many eyes that continued to watch.

Stamatis turned to Nia. 'Lizzie is my girl, and I had every right to intervene since your friend offended her. As for you, Nia, you stay away from Lizzie. I will not have you bothering her any more.'

'Oh, did she come complaining to you? How typical!'

'No, actually, she hasn't. But I'm not stupid. You don't give me enough credit, do you, Nia? I see and know more than you think.'

'Oh yeah? Like what?'

'Like those window shutters in Pitsilos...' He still held Lizzie's hand and put the other on his waist, eyes widening. 'Nowhere else do the handles get smashed about like that! Same with the taps in the bathrooms. Only in your apartments do you seem to have the most careless guests.' He cocked his eye at her. 'Care to explain it?'

Nia stared aghast, then a few of the locals from Messonghi among the crowd began to laugh and snigger. Stamatis seemed to take heart from their reaction and the pitiful look on Nia's face.

He gave a cold smile. 'No? I didn't think so. I rest my case, Nia!' He shook a finger at her. 'Stay away from Lizzie and me. And find someone else to stalk from now on. I am taken!'

As laughter erupted from the crowd again, Nia dropped her gaze to the ground for a few moments. Then, looking the other way, she pulled Tassos by the arm with both hands, trying to drag him away from the scene, but he wouldn't budge. He had planted his feet on the ground, as drunk as he was, obviously hoping for a rematch.

Stamatis stepped towards him and got so close to his face that Lizzie thought for a moment he was going to head-butt him.

Her heart gave a thump so hard she thought it was going to stop. But then, Stamatis only put a finger on the man's chest and tapped it. 'As for you, I don't know anyone who deserved a punch more than you did tonight. And I should have done this years ago, you bastard! Consider this long overdue! Now we're even!'

Lizzie wondered why he said they were even. *What history do these two have?* Just as she began to consider all possible explanations again, she gasped, her hands flying upwards to cover her mouth.

All at once, Tassos threw back his arm and moved to punch Stamatis, but the latter, having the benefit of sobriety and thus being faster, grabbed his arm and held it firmly in mid-air.

The exertion combined with the great amount of alcohol he had consumed, must have taken their toll on Tassos because his face contorted with disgust just as Stamatis let go of his arm. Tassos put an urgent hand over his mouth and turned about face, nearly bumping into Nia, who got out of his way just in time.

Tassos staggered a couple of paces away, then doubled over behind a vacant table and hurled, causing everyone to pull faces of distaste and to look away.

The onlookers began to return to their seats, and Nia moved closer to Tassos to stand with a hand on his back as he continued to throw up. She used her other hand to tap her chest absentmindedly, her eyes focused far as she waited for Tassos to finish what he was doing.

Turning away from the scene, Stamatis moved back to Lizzie, a bright smile on his face. He took her hand, smiled wickedly and whispered, 'That felt great!'

I'm a lady. Never on the first date

'Did you see that? Wow! I cannot believe this just happened!' said Stamatis expressing his glee for the umpteenth time as all five of them made their way back to the pier a little later.

After the awkward scene, they all agreed they'd had enough excitement for one night. Everyone had enjoyed watching Stamatis serve a well-deserved comeuppance to Tassos and Nia, but Stamatis's thrill seemed never-ending.

Lizzie turned to face him as she walked beside him, and as they followed the other three. Stamatis looked so enthused it bordered on manic. He kept raising his hands to his head, raking his hair, sweeping his face with urgent hands and letting out one cheer after another.

But what was more mystifying than all that, was that since leaving the scene many locals had approached him to express their approval and satisfaction for what he'd done.

Especially the men had been very vocal about it. With her limited Greek, Lizzie had realized they were telling him that what he did to Tassos was long overdue or something. That didn't make any sense. But she knew she was missing information... and hoped Aliki would fill her in the moment she sat alone with her for a chat.

This wasn't going to happen tonight, though. Aliki had just announced that she was going to ride back to Messonghi with Babis on his motorcycle. The two of them were only escorting the others to the pier, then leaving on their own.

'I feel liberated! You know?' said Stamatis all of a sudden, taking Lizzie out of her thoughts.

Lizzie turned to him, to find his face animated still.

'I'm so happy for you,' she murmured, but a little annoyed now. She never liked mysteries. Maybe because she'd lost her brother once, smack bang in the middle of one.

'Sorry, Lizzie. I'm boring you, aren't I?' He brushed his fringe back from his brow and licked his lips. He looked simply delicious. Her expression must have softened then because his face melted in response.

He stopped walking, leaving the others to advance forward on their own. He put his hands on her arms, the look in his eyes intense. 'I hope you don't think badly of me for what happened back there, Lizzie. I'm not a violent man, I'm not!'

'I don't think that, Stamatis. Don't be silly.'

'Good. Because, to be honest, the last time I punched someone I was a teenager. And even then I had to do it to defend myself. But what happened here tonight... this...' He shook his head, lips pressed together, but the words wouldn't come out.

'It's okay. That guy deserved it. And I don't mean just for the way he treated me. I can tell it wasn't just that that made you hit him. But you don't need to explain that to me.'

'No. I do. But not tonight. Not because I don't want to, but because what just happened was an amazing breakthrough for me, and I'm still too overwhelmed to talk about it. And it's a long story... Lizzie, you must understand! I felt like a victim for so long ... Like this was final... But I just turned the tables. I just moved on. This is huge for me, Lizzie!'

He gave a big smile and looked away, up ahead where the others were nearing the pier. He turned to her again, his eyes sparkling. 'But I'll tell you all about it once my head has stopped spinning!' He rubbed his mouth with one hand. 'I think I drank quite a lot tonight. You deserve to hear the whole story another day when I'm calm and sober.'

Before Lizzie could speak, to say that this was okay, she heard Tom calling them over. Without a word, Lizzie took Stamatis's hand and offered a sweet smile. Stamatis beamed at her and they hurried to the others, who waited at the base of the pier.

Babis had brought his motorcycle there, and Aliki had already taken a seat behind him, her arms wrapped around his waist, eyes crinkled at the edges as she grinned from ear to ear.

Tom, who stood by the motorcycle, gave a wicked smirk and threw his hands in the air when Lizzie and Stamatis arrived. 'We have to do this again sometime, Stamatis! When is the next festival on? And can you teach me how to throw a punch?' He punched the air with his fists, causing the four to giggle.

※※※※

During the boat ride, the three fell silent, awestruck by the beauty of the stars and the glorious moonlight. The sea, serene, murmured a faint lullaby, lapping against the hull, when the motor died away and the boat approached the pier in Messonghi.

Stamatis broke his warm embrace around Lizzie's shoulders, and she raised her head, squinting at the distant streetlights. It felt like a rude awakening to leave the dark world of the sleepy sea and the starlit sky to approach land again. Numbly, she took Stamatis's hand and he led her out of the boat.

As soon as they all stepped onto the sand, Stamatis enveloped Lizzie in his embrace anew, Tom skipping excitedly beside them as they headed for the apartment.

Stamatis had left his motorcycle on the seafront but insisted on escorting them home, and Tom teased him for being overprotective. As they left the beach behind to walk down a quiet lane, they grew silent. At this hour, when no one was about and everyone was sleeping in their beds, it seemed like the right thing to do.

To Lizzie, it felt wonderful after the bustle of the evening to be shrouded by serenity as she breathed in the chilly night air. Fragrances of flowers and woody herbs from the gardens delighted her sense of smell as owls and other night birds hooted and screeched from the trees.

Even more wonderful, though, than all that, turned out to be Tom's tactfulness as soon as they arrived at their destination.

They went through the garden gate and Tom rushed to the bottom step, then turned around with a wicked smile. 'Right. I'll let you two say bye-bye in privacy.'

Lizzie and Stamatis stifled a snigger. 'Goodnight, Tom. And thanks!' said Stamatis with a wink.

'No. Thank *you*! This was great!' Tom's face was animated with elation.

'Look forward to the boat ride with you tomorrow. I'll teach you to fish in no time.'

'Cool!' Tom made a move to go but stopped mid-step, then turned to them and pointed up with his eyes. 'By the way... Try not to wake up the landlady with your smooching. She's gaga. Better not let her hear you, or she'll evict us on the spot.'

More sniggers ensued as Tom disappeared up the steps to their apartment.

When he was gone, Stamatis took Lizzie's hand, and she followed him under an overhanging trellis. 'Let's stand here, hidden from view, just in case. That landlady sure sounds like someone I don't want to have to mess with.'

'Oh trust me, you don't,' said Lizzie meeting his eyes, to find they had softened. With the faint sound of his breathing in her ears, and the tender touch of his hand around her waist, he leaned in for another kiss, and she lost her bearings of the world again. It swirled around her, then melted, taking away with it for a while all the mysteries that had ever troubled her, and all the worries that stood on her shoulders.

With a second kiss, one that was even more passionate, her knees began to buckle.

With a sigh, he pulled back first. 'I don't want to let you go... but if we stay any more out here, I probably won't be able to control myself.'

She bit her lower lip and laughed mischievously at that, her eyes pinned on his.

He checked his watch, then caressed her cheek to add, 'Besides... If we stay up any longer we'll never get a decent amount of sleep. And I need you to be at your best tomorrow for our fishing expedition!' He put his arms around her and gave her a simple peck this time. 'I'm off... Get some sleep...' He back-stepped, a sweet smile on his lips. 'And, tomorrow, I'll see you again, my love...'

Lizzie blew him a kiss from the bottom of the steps when he turned around at the gate. Then, when he was out of sight, she went up the steps or rather glided along, her mind in a whirl. But, for the first time, she felt happy, truly happy, and full of hope.

❋ ❋ ❋ ❋

The next morning, Lizzie and Tom surfaced quite late. It was gone ten o'clock, but having had only five hours of sleep they felt like the living dead. Lizzie and Tom got their breakfast ready and sat on the balcony to eat. Shortly after they'd finished it, they saw the light go on in Aliki's kitchen.

Aliki must have noticed them sitting there because she drew back her curtains a moment later and waved.

The siblings waved back and Aliki smiled, then yawned. They yawned too, which they all found hysterical, bursting into giggles.

Aliki brought a hand to her ear, mouthing something. 'She's asking you to call her, I think,' said Tom.

'No, I think she said she'll call me.' Lizzie had hardly stopped her sentence when Aliki disappeared from the window. A few moments later, Lizzie's mobile rang.

'Told you so!' said Lizzie and dashed to the kitchen to get her phone.

'Hello Aliki!' she said as soon as she picked up.

'Hi,' croaked Aliki.

'That bad, huh?'

'Only the hangover, everything else okay, trust me!'

'Why don't you come over and tell us?'

'No way. I found it hard to find the kitchen as it was. What did we drink last night exactly?'

Lizzie gave a snort. 'I don't know, but I think it was some kind of rocket fuel.'

'Well, serves us right indulging in free-flowing cheap wine. But it tasted so good last night, didn't it?'

Lizzie agreed, laughing alongside her, then asked, 'How did you sleep then?'

'Like a bear in winter. You?'

'Like a log.'

'Oh good. Headache?'

Lizzie heaved a long sigh. 'Don't ask.'

'Same here. And my tongue has more fur than a fur merchant in Kastoria.'

'Eewww,' said Lizzie scrunching up her face and laughing. She'd never heard of Kastoria, but that didn't stop her from appreciating the joke.

'Yes. That's what I said too when I saw it in the mirror just now.'

'How did it go with Babis yesterday? He's not there, is he?'

'Please. I'm a lady. Never on the first date.'

'Sorry. I didn't mean...'

'Relax. I'm joking.'

'Oh good!'

A loud chuckle, then a pause. '... Besides. He left this morning, around eight.'

'What? Really?'

'You bet, really. Why wait? The man is perfect for me.'

'Oh, I'm so happy for you, Aliki! It's love then?'

'Yes! Oh, yes... I'm so happy, Lizzie! And, what's more... he solved the mystery for me last night.'

'What mystery?'

'You know... about him being so shy at first?'

'Oh yeah... what was that all about?'

'It was Nia! She'd told him that I was no good... that I was cheap... that I was only going to play with him, then leave him!'

'What? That nasty cow!'

'Well said! Babis had been heartbroken from a previous relationship so he was being extra careful... that's why he tried to keep his distance from me even though he really liked me. Nia knew how he felt so she lied to put him off me.'

'But why? Why would she say these awful things about you?'

'Because she sees every woman as an adversary. She wants all the men of the island for herself. She's a psycho. Period.'

'But wait a minute! What changed then? How did he start talking to you, before the festival?'

'If you recall, we all met in his supermarket one evening, when you returned with Stamatis from your visit to his house...'

'Yes...'

'Well, the moment Tom proposed we all go out together to Petriti, Babis grew too excited to contain himself. Besides, he told Stamatis later that evening how he felt about me, and Stamatis assured him that Nia was talking nonsense. He also advised him to go forth and claim my heart without hesitation.'

'Oh bless him... and now it makes sense. But I still can't believe Nia did this...'

Aliki gave a huff. 'I can.'

'Speaking of Nia... I meant to ask you about Tassos...'

'Oh no, please, Lizzie. I know what you're going to ask. But it's not my secret to tell.'

'Wait a minute! That's what you said that time when I asked you why you don't like Nia!'

The other end of the line fell silent.

'Aliki? You there?'

'Yes...'

'Is it the same secret? Does it involve Nia *and* Tassos?'

'Yes, yes it does... But don't ask me any more. I cannot tell you anything, I'm sorry.'

Lizzie ignored the plea, too intrigued to respect it. 'Please tell me. Is this relevant to Stamatis too? Is this why he punched Tassos last night? Did Nia and Tassos do something bad to him in the past?'

For a few moments, Lizzie heard no sound at the other end. She looked at her phone screen, to check if the call had been disconnected when she heard Aliki clear her throat. She stuck the phone back to her ear. 'Aliki?' It was a demand, not a question.

'Look... Stamatis made a real breakthrough last night. It looks like he knew what Tassos had done... And I'm glad he had it in him to punch him in the face. Feel proud of him, Lizzie, because he deserves it. And I'm sure in his own time he will tell you all about it. You'll just have to wait till he's ready to tell you himself.'

'Okay... I will do that then. I will wait for him to tell me. He did say he intended to do it.'

'Oh good.'

'Can I ask you to do something else for me today please?'

'You name it, Lizzie.'

'Can you send out more requests to your contacts on the island? Whoever may be into folklore or history? Writers, bloggers...' She raised a hand and drew cartwheels in the air. '... and everyone's grandparents too?' It was a joke, but not entirely.

She continued, breathless now, as she thought fast, 'The more elderly people we ask, the better our chances to gain some leverage over Phoni. I may be happy I've found Stamatis, Aliki, but my brother is everything to me. If it turns out I can't save him from the clutches of the witch, I'm going to the mountain and she can have me instead. Even if it means Stamatis and I will never have a future...' Her voice trailed off, her eyes pooling with tears.

'Oh, Lizzie... please... Please don't think like that...' soothed Aliki.

'I know... I'm trying not to...' Lizzie wiped her tears with the back of her hand, before continuing in a frail little voice, 'Will you take care of Tom for me if it comes to that, Aliki? Please?'

She stole a glance at the balcony where Tom was sitting happily, his nose buried in a book. A moment later, the sound of a laboured sigh reached her ears from the other end of the line.

'Stop it, Lizzie... you silly girl! It won't come to that, okay? No one's going to the mountain! There's got to be a way to stop Phoni and we will find it! Now let me go and get some coffee in me and then I'll be on the Internet like a shot...' She gave another sigh, then sounded upbeat when she added, 'Come on over in an hour with Tom, okay? We'll research all we can and see where it takes us. And I'll email everyone I know today. Help is out there. Call it intuition but I know it!'

Doctor Tom at your service!

The sea was a striking cobalt blue when Lizzie and Tom sailed away with Stamatis in his boat. The motor buzzed along, the sound mixing in their ears with the echo of water splashing around the hull.

A flock of seagulls kept sweeping across the sky or circling overhead. Lizzie watched them, a wide grin on her face, and tried not to think of ravens or Phoni. Soon, she grew so happy, so carefree on that boat, that she caught herself wishing, over and over again, that this boat ride would never end.

Sitting at the stern with Stamatis and clinging against him, her shoulder tucked under his arm, she felt like she was melting in his tender embrace. The heat of the sun didn't help; it hammered down intensely even though it was well past five p.m.

Lizzie and Tom listened as Stamatis pointed to both sides of the bay while they sailed out towards the open sea. The Old Venetian Fortress in Corfu town seemed so close at this hour that you'd think you could reach out and touch it. On the other side, the bay glinted in the sunlight so much that you couldn't clearly see; the hazy, distorted scene made the headlands look like a bunch of dark green caterpillars heading to the edge of the sparkling water to drink.

Lizzie smiled widely as she took it all in. When Stamatis stopped pointing to the different places he named, he reached out and caressed her cheek with the back of his hand. In his eyes, she saw that he was just as happy as she was.

Her eyes flew to the other side of the boat where Tom sat, his mouth open, trying to catch the droplets of seawater that rose from the prow. He was giggling, eyes dancing with amusement.

'What are you doing, you silly boy? If you're thirsty, I have water right here,' she teased, patting the plastic bag at her feet that contained a large bottle.

Tom looked away with a cheeky grin, and she turned to Stamatis again. Her heart felt full already, but the look in his eyes soothed her soul even further – it was a drug she could never get enough of.

As if he knew, he leaned closer and touched her lips with his own, making the moment perfect. Squeezing her against him, he took her hand and kissed it.

A few moments later, he killed the engine and dropped anchor, causing Tom to stand and go to him and Lizzie, his face alight with enthusiasm to know he could soon be catching his first fish.

Within five minutes, Stamatis had shown Tom how to hook his bait and gave him his fishing rod to use, while he used a line. In the next hour, they both caught a lot of fish, big and small. Every time Stamatis named a fish, Tom giggled. He'd never heard any of these Greek fish names before. The one he loved the most was *mourmoura* because it meant 'murmur' and also 'nagging talk' in Greek.

Tom took one of the *mourmoura* fishes in his hand and shook it gently as if it was talking. He put on a high-pitched mock-angry voice and complained about all sorts of things, making the other two laugh out loud.

In the short silence that ensued, Lizzie wondered how she could tell Stamatis the truth about Tom. It bore down on her that she had to lie that Tom was a distant cousin and not her brother. But how could she tell Stamatis and burden him with her troubles? He seemed to have enough heartache of his own to deal with as it was.

'Darling? You're crying?' she heard, realizing it was him. He'd just brushed her cheek with his fingertips, and only then did it occur to her that tears had been rolling down her face all this time.

She turned away, embarrassed, and wiped the tears with her own hands. 'Don't mind me, Stamatis. I'm happy, that's all...'

He put his hands on either side of her face and turned it gently towards him. 'I hope I had something to do with that, at least?'

'Yes. Of course, you did...'

'Well, if they are tears of joy, I guess it's okay. And, if you let me, Lizzie, I'd like to try to make you happy. Always...'

Tom gave a snorting laugh. 'What are you two mumbling about over there? I hope you're not engaging in naughty talk in the presence of a *child*?'

Stamatis's face brightened, eyes lighting up. 'Oi! Wait till I get to meet your mother! I'll tell her what a big-mouth you are!' He picked up a dirty rag from the floor and tossed it at him.

Tom chuckled when it got him on his arm but, before he could speak, his face ignited with urgency. He gripped the rod with both hands and tugged. 'Hey! I got one! A big one! Stamatis! Help!'

Stamatis rushed to take over, then reeled onto the boat what turned out to be a large tuna fish. All three stared at it for a few moments, mouths agape.

'Wow! I didn't know tuna fish could be so big around here!' said Tom.

'Oh yes! Wait a minute, I have a basket somewhere...'

Stamatis moved to a large compartment under the stern. He opened its door and got a large wicker basket out. Taking the fish in his hands carefully as it gasped, he delivered an effective *coup de grace* with a single blow against the side of the boat. Then, he put the fish in the basket and began to arrange its lifeless body so it lay flat on the bottom. Suddenly, he erupted in a shrill cry of anguish. 'Aaaaarrgh!'

Lizzie's blood chilled in her veins and she moved closer to see what was wrong. Tom was already standing beside Stamatis, his face contorted with terror at the sight of blood in Stamatis's hand. It trickled down to his wrist as he held it up, staining the floor.

By the time Lizzie had come close enough to spot a hook stuck in Stamatis's thumb, Tom had already taken control of the situation. Between gasps, Stamatis was explaining the hook must have been lying forgotten in the wicker basket, half-hidden at the bottom. He hadn't noticed it as he lay the fish inside.

Tom removed the hook from Stamatis's thumb gingerly, eliciting from him a single howl of pain as he did so.

Stamatis ground his teeth, trying to contain his agony, while Tom began to rummage through his freezer bag, which he'd insisted on bringing along with him, just in case. Lizzie had teased him about it, saying they no longer needed to earn any more pebbles from Phoni, but now she realized he was more mature than she could ever be.

Lizzie had been watching, frozen, until now. Being a nurse, the sight of blood didn't bother her, but she'd been stunned to see how proficiently Tom had handled Stamatis's injury. It was like second nature to him, to help people, more so than it had become to her, it seemed.

Finding her voice, she put an arm on Stamatis's back and urged him to sit at the stern so Tom could tend to his wound.

As she waited for Tom to bring what was necessary, she opened her shoulder bag and got a pack of hankies out. Blood was still oozing out of the wound, making a mess on the floor. She sat on the seat beside Stamatis and tried to mop up the blood the best she could.

Finally, Tom approached and began to disinfect Stamatis's thumb. Next, he applied an antiseptic herbal cream of his own concoction and covered the wound with a piece of gauze and a strip of plaster. All the while, Stamatis and Lizzie watched in silence.

Tom spoke first as soon as he was done. 'The cut is rather deep, but not enough to need stitches. You were lucky... And you must have a tetanus jab at the pharmacy as soon as we get back, to be safe,' he said with the air of a practicing physician.

Stamatis seemed unbelieving by what he'd just witnessed and heard. Finally, he raised his eyes from his bandaged thumb and faced Tom. 'Are you sure you're only twelve?'

Tom gave a wicked smile, while Lizzie watched numbly, the terrible secrets she shared with Tom weighing down on her again.

'No, seriously. Where did you learn to do all this?' insisted Stamatis.

'It's a hobby...' Tom pointed to the basket. 'Hey, that's a big fish! Hope you won't eat that on your own!'

'No, of course not. You two should come to my house one evening this week. Let's throw it on the BBQ. It'll be a blast!'

'Will it keep till then?'

'I'll stick it in the freezer, no worries, Tom. I'm an excellent cook. You're safe in these hands!' said Stamatis thrusting both hands forward.

Tom pulled a face of mock-disgust. 'Let's wait till you remove the bandage before you cook for us.'

Stamatis slapped his knee with his good hand, his expression exploding with amusement. 'You! What a jester!'

Tom straightened, looking like the cat that got the cream, and turned to Lizzie. 'Hey, Lizzie, you haven't said anything. Don't you think a BBQ is a great idea?'

Tom's exultant expression snapped Lizzie out of her numb state, and she did her best to sound upbeat. Raising her head, shoulders thrust backwards, she tried her best to smile widely. 'Yes! I think it's fantastic! I can't wait,' she said to Tom, then shifted on the seat and squeezed Stamatis's arm. 'How are you feeling now?'

'I'm okay,' Stamatis said with a shrug, 'I think I'll live. That's what Doctor Tom seems to think anyway.'

Tom didn't reply, just served the two adults with an irresistible smile.

'You know, I don't just owe you for this one, Doc...' he said to Tom, then looked at them both, a single brow raised. 'Haven't you noticed anything unusual about me lately?'

Lizzie was mystified by the question, but Tom widened his eyes and put up a finger. 'Yes! I meant to ask... You don't smoke any more. Is that it?'

'Yes! Those herbal balls you gave me worked like magic.'

'Really?' Lizzie turned her unbelieving eyes first to Stamatis, then to Tom.

'Indeed!' said Stamatis, bright-faced. 'They didn't just wean me off the cigarettes, they made them taste absolutely *disgusting!*' He opened his eyes wide, then stuck out his tongue and pretended to gag. 'After the first and the second one, I only noticed the cigarettes tasted a little different... this carried on to the fourth one, but when I had the fifth... *well!*' He scrunched up his face and gave a frantic wave with his hand.

Tom broke out laughing, and the other two followed suit.

Finally, Stamatis added, 'After the fifth one, it was impossible to smoke and not want to hurl. A strong Pavlovian effect, I must say. So I quit smoking overnight after that... It was a nasty habit. Should have quit it years ago. Thank you, Tom! You made it so easy for me.'

Tom nodded firmly and said, 'Doctor Tom at your service!'

This brought on a round of uproarious laughter, then Tom moved to the bow to pick up the fishing rod. Stamatis took the opportunity to steal a kiss from Lizzie, then pinned his eyes on her, a wicked smile on his lips. 'So, if Tom is to be my doctor, will you be my nurse?' he whispered, then raised his bandaged thumb. 'Kiss it better?'

Lizzie kissed his bandage with a titter, and he squeezed her in his arms. They checked on Tom to find that he was looking out to sea, his line sunk in the water again. From the way he'd turned away, his back to them, it was obvious he'd done it on purpose, to give them some privacy. A very unusual gesture from a child but, then again, her Tom wasn't really one. Even people who weren't in the know had noticed he acted and reasoned like an adult. An overly light-hearted one, but an adult at that.

Relishing the ensuing silence, Lizzie and Stamatis turned to each other, and lost themselves in a passionate kiss.

I knew it. I can read you like a book

As soon as they arrived back at the pier, Lizzie suggested they all go to her apartment for tea. Stamatis didn't have any work obligations, so he accepted gladly. As soon as they arrived at the front yard, they saw Aliki, who raised a hand in greeting from her front door. Charlie stood beside her wagging his tail, mouth gaping open in a goofy smile.

Tom turned to the others. 'It's time for Charlie's walk. I'll go with Aliki. You two enjoy your tea.'

Without waiting for a reply, he walked over to Aliki and sat on his haunches, showering Charlie with affection, to which the pet responded with slobbery kisses and yelps of excitement.

Aliki handed Tom the lead, a mischievous grin on her face. She turned to the others and said, 'Don't expect us anytime soon! We're going to sit somewhere and get some ice cream.' She paused, put a hand on her waist and winked. 'A *really* big one. It'll take us *ages* to eat it. Say… at least an hour?' With that, they were off, Charlie trotting happily beside them.

Lizzie and Stamatis went up the stairs, amazed by the tact of the other two. Being offered some time alone at the house felt like a precious, unexpected gift. Lizzie perceived it that way, and in Stamatis's sparkling eyes she saw he felt the same.

Once in the house, Lizzie strode to the kitchen, Stamatis trailing behind her. She filled the kettle with water and flicked on the switch. As she began to take mugs out of the overhead cupboard, Stamatis came to stand behind her. He put his arms around her and squeezed her to him.

The musky smell of his after shave made Lizzie see stars when she felt his hot breath in her ear. He was now nuzzling her ear lobe and whispering sweet words of adoration. His lips travelled lower, tracing the side of her neck, raising goosebumps in their wake.

At first, Lizzie giggled, her heart swelling with the sheer thrill of being alone in the house with him. But as he didn't stop, her raw desire for him began to take her to new places, and she felt she would lose control. But this wasn't going to happen. She couldn't let it happen.

'Mmm...' She closed her eyes and bit her lower lip, her gut exploding with sweet rapture when he kissed her naked shoulder. She let the teaspoon drop in one of the mugs, the sound of the water bubbling in the kettle akin to the passion inside her that had begun to rise to the point of torture.

She forced herself to open her eyes and turned around, her hands reaching out to land on the strong curves of his biceps. They felt warm under her fingertips, pulsating with vigour. The very idea that she had the power to have him, should she choose to, right there and then, made her head spin. But no. She couldn't afford to think like that.

Lizzie shook her head, eyes closed, trying to sober herself up from her unbearable desire.

'What is it, darling? Are you okay?'

She raised her eyes, meeting his own, to find love and tenderness deepening in them with every passing moment. But instead of making her happy, his affection pained her. *If only he knew the lies I've told him! What am I doing?*

He tilted his head. 'Lizzie? You've had too much sun?' He tapped the tip of her nose with his index finger. 'You silly girl. Next time you must bring a hat.'

Stunned, she didn't react at all to that, and he squeezed her playfully in his embrace, swinging her from side to side. Lizzie allowed herself to sway freely in his arms, enjoying the warmth of his embrace, his light-heartedness. Being bathed in his love felt amazing. It was a balsam to her aching soul, impossible to resist.

He let her go, and she gave a wry smile. 'Yes... Too much sun,' she replied, avoiding his eyes, then spun around to make the tea.

He put his arms around her waist again, but this time, as if he could tell something else was on her mind, he refrained from kissing her again.

Lizzie poured hot water in the mugs and slipped the teabags inside. Then, acting nonchalant, she turned about face and took him by the hand, leading him to the sofa.

As soon as they sat together, she reached for the TV remote. 'Shall I turn it on?' Before she could press a button he took it from her, the side of his mouth rising in an impish smirk, his eyes burning holes in hers like two live embers.

'You must be kidding... Who cares about the stupid TV? All I want to do is look at *you*...' He let the remote drop carelessly back down on the coffee table and put an arm around her, the other hand on her cheek, caressing her, causing her to hyperventilate again.

Just as she was about to try to make conversation, to say how Tom had made them laugh earlier on the boat, he took hold of her with both hands and leaned in for a passionate kiss. The world began to fray into nothing around her as his kiss, urgent and firm, numbed her reservations.

As if they had a will of their own, her arms flew up to his shoulders and pulled him down on top of her. At the same time, she swung her legs up onto the sofa.

With a moan that only served to shift the butterflies in her stomach all the way down to her core, he deepened his kiss, driving her crazy with desire.

He opened his eyes for just one moment, looking into her face adoringly, and propped himself up with one hand so he didn't crush her. Then, he let out a sigh and pressed his lips on hers once more.

Instead of enjoying the moment, her lust for him began to fight inside with her reservations, the tension torturing her, and she thought she'd start screaming any moment now.

This had felt amazing at first, but now, once the first moments of sweet surrender had come and gone, her power of reason had resurfaced, reminding her he knew nothing about Tom, nothing about Phoni. *How can I give him my all if I can't give him my honesty first?*

As he continued to kiss her and nuzzle her neck, Lizzie felt herself sink slowly into oblivion... But that little voice of reason wouldn't let up. *If I let this carry on any longer, I know I'll gladly give myself to him... but after... how will I feel after?*

Lizzie screwed her eyes shut with the rush of his breath in her ears. She willed herself to retain her control as he moaned and whispered sweet nothings, as his lips travelled slowly down her throat to her collarbone, the sensation causing the skin on the back of her neck to break into goosebumps.

What if I told him everything? What's the worst thing that would happen then? And, just like that, Lizzie decided to take the road of honesty even if it meant losing her chance of romance. Somehow, her decision acted as a surge of willpower and she put two firm hands on his chest.

At once, he pulled back, his face hovering over hers. He was hyperventilating, his eyes wild with intensity, chest heaving, mouth agape as he breathed in big gasps. 'What is it, Lizzie? Have I hurt you?' Panic ignited in his eyes. He looked around and behind him, but his thighs and legs were staggered against hers, and he was still propping himself up with one arm so he didn't crush her.

'No...' she murmured softly, caressing the side of his head.

He took her hand in his and kissed it, his eyes softening. 'Then, what is it? And... that thing in the kitchen wasn't about the sun either... was it?'

Lizzie was stunned to hear this question, and it must have been evident in her eyes because he chuckled then and said, 'I knew it. I can read you like a book, Lizzie... Which confirms my suspicion...' He moved up and away, allowing her to sit up.

Lizzie brushed her hair back from her face with an urgent hand and sat beside him on the sofa. He took her hand and held it on top of his thigh inside his own.

When their eyes met again, she said, 'What did you mean just now? What suspicion do you have?'

He gave a bright smile and said, 'What else? That you're my sister soul, of course.'

She felt herself melt as she gazed into his adoring eyes. 'Oh Stamatis...'

'I love you, Lizzie...'

'I love you too, Stamatis... but...'

'But? But, what?' He squeezed her hand in his. 'Tell me, my love... What is troubling you?'

Lizzie pulled her hand gently and he let it go. She raked her hair and stood up. 'I'll go and get the tea... Then I'll tell you everything. I promise. Just wait here... okay?'

Lizzie saw the bewilderment in his eyes. He simply nodded, and she turned away feeling thankful, if only for the few moments she needed to catch her breath. When he was near her, it was like someone kept blasting her brain with dynamite. It made it impossible to think clearly, let alone talk about Phoni and what she'd done to her brother.

She paced to the kitchen window and opened it fully, allowing the cool evening breeze to waft in. The salty air refreshed her senses, and she closed her eyes with gratitude as she breathed it in. Then, without further ado, she prepared the teas and returned to the sofa, determined to break down the barrier of dishonesty that stood between them.

After she'd done that, it would be up to him if he still wanted to be with her or not – if he wanted to be with someone who could very well be swallowed by a mountain any day now, never to be seen again.

It must be like kissing a hedgehog

Lizzie had been talking for fifteen minutes or so, telling the story from the beginning. At some point, before finishing it, she stopped, eager for some feedback. Stamatis hadn't uttered a word all this time, just listened intently.

'Well, Stamatis? What do you think from what you've heard so far? Talk to me... please.'

In lieu of an answer, Stamatis shook his head and let out an audible sigh. From his bulging eyes, she could tell he had trouble processing what she had said.

She sighed too, despite herself. 'It's hard to swallow, I know...'

'You don't say...' He said with a wry smile, then pressed his lips together, his gaze focusing far towards the blank TV screen. With a nervous hand, he raked his hair, the other holding Lizzie's firmly on his lap.

Lizzie swallowed hard, her gaze dropping to their mugs on the table. They'd had a few sips earlier on but, once she began sharing the truth about Tom, their beverages were soon forgotten. Half full, they stood forlornly, side-by-side, their contents long turned cold in the cool breeze that came through the open windows.

'Stamatis? I know it's a lot to take in... And, once again, I'm sorry... I'm sorry that I lied about—'

Stamatis whipped his head around and took her hand in both of his, his eyes huge and pleading. 'Please. Don't apologise. You don't have to. And it's not like this is your average story. I'm sure it's not easy for you to tell it.'

He shifted in his seat and rubbed his chin for a few moments. Seeking her eyes, he added, 'I have to say. I'm having a lot of trouble believing all this!'

'I know... I'd be the same if I were you.'

'Lizzie, I recall you spoke of this witch twenty years ago... And, I do admit, I didn't believe you then... I thought you were being fanciful. And I'm sorry for that. But to tell you the truth, now that I'm an adult, I find it even harder to believe it...' He gave a low, guttural sound and looked away.

'I know...' she said softly.

He turned to face her again and twisted his lips before saying, 'You know, if this story came from anyone else, I'd dismiss it instantly as a fabrication. Or, at best, as a bad joke. But, it's coming from you, so I can't do that.'

'Thank you… for believing me,' she whispered, relieved.

He scrunched up his face. 'So Tom… is your brother?'

'Yes. As I said earlier, somehow, in Phoni's world he never aged a day.'

'Well, I'll be damned! Tom… he's back?' he said mumbling to himself, head bent, then turning to Lizzie, 'I'd never have guessed it was him. Surely, I was astounded by the resemblance when I saw him but…' He scratched his temple, then faced her to add with a faint smile, 'I'm so glad you got your brother back, Lizzie. It must have taken a lot of courage to claim him in that cave at night… I'm sorry I didn't believe you, that *no one* believed you. And, I guess, having seen Tom I have no choice but to believe it's him… even if he's still twelve… but… believing in the existence of a witch that heals the dead… now, that's a tough one.' He shook his head, his brow etched.

'I know… it takes time to digest all that…'

'And Aliki? She knows about all this?'

'Yes… yes, she does. And she's looking on the Internet to help us find ways to fight Phoni back.'

'Fight her? But why? You said you've managed the three healings she demanded. Aren't you free of her now?'

Lizzie twisted her lips, then said, 'No… There's more to the story, Stamatis.' She went on to relay the latest developments and, as she did so, Stamatis's expression grew all the more distressed.

All of a sudden, he opened his eyes wide and jumped back in his seat as if electricity had hit him. 'What? No! No one will ever take you away. Or Tom! Not while there's a breath left in my body, I swear it!'

As if Phoni had materialized before them right then to claim her, his expression grew wild, and he pulled her into his arms, holding her tight. 'That will never happen!'

'Thank you, my love,' she whispered, stunned by the fervour of his response to the possibility of losing her.

Finally, he calmed down a little and let her go, but kept her hand in his, his hold on it firm as if afraid it might slip away. 'She's cunning...' he mumbled after looking absently at the opposite wall for a few moments. 'She knows you and Tom would rather stay together, wherever that may be, than ever get separated. What she really wants is to keep you both!' His voice came out rushed, his words interspersed with gasps of panic. 'But I'll be damned if I let this happen. I'll kill her with my bare hands first!' Once again, he took her into his arms, caressing her hair, his eyes afire with steel determination.

Lizzie fell silent and, for the next few moments, their feelings of desperation as they clung to each other became so intense that she began to cry. Stamatis soothed her with the promise to remain by her side, no matter what. All the while, using the napkins she'd brought with the mugs, he helped her wipe her tears.

For a few moments, they remained in their tight embrace without speaking, spent. Then, she put up a hand and caressed his cheek. His beard felt scratchy, and she wasn't one to like facial hair as it was, but then she'd still love him if he were to turn into Quasimodo overnight. The ridiculous thought, as if she was desperate to lighten her heart, was enough to make her chuckle.

In response, he put a hand on his beard and cringed. 'I know. It's awful, isn't it? That's not me at all. I don't know why I kept it for so long...'

'Do you mean the beard?'

'Yes, I'm sorry. It must be dreadful kissing someone with facial hair. It must be like kissing a hedgehog. Or a broom, at best. I know I wouldn't like it if you had any.'

Meeting his laughing eyes, she put a hand above her upper lip and rubbed at the skin that she waxed on a regular basis. 'Good to know. Saves me from having to seek a better product,' she said causing them both to chortle.

When they fell silent again, he bent his head, resting his forehead on hers, and they closed their eyes for a few moments.

Suddenly, he pulled back, and she opened her eyes to find his were huge and ablaze with an evident revelation. Before Lizzie could ask him about it, he said, 'Lizzie... about that witch...'

'Yes?'

'If there's one person in Corfu who might have heard about her, then that person has to be my father.'

'Your father?' *Of course!' Why didn't I think of this earlier?* Lizzie couldn't believe she hadn't made the connection. Stamatis's father—a retired professor of the Ionian University of Corfu and a fine scholar—was highly knowledgeable in the island's history and the local lore. He'd be very likely to have the information they needed, if there was, indeed, any information on Phoni out there. Lizzie turned to Stamatis, her expression animated. 'But you said he has Alzheimer's... will he be able to tell us anything?'

'Oh, you'd be surprised how clearly he remembers everything from the past... He comes up with the most ancient memories out of the blue. I'm sure all the knowledge from his University days is still stored away safely in that brilliant mind of his.'

'So you think he could answer my questions about Phoni?'

'Yes, I'm quite sure he can do it, as long as we're lucky to catch him at the right moment. My father has his good and bad days, you see...' he scratched his chin, '... actually, I'm going to Corfu town tomorrow to visit him. Come with me and let's hope he'll have a lucid moment to answer our questions. Either way, we have nothing to lose.'

Lizzie gave a squeal of delight, and he opened his arms to hold her, pressing her against him. She felt safe in those moments, and rejuvenated, like a new, exhilarating chapter in her life had just begun. And, having shared her secrets with him felt empowering beyond measure.

When he leaned in to kiss her, she responded with fervour, this time holding nothing back. Inevitably, things heated up in seconds, their mutual passion threatening to contain them whole like a wildfire.

Stamatis broke away suddenly and shook a playful finger at her. 'No, missy. You can forget whatever plans you may have to seduce me here today.' He winked, then added, 'I want to have all the time in the world to do this properly with you the first time, the way my love for you dictates... On a bed, for starters. And with a little more privacy than this.'

He pointed to the door with his head. 'We don't want Tom walking in on us.' He gave a wicked grin. 'I know he's thirty-two and all, but being as innocent as he is, we'd only give him the shock of his life.'

You two look like you've seen a ghost!

Lizzie and Stamatis arrived at the retirement home in Corfu town early the next morning. The receptionist called a nurse, whom Stamatis knew. She greeted them cordially, then led them to Mr Lambros's room.

They found him sitting in an armchair by the window, looking at the sparse traffic on the road.

Standing at the door with the others, the nurse gave an amicable smile and said softly, 'It's still early for him to go downstairs.'

'Yes, I know,' said Stamatis and, turning to Lizzie, added, 'The guests are escorted to the hall downstairs at ten a.m. every morning. If the weather's nice they get to sit in the garden outside to enjoy the sunshine and get some fresh air.'

'That's nice,' said Lizzie.

'Yes, we do our best,' said the nurse, then entered the room and the others followed. She put a gentle hand on the old man's shoulder. 'Hey, Mr Lambros! Look who's come to see you today.'

He turned around slowly, shifting in his armchair.

The nurse raised her brows as they all waited, and whispered to the two, 'Let's hope that this is a good day.'

By the time Mr Lambros had turned in his seat to gaze at the others with beady eyes, the three were standing over him with big smiles plastered on their faces.

'Hi, Dad!' said Stamatis, a hand resting on his father's shoulder.

'Dimitris! Good to see you! How's work?' he said with a bright smile.

The nurse pressed her lips together, throwing a meaningful glance at the other two.

'Dimitris? Please tell me that's your middle name?' whispered Lizzie in Stamatis's ear.

Stamatis was shaking hands with his father at the time, exchanging pleasantries. He leaned to her ear to explain, 'Sadly, that's his brother. He's deceased. But I hear I looked like him a lot... and he often mistakes me for him. Shares all sorts of old stories of the two with me. You wouldn't believe how far back he remembers.'

'And this young lady? Who are you?' asked Mr Lambros, causing them to turn to him again with jovial smiles.

Stamatis gave a sweet smile. 'This is a friend. Her name is Lizzie. She's from England.'

Mr Lambros extended his hand, to speak in his perfectly enunciated English that Lizzie remembered so well from that old holiday. 'Pleased to meet you, Lizzie. How are you?'

The nurse left the room, saying she'd be back at ten o'clock to escort Mr Lambros downstairs via the elevator. As soon as they were alone, Stamatis dragged two chairs that stood near the wall so the three of them could sit closely together.

Stamatis picked up what looked like an old photograph album. It lay on top of a cabinet a little further away from the bedside table. Stamatis had explained to Lizzie earlier that his father enjoyed seeing the photos on his better days. On his really good ones, when he remembered Stamatis as his own son, the two of them would leaf through the album together and share their family memories of Stamatis's mother and his grandparents too. On the bad days, Mr Lambros didn't like to give the book a second look, and these were many.

The album was dog-eared and tattered, but Lizzie could see it for what it was – a precious compass that Stamatis and his father could use, whenever the tempests in the latter's mind allowed it. That way, they could grant themselves a small window of time where they could sit together again; a father and a son, just reminiscing and enjoying each other's company, for a few precious moments at a time.

As she watched them sitting side-by-side leafing through their old family album, Lizzie pondered on how unfair life could be. Why should this man be robbed of his memories? That was so cruel... Not just to him, but also to his loved ones, and especially Stamatis. She had known a fair share of tragedy, of inequity, herself.

It dawned on her then that these are things we can never avoid. All one can do is enjoy every day as if it were the only gift life had ever given them. If catastrophe came one day to strike, to shatter one's life, even then they'd have the choice to deal with it with strength and dignity; the best they could.

These thoughts left her with the certainty that no matter how long or short, the time she had left to enjoy her love with Stamatis was more precious than gold – a real lifeline. Whatever doubts she'd had up until then about resisting the love he offered her had somehow vanished into thin air, just by watching Stamatis try to capture a moment of recognition of his own identity in his father's eyes.

The heartrending scene that transpired before her made her clearly see that when it comes to love it is of no importance how long happiness is likely to last. All that matters is love itself. And, even if it comes a day at a time, it still has the same merit as a love that lasts a lifetime, if only we hold it precious in our hearts.

The sound of laughter reached her ears and snapped her out of her deep thoughts. From what she could tell, Mr Lambros was sharing an old memory of his brother Dimitris. Father and son were chortling about it.

Lizzie smiled brightly and leaned back in her chair, relaxing, as she watched them. Mr Lambros was in good spirits, and it delighted her to see it. Stamatis's face was bright too, even though his father still called him by the name of Dimitris. The thought caused her heartstrings to tug inside her chest.

She was about to fall back into a reverie, being so deep in her thoughts, when Mr Lambros turned to her to say, 'Margaret? Where are Lizzie and Tom?' He glanced at the door, then back at Lizzie. 'Didn't you bring them along this summer?'

Margaret? He thinks I'm my mother? Before she could say anything, Mr Lambros turned to Stamatis.

'Your mother is in the fields this morning. You'll have to help Mrs Margaret check in at the house, Stamatis. Go on, my boy! She must be tired from the trip.'

Aghast, Stamatis and Lizzie stared back at him, lost for words, causing Mr Lambros to chuckle. 'What is it? You two look like you've seen a ghost!'

Please tell me what you know...

Lizzie leaned closer to the old man. 'You mentioned Tom earlier, Mr Lambros. Surely you remember we lost him? On the mountain?'

Mr Lambros stared blankly at her for a few moments, then slowly lowered his head to shake it forlornly. 'Aah... of course. You lost him. Poor thing...' He raised his head again to gaze into her eyes. 'I'm so sorry, Margaret. He was such a good boy.'

Stamatis dragged his chair a little closer and placed a firm hand on his father's shoulder, shaking it gently for a while as if desperate to help him focus his mind. 'Father... this is not Mrs Margaret. This is Lizzie. Tom's sister. It's been many years since Tom has gone missing, if you recall.'

Mr Lambros's eyes lit up. 'You're Lizzie?'

Lizzie gave a tight-lipped smile, her eyes dancing with hope. 'Yes, yes I am. Lovely to see you again, Mr Lambros, after so long.' She offered her hand, and he shook it firmly.

Now, the delight in his eyes and his cordial smile were those of a man in full possession of his faculties, causing hope to ignite in her heart. Nostalgia was palpable in his expression as if time had a meaning for him again. But alas, as wonderful as it was to be able to have this short exchange with him, to introduce herself properly, these precious moments ended in the blink of an eye.

Mr Lambros gave a little sigh, his face dropping, and he looked out of the window again.

Stamatis exchanged a glance with Lizzie and shook his head. He seemed just as downhearted as she was, but not ready to give up yet.

'Father?'

'Hmm?' came the non-committal answer from Mr Lambros, who now seemed to gaze at the line of cypress trees in the lush garden below. The top branches swayed in the breeze hypnotically under a bright blue sky that was dotted with sparse cotton clouds.

'Dad, Lizzie has a question to ask you.'

At the sound of the name, Mr Lambros turned to them again, confusion alight in his eyes. 'Lizzie?'

'Yes, Dad. Remember little Lizzie? From the guest house years ago? She's come back, a woman now, as you can see.'

The old man smiled and shook hands with Lizzie again. Her gut felt clenched, about to flip over, but she managed a sweet smile. Mr Lambros seemed lost in his own thoughts now, his handshake feeble, and she had the impression he still wasn't sure who she was. 'Do you remember Tom, my brother, Mr Lambros?'

'Ah yes, Tom... Such a lovely boy. Shame he was taken from you.'

Lizzie's heart leapt. She exchanged an urgent glance with Stamatis and saw the hope that coloured his expression. 'Taken? What do you mean, he was taken?'

Mr Lambros gave a deep frown. 'I'm not sure, of course, I can only surmise because his sister, Lizzie, told everyone at the time that a witch had taken him. His parents were very concerned, all of us were. Why would she resort to this ridiculous story, we all thought?'

'So you didn't believe her story?' asked Stamatis as soon as his enthusiasm allowed him to find his voice again.

Mr Lambros shook his head firmly. 'No, of course not. This is why we were concerned. We thought the shock of the experience of losing her brother in that cave may have been the reason why her mind had created this fabrication, but later...'

'Later?' asked Lizzie urgently. His pause had caused panic to strike in the pit of her stomach that he might lose the thread, reverting to oblivion, whatever valuable information he had to share lost forever in the mists of his confused mind.

Mr Lambros pinned his eyes on her. 'You see, Margaret... I discovered things later on in life that suggested these weren't fabrications, after all... but Lizzie was in England then. And you never came back to the house. There was no way I could talk to her, to tell her how sorry I was that I didn't... that *we* didn't believe her back then.'

Lizzie gave a gasp and brought a hand over her mouth. *He knows!* She leaned forward and squeezed his arm gently. 'Please! Please tell me what you know... It may help to save Tom!'

'Tom?'

'Yes! We've found him, you see...'

'You've found him? Oh, thank God! Is he okay?'

'Yes, he is! But we need help to get him freed from Phoni for good. He lives with me in Messonghi, but she won't let us leave the island... She threatens to retaliate if we do.' She used the word 'Phoni' to see if he knew of her, but the confusion in his eyes told her otherwise.

'Who's Phoni?'

'The witch.'

'In the mountain? In Martaouna?'

'Yes. That's where her cave is. If you recall, the police searched it thoroughly. But there was no way they could have found Tom in the depths of the spring... Phoni, the witch, took him via the spring, deep into the earth where she dwells. Can you help us? What can you tell us about her?'

'I know about the witch... but I didn't know her name was Phoni. All the references I found after your family returned to England mentioned her as the Raven Witch.'

Raven? It has to be her! 'Tell us what you know about her please...'

Stamatis leaned forward, his eyes pleading. 'Yes, Dad. Tell us! It's important. It will help both Tom and Lizzie to lead a happy life again after what the witch has done to them.'

'Lizzie? Is that you? I didn't recognize you earlier, I am sorry.' Mr Lambros put out his hand and she held it tenderly.

'Yes, Mr Lambros. I am Lizzie. And I've taken Tom from Phoni... The Raven Witch, as you called her. But she's threatening to never let us go free. We need to get rid of her once and for all! Can you help us please?'

'Oh, Lizzie! Do you remember? You were forever reading books of Greek myths... and I thought... as fanciful as you were back then... I am so sorry.'

'Yes... I did love those books you let me read... Especially the pictures. They were so—'

Mr Lambros snapped his fingers. 'I remember now... of course! You did tell us back then that the witch called herself Phoni. But because the name points to Persephone, the daughter of Goddess Dimitra that Hades took to the Underworld, we thought it was a fanciful tale...'

'It's okay... It's okay...' Lizzie squeezed his hand in hers, and placed the other on his arm, patting it, urging him to calm down.

He grew more upset by the second and Stamatis seemed as concerned as she was. He had begun to coax his father as well to not feel bad about it.

'Oh... But we did all fail you, Lizzie. You insisted that Tom was taken by a witch, but with the police report and everyone's logic suggesting he'd simply fallen into the spring and drowned, none of us could believe you.'

'I know... I know... but it's okay. I understand.'

'And it bugged me... it bugged me because they never found the body. But even that didn't mean much to the police. They said it was impossible to get to the body because the spring water comes through large fissures in the aquifer below. The fissures went deep into the mountain rock and were impossible to explore. Two divers tried at the time and nearly drowned, so the search was called off.

'But I never forgot! I never forgot your story, Lizzie. So I researched for at least one decade after you left, on and off... And found out all about the Raven Witch. I felt so ashamed then that I let you down... So I never told a soul about it. Not even my family...' He turned to Stamatis. 'I'm sorry, son.'

Stamatis's eyes melted to hear his father call him that. He seemed too moved to speak and, instead, squeezed his father's shoulder gently. Then, he asked, 'So what is this Raven Witch exactly?'

'Not of this world, my boy. She belongs to the Underworld.'

Lizzie's brows shot up. 'The Underworld? As in... Healer of the Underworld?'

'That's right. They say she's a dead woman herself, and that she has tremendous powers of dark magic. She's not your average Healer, that's for sure.'

'So she lives *in* the Underworld?' asked Stamatis.

'No... not in the Underworld per se... Rather in a place that serves as the gateway between the Underworld and our world. And what she does there is she heals the souls of the dead who are on their way to the Underworld.'

'I don't get it. What healing is necessary to the dead?' asked Stamatis.

'All sorts, from what I have read. Some are in shock, the victims of violent accidents, murders or wars, and others have died after long-drawn out or painful illnesses. And some do not even realize they are dead. By calming their spirit and treating any problems their semi-physical semi-ethereal bodies may have, the Healers help them come to terms with their injuries or illnesses and, ultimately, with the end of their lives.'

'You said "the Healers"... Are there many Raven Witches, Mr Lambros?'

'No, Lizzie... there are many Healers of the Underworld, but only one Raven Witch. At least in Corfu. When I read during my research that she snatches children, that's how I came to understand what happened to Tom. And to believe you, Lizzie... This is what makes Phoni evil, unlike the other Healers.

'You see, she's not supposed to snatch living children. The Healers are allowed to recruit helpers only among the dead, those who wish to stay in their semi-physical, semi-ethereal form and never go to the Underworld. But, over the centuries, the Raven Witch has been stealing living children to help her with her work instead.'

'*The centuries?* Just how old is she, Dad?'

Mr Lambros shrugged his shoulders. 'Who knows?'

Stamatis and Lizzie fell silent, amazed, so Mr Lambros continued, 'One day, I got hold of an ancient volume in the Municipal Library of Corfu... The book mentioned that the Raven Witch was sighted in a cave in the foothills of a mountain in south Corfu. A drawing on the same page depicted a mountain shape that looked like Martaouna, an arrow pointing to it. The drawing depicted another mountain, a higher peak, to its left and a lake behind it. Assuming that these were Mountain Chlomos and Lake Korission respectively, I came to the conclusion that the mountain in question was Martaouna.'

'Did your research provide any information as to how one could defeat the Raven Witch? You know... fight back?' asked Lizzie.

'Fight back?'

'Yes. Any weak points?'

'Ordinary people like you and I wouldn't be able to fight off this vile creature, but there are some humans among us who are highly trained from birth to do this.'

Lizzie's heart gave a thump. 'Really? Who would that be?'

'They are called Necrojudges...'

'Necrojudges? And they're human?' asked Stamatis, his face igniting with hope.

'Yes, like you and me. But they are very special people... well, women. They can only be women. And they can do magical things, to match the magic of the witch, and to drive her away.'

'Where do we find one? Do you know, Mr Lambros?'

'I'm sorry... I tried many times to find one, to get some answers about your brother, but I couldn't. All I found was a reference in the Municipal Library about two Necrojudges who were born and raised on the island centuries ago... but they were just stories... nothing else.'

'What else do we know about them? Would there be one living in Corfu these days?'

'Well, they exist among us... but they make themselves known only as they wish. They learn their skills from their grandmothers and are born with natural gifts. Every Necrojudge teaches her first granddaughter and so forth, and for every one that passes to the other side, another one is born.

'They say there's a Necrojudge for every Healer, living in the same area, checking on their practices for anything untoward... which means that there must be a Necrojudge living in or near Martaouna. We just don't know who she is.'

There was a knock at the door then, and they all turned to see the same nurse, who'd stuck her head in, a cheerful smile on her face. 'Sorry to interrupt you, all. Just to say, I can escort Mr Lambros downstairs, if you need me to. You can all sit outside, if you like. It's very pleasant out there today.'

'Thank you,' replied Stamatis. 'We'll take him downstairs in a while.'

'Great. And I must say, you're looking breezy today, Mr Lambros. Mrs Mary will be glad to see you in good spirits. I know she's looking forward to playing checkers with you again. It's been a while.'

Once she was gone, Lizzie and Stamatis turned to Mr Lambros to find he had a bright smile on his lips.

'Mrs Mary?' asked Stamatis smirking. 'You made a new friend?'

'Yes. She's very nice,' he replied with a bright smile.

Lizzie patted the old man's hand. 'Thank you for the information you gave us, Mr Lambros. It's been really helpful.'

'What? About Mary?' said the old man, and raised himself up from the chair slowly to waver on his legs. Stamatis shot up to help him.

'No, about—' Lizzie stopped midsentence when she realised he'd lost the thread of their earlier conversation. She exchanged a glance with Stamatis and saw in his eyes the same enthusiasm that she felt. His father had just given them confirmation of what they knew and valuable new information on top of it.

'Thank you, Dimitris,' said Mr Lambros and began to walk towards the door aided by the other two, who held him by the arms. He had a twinkle in his eye, but it was a poor match for the universe of exploding stars in the eyes of the other two.

Lizzie's heart palpitated, her mind churning with plans. They had to visit Aliki. If she couldn't find the nearest Necrojudge through her many Internet contacts on Corfu, then no one could.

He doesn't smell of raw fish like you do

Stamatis and Lizzie rode back to Messonghi on his motorcycle and headed straight to her place. As soon as they parked outside, they heard Tom's jovial greeting coming from the courtyard.

They went in through the gate, saying hi to Tom, who was holding a tennis ball, Charlie leaping and yelping at his feet. He put the ball in his shorts pocket and ordered Charlie to sit. When the dog obeyed, he patted him on the head, then turned to the others, his face animated. 'Well? What did Mr Lambros say?'

'He's given us new information!' said Lizzie causing Tom's eyes to brighten even further.

'Yeah? Like what?'

'Patience, Tom! Let's go see Aliki and we'll tell you both.' Stamatis put a tender arm around Tom's shoulders, his heart swelling with affection every time he looked at him, now that he knew his true identity.

Never breaking their stride, they all entered Aliki's apartment, Charlie wagging his tail as he followed.

They called out to Aliki, announcing their arrival, and Tom beckoned them to her bedroom where, like any other weekday, she'd been working on her computer all day.

Aliki's face was alight with anticipation when they entered her room.

'Hi! We have big news!' said Lizzie first, unable to contain her excitement any longer.

'Do tell!' said Aliki springing upright. The four stood together in the middle of the room, while Charlie went to lie down close by.

Without further ado, Lizzie and Stamatis took turns to relay what Mr Lambros had said. At the sound of the word "Necrojudges", Aliki's eyes ignited with mystification, then narrowed into slits, an index finger resting on top of her closed lips. 'Necrojudges...' she mumbled.

Lizzie gasped, her voice a little more than a whisper when she said, 'You've heard about them before?'

Aliki pressed her lips together, her brow deeply etched. 'I don't know... I'm not sure.... Let me see.' She sat at her computer desk and the others approached slowly to stand behind her in a line. As she began clicking away on the menu of her browser window, they didn't emit a single peep, for fear they might break her concentration.

A few unbearable moments later, during which Aliki accessed her browsing history and opened a few blog pages, she suddenly snapped her fingers. 'Aha! I knew I'd seen this word somewhere!'

The other three bent forward in perfect sync to take a better look at the screen.

'You mean the word "Necrojudges"? Where is it mentioned?' asked Lizzie breathlessly.

'Here!' Aliki pointed to the word with a flourish. It was positioned halfway down in a blog post titled "Legends of a Secret Greece – Underground Worlds and Ancient Healers".

Lizzie couldn't believe her eyes. On either side of her, Stamatis and Tom were peering at the screen, looking just as dumbstruck as she was.

'I'd forgotten all about it... I read this post months ago. It even mentions the Healers! Why didn't I make the connection? It's all right here in black and white, look!' exclaimed Aliki pointing vaguely at the screen again.

Before anyone could ask what she was referring to in particular, she started reading from the screen, pointing at every word as she read for the others to follow.

"And even though the Healers are allowed to visit our world so they can refresh their stock of plants necessary for their underground healing practices, their actions are monitored by The Necrojudges, who dwell among us."

A pause ensued, where they all exchanged mute glances, then erupted in cheers and frantic slaps on Aliki's back.

When they fell silent again, eager to hear more, Aliki returned her gaze to the screen and resumed reading.

"Unlike the Healers, the Necrojudges are human. These gifted women are endowed with magical powers inherited at birth. They also possess secret knowledge and skills that are passed on to them from their grandmothers. Only the Necrojudges have the power to discipline a Healer that may have gone rogue or done something

untoward. Indeed, it is only up to the Necrojudges to keep the Healers in check. And this is fortunate, as many a time the Healers have been known to do evil deeds in our world, such as kidnapping small children."

Aliki stopped reading and turned back in her seat to look at them all, her face beaming.

'Oh my God! I cannot believe it!' said Lizzie, her hands cupped over her mouth.

Stamatis turned to Tom, patting his head. 'See? I told you we'd find a way!' He squeezed Lizzie's arm next, his eyes overflowing with emotion. 'This is it, darling! All we have to do now is find a friendly neighbourhood *Necrojudge*,' he added with a wink to make a joke.

But Lizzie didn't smile. Instead, she twisted her lips at the realization that this might not be so easy to do. 'But how do we find one?'

'The administrator of the blog might know,' cut in Aliki. 'I've chatted to him in the past as I often comment on his posts. I love his work... He writes largely about legends and mysteries and is a really nice guy. I can try asking him...'

'Is he based here on Corfu?' asked Lizzie, chewing her lips.

'Somewhere in the north of the island, if I recall. Certainly nowhere near here.'

'Worth a try, though, Lizzie, don't you think?' said Stamatis. His eyes were twinkling with a palpable effort to encourage her.

Lizzie lowered her head and nodded firmly once. She felt bad for her pessimism, despite them being so close to a possible solution. But it was exactly that... It felt too good to be true that they were so close to fighting back and getting rid of Phoni forever. But she had to try to believe. She had to try not to dampen the others' spirits, at least. 'Yes, of course it's worth a try asking the guy.' She managed a cheerful little smile. 'What do we have to lose, right?'

'Exactly,' said Aliki.

Lizzie turned to Tom. 'Do you recall hearing anything about a Necrojudge while you lived with Phoni?'

Tom shrugged. 'Sorry... I have no recollection of such a thing.'

'Do you remember Phoni mentioning anything remotely relevant to a foe of some kind?' pressed Stamatis.

Tom served him with an apologetic glance before lowering his eyes. 'No, I'm afraid not... She never mentioned much to me or to the other children, other than what was needed to be done for work. She'd come and go a couple of times every day, just monitoring us and giving orders. That's it.' He huffed. 'She wasn't exactly the nurturing type or one to enjoy a good conversation,' he added, sarcasm colouring his voice.

'Ok! Let me write to the guy then! See what he can tell us.' Aliki turned to the screen and began to speed-type a short message on the blog's contact page. Seconds later, she turned to the others, her face glowing. 'Done! Now we wait. Come to the living room...' She beckoned them to follow. 'You two must be dying for a refreshment after your motorcycle ride in the heat.'

❀ ❀ ❀ ❀

A few minutes later, as they chatted over a glass of chilled lemonade, Aliki suddenly froze and straightened in her seat. 'My computer! It just pinged with a new email message. It may be him!' she said breathlessly as she rushed to her room.

Everyone followed her, their excited sounds reverberating against the walls, including Charlie's. His frantic barking echoed deafening within the confines of the apartment in the face of such commotion.

An eerie silence ensued when Lizzie, Stamatis, and Tom huddled behind Aliki's desk chair and leaned towards the computer screen. She'd just announced the message was indeed from her blogger friend. Slowly and clearly, she began to read.

"Hi, Aliki! Hope all is well down there in Messonghi. Can't complain about my life here in Acharavi, though the beach is a big distraction haha. Anyway, about your question. Yes! I know for a fact there is a Necrojudge in your area because the guy who was my source for the article actually told me so. I don't know who she is as he wouldn't tell me... BUT! I can tell you how you can get in contact with her. My source told me all about it, and even though I thought it was quaint at first, I decided to leave that bit out of my article in the end."

At this point, Aliki made a pause and turned to the others rolling her eyes, then made a gesture of shooting herself in the head. 'Agh! Bloggers! Always blabbering!' She widened her eyes to the sound of the others chuckling. They all brimmed over with anticipation to hear the rest of the guy's message. Finally, Aliki turned back to the screen and resumed reading.

"Ok! So what you should do: Make some printed ads on green A4 paper. I repeat, the colour has to be green! Choose the most central streets in Messonghi and mount a couple of ads on each. My source mentioned that the Necrojudge frequents this village often, if not daily, so you're in luck!

The ad should be simple and include only this: The name of the witch (Phoni or the Raven Witch, in your case) and, underneath, the date you want the Necrojudge to meet you. You don't have to mention the time or the place. By default, this is midnight and the cave of the witch in your area.

I know it sounds crazy... but apparently it works and the beauty of it is that people who are not in the know will hardly notice your ads, let alone care to know what the writing means. But, for the Necrojudge, this will make perfect sense, of course. Put these ads up and she will come. Just make sure to word the ad exactly as I said. Good luck, and great hearing from you!"

'That's it. Wow! What do you think of that, guys?' said Aliki, turning to the others again.

Everyone was chattering excitedly now, their hopes catapulted to new heights. Aliki offered to produce the ads on her printer and said she knew of a shop in Moraitika that sold green printing paper.

Lizzie and Stamatis volunteered to put up the ads. The lane that led to the beach across from the pier was quite busy, so they had to put a couple there. More would have to go along the central road that ran through Messonghi. For good measure, Stamatis suggested they put a couple of ads in Spileo as well, and more at the big crossroads outside Messonghi where the municipal tap was.

They agreed on everything except for one thing. Tom wasn't happy that the others wouldn't let him participate in putting up the ads.

Stamatis put a tender hand on his shoulder. 'I'm sorry, Tom. It must be tough looking like a boy when you're not...'

'Yes, Tom...' cut in Lizzie squeezing his other shoulder gently. 'We know it's hard... but just think. It's not exactly legal to put up printed ads in public places. What if we got asked about them, or worse still, what if someone from the police saw us? I can't let you get into trouble with the law. Can't you see that?'

Tom saw her point, so they all agreed that Stamatis and Lizzie would do this alone in the wee hours of the morning when the roads were deserted.

'Wait a minute!' piped up Tom. 'What about the date? Which one do we choose to summon the Necrojudge?'

'That's a point...' said Lizzie frowning. 'What's the date today?'

Aliki glanced at her computer screen and told her, and Lizzie announced that in four days they'd have to give their answer to Phoni.

Everyone fell silent, and Lizzie's brow furrowed as she concentrated, thinking aloud. 'The witch said she needed a week to tell us if she could give Tom the looks of the thirty-two-year-old he never got to grow into.... So, if she finds a fix and visits us sooner to tell us so, then Tom and I won't have an excuse to procrastinate further. It makes sense, therefore, to seek help from the Necrojudge as early as we can.'

'Yes. Definitely. But we shouldn't give the Necrojudge too short a window either to see the ad,' said Stamatis.

'Three days then?' suggested Aliki.

'No... That's too long. What if she needs more than the one remaining day to help us? And, as I said, we don't want to risk Phoni paying us a visit sooner than expected.' Lizzie cringed at the thought, her features tightening. 'We can't allow this to happen!' She took in a laboured breath. 'I propose we ask the Necrojudge to meet us the day after tomorrow.'

They all agreed to that, and hoped that the Necrojudge would visit the village during that time.

Now they had decided on everything they grew so excited they didn't know what to do with themselves. Charlie stood among them with his mouth open, tongue hanging out as he took turns to look at them all, his soft brown eyes twinkling under the overhead light.

'Come on, let's get back to our drinks, then I'll take him for a quick walk,' said Aliki pointing to her pet. She beckoned them to follow and added with a mischievous smile, 'I say we spike the lemonade to celebrate a little!'

'Good idea,' said Stamatis, squeezing Lizzie up against him with one hand, and Tom with the other, as they followed Aliki out of the room. 'Afterwards, I'll go to Moraitika and get the green paper. I know where the shop is.'

Aliki dashed to the kitchen with the promise to bring the perfect ingredient for the lemonade, while the others sat on the sofa.

Lizzie turned to Stamatis to tease him. 'Tonight. You and me. Dress in black. Take no chances.' She made waves in mid-air, eyes widening, her face and voice taking on the intensity of a circus ringmaster presenting the most perilous act of the show. 'Let's roam the streets tonight looking invisible... mixing with the shadows!'

He gave a guffaw. 'Cool!'

Cradled in Stamatis's arms, she raised her head to look at him. He seemed so heart-stoppingly handsome the way he smiled like that... his eyes twinkling in the sunlight that streamed through the window. It made her heart bloom. She still had trouble believing he was all hers.

Lizzie giggled. 'Oh, Stamatis! I can just see you dressed like Ethan Hunt tonight! Minus the skylight, the harness, and the matching music, of course.' She bit her tongue mischievously, causing the others to howl with laughter.

Aliki, who was on her way over and had heard, didn't need much encouragement to engage in playful banter. She stood before them, a bottle in hand, and said, 'Stamatis, I gotta say! You're definitely more handsome than Tom Cruise. However, he doesn't smell of raw fish like you do!'

Stamatis rolled his eyes, and Tom began to hum the theme from Mission Impossible, one of the many movies he'd watched in the past weeks.

'You traitor! I thought you were my friend!' said Stamatis, causing everyone to erupt in howls of laughter.

It's like thanking the sun for shining

Lizzie and Stamatis put up the ads around Messonghi the same night. Now, all they had to do was wait. The next two days felt like a month of Sundays, the anticipation unbearable at times, but they had fun too – swimming in the morning with Tom, then going out for a meal in the evening with Aliki.

Lizzie and Stamatis managed to steal some time alone too, taking long walks or sitting at a beach bar till late at night. The two of them felt the bond of their love grow deeper and deeper with every hour they spent together, and it made them feel strong in the face of the perilous endeavour that lay ahead.

Before they knew it, the evening where they hoped to meet the Necrojudge had come. A few minutes before midnight, Lizzie and Stamatis took the uphill road on his motorcycle, their minds whirling with questions. What will the Necrojudge be like? Will she be kind and helpful? And, more importantly, will she be able to assist them at such short notice, if at all?

As they rode uphill past village houses and fields, Lizzie recalled her earlier conversation with Tom. He had insisted on walking with Aliki to join them, but she'd been adamant that he should stay safe at home.

Once again, Lizzie began to worry about the Necrojudge. Would she be there? They had no proof that she'd seen the ad. All they could do was hope.

When they arrived at the olive grove, their faces brightened at the sight of an old banger – a rusty, white VW Beetle parked at the roadside. They parked the motorcycle behind it, then rushed there to peer through its windows in the semi-darkness.

'Can you see anything inside? Anything that might suggest this belongs to the Necrojudge? I can't see anything, it's too dark...' said Stamatis in a whisper.

Lizzie gave a loud chuckle. 'What do you expect to see in there exactly? A cauldron? Frog legs? Bat wings?'

He shushed her playfully and looked all around, worried anyone might hear, even though they were alone in the middle of nowhere. His eyes scanned the dark car windows, then the olive grove again. 'I can't see her in the trees. Maybe she's at the other end of the grove,' he said in a low voice, adding after a short pause, 'Thank goodness the moonlight is strong enough tonight for us to see where we're going.'

After another good look in the car that still didn't do much to satisfy their curiosity, Lizzie turned to Stamatis. 'Okay. She must be waiting for us by the cave. Let's go.' As they began to walk through the trees hand-in-hand, she added, '*If* this is her car, that is. *If* she is here.'

'Uh-oh. Don't say that!' he said wagging a finger at her. '*Of course,* she is. It can't be any other way.'

Lizzie gave a sweet smile at that, and he responded by squeezing her hand in his fondly.

Suddenly, they heard a crunching sound, like someone had stepped on a dry branch. It caused them both to freeze on the spot mid-stride, falling silent to listen.

Lizzie opened her mouth to ask Stamatis if he could hear anything when she heard a sweet voice coming from the far end of the grove. '*Kalos irthate.* Welcome.'

Finding their voices, they both said hello even though they couldn't see anyone up ahead, and resumed advancing forward.

Rushing around the last bend on the path, Lizzie made out the figure of a woman standing at the far end. She was in her mid-seventies, plump, of medium height, and wore a scarf over her head. Her chosen attire was a simple combination of a cotton blouse and a skirt. When she began to walk towards them, her shoulders back, head held high, she seemed quite sprightly.

She met them halfway and extended her hand to shake. Lizzie shook it first, then Stamatis.

'Hi!' said Stamatis.

'Hello! Thank you for coming,' said Lizzie.

'Hello there! You're English!' said the woman in Lizzie's native language. 'Pleased to meet you both. Come, children! Let's stand here under the moonlight so I can see your faces, and you mine. Let our souls meet, so to speak.'

'Our souls?' asked Lizzie numbly.

'Through our eyes, child! That's how our souls can get to know each other,' the woman answered matter-of-factly.

She led them to the edge of the grove, then extended a hand before them as if to stop them from going any further. 'That's enough. Still under the trees, but away from the thick canopy so the moonlight allows us to see each other. As you obviously are aware...'

She swept her arm around to point at the opening of the cave across the small clearing, her face igniting with disdain. 'The wretched creature dwells in there. Best to stay as far from it as possible. Not for mine, but for *your* sakes. I am impervious to Phoni's tricks and the spying powers of her lackeys, those damned ravens of hers... But you will be safe standing here. If not because of me, surely because of the sacred trees of Athena. The purifying power of the olive trees will shield us from the witch's evil...' She raised both hands to point at the olive trees with majestic sweeping movements.

'Really? The olive trees can do that?' asked Lizzie.

'Of course! Why do you think the cave is located beside the grove?' She gave a knowing smile. 'You look like good kids, so I'm sure this will make sense to you: for every evil in the world, Life, somehow, creates something purely good to counteract it. So for the evil witch that uses this cave as her gateway to her world and back, this olive grove has grown here as a sanctuary, a counteracting benevolent refuge offered to those, like you and me, who may need it.'

She paused for a few moments, a hand hovering mid-air, a benign smile spreading across her mildly wrinkled face.

Under the radiant moonlight, Lizzie studied the woman's eyes and surmised she was a person of great kindness. This woman cared for them. Deeply. A huge weight lifted off her shoulders, and a sigh, heavy and long, escaped her lips despite herself.

The woman placed a tender hand on Lizzie's cheek, cupping it tenderly. 'I can see it is *you* who has been affected mostly. But don't worry. Help is here, my darling. We Necrojudges have been here since the dawn of time to help people against the evil of the likes of *her*.' She pointed a finger over her shoulder, pressing her lips together. Before either of the others could speak, her eyes widened, and she tapped herself on her chest. 'Oh, my! Do forgive me. I haven't introduced myself yet. My name is Valia.'

Lizzie offered her name and Stamatis's too, a big smile on her face. This woman was so easy to talk to.

'So, tell me. What's happened to you, precious girl? Did you lose a child in your family because of Phoni?'

Lizzie's eyes turned huge. 'How did you know?'

'Because with Phoni in the vicinity, that's the designated crime. And since you asked for a Necrojudge and not the police, I presume this is what's happened to you.'

'Indeed. It's my brother, Tom. Phoni took him twenty years ago...'

Valia's eyes widened. 'What? And you waited all this time to tell me, child?'

Stamatis put out a hand, drawing her attention. 'Look, Mrs Valia, let's cut the story short because, to tell you the truth, I'm not feeling safe here near this damned cave, no matter what you say – no offense. But not for me. For Lizzie. She's everything to me.' He leaned closer to Lizzie and put a protective arm around her, causing her to rest her head on his shoulder.

He turned to meet her eyes for a moment, and her heart melted. Lost for words, all she could do was watch as he continued to speak.

'If anything happens to my Lizzie, I don't know what I'll do! Probably come here and scorch the place, cement the entrance of the cave and—'

'No! No anger, my child! This attracts her ravens like nectar draws the honeybees! It will bring them here in droves if you don't calm yourself down!' Valia touched a round talisman around her neck that had a large amber stone at its centre. After a few moments of stroking it absentmindedly, she added, 'And if this happens, and Phoni finds us here, just the three of us, then not even *I* will be able to help you.'

Stamatis pursed his lips and Lizzie coaxed him with her eyes to take the woman's advice.

'I'm sorry... It's just that... Lizzie and her family didn't know anything about Necrojudges at the time of Tom's kidnapping. My family didn't either...'

'How far do you two go back?'

Stamatis gave a beaming smile. 'All our lives, it seems...'

'That's good. It strengthens your bond...' She stepped closer and took their hands, cupping them together inside her own over her chest. She closed her eyes for a few moments, her face serene.

When she opened her eyes again, a shadow crossed her face for a split second, then she let go of their hands. 'I can see that you have a bond that transcends this world, this life. By far...'

'Really? How do you mean?' asked Lizzie.

'Lizzie, please...' said Stamatis, then turned to Valia. 'Can I just carry on with what I was saying earlier?'

'Yes, by all means, young man.'

'Well, as I said, no one knew back then... so no one summoned you twenty years ago like we just did. Lizzie was present when Phoni took Tom, but even though she told everybody what she saw, no one believed her. Me included... So, you see, we're all paying the price now. The price of ignorance and distrust. Lizzie has been paying this price all her life. But no more. And I am so proud of her! Why? Because she came here, twenty years later, and as Phoni had promised, she gave her back her brother then!'

Valia's jaw went slack, her eyes wide, glazing over. Finally, she regained her composure and said, 'That's a first! I don't believe it!'

Lizzie then took over to relay to Valia the rest of the story. When she mentioned that Phoni had asked her to choose between herself and Tom, Stamatis squeezed Lizzie against him and piped up, 'But this will *never* happen, Mrs Valia! I won't let Phoni take either of them! And this is where you come in. As we say in Greece, *ta polla logia eine ftohia.* Too many words make a man poor. So just, please. Tell us... Can you help us?'

Valia gave a cryptic smile. 'Believe me when I say, I am your only hope.'

'So you can help?' asked Lizzie.

'Of course. I wouldn't be a Necrojudge if I couldn't.'

'I hope you don't mind me asking,' piped up Lizzie, then twisted her lips. 'Have you... ever met Phoni? Have you done this before?'

'I've met her, but this will be the first time I actually take a stand against her to protect people she has wronged. When I was a teenager, though, I witnessed my grandmother judge her for a kidnapping that she did.'

Stamatis gave a frown. 'She judged her?'

'Yes.'

'Like in the normal sense of the word?'

'From what I know, young man, there's only one way to judge someone. I have the power to both incarcerate Phoni and to discipline her. God endowed me with this power and I intend to use it, may God be my witness.'

'When can we do this, Mrs Valia?' interrupted Lizzie, then carried on by explaining the window they had until Phoni was expected to make another appearance in her house, in order to hear her answer.

When Lizzie finished, Valia shook her head, her exasperation palpable. 'She's got so much nerve to give you this impossible choice to ponder upon! But never you mind! We will teach her a lesson. Tomorrow night. Meet me right here at midnight and I'll expel her into the earth for good.'

'Tomorrow?' asked Stamatis to confirm. His eyes sought Lizzie's, his expression ablaze with enthusiasm.

'Yes. No time to lose,' continued Valia. 'But you must bring Tom along. And someone else that you trust too. Someone who cares for you. Otherwise, this won't work.'

'I can understand Tom must be present, but why do we need to bring someone else?' said Lizzie.

'We need a total of five for the ritual I must perform.'

'We can bring our friend, Aliki. She'll be happy to lend a hand,' said Stamatis, and Lizzie nodded her assent.

'Excellent! Now, if you don't mind, let's start walking back to the road. I've left my grandchildren sleeping alone at home so I can't be long.'

'They live with you? That's nice,' commented Lizzie as the three of them began to walk through the grove.

'They don't normally. But tonight their mother had to work at their family taverna with her husband – my son – so she left me the children on her way there to spend the night with me.'

'Is the taverna in Messonghi?' said Stamatis, just making conversation.

Valia hesitated for a few moments, then finally said, 'No, it's in Chlomos, actually. That's... where my house is too. Up the mountain, past Agios Dimitrios.'

'Yes, I know where Chlomos is.' He gave a chuckle at the thought that she should give him directions to it. 'And this explains why I haven't seen you before,' said Stamatis breezily. 'I live in Spileo, down the road from here and—'

Valia put up a hand, cutting him short. 'I don't mean to be rude, but I'd rather we didn't share too much about ourselves. I have my reasons.'

'Yes, yes of course,' said Stamatis, then fell silent, but he gave Lizzie a lingering look behind Valia's back, and she responded with a mute gaze. Neither of them could understand the reason for the woman's request, but they had to respect it all the same.

When they reached the road, Valia went straight for the decrepit VW beetle and opened the driver's door. She hadn't locked it. She was about to get in when Lizzie cleared her throat and said, 'Before you go, Mrs Valia, can I ask you a question?'

Valia turned to her. 'Of course, child.'

'What is the worst thing that could happen tomorrow night?'

Sensing her apprehension, Stamatis reached over and put a hand on her shoulder, squeezing, and Lizzie responded by patting his hand.

'Well,' Valia said, 'Phoni could escape our attention and snatch Tom, then jump into the spring. She can be fast, despite her age, trust me. And that is why I'll have Stamatis and your friend hold Tom firmly by his hands.' She turned to Stamatis and pointed sharply. 'And you shouldn't let go of Tom, no matter what!'

'I can hold his hand!' said Lizzie before Stamatis could respond.

'No! I need you by my side. There's a reason for that. But don't let yourself worry. It'll be all right.' She paused for a few moments, allowing the words to sink in.

Valia heaved a sigh, then added, 'There's a reason Necrojudges exist. It's because we keep those devils, the likes of Phoni, under check. She won't get away with it, mark my words. Now that I'm here, she won't be able to claim you or your brother ever again. You are free already.'

The words felt like balsam in Lizzie's soul. Stamatis put his arms around her, and she revelled in his embrace.

'So what will happen to her?' asked Stamatis. 'Will you kill her?'

Valia gave a low laugh. 'I wish. But no. She's not human to kill... But I can expel her. I can send her back to where she came from for a while... and hopefully, when she's allowed to walk on this land again, she will have learned her lesson.'

'I know you need to leave soon, but...' asked Lizzie, hesitation colouring her voice, but Valia offered an encouraging smile, so she added, '...I was wondering... how long has Phoni been doing this? Stealing children, I mean?'

'All her life, it seems. And that spans several centuries, from what I know. Phoni herself was kidnapped when she was a human child by her predecessor. In time she took her post and started doing the same to other children. You'd have thought that someone who knew what it was like, to be snatched and taken away from their life and family, would know better but... what normal person can wrap their mind around an evil act? Impossible!'

'Why is she still allowed to do this?' asked Lizzie.

Valia shrugged. 'Who knows? Why is any evil allowed to exist in this world?'

'So, is she superhuman? How does she have these powers?' asked Stamatis.

'She's a witch, a Healer of the Underworld. And dead herself, except she's never crossed to the other side. She's doing what she's supposed to do, which is to heal the souls that descend to the Underworld, but she went rogue.

'Unlike the other Healers who do the same godly work all over the world, helping souls find their way to the Underworld with as much peace and comfort as possible, this one kidnaps human children to help her, because they have more physical strength than the dead in the semi-ethereal state she's entitled to recruit.

'And even though this makes her better at her job, if you will, it has kept her perpetually in trouble with the Necrojudges here throughout the millennia. I believe all my ancestors have had to judge her at least once. It seems, this time, she'll answer to me. She certainly hasn't learned her lesson yet.'

Stunned, Lizzie and Stamatis exchanged mute glances.

Valia sat in the driver's seat, started the engine and rolled down the window, then closed the door. 'Good night then. I'll see you tomorrow. Have faith. Like all things we seek in life, make sure to see it in your mind's eye as if it's already happened.'

'Thanks for the tip. I'll try it. I'll try anything...' said Lizzie with a tired smile. She'd come to stand with Stamatis before the car window.

'Keep the faith and it'll all be all right, child. I promise.' Valia was about to roll the car forward when Lizzie put up a hand, catching her attention.

'Mrs Valia!' Lizzie took a step closer and stooped low to meet the woman's eye level. 'Thank you so much for helping us... I don't know what we'd have done if you hadn't stepped up for the task.'

'Don't mention it, child. Doing this is not just a kindness. It's my destiny and my reason of existence. Thanking me is... it's like thanking the sun for shining and the rain for falling.'

'You know, I'm amazed... I hadn't heard about you until recently... and you say Necrojudges exist all over the world?'

'Yes, because, trust me, there are many Phonis in the world. And when the first Healer went rogue, God created the Necrojudges to protect the people.'

She must have seen the dumbfounded expression in Lizzie's face then because she reached out and took the girl's hand, then added, 'Child, on our good Earth you will find a plant to cure every ailment, every disease. So it is with evil acts, and evil situations: God brings forth his angels, and others among His benevolent creations, and they intervene directly or inspire the people to take action against evil. So this is what is happening here with you and me. Nothing more. Nothing less.'

With these words, Valia let go of Lizzie's hand, waved them both a quick goodbye and drove off uphill back to her village.

Alone with Stamatis in the wilderness, under the silvery moon, Lizzie fell into his arms and wept tears of relief as he stroked her hair and whispered words of love.

Dark, glistening eyes

Lizzie woke up in her bed the next morning feeling numb, her mind churning with a plethora of thoughts, mainly ones that struck terror in her heart. She tried, just as Stamatis had made her promise, to keep positive, to believe this was going to be the day when they'd all be free to carry on with their lives. But it was hard, all the same, not to think of the dangers.

She propped herself up on her elbows and rested her eyes on the closed window shutters. The morning sunlight seemed strong outside, even though it was a little after eight o' clock. The birds were singing just like any other day. Yet, this was no ordinary day. *This could be the beginning of a devastating end... Anything could happen at midnight.*

Mrs Valia required her and Tom, Stamatis and Aliki to be at the cave when she'd summon Phoni tonight... But what if the witch had an ace up her sleeve? What if one or more of them wound up trapped in the mountain, or even dead?

Lizzie shook her head fiercely and jumped out of bed. She slipped her sandals on and went to the window to open the shutters. The sunlight rushed in, streaming gloriously all the way to the wardrobe on the other side of the room. A warm breeze tickled her face, and she managed the ghost of a smile, despite her dark thoughts. She turned around and pricked her ears. Not a peep from the living room.

Aliki had stayed in the apartment the previous night to keep Tom safe while Lizzie and Stamatis were on the mountain with Mrs Valia.

When Lizzie returned a little after one a.m. she found Aliki dozing in an armchair while Tom slept on the sofa bed. *Bless her... We owe her so much!* If it hadn't been for her local connections Lizzie doubted they'd have found Mrs Valia.

As for Stamatis... he'd been her tower of strength... her lifeline. Deep heartache awaited her, she knew, when she'd soon have to leave him behind.

She'd have to go to England with Tom so her family could reunite properly, but then, what would she do? Would Tom be okay in England without her? How soon could she return to Corfu again to be with Stamatis?

Maybe Tom could come with her... He felt perfectly at home on the island, just like she did. But their parents... they'd want to keep Tom in England, surely... Or maybe they wouldn't care...

Unbearable, painful memories from the past flooded her mind, making her angry at her parents. *They didn't believe me! They put me in a mental health clinic, for god's sake! Mum said it was so they could help me. But it was dreadful... what they did to me. The therapies, the drugs, the sheer misery of the place. All for nothing. Because I didn't imagine it! I was telling the truth! And now... now, when they see Tom still looking twelve, how can I expect them to believe it's him? Could it be that they will accuse me of being a liar all over again?*

Her parents were realists... with a sheer aversion towards anything fantastical. They didn't even believe in God, let alone witches. They'd never have sought the assistance of a Necrojudge even if someone had offered the information that they existed. *No! My brother stood no chance from day one!* He was condemned to be left in the hands of Phoni, helpless... because of their parents. Those ignorant realists, who'd never allow themselves to believe in the unseen.

This is why once they'd called the police and arrived at a dead end, they'd given up on their son, just like that, and left the island. *And they never came back. But I did. I did... So, why should my family back home need to know? What if we never left the island? What if we stayed here... with Stamatis? But... wouldn't this be unfair on my brother? Never to see his parents again? His aunts, uncles, and cousins? His grandparents? He says he misses them all, that he bears no grudges to Mum and Dad... Oh, God! What do I do?*

She had just dressed in a t-shirt and a pair of shorts and came to stand before the mirror. She picked up her hair brush and threw a sympathetic glance at her grim expression just as a migraine stabbed her in her left temple, causing her to wince.

It's a dead end... Even if we defeat Phoni tonight, Tom's and my life will remain irreversibly affected by her. So much has been lost... So much that we can never regain. How do you recapture twenty years? How do I even introduce my twin brother to the family when he looks young enough to be my son?

With a heavy heart, she brushed her hair quickly, averting her eyes from her reflection in the mirror. Regardless of what's happened and how much Tom and she had already lost, what mattered now, first and foremost, was to get Phoni out of the way. *For good! The rest, I'll just have to address later.*

※※※※

Just after five p.m., Lizzie stood outside Stamatis's garden gate and rang his phone a couple of times, then ended the call, to notify him of her arrival. He was expecting her, so they could have some alone-time together. He'd offered to pick her up from her apartment on his motorcycle but she'd insisted the long walk in the fresh air would do her good. It had certainly helped to ease her anxiety a little.

Aliki had taken Tom to Corfu town so he could buy some clothes. They hoped he'd find some that'd be suitable for cold weather. Tom was eager to visit England again, but couldn't pack the only clothes he owned, which consisted of a small selection of t-shirts, shorts and flip flops.

Lizzie gave a wry smile as she thought of all that. She still wasn't sure if taking Tom back to England was a good idea, but he wanted to do it, so she had to respect his wish. They had it all planned. If all went well tonight, the next morning she'd take him to the police, claiming she'd found him wandering in the mountain, a boy with amnesia who was British from what she understood.

Then, via the British Vice Consulate in Corfu town, she hoped to get him the necessary papers so he could fly to England with her. From there, things would have to work themselves out. She and Tom would have to stay together, somehow. She'd consider no other possibility.

Stamatis emerged from his open front door and waved across the distance, snapping her out of her deep thoughts. Smiling to his ears, he hurried along the concrete path to open the gate. 'My love!' He unlocked the gate and, as soon as she stepped through it, pulled her into his arms.

He offered his lips and she drank from them, thirsty for his love and the feeling of bliss it gave her. It numbed all her fears, all her apprehensions, and had become a drug to her. She wouldn't mind overdosing on it today.

She was no fool. Tonight was the big night at the cave... and they were running out of time to live their romance fully, in case something terrible happened when they met Phoni. That's why she was desperate to give herself to him, body and soul, even this once, before tonight, just in case.

Lizzie felt their mutual sexual desire sizzling in the air, crackling like electricity on their skin as they touched. She could see it in the twinkle of his eye; he wanted the same, and her heart sang with sweet anticipation.

With laughing eyes and holding her by the hand, Stamatis led her into the house, then upstairs. To her surprise, instead of his bedroom, he took her to his balcony gesturing her to take a seat in one of the comfortable wicker armchairs.

A gentleman. I love it... Or maybe it's a ploy. He's playing hard to get, to get me even more worked up! Lizzie smiled to herself as she sat down and couldn't help giggling when he gave her a puzzled look.

'What?' He seemed none the wiser.

'Nothing,' she said, smiling sweetly.

'You must be thirsty from the climb. What will you have? I have water, tea... or maybe orange juice?'

'Orange juice would be great, thank you.'

He disappeared down the stairs and returned a minute later, two glasses of orange juice in his hands. He gave her one of them and sat beside her.

She drank half of the glass in one go and gave a deep sigh as she put the glass on the table.

'I think you were thirsty.'

She wiped the side of her mouth with her fingertips and smirked. 'Yep. You can say that again.'

His face turned sombre as he leaned towards her, the back of his hand caressing her cheek. 'So? How are you feeling about tonight? You're keeping strong, I hope? Optimistic and all that?'

Lizzie drank from her glass again, then pursed her lips. *What do I say? I can't lie to him...*

'That bad, huh? Don't do it, *Lizzie mou...*'

Lizzie knew of the Greek "mou" that means "my". The Greeks use it after names to show affection. The sound of it made her heart melt. She put out a hand and caressed his hair, and he leaned in for a kiss. It was tender, sweet, wonderful, and it made her feel alive... No, not just alive; every time he held or kissed her, somehow, he'd leave her feeling indestructible.

She tilted her head back and smiled, her eyes closed. 'Please. Don't stop. Kiss me again.'

He chortled, then obliged her, this time kissing her with a passion that made her gut ignite with heat. Like hot lava it trickled down, reaching her core, trailing down her thighs, making her lose all sense of time and place.

That's when they heard a cawing sound and snapped their eyes open to find a raven perched on the rail at the other end of the balcony. The bird sat there, turning its head this way and that, watching them intently with its dark, glistening eyes.

Lizzie grabbed a newspaper that lay on the table, cursing, about to stand and use it to swat the bird away, but Stamatis put up a hand to stop her, his eyes bright with alarm.

'Don't be hostile to it,' he whispered urgently. 'What if it's *her*? You don't want to raise suspicions. As far as she knows, you're looking at striking a deal. She doesn't know we've arranged for *you-know-who* to set her straight, right?'

Lizzie nodded. This made sense. She put the newspaper back on the table and looked at the bird one more time. It still watched them, silently now, and she hoped it hadn't perceived her earlier action as hostility. *I'm so stupid sometimes!* She had to stop being so impulsive, so hot-headed. But she couldn't help it. She'd had a gutful of Phoni and her black-feathered spies.

But it wasn't just that. Her moment of bliss was gone because of the damned bird. It had shifted the mood between them. Stamatis was looking at her warmly enough, but the fire of passion in his eyes had vanished.

She sat back in her chair and gave a long sigh, causing Stamatis, who'd just drained his glass, to look at her with a mischievous grin. 'Don't worry, Lizzie. Let it watch. Who cares? Just stay cool...' He winked and added in a whisper, 'Remember... we have the upper hand.'

'Yes, you're right. I'm sorry.' She finished the dregs in her glass and, holding hands, they sat in silence for a few moments. Lizzie tried all she could to relax while she watched the bird from the corner of her eye.

Finally, the raven flew away.

Lizzie clutched her chest. 'Phew! After you said, I was so worried it might transform into Phoni... though it didn't have the white streak, but you never know with her.' She gave a little wave. 'Anyway. I'm so glad it's gone.'

'Don't worry. The week she gave you expires tomorrow. That's why we're doing this tonight. Besides, she wouldn't show herself in front of me, would she?'

'Of course. How right you are! I envy you, Stamatis. I wish I were as cool as you are so I could think straight too...' She turned her gaze towards the mountain. 'I cannot believe how close her darn cave is to your house. Unseen... hidden...'

'Not so hidden if you think about it...'

'What do you mean?'

He raked his hair and gave a lopsided smile. 'I've been thinking... my village's name is Spileo. And the word in Greek means 'Cave'... Do you suppose the people who named this place knew our secret?'

'I didn't know that!' she said wide-eyed, then, tilting her head, added, 'Well, I suppose... it's possible.'

'Or maybe not. Maybe it's just coincidence. Every place has to mean something, I guess...'

'Every place? Really?'

'Certainly. A name for a place should mean something, don't you think?'

Lizzie raised a brow. 'Well? What does Messonghi mean then?'

'That's easy. Middle Earth.'

'You're jesting.'

'No, I'm not!'

'So, what does that mean? That Gandalf and a bunch of hobbits could be living next door to me?'

'No, clever clogs!' He grabbed her and started to tickle her waist, causing her to howl, her gut tightening unbearably as she gasped for air. Finally, he stopped, allowing her to breathe easily again.

'You brute! Never do this again!' she protested playfully, tapping her fist on his chest only to hit what felt like a concrete wall where his pecs bulged under his tight-fitting t-shirt.

She met his eyes that had exploded with laughter. Then, he put an arm around her, and they turned to gaze at the coast. Mist sat low over the water in the distant horizon, colouring it grey, the sea tranquil, like a sheet of glass, the sun already on its ancient path to kiss the sea and fill the sky with wonder.

Villages force you to act this way

Stamatis entered his bedroom with Lizzie, hand-in-hand, and led her to sit on the side of his double bed, then reached for the bedside light and turned it on.

'This is it... my *boudoir*, so to speak,' he said, a wicked smile on his face, as he took a seat beside her.

'It's a lovely room...'

His face turned sombre. 'Just so you know... I bought this bed when I moved in here... *After* Kiki passed away. I... I'm the only person who ever lay on it.'

Lizzie gazed into his eyes mutely for a few moments, her heart melting with love for him. 'I see...' It sufficed her to say, too moved to express how thankful she felt for his thoughtfulness. It hadn't even crossed her mind to wonder about that.

As he watched her, she looked around her appreciatively. The decoration was simple, the furniture only few; just two bedside tables on either side of the bed, a built-in wardrobe by the door, an armchair near the window and a dresser beside it with a wall-mounted mirror above it.

A few clothes were draped carelessly over the back of the armchair, and an untidy stack of magazines stood on top of the dresser. Two portraits hung on the walls in dark wood frames. One was of his grandmother, the other of his parents.

She turned to look at him and met his deep gaze, losing herself in it instantly.

The shutters were almost fully shut allowing just enough light to see clearly. It was deliciously cool in the room, so comfortable that a luxurious sigh escaped her lips.

'What is it?'

'I love this room. It grows on me with every passing minute.'

'I'm glad to hear it.' He leaned in, so close that when he spoke she felt his warm breath on her lips. 'Oh, Lizzie... if only you knew for how long I've been dreaming about this...'

Before she could respond, to say that she'd been doing the same, he took her in his arms and kissed her, and she let herself fall on the fragrant linen as he lay upon her.

His hands, urgent now, caressed her face and neck as their kiss grew deeper. Soon, with their hearts thumping in their chests and soft moans escaping their lips in quick succession, they began to undress and explore each other's bodies. As they surrendered themselves to their fiery passion, time came to a standstill, the world shrinking to the size of their embrace.

※※※※

After their moments of ecstasy had come and gone, they stayed in each other's arms for a while, their bodies limp. Lizzie listened to the chirping of the birds in the garden below and to the soft sound of his breathing as he caressed her hair with a gentle hand.

'Do you mind if I leave you on your own for a while?' he said suddenly. 'There's something I need to do.'

Lizzie registered his cryptic smile and chuckled. 'Why? Where are you going?'

'Not far. Just to the bathroom. I won't be long.'

'Oh. Of course.'

He slipped his shorts back on, then left the room in a hurry.

As soon as he left, Lizzie grew conscious of her nakedness as she caught sight of herself in the mirror across the room. She put on her clothes—just a summer dress—and sat up on the bed against the headboard, her eyes returning to the mirror. Soon, she found herself smiling at her reflection. Even though it had just happened she still couldn't believe it. *Stamatis. Mine. Oh-my-god.*

Lost in her thoughts that soon took her to Phoni and the perilous night ahead of them all, she lost track of the passage of time but could hear a tap running, on and off, and presumed that was Stamatis in the bathroom. She hadn't heard a flush, just the tap. *What's that all about?*

Then, the door creaked open and in stepped a man she didn't recognize. A pang of alarm seized her, causing her to gasp and clutch her chest, eyes bulging.

Stamatis, the man at the door all along, broke into a guffaw. 'It's me! Relax! Oh! Your face!' he said, pointing at her, then laughed some more.

Lizzie stared incredulous as he came to sit on the bed.

'What? You shaved your beard? Just like that? Why?'

'No, not just like that, Lizzie...' He caressed her cheek, then sat back against the headboard beside her. He took her hand and kissed it, then placed it on his lap and gave a long sigh.

'You see, Lizzie... I didn't just decide to shave my beard. I meant to, for quite some time now, but it felt wrong. I wasn't ready to do it... not until I could make you mine, and prove to myself that I've actually moved on.'

'Is this about Kiki? If it is, by all means, I understand. I expect it takes a long time to get over the loss of a spouse...'

'No, Lizzie... You don't understand. This is about her, but it has nothing to do with me mourning over her death.'

'It doesn't?'

He shook his head profusely. 'No.'

'So, what is this about?'

'Lizzie... Kiki was not the kind of wife you'd expect.'

'How do you mean?'

His expression was pained when he turned to her. 'She wasn't a faithful one, for a start. She was cheating on me, Lizzie.'

'Really? And you knew?'

He shook his head. 'I found out the day that she died.'

She raised her brows, her voice a little more than a whisper. 'What?'

'Kiki was involved in a car crash...'

Lizzie nodded in lieu of an answer.

He gave a laboured sigh. 'She was in the car with a guy.' He flinched, then carried on, 'As it turned out, they were returning to the bar from his house that night... whereas I thought she was at the bar all night, working.'

'She worked in a bar?'

'Yes. Except she worked *his* bar too from time to time...' he said with a wry smile.

Lizzie didn't smile at that; she felt sick, all of a sudden.

'And what about the guy? Did he die too?' she asked after a while.

'No. He survived... just so he can laugh in my face about it... the bastard!' He turned to her, his eyes two live embers. 'And... what's more... you know him.'

'I do? Who is he?'

'Tassos.'

'That idiot from Petriti?'

'The very same.'

'Oh.' Now it made sense... It all made sense. 'I cannot believe it! Kiki cheated on you with *him*?'

'That's right. With that *redikolo*... that ridiculous poser.' He gave a bitter smile. 'You don't look impressed.'

'I'd love to tell you what I think about that... but I won't speak ill of the dead. I'll just say I cannot imagine any sane person could ever choose that loser over you.'

'Well, Kiki did... and that's not all.'

Lizzie tilted her head. 'What else is there?'

'Only the fact that it came out in the open after her death. Suddenly I was a cheated husband and a widower at the same time. Everyone in Messonghi soon found out—I'm guessing because of Tassos—and I had to be seen mourning about Kiki's death despite that. I had to hide my own shame and be seen respecting her memory, all for the sake of keeping up appearances.'

'What? But surely you didn't have to!'

'Oh, I beg to differ. Villages force you to act this way. Besides, my parents didn't know. If anyone here at Spileo found out, then they probably never told them out of respect. That was my saving grace...'

'That was lucky.'

'Yes, it was... So I pretended to be mourning the loss of Kiki for my parents' sake too. Thankfully, her family live in Salonica, so I didn't have to face them again after the funeral. But the false pretences, listening to people's sneers behind my back, and my wife's deceit, of course... all that hurt me, Lizzie, it hurt my dignity to the core.' He raked his hair with an urgent hand. 'I found it impossible to deal with what happened... Had she not died, I'd have been able to divorce her, do anything I could to move on, but she went and died on me!'

Lizzie got hold of his shoulder and shook it gently. 'Hush... it's over now...'

'Thank you, I know... I know, my darling. That's why I'm here, beside you, clean shaven again.' He brushed his smooth, fragrant cheek with the palm of his hand and gave a feeble smile. 'I feel reborn, if you must know.'

She forced a smile to lighten the mood, even though her heart twinged with sympathy. 'You silly boy...' she said, tousling his hair. 'You should have told me earlier. I'd happily have gone all horizontal on you sooner.'

'I know, right?' He gave a wry smile, then gave a soft sigh. 'That damned beard had become a part of me, you know? But it was a part I didn't want any more, except I didn't feel ready to let it go. I had grown it to mourn my wife's loss like any other husband would have done here, but in time it became my way to hide my pain, not for her loss, but for her betrayal... When my mother passed away too I found myself feeling too trapped in this place to bear it. I guess it was evident because my father, for my sake, urged me then to leave the island...'

'Is that when you went to work in Ioannina?'

'That's right... I left him behind to do that. Bless him, he'd said he didn't mind but, of course, when he got sick I had to come back to be here for him. By then, it was expected of me to shave the beard of mourning and move on with my life, but I just couldn't do it. So I decided to keep it and told everyone who asked that I'd grown to like it. Except I didn't, but it served a purpose...'

'What purpose?'

He shrugged, eyes glued to their entwined hands on his lap. 'In a way, it felt like as long as I had it, people would respect my privacy and leave me alone, you know?' He turned to look at her, only for a moment, then lowered his gaze again.

'I'd heard so much nasty stuff going around about me by then... Most of it said by Tassos... And other people were saying I was a fool to be taken for a ride for so long... that Kiki was laughing in my face while she partied with this guy. In a way, it's my fault they met!' He snapped his head up, seeking her eyes, his own feverish.

'Your fault? How was it your fault, Stamatis?'

'Kiki wasn't happy to clean the rooms. She'd complain about my mother all day long and said the work was demeaning for her. So we argued all the time... and she begged me to let her work in a bar instead. To keep her happy I employed someone to help my mother clean the rooms and I let her work in the damned bar... and that is where she met that idiot.'

'I see... but this doesn't make you responsible for what followed. You've done nothing wrong, Stamatis. Nor are you responsible for her passing.'

'Oh... if only all those years you had been around, Lizzie! It would have saved me from so much heartache! Had you come back again and again over the years with your family we'd never have lost touch. Had Tom never gone missing, I'd never have got married to Kiki.... You and I would have been together... *stayed* together. From the beginning...'

'Hush... Don't say any more! Please! I can't bear the thought of you in pain for so long. But it's okay... I'm here now...' she whispered, a loving arm on his chest, but he shook his head. He wasn't done yet. He needed to keep going so she let him.

'For so long, I felt like I'd become a dead man, Lizzie! Like I died too when she did.'

'No, don't say that...'

'But I did... I did... and I didn't want to return to the land of the living, to meet another woman, for fear this would happen again. I felt ridiculed... I didn't want to date anyone, not even to make new friends. They all knew, Lizzie... they all knew. And they kept laughing behind my back.' He turned to face her, unashamed, even though his eyes were full of tears.

'Oh, my love...' Lizzie wiped his tears and kissed his cheeks, then his mouth, as he whispered words of love and thanks.

When she pulled back, she saw his lips curl up into a thin smile.

'That's better!' she said, pinching his chin. With the back of her hand, she brushed the smooth skin of his clean-shaven cheek. 'Oh, you smell so good... what is it?'

'Just after-shave. Citrus Fruits and Musk, according to the label. Glad you like it. There'll be plenty of that from now on.' He winked, then heaved a long sigh. 'So, do you see now? Do you see why I love you? Why I owe you so much? You make me happy, and I thought it could never happen again. You worked a miracle on me, Lizzie. You gave me my life back, and my own sense of dignity.'

Lizzie took his face in her hands and gave him a lingering kiss, then pulled back and smiled to her ears. 'I gave you your life back? Oh, you can say that again! Now the beard's gone, it's like I've just found my childhood friend again. So much so, that I'm undecided. Should I call you Stamatis or Stamata from now on?'

She saw his eyes ignite with merriment and stuck her tongue out. He responded by letting out a roar, then started to attack her midriff with tickles and pinches.

Lizzie bent over, then slid down the bed on her back, squealing, howling, and begging him to stop tickling.

'Serves you right, Your Highness, Queen Elizabeth!' he said with a chortle when he stopped, collapsing on top of her, letting his full weight fall upon her.

She complained, just like he expected, so he laughed and lifted himself up. 'My apologies, Your Highness. But you had it coming.' She pulled a face of mock annoyance, and he offered his hand to help her sit up beside him again.

'You brute!' she joked, elbowing him, and he elbowed her gently back, then they fell silent for a few moments. 'Oh... I could so get used to this...' she said dreamily as she raised her hand, her fingertips tracing the line of his strong jaw. When they reached his chin, he jerked, opened his mouth and pecked at her fingers, causing her to giggle.

'What's that?' he asked. 'What could you get used to?'

'Sleeping with someone as gorgeous as you,' she said with a smirk, then batted her eyelashes at him playfully.

He put his arms around her waist and lifted her effortlessly onto his lap. 'Don't tempt me, missy. Because there's loads more where that came from.'

'Oh, trust me. I know. And I look forward to it.'

He pushed her gently out of the bed and into a standing position, then slapped her bottom playfully. 'But not now, lest your brother will think I've kidnapped you or something.'

Lizzie checked her watch. 'Damn! He and Aliki must be back from Corfu town by now. Can you give me a ride home please?'

'Of course! But we're sticking to the plan, right? BBQ here tonight? I've already defrosted the fish we caught the other day.'

'Yes! Tom's looking forward to the BBQ!'

'So we're staying here afterwards like we said? All four of us?' he asked as he put on his shirt.

'Yes. We'll watch TV or something, like you said, till about half past eleven, then walk up the mountain to meet Mrs Valia for midnight.'

They held each other in silence for a while as they pondered on the difficult task ahead. Lizzie could tell he was just as worried as she was about meeting Phoni. Still, they had to stay upbeat and hope for the best. What good would it do to go mad with worry?

Lizzie forced a feeble smile and took his hand. 'Let's go. And you don't have to stay in Messonghi for long – or at all –if you don't want to.'

'Sure. I'll get the BBQ ready back here. Come over around eight with Tom and Aliki. I'll still be cooking the BBQ then. You girls can make the *salata* and the *patates*, while we men prepare the protein.'

She cocked her eye at him. 'I knew it. You wanted me for the kitchen all along like a typical Greek man, didn't you?'

He gave a smirk. 'Not just a Greek. You know what all men say... "Brides are dressed in white because the colour doesn't clash with the kitchen appliances".'

She raised her brows and smiled wickedly. 'Brides? Is that the plan then? For you and me?'

'If you play your cards right. I expect *pastichio*, *moussaka* and a lamb roast, with homemade *tzatziki*, every week. None of that brown watery stuff you Brits make back home.'

This time, it was Lizzie who attacked his midriff, but no matter how much she tried, she couldn't get past the hard muscles to find soft flesh to tickle. All the while, he grinned at her, his tongue bulging under his bottom lip.

'Oh, *Stamata*! I give up!' she said, grunting playfully, then marched to the door. She spun around, rolled her eyes and beckoned him to follow.

Stamatis gave an impish smirk. 'Your Highness, sorry to say, you shouldn't have used that word. Here comes the punishment!' he exclaimed, hands extended before him, fingers curled up, ready to catch her.

His heavy footsteps and her squeals reverberated against the walls as he chased her down the landing.

Good old karma works on auto-pilot

Lizzie and Stamatis entered the courtyard and went straight to Aliki's apartment to see her and Tom. They rang the doorbell sniggering, impatient to see their reaction to Stamatis's new look.

Just as they expected, Aliki froze when she opened the door. Tom, who poked his head around her big form, widened his eyes, mouth agape.

'Oh my goodness!' said Aliki finally.

'You shaved your beard!' said Tom.

The two walked in, chortling, as Aliki beckoned them to the sofa so they could all sit down.

Charlie, who had been lying on the cotton rug by the coffee table, stood and began to bark, tail wagging excitedly. Once Lizzie and Stamatis had taken turns to pet him, he calmed down and lay by their feet when they sat.

'Phew, I'm glad it's you, Stamatis. For a moment back there I thought my sister got a new boyfriend!' teased Tom.

Aliki leaned forward with a wink. 'Tell the truth! Did Lizzie twist your arm to do it?'

'No, it wasn't me! He just went to the bathroom and shaved the beard unprompted. He gave me a start when he came out!'

'That's right; it was all me, I assure you!' said Stamatis to Aliki and Tom. He pulled Lizzie against him and squeezed her lovingly, eyes bright like two exploding stars.

Aliki beamed at them both for a few moments, then said, 'You look great, my friend... My only worry is that you will be headhunted by a modelling agency and whisked off to Paris, Milan or New York, and I'll have to spend the rest of my days consoling my friend over here!' She pointed at Lizzie and they all dissolved into giggles.

Stamatis stood again, announcing he had to go back and get some odds and ends done, then start the BBQ. The others stood and cheered, saying how they couldn't wait to taste the fresh fish the three had caught the other day, especially the large tuna fish. Stamatis said he'd cook it in thick slices with lashings of olive oil, lemon juice, and oregano, making them all ravenous.

As soon as he was gone, Tom opened his shopping bags to show Lizzie the clothes he'd bought in Corfu town. Long sleeve tops, perfect for autumn weather, and even a woolly jumper. More bags contained a pair of jeans, a pair of pyjamas, a light jacket, a scarf, socks and underwear, and a pair of sneakers.

'Wow, you're all set for English weather! And they are wonderful. *Meya!* Enjoy them with health,' she wished him, the Greek way.

Aliki stood and walked to the kitchen, saying she'd bring some fruit juice for them all. 'Oh no!' she uttered with dismay moments later.

'What is it?' Lizzie asked from the sofa where she sat with Tom, still admiring his new purchases.

Aliki returned to the living room and went straight to the cabinet by her front door. She picked up her purse and keys and turned to them. 'The carton is empty but I'm not surprised. It's so sweltering hot today, and I've been drinking lots. Sorry, guys... I'll get a fresh carton. Back in a jiffy.'

'You don't have to go. A cup of tea would do nicely.'

'A hot drink on a day like this? No way, Lizzie.' She gave a dismissive wave, then winked. 'Besides. It's a chance to see Babis again!'

With that, she was gone, eager, it seemed, to get to the supermarket a moment sooner. Lizzie smiled to herself. Since the night in Petriti, Aliki's romance with Babis had been blooming alongside that of her own.

'Lizzie? All okay?' asked Tom.

She turned to find him looking concerned and raised a fist to push back his chin. 'Of course... matey.'

Tom kept his eyes on her, looking unsure that she meant it.

'No. Really, I'm okay.'

'Thank you for saying yes to us going back to England...'

'Oh Tom... Of course, we are going. How can I deprive you of seeing our parents again?'

'But you're worried that they might reject me, aren't you? That they may think it can't possibly be me. I know you are. But you're still doing it. For me.'

Lizzie put a gentle hand on his shoulder. 'Of course. Anything for you, Tom.' She forced a smile. 'You and I are going to give it a go. For the sake of our family. For what it once used to be. And if they don't believe us, at least we'll have tried. And you will have seen them again, no matter what they will do or say. And, if they reject us, we'll come straight back here. Together. Where we belong.'

'And if they take us in? If they believe us?'

'Then all the merrier for us, Tom.'

'But what about you and Stamatis then? You seem so happy together. He will miss you when you go... and you... Lizzie, you're radiant! Look at you! How can you live without him?'

'I won't have to live without him, Tom. I'm sure I will be back soon. He will wait for me... Let's settle you back in England first... we shall see. Don't worry about me.'

Charlie, who had been napping on the rug, stirred then, and they looked at him, smiling. His coat looked shiny, perfect. Lizzie thought back to the time when it was in a bad state. Tom had used the perfect remedy for him. Thoughts of the four healings they'd done, with perfect timing, flooded her mind. They had been through so much...

'Lizzie?'

She turned to her brother, who was smiling wryly. 'Yes, Tom?'

'If only there was a herb I could use to make myself thirty-two... the way I should be looking... then things would be so much easier for you. You wouldn't have to worry about our parents calling you a liar again... saying that you're crazy...'

Lizzie shook her head, then gave him an encouraging smile. 'No, Tom... There is no herb like that. Which means we will have to put our parents to the test. And let's hope, for your sake first and foremost, that this time around they will pass it.'

A few moments later, Aliki breezed in through the door, her face animated with excitement. She stopped before the others for just a few moments, her eyes widening. 'Oh, Lizzie! Wait till you hear what Babis just told me!'

'What?' Lizzie and Tom uttered in unison.

Aliki wagged her index finger. 'Uh-uh. You and me, Lizzie. Talk alone later. Sorry, Tom. Girlie talk.'

Tom huffed playfully and Aliki disappeared into the kitchen to return a few moments later with the refreshments on a tray. 'Finally! It's got a little cooler now that the sun has started to set,' she said when she placed the tray on the table and sat down. 'After we've had our drinks, I'll have to go and walk Charlie. You guys can come with me, if you like.'

Tom nodded excitedly at her suggestion as he took one of the glasses.

Lizzie cradled hers on her lap, chewing her lips as she watched the other two drink. When Aliki put her glass down on the table, Lizzie turned to her, leaning closer. 'Actually, I was thinking, what if Tom walks Charlie on his own? I'd like to discuss something with you too.'

Tom drained his glass, then rolled his eyes. 'More girlie talk. I get it.'

Aliki giggled in response while Lizzie put out a hand to Tom, smirking. He put up one too and they did a high five.

'You're the best, Tom,' said Lizzie.

'I know,' he said matter-of-factly as he moved to get the dog lead that hung by the door. Within a few moments, he and Charlie were standing at the open door, the dog barking and whirling excitedly beside him.

As soon as he was gone, Aliki faced Lizzie, her expression exuberant. 'Okay. You tell me first, then I'll tell you what I have to say.'

Lizzie sat straight, then thought for a minute, trying to find the right words. 'Aliki, the morning after the festival in Petriti, I asked you what Stamatis has against Tassos, and you told me it wasn't your secret to tell.'

Aliki gave a knowing smile. 'Uh-huh...'

'And then, you admitted that the same secret involves Nia too...'

'Yes, that's right.' Aliki tilted her head and eyed Lizzie sideways. 'Where are you going with this? Speak up, girlfriend. What do you know?'

'Stamatis told me more about Kiki today. He mentioned that she had an affair with Tassos.'

Aliki gave a soft sigh. 'Ah. So you know.'

'He said the whole of Messonghi does.'

'Sadly, it's true.'

'And what about Nia? What does she have to do with this? Is she an item with Tassos? Is that it?'

'No. These two have always been just friends, from what I know.'

'So what is it? Why don't you like her? Other than the obvious reasons, of course... Forgive me, but... I have the impression that you've left something unsaid, and that this has something to do with her and Stamatis.' She cocked her eye at Aliki. 'Am I right?'

Aliki twisted her lips. 'Oh damn... I can't lie. Yes, it does.'

Lizzie leaned forward. 'Well, if you're willing to share, I promise I won't tell Stamatis or anyone else. I just need to know everything there is to know about Nia. Just in case she tries anything nasty in future.'

Aliki gave a little wave, then chortled. 'Oh... don't you worry about Nia any more.'

'Why?'

'I'll tell you why in a minute. But first, to answer your question... Yes. I don't like Nia because I know something that she shared with me once. And it doesn't sound like you and Stamatis know about it.'

'Which is?'

'That she was the one who pushed Kiki into the arms of Tassos in the first place.'

Lizzie couldn't believe her ears. Her voice sounded squeaky when she said, 'She did?'

'Yep.'

'So she could have her chance with Stamatis?'

'You guessed it.'

'What a psycho!'

Aliki gave a firm nod. 'Indeed. Nia and Kiki were close friends back then. Nia knew Kiki had fallen out of love with Stamatis long ago, and she saw her chance to claim him anew. So she put her plan into action... She tried and tried to convince Kiki that she ought to stop working at the guest house, that a fun place like a bar would be perfect for her, and all that crap.

'She knew Tassos was working in a bar, and as he was gorgeous, yet shallow and promiscuous, she believed there was a good chance that Kiki might fancy him enough to have an affair with him. Somehow, she intervened and got Kiki a job in that bar that summer. It was the high season and they needed the extra hands, plus she knew the owner.'

'How convenient...' said Lizzie bitterly.

'Yes, I guess it all worked out in Nia's favour at the time... So, she started to lie to both Kiki and Tassos, telling each one that the other was infatuated with them until she got them to go out together. Kiki was a beautiful woman... but not one of great ethos. Plus, she felt resentful towards Stamatis and his parents for the long years of "mindless work at the guest house" as she put it to Nia at the time... So she found in Tassos her perfect chance for a romance behind her husband's back.'

'Did she intend to leave Stamatis? Or at least tell him about Tassos at any point?'

'That, we will never know. But what I do know from what Nia told me is that Kiki had fallen head over heels in love with Tassos and that, somehow, he'd grown madly in love with her too. Tassos knew how fed up she was with her married life.

'After her death, he became so upset, I guess, in a sick way, that it gave him pleasure to hurt Stamatis even though he wasn't responsible for her passing. Tassos talked nastily about Stamatis to everyone who'd listen... marring his name... especially as he deliberately added a lot of lies to make his stories more impressive. I believe in several of them, Stamatis was supposed to beat Kiki regularly. A blatant lie, of course...'

'Oh-my-god! I cannot believe I'm hearing this! And Nia said all that to you back when you first met? When you were going out for the odd drink together?'

'Yes. Sadly so. I had no idea what a conniving piece of work she was. But once she confessed all that to me one evening after a few drinks, believe me, I never gave her the time of day again. But... you know what they say.... Karma has a way of biting you in the ass when you least expect it.'

Something in Aliki's meaningful gaze caused Lizzie to ask, 'Why do you say that?'

'It's what I wanted to tell you earlier. Guess what Babis just told me...'

'About Nia?'

'Yes! She left Corfu this afternoon. For good. As we speak, she's on the ferry to Igoumenitsa. She's taking a coach back to her village in Preveza from there.'

'She left Corfu? Just like that? But why?'

'Tassos. They had a big fight and… it seems that he, being a sleaze ball and all, decided to do to her what he'd been doing to Stamatis all those years.'

'Lie about her?'

'That's an understatement. But yes.'

'Why? What happened?'

'They had a big fight back at his house when they left Petriti on the night of the festival, five days ago… If you recall, they were both heavily intoxicated. He, especially.'

'And?'

'What followed in his house between them… I guess it made him mad. And from the following day, he began to spread rumours and monstrous lies about her.'

'But why? I don't understand.'

'Apparently, they went back to his house for a night cap and to recover after that nasty incident at the festival. From what Nia told Babis, Tassos was very angry and felt humiliated because of the way Stamatis had treated him in front of everybody. He kept cursing, shouting… and then, just like that, he assaulted Nia. Quite forcefully too. You know… sexually.'

Lizzie's eyes widened. '*What?*'

'Yes… And Nia said that she got very lucky. Had it not been for a vase on a table nearby that she managed to grab and strike him on the head with, rendering him unconscious, he might have even raped her. From what she heard later on, a friend found him passed out on the couch the next morning, blood smeared all over his face. They took him to the hospital and he had a few stitches on the side of his scalp. Nia told Babis that this is where her real nightmare began… Since that morning, Tassos has been walking past Pitsilos all the time, calling her names and shouting, threatening to beat her up.'

'But why? What did he have against her? Apart from the stitches, that is?'

'Well, even *that* he had coming! But in his eyes, she was a cheap woman who had dangled her sexuality before him and then assaulted him when he moved closer. That's the story he told everyone, and I guess, also to himself – to justify what he'd done.'

'Un-be-lievable.'

'Oh believe it... it's all true. So next thing Nia knew, everyone was relaying to her the lies he'd spread about her... that she was— and I'm going to use the tame versions of the words— promiscuous, easy, crazy, and nasty.'

'Oh-no. Poor Nia.'

'Poor Nia? Seriously? You're forgetting how much misery she's caused Stamatis?'

'Yes, I know. But still...'

'You're too good, Lizzie. Too kind. Personally, I'm glad she got her comeuppance. Even late. She deserves every bit of misery she's gone through. She's the one that put Tassos in the picture, and she relished all he'd been doing to Stamatis. She probably enjoyed watching him suffer, watching him live his days defeated and lonely. She probably thought he deserved it because he didn't choose to be with her. What a psychopath! I'm only sorry for Preveza, you know? I hope the poor devils over there know what they're in for.'

After a few moments of quiet contemplation, Lizzie heaved a long sigh, then said, 'Well... I hope she'll be happier in her village. Maybe the lesson she learned here will make her a better person, who knows? That said, I do admit, it's nice to know I don't have to see her face again.'

'Don't fool yourself. She'll never change... Oh, Lizzie! You always see the best in people. My Babis is the same... A heart of gold, he has. And how did Nia repay him? She lied to him about me when he told her he fancied me. Nasty piece of work she was! Despicable. So you and Babis can sympathize with her all you want. As for me, I say one thing and one thing only to her: Good riddance, *darlin'*!'

Lizzie gave a frown. 'And what about Tassos?'

'What about him?'

'He won... The moment Nia succumbed and left this place.'

'No, he hasn't. A nasty son-of-a-gun like him can only live a poor existence, no matter how much he tries. Plus, he has a predetermined *rendez-vous* with a spectacular bite in the ass. Trust me. It's only a matter of time.' She winked, a wicked smile spreading across her face. 'Good old karma works on auto-pilot. And it never disappoints.'

I dare think you haven't done this before

Stamatis and Lizzie walked hand-in-hand uphill with Aliki and Tom. Once they'd left Spileo behind, the moon provided just enough light to see where they were going. Stamatis lit a powerful electric torch at that point, having come fully prepared.

When they reached the olive grove, they saw Valia's parked car and took heart, giving little cheers as they smiled to each other. Quickening their steps, they entered the olive grove where they grew silent as they moved ahead, aware that they were nearing the cave.

Just like the previous time, Valia waited at the edge of the grove. Her attire took them aback. Far from wearing normal clothes like last time, tonight she was dressed in a hooded blood-red coat, the hood covering her head. The coat was made of velvet and reached down to her ankles. Fastened with only one button at the top, it was wide enough to look like a cloak.

On her feet, she wore a pair of flat, red sandals made of leather. Her grey, wispy hair fell loosely over her shoulders. When she opened her arms wide to welcome them, a shirt came into view on the inside of her coat, its milky-white fabric catching the faint moonbeams to sparkle eerily.

As Lizzie took Tom by the hand to approach Mrs Valia first, she felt magnetized by her eyes. She was smiling at them, her arms still open in welcome.

'Hello!' she said when Lizzie and Tom reached her, the other two following closely behind. Valia placed a gentle hand on Tom's head but, strangely enough, once she'd patted it she didn't remove her hand. Instead, it lingered there as she closed her eyes. 'A-ha... Interesting... she murmured, then opened her eyes again.

'What is interesting?' asked Lizzie.

'Nice to meet you, Tom,' said Valia, ignoring Lizzie's question.

'Nice to meet you, too,' he replied, then Valia acknowledged Aliki and Stamatis. The latter made the introductions.

Lizzie was stunned to silence. *What did she mean earlier? And why didn't she answer me?* As they all began to walk towards the cave, Lizzie mulled it over, wondering if she should ask her again, when Valia suddenly halted and turned around, just as they reached the entrance of the cave.

Valia squeezed Lizzie's arm gently. 'I know you are full of questions. But I need you to trust me, Lizzie. I've been doing this all my life, and so did the women in my bloodline since the world began. Trust that I'm here to do the best there is for you and your brother.' She tilted her head, her eyes warm, twinkling like embers in the hearth. 'Can you do that for me?'

Lizzie nodded, but still felt strange about all this, and shamed, in a way. It occurred to her that, somehow, this white witch could read minds. *I guess I'll never know what she meant earlier... But is it worth worrying about it? No. What's important is that Tom and I can carry on with our lives. Free. As if this nightmare had never happened...*

'Good girl... That's exactly what we're here for,' said Valia, breaking her reverie.

Lizzie met her eyes and saw that they were laughing. 'Mrs Valia...' She placed her hand on the old woman's arm. 'Is there a way we can help the other children too? Tom said there were many trapped in Phoni's world...'

Valia shook her head ruefully, lips pressed together. 'I know... those poor souls! For centuries on end she's been doing this. But alas! I can't force Phoni to return them unless the relatives of each child come to me for help. I imagine many of the children were snatched centuries ago, though, their families no longer alive...'

'So there's no hope for them?'

'I'm afraid not. Unless, of course, Phoni offers to return the children, but that, of course... is wishful thinking.'

Lizzie bent her head, her heartstrings tugging with upset to hear this. When Valia placed her hand on Lizzie's shoulder, it caused her to look up again to meet the old woman's serene gaze. 'Let's concentrate on your brother tonight... Don't allow sadness to break your focus. I need you to try your best for Tom tonight, come what may.'

Lizzie nodded fiercely. 'Yes, yes! Of course! I'm sorry...'

Valia smiled at that, then dropped her gaze to the lit torch Stamatis was holding. 'You can turn that off now, we don't need it. The moonlight is strong enough.' She gave a wicked smile. 'And I've brought my own lights too... You'll all see in a minute.'

Stamatis switched the torch off, and Lizzie turned to the others to receive encouraging smiles from them all. Still, from what she could decipher from their expressions and gait, she wasn't the only one who felt worried.

Now that she was about to enter the cave, Aliki seemed terrified. Lizzie hoped she wouldn't back down at the last minute.

Tom looked intrepid bordering on excited... Lizzie was thankful for that. As for Stamatis, he had his eyes pinned on Lizzie, his hand squeezing hers tight. From the look in his eyes alone she could tell he was worried. Not for himself though, but for her. He stood tall, rigid, ready to do anything he could to help her. *My guardian angel...*

Lizzie turned her attention to Valia again, realizing that she was chanting something incomprehensible while everyone waited. All the while, she was holding the amber talisman that she wore around her neck, turning it towards the sky, and it caught the moonlight, casting a ghostly yellow light on the entrance of the cave that was mesmerizing to watch.

Swirls of dust particles danced in mid-air, bathed in that eerie yellow light that shone. As Valia inched forward turning the talisman in her hand this way and that, the light beam it cast deep into the cave exposed all its nooks and crannies. Rocks, dirt, and the spring, of course... it had swallowed whole the baby goat that fateful day... Then Phoni had emerged from it to change her and Tom's destinies forever.

'Oh! Of course! The goats!' exclaimed Valia, snapping Lizzie out of her trance.

'The goats? What goats?' asked everyone in unison.

Valia tapped the side of her head. 'Old age can be a pain. You, youngsters, will know what I mean, someday.' She turned to Tom and pointed to a huge rock formation outside that was surrounded by bushes. 'Go behind the rock and get me the baby goats I left there, please. There's a good lad.'

Tom did as he was told and came back moments later with two baby goats tied to a tether.

'Mrs Valia, please tell me these goats will not be harmed!' said Aliki, her eyes alight with shock.

Valia raised her hand and smiled. 'Please, give me some credit. I am a white witch. I respect life.'

Aliki put a hand on her heaving chest, relief visibly washing over her. Everyone else seemed to feel the same.

Valia gave a soft sigh. 'Listen. Lizzie and Tom, you come inside with me. You,' she pointed to Stamatis and Aliki, 'Stay out here, hidden from view. I don't want Phoni to see you, to know you're here until it's time. When I shout out "now", I want you to hurry inside, grab Tom by the hands and hold him between you. Don't break that bond, whatever happens. Is that understood?'

Stamatis and Aliki nodded fiercely, and Valia beckoned the two siblings to follow her inside the cave. They did so, Tom holding the goats by the tether.

It was gloomy inside, now that Valia wasn't using her amber stone any more to show the way. With great difficulty, Lizzie could just make out the edge of the spring.

'Let's stop here a while,' said Valia after they'd taken a few steps. 'Let our eyes get accustomed to the darkness. The moon is strong enough and will allow us to see clearly in a while.'

Lizzie and Tom murmured a numb "okay", then the three fell quiet as they stood in the gloominess. Only the soft sound of their breathing and the odd bleat from the goats disturbed the quiet.

A couple of minutes later, just like Valia had said, the interior of the cave revealed itself before Lizzie's eyes, crystal clear. Whereas before she couldn't see the spring, now she was transfixed by the sight of its still surface shimmering in the moonlight that streamed through the entrance. 'Beautiful...' she whispered, despite herself.

'It's true. Beauty is everywhere in this world. And we can see it, if only we allow ourselves to, even in our darkest moments,' said Valia. 'I'm glad you can do that. It means that my time here is worthwhile.'

Tom smiled at that, then looked down to check on the baby goats that moved around him, and he spent a few moments untangling the rope. He picked up the slack, giving the goats just enough space to stand comfortably beside him. 'Mrs Valia, what are the goats for?'

'To summon Phoni, of course.' She put out a hand. 'Give them to me, Tom. You and your sister, go and hide behind that rock over there.'

Lizzie and Tom turned to where she was pointing. The rock was large enough for both of them to hide behind. It was situated at the far end of the cave, away from the spring. *As far from Phoni as possible, thank goodness!*

Tom handed the goats to Valia and hurried to the rock with his sister. As soon as they hid behind it, Valia took the goats to the spring, and they lowered their little heads to drink. The moment their lips came into contact with the water, the surface of the spring began to bubble, causing Lizzie's breath to catch in her throat as she watched with Tom.

An eerie green light emanated from the depths of the spring, and then, in a mighty splash of foamy water, Phoni came into view standing in the middle of the spring, up to her waist in the glowing water.

Phoni's eyes narrowed into slits, lips twisted with malice, wrinkled chin protruded and wagging, even though no sound came out of her. She didn't seem to have noticed Valia, only the baby goats. Somehow, in one giant leap over the water as if she could walk on air, she reached the edge of the spring and snatched the animals, gripping one in each hand, her talons sinking into their perfectly white fur.

Lizzie brought her fist up and put it into her mouth willing herself not to scream in horror. *Mrs Valia said she wouldn't let the goats come to harm! What's just happened?*

Valia stepped forward, her sandals getting wet and, somehow, her open hand emitted what looked like a fire bolt. This caused the goats to disappear from Phoni's hands, and to reappear at the entrance of the cave. Valia spun around, facing them, to raise the talisman of the amber crystal in her hand. It caught the moonlight and shone yellow light into the goats' eyes, causing them to run off in panic, bleating loudly.

Valia turned to Phoni again, her gait exuding confidence. Lizzie couldn't believe her eyes. She'd never seen a woman of her age looking so defiant, let alone in the face of this diabolical witch that eyed her with pure malevolence.

Phoni splashed noisily out of the spring, shaking her gnarled hands mid-air. 'Necrojudge, what is your name? Why are you here? I've done nothing wrong!'

'Valia is my name. And I beg to differ!' Valia turned around. 'Lizzie, Tom! Come out!'

The two siblings came from behind the rock and walked side-by-side to the edge of the spring where both Valia and Phoni stood.

As soon as they approached, Phoni cringed, a low guttural sound coming out of her twisted lips.

Valia raised her chin and pointed to Lizzie. 'This woman tells me you snatched her brother and kept him for twenty years!'

'That's a lie! I don't know these two!' said Phoni avoiding their eyes, hands flailing about.

'Don't add insult to injury for these poor souls! You thief! Silence!' Valia placed a hand inside her coat and, impossibly, took out a large staff. It was made of wood, olive perhaps... A sphere of quartz crystal stood on its top. Inside it, a round polished lapis lazuli stone swam in some kind of transparent yellow liquid. Valia struck the staff once on the ground, and the lapis lazuli stone erupted with bright blue light. It radiated all over the cave, filling it with an eerie blue luminescence.

Phoni gave an ear-piercing shriek and took two steps back, her heels at the edge of the water. Then, the blue light subsided and Phoni looked daggers at Valia, a toothy grin spreading across her face. It revealed rotten teeth and gaps where others had long gone.

'What's this?' she uttered, spit flowing out of her dark, almost all-black lips. 'You are two people short, Necrojudge! I dare think you haven't done this before!' With that, Phoni began to laugh maniacally, her head tilted back, hands on her hips.

'*NOW!*' shouted Valia and, in a heartbeat, Stamatis and Aliki entered the cave, hurrying towards Tom.

Phoni's face fell, terror igniting in her eyes.

It's worth a try or I am lost!

Before Phoni could react, Valia put her hand in her coat pocket and took out a large crystal that emitted a bright green light.

As soon as Phoni saw it, she collapsed to the dirt writhing and wailing.

Valia sprang forward and dropped the glowing crystal by Phoni's feet, then joined hands with Lizzie. Behind them, Stamatis and Aliki were holding hands with Tom, who stood between them, as instructed.

Valia looked over her shoulder and nodded to the three. 'Grip tight! Don't break the chain of hands!'

Everyone nodded firmly and Valia turned her attention to Phoni again, raising the staff high in her hand. She began to chant, her voice booming, reverberating against the walls.

"Out of this fair, earthly plane I expel you, far from the reaches of man, up on the highest mountains and in the depths of the farthest seas, where no ray of sunshine ever shines, where no man's voice has ever been heard. There, I condemn you to go! Scatter in a million pieces, wind to the wind, earth to the earth and darkness back to darkness!"

As Valia spoke, the light coming from her staff grew deeper and deeper blue, filling the cave with pulsating strong light, so strong, in fact, that the others had trouble keeping their eyes open.

All the while, the green crystal by Phoni's feet began to emit its light in a flowing swirling pattern. On and on, it advanced over the witch's body starting from her feet. Phoni brought up her hands to protect her bulging eyes, but when the light reached them, her hands fell limp to her sides. The light, somehow, entered through her eyes causing her to writhe again as she gave a long-drawn out, deafening wail.

Within seconds, her form had turned into a mixture of green light and smoke, which swirled and flowed the opposite way it had come, disappearing into the crystal. Phoni's desperate screams still echoed in the air for a few moments after she was gone.

Valia bent over and picked up the crystal, a satisfied smile on her face while Lizzie and the others stood rigid, still trying to process what they'd just witnessed.

Finally, Lizzie managed to find her voice. 'Valia, you said you were going to expel her into the earth for good! What is this crystal you just used to... to... put her inside?'

'Yes, Valia!' cut in Stamatis pacing forward, without letting go of Tom's hand. Aliki trailed behind as she still held hands with Tom too.

Stamatis looked livid. 'Why did you trap her in this crystal? Is it safe? What if she escapes from that?'

Valia turned to face them all, her expression serene. 'You can let go of Tom now. The danger is over...'

Stamatis and Aliki did as they were told, but before anyone could speak, Tom broke into sobs. They all turned to look at him to find him shivering, rubbing his eyes with the heels of his hands.

Valia knelt before him and cupped his cheek with a tender hand. As everyone watched, spent, Valia produced a hankie from her coat pocket and offered it to him. 'Don't cry, Tom. I'm here to help you, remember?'

Tom sniffed, then blew his nose. 'Mrs Valia, I just need to know that it's over. Please say that it is... I'm done with surprises. I'm done with this madness. I just want to take my sister away from this wretched cave, and never have to come back. Can you do that?'

Valia gave him a sweet smile and caressed his head. 'It's okay, Tom. You're at the end of your turmoil, I promise. I'm here. I will fix everything now, for both of you.'

'But, how?' cut in Lizzie. 'What are you going to do with the crystal? With Phoni? Why did you lie to us? I don't understand!'

Valia sighed and stood up. She took Tom's hand in hers and asked Stamatis and Aliki to stand back. Then, she handed Lizzie the crystal. 'Take it!' she told her. 'Take it and find your happiness again!'

Lizzie looked at the crystal that glowed brilliantly in her hand, and it made the hairs stand on end on the back of her neck. Just the thought that Phoni was inside it, possibly trying to escape that very moment, caused her to tremble like a leaf.

'Why are you giving this to me? What do you have in mind to do?' she mumbled.

Before anyone could react, Valia, who still held Tom's hand, grabbed Lizzie's too and began to stride towards the spring.

'What are you doing? Let me go! Let us both go!' Lizzie dug her heels in the ground but was too terrified to let go of the crystal so she held it tightly.

With an astonishing super-strength, Valia managed to reach the spring, practically dragging Lizzie and Tom by their hands despite their strong resistance, their wails deafening as they protested.

Probably frozen by shock until then, Stamatis and Aliki suddenly rushed forward, yelling for Valia to let the others go.

Valia let out a mighty roar, her form pulsating with vigour. Somehow, this set Lizzie and Tom free, who collapsed to the ground, terrified.

A cloud of bats formed where Valia used to stand, causing everyone to stare, mouths agape. Valia had disappeared before their eyes, and the bats began to fly in circles low over their heads, sending all four kneeling or lying on the ground, cringing, their hands covering their heads.

Startled by the sight, and the thrashing sound of the bat wings that chilled her blood, Lizzie let the crystal drop, and it rolled into the spring.

As soon as it sank, the water began to bubble, erupting in a green flash of light. Phoni emerged through it, her features pinched with spite. 'You! All of you! How dare you enter my cave and try to capture me?'

Lizzie, who sat on the ground, stared at Phoni, her eyes bulging, whole body shuddering. *What chance do we have now that Valia has left us? Possibly cheated us too? We're as good as dead! All of us!* Lizzie put out a hand and took hold of Tom's shoulder, pulling him to her. *If I'm going to die or be captured by the witch, then, either way, I'll face it with my brother!*

Stamatis and Aliki approached the two siblings on all fours under the cloud of bats, and they all huddled on the ground together.

Phoni eyed them all with disdain. She put out her wrinkly hands, black smoke coming out of her talons. Two streams of smoke rose high, above the whirling colony of bats, and transformed into two giant buzzards.

They flew even higher, their backs almost touching the ceiling of the cave. Then, in perfect formation, they swooped down towards the people, but the cloud of bats split into two and rose up to meet them. Next, the bats formed a black sphere of flapping wings and shrieking mouths that trapped Phoni's creations inside. The sphere whirled, round and round, the buzzards unseen now inside it.

Then, a black, gyrating shadow separated from the sphere, fell to the ground and, in a split second, Valia appeared again before their eyes.

At the same time, the colony of bats disappeared through the opening of the cave, the buzzards of the witch nowhere to be seen.

Phoni let out a harrowing scream to see this development and began to retreat further into the deep water.

'Fool! Valia shouted at Lizzie taking hold of her hand. 'Why didn't you trust me? Careless, stupid girl! It's because of you that this demon is released anew!'

'But, what was I to do? You were dragging us to the water—'

'To free you, *yes*! And to expel this demon into the pit of the earth like I'd promised. Lizzie, *please*! This time, trust me! Now! We have no time!'

Spent, Lizzie nodded, and so did the others in silence.

'Now, stand! All of you!' she ordered the four, beckoning with two urgent hands. When they obliged her, her chin hardened, then she thrust her hands forward. 'Now, hold my hand firmly, Lizzie! You too, Tom! Now!'

Lizzie did as she was told, then turned her gaze towards Stamatis and Aliki. They looked numb as if they were convinced this was a dream. Yet, Stamatis's eyes were pinned on Lizzie across the distance, burning with feeling, feverish.

His pained expression made Lizzie's heart break, but unless she trusted Valia, she knew inside her heart she'd never see him again, and that their love would never have a future.

'I love you, Stamatis!' she cried out, having just a split second to register love and hope in his eyes before Valia pulled her by the hand, forcing her to look in front of her again.

As Valia led Lizzie and Tom into the spring, she said softly, 'Trust me, you two... You *have* to trust me now. I only want for you what's good, what God intended.' She looked over her shoulder, instructing Stamatis and Aliki to stay where they were.

Lizzie allowed Valia to take her into the water, even though Phoni still stood in the middle of it, immersed up to her chin, her eyes narrowed into slits. She made for a terrifying sight, the stuff of nightmares but, somehow, in Valia's presence, Lizzie finally felt confident, fearless, at peace.

✶ ✶ ✶ ✶

Phoni watched as the Necrojudge brought the two siblings into the water. She knew what that meant. She'd noticed the amber stone in the Nerojudge's talisman... and the green crystal that had trapped her earlier was somewhere in the water now... Phoni knew this crystal meant imprisonment for her. For a very long time indeed. And she wasn't going to let that happen.

Phoni bellowed out a spell and the water began to bubble furiously. *Time to get me some leverage. It's worth a try or I am lost!*

Eyes ignited with panic

Lizzie stood in the water up to her calves with Valia and Tom and couldn't believe her eyes. A large number of children had just emerged from the water, and were now hovering in mid-air over the spring, all around Phoni. They looked ethereal in form, definitely not flesh and blood, but their eyes seemed human enough, their expressions ablaze with joy.

'Here!' shouted Phoni, but for the first time, her voice sounded frail. 'Take as many as you want. Just let me be!'

Valia didn't respond to that. Her eyes were pinned on the children, tears flowing down her cheeks to see all the lives Phoni had stolen across the centuries. There were dozens and dozens of them, small children of all ages and even some teenagers.

Lizzie's heart tugged with the same ache, and she turned to Tom, wondering how this sight was affecting him.

✳✳✳✳

Tom stared at the children, a low murmur escaping his lips. It was a lament, for all that was lost, for all these children and for him too. Suddenly, he remembered, and found that he knew all of them by name. He'd been living with them all those years... Whereas, before, his memories of life with Phoni had been sparse and clouded over, now he remembered everything that had transpired in the depths of the earth with perfect clarity.

In his mind's eye, he saw the crowds of the dead walking the path to the Underworld... the water he carried with the other children from a spring so they could moisten the dead people's dried-out lips. He recalled the sponge he carried in his pocket to wash their wounds, and the plants that grew alongside all the paths he visited, the leaves of which he boiled and applied to their sores.

Hot tears flowed out of his eyes, his sobs causing his chest to shudder. He wasn't upset, just too happy to bear it. Because he knew then, without a shadow of a doubt, that Valia was going to save all the children, him included.

✳✳✳✳

Lizzie's heart constricted with feeling to see her brother cry, and she tried to get closer to him, but Valia didn't let her.

'Don't let go of my hand. Now is the time. This is where we send this abomination back to where she came from!'

Bolts of sparkling yellow light, bright like the summer sun, emerged from the talisman on Valia's chest, and the hovering children turned into doves with spotless, all-white wings.

Phoni began to shriek at an ear-piercing pitch.

'Go, children!' shouted Valia, ignoring Phoni, who had started to wail and protest at the sound of these words.

'You are finally free!' continued Valia. 'May your souls be at peace. I bless you and bless you with all that is good. Fly out of this wretched cave and into the night, reach the stars where you belong and, from there, fly directly to heaven! You are spared from the underground passage meant for the souls that leave this earth. I bless you to fly straight into your parents' loving arms! Your lives were once stolen from you here, but your peace and joy in heaven will be eternal!'

By the time she'd finished, every single one of the doves had flown out of the cave.

'No!' shrieked Phoni from the deep water. 'How am I supposed to do my work without them now? What have you done?'

Valia tilted her head back, her face hard like stone. 'Phoni! You were supposed to take souls among the dead for this task. Not the living! Let alone innocent children! You've deprived so many living souls of their right to live their lives on this earth and not in it! But this is where I come in... to remind you that you've strayed! And, as of tonight, these two souls will also be free from your evil grasp!' She pointed with her head to Lizzie, then Tom, as she held them by their hands, then looked daggers back at Phoni.

'As for you, tonight, I'm sending you back down into the bowels of the Earth to be disciplined! Your punishment is this: You cannot use this spring, your gateway, for one hundred years!'

Phoni's eyes ignited with panic, and she waded through the water, trying to get closer fast, all the while her hands brought together in a pleading gesture. 'No! Please! Spare me from this harsh penalty. Please, Necrojudge! What about the dead? How am I to get all the herbs I need without access to the mountain for one hundred years?'

'Enough! There are other Healers, ones with higher morals than yours. And you will serve under one of them, until your sentence is over.' Before her, Phoni seemed horrified, too stunned to speak.

Valia widened her eyes, her voice booming when she added, 'But beware, Raven Witch! When this spring is reformed, if you come out and steal another of my children, my next punishment will make this one sound like a treat! Do you understand?'

Before Phoni could respond, Valia brought her arms forward abruptly, sending Lizzie and Tom flying into the water with the kind of force that you'd only expect from a supernatural being.

※ ※ ※ ※

Valia gave a satisfied smile. Lizzie and Tom had disappeared under the water's surface moments ago and hadn't come back up.

Stamatis and Aliki dashed to the edge of the spring screaming Lizzie and Tom's names with anguish, but Valia ignored them.

Instead, she turned her full attention to Phoni, who was cowering in the spring, the water up to her gnarly knees. Undeterred by the pathetic sight, Valia picked up her staff that now shone its blue light softly. She walked into the spring and aimed her staff at Phoni just as the latter released an agonizing scream.

In a flash of blue light, the Raven Witch disappeared under the water.

Taking her time, Valia came out of the spring. Stamatis and Aliki rushed to her, their faces afire with distress, begging her to bring Lizzie and Tom back, but she didn't say a word to them, didn't even turn to look their way.

Instead, the Necrojudge shook her sandaled feet and stomped them on the ground to remove any leftover drops of water. Then, she turned to Stamatis and Aliki to say, 'I bless you both. Be at peace now. It's over.'

With an expression of steel determination, Valia struck the staff on the ground. The cave shook and the blinding flash of light emitted from the blue stone made her close her eyes.

Valia opened her eyes again, sighed deeply, and looked around her. She was all alone in the cave. But that was no surprise to her.

Slowly, as if she had no worries in the world, she looked down at her sandaled feet. They were bone dry. The spring was gone too. By her right shoe, a big spider scurried away on the dusty soil.

※ ※ ※ ※

The first thing Lizzie saw when she opened her eyes was the humid, mossy ceiling of the cave, and she realized, puzzled, that she was lying on her back. Then, she heard someone cough.

She sat up and saw Tom. He was hunched over beside her on the ground, spluttering and spitting water out of his mouth. Instinctively, she brought a hand to her lips and remembered a few moments ago she'd been doing the same. *What happened? I can't remember a thing!* 'Tom, are you okay?'

Tom was fine but looked just as shocked as she was. The cave was eerily quiet and Lizzie had the impression that more people were supposed to be there, except she couldn't tell who that might be.

'Is it me, or did we come with other people in here?'

'Who? Stamatis?' asked Tom. 'I'm not sure... What do you think, Lizzie?'

Lizzie shrugged her shoulders. She had no idea either.

Shocked into silence, and not even knowing why they felt like that, they stood by the edge of the spring for a while, just watching the surface of the water that sparkled like liquid silver, perfectly still.

Finally, they turned on their heels and walked out of the cave into the bright sunlight. When they got out, they saw two baby goats jumping about on the grass. The sight made them laugh but brought tears to their eyes too. Neither of them could tell why.

Tom turned to Lizzie, his blue eyes bright in the glorious sunshine. 'You won't tell Mum and Dad you saw me cry just now, will you, Lizzie?'

Lizzie smiled, gazing into her brother's eyes with adoration. 'Don't be silly, Tom. To tell you the truth, I'm not sure I want to tell them anything about the cave. Do you remember what happened in there?'

Tom scrunched up his face. 'No... Do you?'

Lizzie gave a shudder. 'Promise we'll never go back in there?'

'Promise! And we should never tell anyone we went there either. Agreed?' He offered her his hand and they shook on it, nodding fiercely at each other.

'Now, come!' said Tom. 'I'm starving! Mum said she'd make a roast for lunch today!'

They hurried through the olive grove, leaving the cave forever behind, the sound of crickets loud in their ears. Side by side, they made their way downhill to the guest house, their little sandaled feet scuffling on the stones as they went.

'Stamatis said we can go to play at his grove this afternoon...'

Lizzie tilted her head, a cute smile on her face, her eyes bright in the sunshine. 'Good! I like it there...'

'Will you promise to be kinder to him this time, Lizzie? Don't call him Stamata any more. He doesn't like it. All right, *kontessa*?' He gave a cheeky grin.

Lizzie huffed, then smiled sweetly. She took his hand and they picked up their pace. It was close to one o' clock. At the thought of her mother's roast, her stomach began to grumble.

When you do all that gooey stuff

Twenty years later

Lizzie sat back in her chair at Gorgona, her cup of Greek coffee cooling in the salty breeze.

Mr Petros had just brought it out, then dashed back in without further ado. She turned her gaze towards the mountain of Martaouna, its pyramid shape prominent at this hour. It always came alive in the late afternoon as the hammering of the sun eased, its rays tender, like a caress, bathing everything in this sweet light, tinting it with gold.

The view of the mountain brought with it that vague feeling of wistfulness that hit her, without fail, every time she gazed at it. *The cave... What happened in there that morning?* She and Tom had never entered it again. Over the years they'd often spoken about it but had never come up with any answers. It had remained a mystery, and they'd kept it to themselves.

'Hey!' she heard and turned around. It was Stamatis. Her Stamatis. The love of her life.

'Are you done already?' she said as he came to sit beside her. She beamed at him. It was like a compulsion. Ten years married to him and she still pinched herself. Because every year that had passed she had felt blessed to have him. And the blessings had kept coming. Often, she wondered what she'd done to be so lucky in love, so lucky in life. As if she'd been touched by a saint, blessed by the angels... Somehow, she'd always felt that way.

Stamatis waved dismissively. 'You know Mr Petros! He always exaggerates. It was a case of changing a rubber ring. Once I did it, the tap was fixed.'

Lizzie took his face in her hands and pecked his lips. 'What an amazing handyman! And all mine! My perfect guy!'

His eyes twinkled with elation and, as soon as she removed her hands, he leaned closer. 'Have I ever told you how much I love you, Lizzie?'

She rolled her eyes. 'Only every day!'

He tilted his head. 'Did I tell you today? I can't remember.'

'You probably did.'

'Well, it doesn't hurt to tell you once more, does it? I love you. I looooovvvve you!' He leaned in and kissed her, and it was hard for Lizzie to kiss him back while she laughed alongside him, but she did try.

'Oh no! Not again! Will you please stop?'

They turned to the sand at the edge of Gorgona's façade to find their nine-year-old daughter, Penny, and their six year-old son, Lambros, staring.

'It's embarrassing!' complained Penny, crossing her arms over her chest. 'You won't do it before my cousin, will you? She laughs when you do all that gooey stuff!'

'Well, Uncle Tom kisses Aunt Janet and you laugh too, so what's the problem?' said Lizzie, trying to keep a straight face.

Penny had no answer to that, so she and Lambros turned their attention to their buckets and spades again.

Lizzie laced her arms around Stamatis's neck and tilted her head back, her expression teasing as she whispered, 'We should never have named our girl after your mother, Penelope. Your *mama* may no longer be with us, but I'll say it... She certainly loved to moan.' She cocked her eye at him. 'Seems our daughter got the trait too. Traits get passed on along with the names, or so I hear.'

'Well, at least we did things right with Lambros. If your theory is correct, then he can only turn into a respectable academic like my dad.'

Lizzie nodded wistfully, fond memories of her father-in-law flooding her mind. He had passed away shortly after his wife had, a few years back.

'Hey, chin up! Tom and his family are arriving any minute! You don't want your brother to see you looking down in the mouth, do you?' Stamatis elbowed her and she elbowed him back. For a while, they did this back and forth, causing Penny from the sand to grunt and roll her eyes again, before turning to her brother anew. Their sand castle was almost done and they were getting excited.

Stamatis exchanged a knowing smile with Lizzie, then checked his watch. 'You said Tom's flight has landed, right?'

'Yes, he texted me from the airport. They were heading for the taxi queue.' She checked the text message on her phone. 'Three quarters of an hour ago. Should be here any second. I told them to come straight to Gorgona.'

Stamatis sat back in his chair and let a luxurious sigh. 'Ah... this is the life...'

Smiling, Lizzie straightened in her chair, then sipped her coffee. When she put it back down she smiled with relish. 'Aah... I agree. They don't make this coffee back in England.'

Stamatis reached out and took her hand, caressing it with his fingertips. Lizzie lost herself in his eyes for a few moments. Her gaze then travelled lower to the strong muscles and sinews bulging in his neck, shoulders, and torso.

She'd known him all her life, watched him grow every year. They'd spent all their summers together as she and her family kept coming back every year to stay at the guest house. Her childhood friendship with Stamatis had blossomed into a flaming romance when she reached sixteen and he was seventeen. They had become sweethearts then and, somehow, they were still sweethearts now.

Her love for him had only been raging since then with every passing year. And, even though she took him to bed every night, he still lit up the passion in their lives effortlessly, her carnal desire for him never-ending. *What have I ever done to be so blessed? I must have been a saint in a previous life... Either that or someone who'd suffered too much!*

'Lizzie...' she heard and turned to find Stamatis eyeing her with curiosity.

'Yes?' she asked with a frown.

'Are you happy? Living in Corfu, I mean, instead of the UK?'

'Of course! This is paradise to me... Why would I prefer to live in England? Besides, this is where you are. Where I met you...' She leaned in and caressed his chin.

'But don't you miss England? Your family? I know you're not that close to your parents, but surely you miss Tom?'

'Yes, of course I miss Tom. But he comes to stay for at least a fortnight every summer.'

'But what about our life here?'

'What about it?'

'Well, I'm thinking of the sacrifices you've made... You quit your nursing studies to come and live here and wound up running the family guest house with my parents and me, instead of working in some hospital...'

'And what's wrong with that? I chose to be with you, silly. And I never regretted it!'

'But... don't you mind that I can't give you more?'

'But you've given me *everything*! Your love, our beautiful children, a roof over my head, and the guest house that provides us with a steady income. If anything, it's you who has it bad, having to do all these odd jobs on top to earn a little extra.'

'And I don't mind it one bit. I only mind that I can't give you the kind of life that Tom has given his wife.'

'Oh, Stamatis! If you mean their big house in Kensington and their highly paid jobs, I don't care about all that.' She squeezed his hand and gazed deeply into his eyes. 'All I care about is you. And where you are is the only place I want to be. Simply because you're in it. And that's enough...' She gave a playful smile. 'And now, enough of that, or I will call you *Stamata!*'

He chortled, then began to stroke her hair, and she tilted her head towards him like a flower looking for the sun.

'Oh, Lizzie... I love you a thousand times more than when I first met you...'

Lizzie cocked her eye at him and gave a lopsided smile. 'Well, you didn't exactly love me back then. At the time, if I recall, the purpose of your existence seemed to be teasing me till I got blue in the face.'

They burst into guffaws, then Lizzie noticed a woman staring. She was sitting outside Pitsilos Apartments. She ran the place, being the niece of the owners. Lizzie didn't like her, she never had, and didn't even know her name.

'She's staring again... that girl, next door,' said Lizzie, looking the other way.

'Who? The Pitsilos girl?' he replied without looking that way either.

'Hm-mm...'

He shrugged. 'So? That girl is weird... Weird people do weird things. Let her stare. Who cares?'

'You're only saying that to put me off the scent...' She smiled wickedly. 'I see the way she looks at you. Like she wants to gobble you all up!'

He gave a mischievous grin. 'And what if she does? I only have eyes for you!' With that, he began to tickle her, causing her to howl with laughter.

From the sand, their children, who were gathering pebbles to decorate the perimeter of their sand castle, stopped playing to watch them. 'Stop already! You're so embarrassing!' complained Penny.

Like a dog with no teeth

Valia sat at a remote table at Gorgona watching Lizzie and her family. Beside her, sat her thirteen-year-old granddaughter Eva, a beautiful young girl with wavy, long blond hair. They were eating ice cream from glass bowls.

Eva had nearly finished eating hers, while Valia had about half left. Both had been watching Lizzie, Stamatis and the children all this time, chuckling to themselves. Finally, they turned to each other, smiling knowingly.

Eva finished her ice cream and dropped the teaspoon in the bowl, then tossed a thick strand of hair behind her shoulder. She ventured another look at Lizzie and Stamatis, who watched their children play in silence, their beaming smiles speaking volumes about their happiness.

'*Yiayia*, tell me again, why did you *have* to take Lizzie and her brother out from that timeline? Couldn't you have kept them there, rather than return them to the time where Tom was taken?'

Valia gave a laborious sigh, her eyes pinned on the loving couple still. 'I could have kept them there... but there was so much wrong with that universe...'

'Like, what?'

'Well, to start with, Tom had been robbed of twenty years of his life. Lizzie had been traumatized too and not just because Tom had been taken. Let us not forget her parents had let her down and hurt her irreversibly.'

'What would have happened had you left them there? Did you visit that timeline any further? Do you know?'

'Of course, I did. We Necrojudges never make a decision unless we've done a thorough research first. And I'll have you know that that universe would have ended in total disaster. Had I only imprisoned Phoni but left Lizzie and Tom in that world, Lizzie would have taken her brother back to England and their parents would have rejected them.'

'What? No!'

'Yes... Their parents called Lizzie a liar and a fantasist all over again. It devastated her. No... it crushed her! She tried so hard to put sense into their heads, to get them to accept Tom. It was draining for her, but it was to no avail. Then, there was that road accident... She drank a lot that night... back in England... The accident took her life. She died instantly.'

'Oh no!'

Valia waved dismissively. 'Don't worry, darling. It was just a glimpse during my research. It never actually happened.'

Eva clutched her chest and sighed. 'Oh, thank goodness for that!'

'Do you want to know what happened to Tom in that glimpse after Lizzie died?'

'Of course!'

Valia put a finger on her lips, her eyes twinkling. 'Well, this is where it got really interesting... it took me aback and, let me tell you, not a lot surprises me any more. After Lizzie's passing, Tom returned to Corfu on his own.'

'Really?'

'Yes! He felt like he owed it to Lizzie to cut all ties with his parents. And, you know, he did it just as they'd started to warm up to him considering the possibility that he was their long lost son, after all.'

'It took for Lizzie to die for them to accept him?'

'Sadly so...'

'And what did he do once he got back here?'

Valia's eyes lit up. 'Aliki took him in! Can you believe it?'

'Really? How sweet of Aliki! And Stamatis? What happened to him?'

Valia shook her head. 'After Lizzie's passing... he... well, you can imagine... I don't even want to talk about it, if you don't mind.' She shrugged. 'But, as I said, what I saw was just a glimpse... when it was still a possibility. But that timeline doesn't exist any more. Because I intervened. And, as a result, I changed their lives for the better. Look at them! Just look at them now!'

They both turned to admire the sight of Lizzie and Stamatis holding each other quietly while their children played.

Finally, Eva said, *'Yiayia*? I have one more question.'

'Yes, darling?'

'What happened to Stamatis and Aliki after you took Lizzie and Tom back twenty years?'

'What do you mean, what happened to them?'

'Well? You said they disappeared from the cave. Where did they go?'

'They didn't go anywhere, darling. Once Lizzie and Tom went back, it was like Stamatis and Aliki had never been in the cave in the first place.'

'But, how come?'

'It's because I changed the course of their lives when I took Lizzie and Tom back... Do you understand?'

'Yes, I think so...'

Valia saw it in her eyes that she was confused still. 'For example, Lizzie married Stamatis because of what I did... yes?'

'Uh-huh...'

'So he never married Kiki, he never became a widower, he never met Lizzie again, the Lizzie who had lost a brother. So he never visited the cave that night! Do you get it now?'

'Ah! Yes... I think.' A short pause. 'So where was he that night?'

'In his bed sleeping, I expect. With his wife, Lizzie.'

Another short pause. 'Oh, *Yiayia*! I don't know why, but every time I ask these kinds of questions I always wind up feeling like a dummy.'

'Don't worry, darling. That's why the training takes years to complete. I dare think the good Lord will give me a few more years to train you properly. We are doing God's wholesome work. Have faith. You will learn the ropes in no time, just like I did, and so many of your great-grandmothers before you.'

Valia caressed the girl's head, the latter's face beaming. After a few moments, Eva gave a frown and said, '*Yiayia*... what about Aliki? She was such good friends with Lizzie and Tom! What happened to her in this world?'

'Oh don't worry... Aliki lives here like she did in that other timeline. The only difference is she hasn't met Lizzie and Tom. Yet!' She winked.

Eva's eyes lit up and she straightened in her chair. 'Yet?'

Valia gave a wide grin. 'Yes. They'll meet very soon. Their friend Babis, who owns the supermarket, is getting married this Sunday. Lizzie and Stamatis are invited to the wedding. Tom's going too. And guess who the blushing bride is?'

'Aliki?'

'Yes! I can foresee that Lizzie and Tom will love chatting to this bubbly Greek-American girl, and they'll strike up a friendship with her that will last a lifetime. Even Charlie will get to meet them all.'

'The doggie? Is his coat okay?'

'Yes, actually! Aliki found a local naturopath with wonderful skills via Babis. He fixed Charlie's skin problem in no time.'

'I can't believe it, *Yiayia*! This world is perfect! You saved them all! Even the doggie!'

'Yes... even the doggie...' said Valia with a sweet smile, and pinched her granddaughter's cheek.

'So... Phoni is still serving her time as we speak?'

'Yes... I gave her one hundred years. She has eighty more to go.'

'And if she steals another child after that?'

'Let's just say that if she does I will know. When I trapped her in the green crystal I made it easy to expel her to the Underworld, but I also enabled myself to track her deeds in future. It's a spell I've developed myself. Never been tried before, but it's working so far...' She gave a smug smile and rubbed her hands together.

'So you know where she is now?'

'Yes. She's doing the healing work herself under the command of one of the harshest Healers in Greece. No one else wanted to work for her so Phoni had to take it since... let's just say... no one else wanted to employ her. Her bad reputation had spread far and wide over the centuries.'

'Why did she have to work at all, though? I don't understand.'

'Because she is a Healer of the Underworld. She has to do the work. The same goes for us Necrojudges. Duty calls for each one of us. We were made that way. Our work is our reason for being. The Raven Witch had to work somewhere else since her water spring is gone.'

'But wasn't she looking to retire?'

'She can't retire unless she trains someone else to take her place first. These are the rules. But instead of training someone among the dead all this time, she'd been stealing living children hoping to find the perfect one to take her place. Now she's paying the price. If she wants to find an apprentice, she'll have to choose someone from the Underworld. And she'd better work hard to gain some good reputation, otherwise, I foresee she'll have to keep working till her bones grind into powder.'

Eva tittered, her laughing eyes crinkling at the sides. 'And this Healer she's working under right now is harsh, you say?'

'Yes, quite harsh. Phoni's life nowadays would make Tom's last twenty years seem like a trip to Disneyland by comparison.'

Eva roared with laughter, then said, 'I'm laughing at her expense, I know, but I can't help feeling sorry for her too.'

Valia peered at her solemnly for a few moments, then said, 'It makes sense. Because you're a good person. But she's not.' She heaved a long sigh, then added, 'Man is born with the freedom of choice. As a child, Phoni didn't choose to be kidnapped, of course, but she did make a choice to stay in that foul circle. Just because she had tasted the pain of being snatched away from this world, she cannot be given any leniency for doing this to other people. Simple as that.'

Eva pondered on these words for a few moments before meeting her grandmother's eyes again. 'Can I ask one last question, *Yiayia*?'

Valia nodded encouragingly. She had all the patience in the world to explain things to her.

'What about Nia? Is she a threat to Lizzie and her family?'

'Oh. Her.' Valia scrunched up her face with disdain, then shrugged. 'Nia will always be Nia. Except, in this timeline, she will never get to hurt Stamatis. This time she'll never touch their lives. To them, she's harmless now. Like a dog with no teeth.'

'That's cute, *Yiayia*. You say the funniest things!'

Valia rolled her eyes. 'I guess I keep myself entertained... Being able to skip from universe to universe offers a lot of chances for finding merriment.'

'Thank you for bringing me with you here, *Yiayia*! My first time to another world! This is so exciting!'

'Well, this is only the first of many cross-universe travels to come.'

Eva gave an excited squeal, and Valia beamed at her for a few moments. She certainly was the apple of her eye. Suddenly, the old woman slapped her knee. 'Now, are you ready to go?' Valia removed her amber crystal talisman from her pocket and handed it to Eva. 'Your turn to do it this time. I want you to get the hang of it.'

'Gladly!' said Eva. 'This world may be perfect for Lizzie and her family, but it got a little strange for me earlier, as you know.'

Valia chortled. 'You mean your mother not recognising you on the way here?'

Eva grunted playfully. 'Don't laugh, *Yiayia*! It's not funny! I walked straight past her, and she didn't even look at me. Fancy that!'

'Didn't I tell you? Your mother chose to never marry in this timeline.' She flicked her wrist. 'Oh, you'll get used to it. In my cross-universe travels, I've seen it all...'

They got up and walked away from the table. When they stepped onto the sand, Valia turned one last time to look over her shoulder. She couldn't get enough of the outcome of her work, one of the most idyllic endings she could ever give to a local who had asked for her help.

Once more, the sight of Lizzie and Stamatis melting with love in each other's arms caused her old heart to swell with feeling.

Then, she took her granddaughter's hand and they walked away. They turned the corner into a small deserted lane and, with a flash of yellow light, they were gone.

❋❋❋❋

Back at Gorgona, the air was filled with excited squeals. A taxi had parked in the lane outside moments ago. Tom and his family had emerged from it, then rushed to the taverna to meet their loved ones.

Lizzie fell into Tom's arms and, after kissing each other the Greek way on both cheeks, they swayed from side to side in a tight embrace.

Tom's daughter, after greeting her aunt and uncle, went straight to the beach to greet her cousins and to sit together on the sand to chat and play.

Mr Petros heard the commotion and came out, his arms open wide to welcome Tom and his wife, Janet. Then, he rushed back in, only to come out again a few minutes later with shots of *tsipouro* and a large platter of meze for them all.

After everyone had had a few nibbles, Tom went to sit on the sand and talk with the kids for a while, then returned to stand at the railing and gaze at the stunning view of the bay, his back to the table where the other adults sat.

Lizzie saw him standing there, a fully grown man, and she wondered once again where the years had gone. It seemed like yesterday when he was still a little boy, playing with her on the mountain near the guest house.

She walked up to her brother to loop her arms around his waist, and he responded by squeezing her against him lovingly. They stood there for a while, admiring the view of the bay and the lush mountains together.

Lizzie turned to him to find his expression was wistful as he looked towards Martaouna. Before she could speak, he turned to her. He seemed dazed, the ghost of a smile on his lips.

'Tired from the trip, Tom? We'll go home soon, then you can rest properly, if you like.'

'Oh no, it's not that...' He turned his gaze towards the mountain again, this time caressing it with his eyes. 'What happened in that cave, Lizzie?' he added, turning to face her.

'I don't know, Tom... I guess we will never find out. But why does it bother you so much?'

'It doesn't, as such... it just feels like we're missing something, that's all...'

Lizzie gave a howl of laughter, pulling away from their embrace. 'Missing? Missing, what? Look at *this,* Tom!' She beckoned him to turn around, then put a loving arm around his waist.

Their large family was gathered at the table, including the kids. Mr Petros had brought all three of them ice cream and they were eating greedily, giggling at each other's chocolate-smeared faces.

From the table, Stamatis caught Lizzie's eye and winked at her, his eyes sparkling, causing her to break into a huge smile, her heart exploding with joy to see them all sitting together, reunited again. Everything she ever wanted from this world was right here, within her reach.

As if on cue, Tom spoke then, breaking her reverie. 'How right you are, Lizzie... Of course, we're missing nothing!' He gazed into his sister's face for a few moments, his adoration for her palpable, then grinned from ear to ear and added, 'What else could we ever ask for?'

THE END

Thank you for reading The Raven Witch of Corfu. Keep turning the pages for recommended reads, a note from the author and more!

Did you know? Every time one of my readers forgets to write a review, a Corfiot gets so upset that they forget to pick the olives from their trees. It just breaks my heart! Tell me what you thought of my book and help the Corfiots continue to pour olive oil in their salads!

Please leave a short review on Amazon. It will be greatly appreciated!
US: http://www.amazon.com/dp/B07J4V96RP
UK: https://www.amazon.co.uk/dp/B07J4V96RP

More from this author

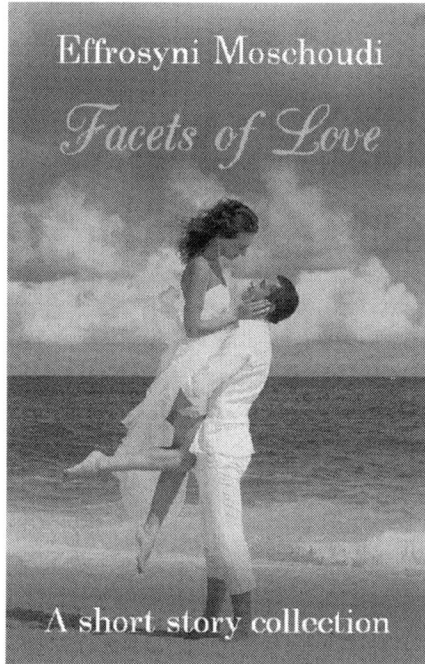

FREE eBOOK!

Treat yourself today to this wonderful collection of short stories that highlight various kinds of love. Not just the romantic kind, but also love for family, pets, and country. Facets of Love will introduce you to stunning locations around Greece. The fantasy elements contained in some of the stories are bound to enchant you!

"I loved the variety of voices, characters and motifs I encountered. From blooming love, second chance love, to the innocence of children, grandma's wise words, to Greek pride."
~Alina's Bookish Hideout Blog

Visit: http://effrosyniwrites.com/yours-for-free/

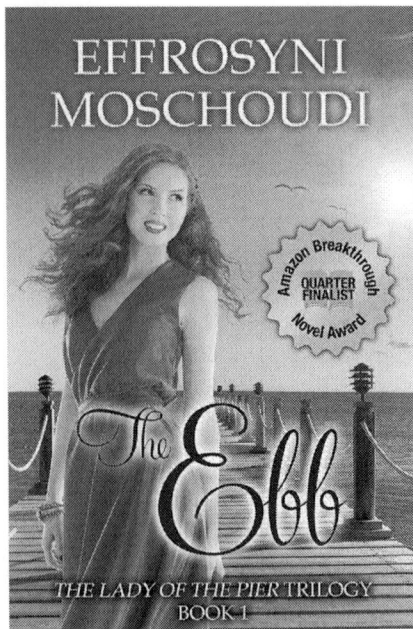

When Sofia falls in love, a mourning spirit begins to haunt her...

CORFU, 1987: During her summer holidays, Sofia Aspioti meets Danny Markson, a charming flirt who makes her laugh. Although she's worried about village gossip, she falls desperately in love. That's when strange dreams about a woman dressed in black begin to haunt her. Who is this grieving woman, and how is her lament related to Sofia's feelings for Danny?

BRIGHTON, 1937: Dreaming of wealth and happiness, Laura Mayfield arrives in Brighton to pursue a new life. She falls for Christian Searle, a young worker at the theatre, but when she's offered a chance to perform there, Charles Willard, a wealthy aristocrat, starts to pursue her relentlessly. Will Laura choose love... or money?

Amazon US: http://www.amazon.com/dp/B00LGNYEPC
Amazon UK: https://www.amazon.co.uk/dp/B00LGNYEPC

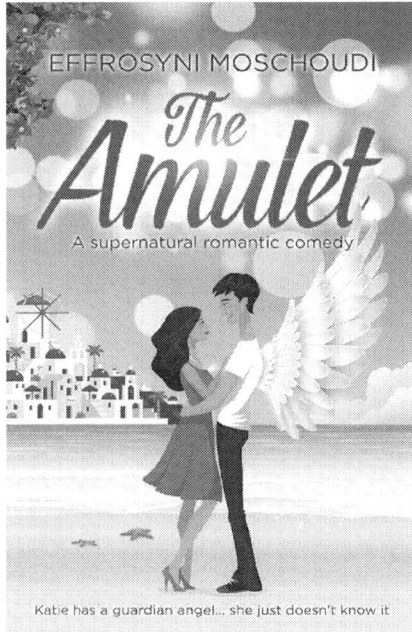

Katie has a guardian angel... she just doesn't know it

Katie has a guardian angel . . . she just doesn't know it

When Katie loses her Athens office job, a gypsy woman hands her an amulet for good luck. Next, she gets hired as hotel receptionist on the Greek island of Sifnos and everything seems perfect, except for the overbearing hotel owner, Mrs. Matina. One of the guests, heart-stoppingly handsome Aggelos, keeps saving the day whenever Katie needs help. As she falls in love, she grows all the more intrigued by him and his quirky friends, including a little girl who keeps turning up on her own. Add a psychic, half-mad elderly woman into the mix and you're in for a few laughs. Things are not what they seem in this small, family hotel and get even more complicated when the gypsy woman shows up again. Will Katie ever work out that Aggelos is a guardian angel that came with the amulet? And if she does, will she be able to keep him? It may take a miracle. But on an island as magical as Sifnos, anything is possible!

Amazon US: http://www.amazon.com/dp/B01MCZ2UOU
Amazon UK: https://www.amazon.co.uk/dp/B01MCZ2UOU

A note from the author

I was inspired to write The Raven Witch of Corfu one blissful morning in August 2016. As I swam by the pier in Messonghi, I grew all the more enchanted by the up-close view to the mountain of Martaouna.

My mind filled with thoughts while I absorbed its beauty and magnificence and I wondered, *What if it's not all good? What if a terrible evil lurked in its depths?* All at once, Phoni sprang out from my head and dived into the sea beside me to have a chat. The rest, you know...

I hope you've enjoyed the story as much as I've enjoyed writing it. Everything about it is fictitious, including the cave, and the legends about ravens, Healers or Necrojudges. As far as I know anyway. Who knows? Maybe I should buy a pack of green A4 paper to summon a Necrojudge, then walk up to Spileo late one night and see what happens...

Were you interested in the mentions of St Spyridon's miracles and legends in the book? To read more, see my post: http://bit.ly/1NskasM

I hope you've enjoyed the many references to Greek food in this book! For my delicious Greek recipes, go here: http://bit.ly/1L9GuKu

Acknowledgements

This manuscript has been polished by a group of talented writers and avid bookworms - precious friends in every case that I feel blessed to have. In this mad world that we live in, where spare time forever seems to be an elusive dream, the mere fact that these awesome people took the time to help me means the world to me. So a big thank you goes, first of all, to my precious beta readers, in no particular order: Colleen Chesebro, MM Jaye, Wendy Gilops, Cheryl Worrall, Marina Mitchell, Louise Mullarkey, Hilary Whitton Paipeti, Jean Symonds and Anne Bateman.

As always, I offer heaps of gratitude to my in-house editor and 'sponsor', my husband Andy. If anything, for believing in me and for continuing to pick me up whenever I am down.

To all my readers and fans, a big thank you for reading through my list and for urging me to "hurry and write the next one" during last year's health troubles. They had brought my work to a standstill, but your urgency gave me the oomph I needed to get there faster.

Last, but not least, a super-thank you to you, dear new reader. I am well aware that there are millions of books on Amazon, so I am deeply honoured that you've chosen one of mine. I hope I didn't disappoint.

About the author

Effrosyni Moschoudi was born and raised in Athens, Greece. As a child, she loved to sit alone in her garden scribbling rhymes about flowers, butterflies, and ants. Today, she writes books for the romantics at heart. She lives in a quaint seaside town near Athens with her husband Andy and a ridiculous amount of books and DVDs.

Her debut novel, The Necklace of Goddess Athena, has won a silver medal in the 2017 book awards of Readers' Favorite. The Ebb, her romance set in Corfu that's inspired from her summers there in the 1980s, is an ABNA Q-Finalist.

Effrosyni is a member of the writer's groups eNovel Authors at Work, ASMSG and The Fantasy & Scifi Network. Her novels are Amazon bestsellers, having hit #1 several times, and are available in kindle and paperback format.

Go here to grab FREE PDF books by this author: http://effrosyniwrites.com/free-stuff/

Visit Effrosyni's website for her travel guide to Corfu and a plethora of blog posts about her life in Greece. Make sure to join her newsletter to receive her news and special offers: http://www.effrosyniwrites.com

**Email her at contact@effrosyniwrites.com or ladyofthepier@gmail.com

**Friend her on Facebook:
https://www.facebook.com/efrosini.moschoudi

**Like her Facebook page:
https://www.facebook.com/authoreffrosyni

**Follow her on Twitter: https://twitter.com/frostiemoss

**Find her on Goodreads:
https://www.goodreads.com/author/show/7362780.Effrosyni_Moschoudi

**Follow her blogs. The first one below is perfect for bookworms (many author interviews and book reviews). On the second blog, you'll find her yummy Greek recipes!
http://www.effrosyniwrites.com
http://www.effrosinimoss.wordpress.com

Fabulous reads by other authors

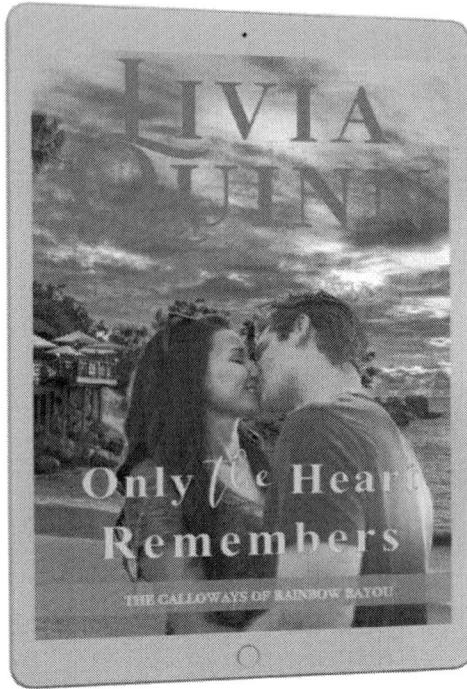

Love happens.... when you least expect it!

Brenna just got home to the Rainbow Bayou a few months ago and now the first storm of the season delivers a surprise. She's got a very bad feeling and when that happens, she pays attention. As a stranger tries to enter her cabin during the storm, she whacks him with a fireplace iron creating an even bigger problem—he awakens thinking she and he are a couple. As memories from his past surface and their feelings intensify, Brenna is shocked to find clues about him that threaten their future together...

Visit Amazon US: https://www.amazon.com/dp/B07GMRZ5T3
Visit Amazon UK: https://www.amazon.co.uk/dp/B07GMRZ5T3
Other stores: https://bit.ly/2DF1mNC

A science fiction crime adventure with plenty of humor and romance!

A souvlaki and some sun. That is all Detective Mika Pensive wanted from her fun weekend away on the Greek islands. Instead, she finds herself caught up in a sinister plot, hatched by a reclusive billionaire with a penchant for illegal genetic engineering. As if that wasn't bad enough, she has to put up with her new partner, Leo. Leo is an android—or toaster, as people scornfully call his kind. The only thing that could make things even worse would be for the headstrong Mika to fall for Leo. But people don't fall for toasters—do they?

Amazon US: https://www.amazon.com/dp/B07FP99KSS
Amazon UK: https://www.amazon.co.uk/dp/B07FP99KSS

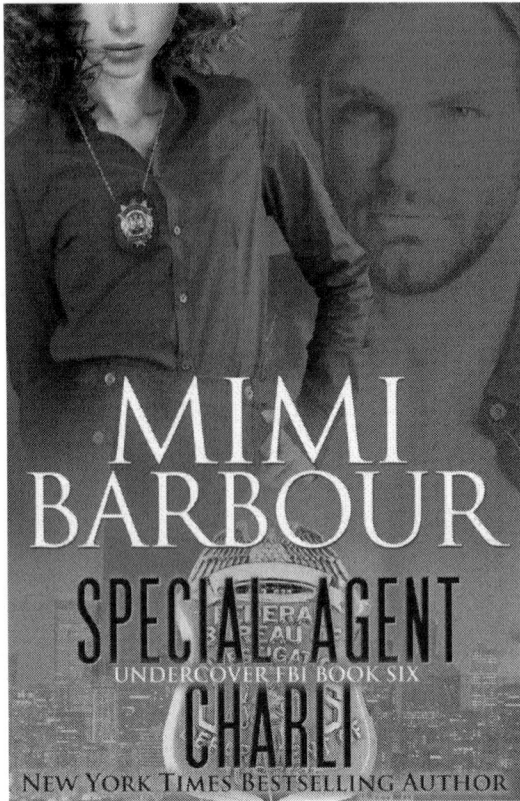

Heaven knows, she doesn't deserve this mess...

Charli's stressed to the max from a case that went down badly. So why does fate stick her with a kid who sees a murder and is the only identifier of the notorious killer? And... the girl will only go into witness protection if her bodyguard is Charli? To make matters worse, Charli has to break a promise to her Gramps, and... accept the local Police Major as her fictitious fiancé, a hotshot womanizer, the type of male she most detests. Can life get much worse?

Oh yeah...

Amazon US: https://www.amazon.com/dp/B07FLLG4D9/
Amazon UK: https://www.amazon.co.uk/dp/B07FLLG4D9

Printed in Great Britain
by Amazon